**"I've dreamed of holding you li[...] since the gala," he said, his voic[...] emotion.**

They had danced together, but Ellie didn't think this was the time to remind him of that.

Then his face blurred as it came closer to hers. Her eyelids fluttered closed as Blake's mouth touched hers. His lips were soft, seeking, teasing. He moved his head from one side to the other, kissing her on the left and right of her mouth. Ellie could feel the heat rising in her face, feel the pounding of her heart. Her neck and ears were hot enough to melt. And the wind must have picked up, because she suddenly heard it roaring.

Ellie's arms circled Blake's neck, and her body melted into his. His arms banded her waist, then traveled smoothly up her back. His mouth crushed hers as if it was hungry for the sweetness only she could provide. Desire and wonder flooded through her as something so elemental, so right, pulsed within her. She'd been kissed before. But she'd wanted Blake to kiss her. It was their first, although she was unsure if there would ever be a second. But this was not a first kiss, not an initiation or a getting-to-know-you sampling of need. This wa[...] Blake w[...] only to her, [...] see him ag[...] every other m[...]

**Shirley Hailstock** began her writing life as a lover of reading. She likes nothing better than to find a quiet corner where she can get lost in a book, explore new worlds and visit places she never expected to see. As an author, she can not only visit those places, but she can be the heroine of her own stories. The author of forty novels and novellas, Shirley has received numerous awards, including a National Readers' Choice Award, a Romance Writers of America's Emma Merritt Award and an *RT Book Reviews* Career Achievement Award. Shirley's books have appeared on several bestseller lists, including the *Glamour*, *Essence* and *Library Journal* lists. She is a past president of Romance Writers of America.

**Books by Shirley Hailstock**

**Harlequin Kimani Romance**

*His Love Match*
*Someone Like You*
*All He Needs*
*Love in Logan Beach*
*Love in San Francisco*

Visit the Author Profile page
at Harlequin.com for more titles.

# SHIRLEY HAILSTOCK
and
# JANICE SIMS

*Love in San Francisco &*
*Unconditionally*

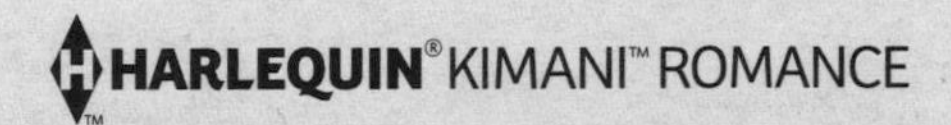

ISBN-13: 978-1-335-43301-5

Love in San Francisco & Unconditionally



Recycling programs for this product may not exist in your area.



This edition published by arrangement with Harlequin Books S.A.

For questions and comments about the quality of this book, please contact us at CustomerService@Harlequin.com.

**Printed in U.S.A.**

# CONTENTS

To Mrs. Marion A. Smith, a fan.
May she rest in peace.

# LOVE IN SAN FRANCISCO

Shirley Hailstock

Dear Reader,

There are cities that inspire writers. After visiting San Francisco, I knew I had to set a book there. When I was plotting the House of Thorn series, Blake insisted that his store be in the city by the bay.

The idea of his story came from a past incident. It had nothing to do with the events of Blake and Ellie's connection. I taught at a university and I spent a long night discussing options with a student on how a small accident could derail his future plans. Blake's life was derailed the night of his accident. And like an alternate timeline, it put him on a different emotional trail. Then Ellie walks into his life, challenging his emotions and holding a secret that could either free him or again change the direction of his life.

I hope you enjoy this second book in the House of Thorn series.

Sincerely yours,

*Shirley Hailstock*

# *Chapter 1*

Elliana Hamilton loved parties. They were usually a lot of fun, unless it was *your* party and you were the host. And this was Ellie's annual fund-raiser. But it was more than that. This was her evaluation. The Thorns, her employers, were expected at any moment. Ellie's stress level increased at the mere thought of them. Nothing could go wrong, she told herself for the umpteenth time that day. She was in the hot seat. Every detail had to go as planned.

Ellie stood at the top of the stairs. A couple appeared at the door. She drew in a breath and released it as she recognized the couple. It wasn't the Thorns. Suddenly she questioned her decision to go with holding the affair at the Riverton Mansion. The place was absolutely majestic. The staircase alone was worthy of

*Architectural Digest.* Yet if she had to run up and down it one more time, she was going to have to change her shoes—or her legs. She didn't know which, but one of them had to go. Whoever thought to put the workroom on a separate level from the activities had to be a man with no sense of engineering or workflow. Her shoes usually fitted like soft gloves, but with this much abuse, her feet were protesting. Unfortunately she couldn't complain, at least not out loud.

Seeing Darlene, one of her assistants, Ellie headed for her. "Here are the ribbons," she said, handing the colorful collection to her.

"Everything's going to be fine," the woman said, obviously homing in on Ellie's stress level. "I think the Thorns are arriving."

Ellie tensed at the sound of their names.

"Breathe," Darlene said.

The Thorns ran a chain of department stores. Ellie was the executive director of their charity, the Deborah Thorn Give It to the Girl Foundation. Every year the entire family came for the fund-raiser that supported the charity's programs. Well, almost all of them. The manager of the House of Thorn San Francisco hadn't appeared once during Ellie's three-year tenure.

When she first took the job, she'd avoided the store, feeling she'd inadvertently run into Blake Thorn, but after a while she felt it was unprofessional to be in the same city and not introduce herself. She'd made several failed attempts. He was always away when she tried to reach him. Maybe he knew who she was and didn't want to see her. The thought struck her, adding to her stress level. Calming down, she told herself he hadn't come in the past. Why should she expect to see him tonight?

Doing as Darlene suggested, Ellie took a deep breath and headed for the door. The first person to come through was definitely one of the Thorns. The resemblance to his father was unmistakable. Ellie had seen him once before, but she'd been too distraught to give him much attention. It had to be Blake.

Ellie's breath caught in her throat and she stopped with her foot in the air, balancing on one high heel. She was suddenly glad she'd climbed those stairs, or she'd have missed seeing him.

She forgot about her feet. His presence arrested her attention, and everything around her seemed to stop. His gaze changed from daydreaming to focusing on her. Ellie didn't even think of moving her eyes from his. They were tied together, bonded by invisible threads to each other.

His eyes were dark brown pools that oozed bedroom, and despite herself Ellie felt a sense of arousal. Ellie wondered how any woman could get work done if he turned those sexy eyes on her. It was hard to judge his height from where she stood at the top of the staircase, but she'd bet if she walked up to him, even wearing her heels, she'd still have to look up to see his face.

Broad shoulders spoke of daily workouts, as did the strength of his legs, which she could appreciate through the tuxedo he wore. And if "the clothes made the man" was a true statement, it applied to him tenfold.

"Time to go down," Darlene whispered.

Blake held the door for the others, allowing the entire family to file in, all wearing bright smiles. Ellie swallowed and took another breath. She put on a smile, descended the stairs and went to greet them. Her gown made a slight twinkling sound as she moved. She loved the way it felt about her legs. It gave her the confidence to begin her night.

"Ellie," Mrs. Thorn said, greeting her with a large smile. "Wonderful to see you again." The two women hugged.

Katherine Thorn introduced Ellie to her family. Except for one of them—the one who really didn't want to be there—Ellie had met them before. "This is Blake. He's right here at the San Francisco store, but I don't think you've met before."

Ellie glanced at Mrs. Thorn, then smiled and shook hands with Blake. She knew his name, knew who he was, what he looked like. Apparently he didn't know her. His hand held hers a moment too long. It was warm, but not as soft as she had expected. It wasn't the hand of a man who sat at a desk all day. Blake Thorn clearly worked with his hands.

She liked that. She'd met a lot of donors in her time. Most of them had soft hands. Somehow this workman appealed to her.

"And this is Rose," David said, pulling his wife close to him and slipping his arm around her waist.

"I heard you were recently married," Ellie told him. Then she directed her attention to the dark-haired woman. "Congratulations." They shook hands. "Go on in. There's a table waiting for you near the front. Enjoy yourselves." She gestured toward the main room.

As she moved to the side, she bumped into Blake. Ellie looked up, ready to apologize, but stemmed the thought as soon as she gazed into his dark brown and piercing eyes. He didn't smile or speak. His hand had jutted out to steady her, but stopped prior to actually making contact. Yet Ellie felt it anyway.

"I'm… I'm sorry," she stuttered.

He remained quiet, but she thought she saw a slight bob of his head.

"Please excuse me," he said.

With his first words, he left her. Ellie's gaze followed him as he returned to the entrance, where a strikingly beautiful woman had just come in. He embraced her, kissing her on the cheek and smiling. It was the first time he'd smiled. Despite Ellie's stress, her stomach did an indescribable flop. She put her hand on it for a second.

"Are you all right?" Darlene appeared at her side.

"Fine," Ellie said.

"Good. Just relax and the night will go by faster than you think."

*One can only hope*, Ellie thought. She turned. Blake and the beautiful woman were talking to another couple near the dance floor. Ellie put her mind to work. She had to check everything. There was entertainment later in the evening. Right now the band was playing. She'd talked to the band leader, making sure the song "Endless Love" was not on their playlist.

Ellie had enough on her mind. She didn't need to

hear an oldie that her father had loved, especially one that had been playing the night of the accident. It would bring memories of him back. Those memories always made her sad. And tonight she needed no distractions. Thankfully, the band leader said it was not among his plans. Ellie smiled. She had a surprise in store for the donors later. And tonight, everyone was a donor.

She found the Thorns, excluding Blake, and feeling more relaxed, went over to check on them.

"Ellie, this is an absolutely beautiful place," Rose Thorn said as she looked around. "I've never been to San Francisco before. I hope to see a few of the sights before we have to fly back."

"It's a beautiful city. See as much as you can. And call me if you need a guide."

"I'm going to be guiding her," David said, coming up to join them. "We're making it a second honeymoon."

Ellie looked confused. "I thought you were only married a few months ago."

Rose laughed, "Three months." She glanced at her husband. "David calls it a second honeymoon every time we leave the house."

Ellie thought that was so romantic. They were obviously in love. She'd never felt like that about anyone. She knew she was missing something, and hoped someone would one day love her like David obviously loved Rose.

"Is there anything you need before I go?" Ellie asked.

"We're fine," David and Rose said at the same time. They all laughed.

Ellie moved to the other Thorns to make sure they were fine, as well. She knew she had to speak to several people about donating to the foundation and wanted to get it done before they sat down to dinner.

Katherine took her arm and pulled her aside. Ellie felt as if a bomb was about to drop.

"Ellie, don't worry about us," Katherine told her. "Do what you have to do and have some fun." This last part she said with happy emphasis, squeezing Ellie's arm.

Ellie smiled and relaxed. "I'll try," she said. Taking a step back, she turned to find herself face-to-face with Blake.

No one had ever looked so surprised to see him as the woman standing in front of Blake did. His mother, with whom she'd been speaking, gave him a sly smile and melted back into a group of people next to his dad. The expression on Elliana's face changed to something more serene.

"Excuse me. I didn't know anyone was behind me."

He ignored her comment. Blake hadn't intended to surprise her. He hadn't thought she'd turn that quickly, although he'd seen her moving at the speed of light, taking care of whatever detail called for her attention.

"Is there anything I can get you?" she asked. Blake felt as if he were being dismissed.

He shook his head.

"Well, I suppose you want to rejoin your party."

There was that dismissive tone again. It irritated him. Elliana, or Ellie as his mother had called her, had a familiar look about her. Blake was sure he hadn't met her before. He'd surely remember those light brown eyes, high cheekbones and that lustrous hair. It was black and long. Although it was coiled on top of her head, several curls swung free along her temples and a section on the back lay about her shoulders, looking so crushable, he had to curl his fingers to keep from reaching for it.

She moved to step around him. Blake stepped in front of her, another action he hadn't intended.

"This is a beautiful place to hold a charity function." He looked around at the high ceiling, the brilliantly lit chandeliers, the textured wallpaper.

Ellie smiled proudly. "Have you been here before?"

"Once or twice. It's very expensive." He expected a reaction, but saw none. "Wouldn't having this gala at a little less expensive place put more contributions into the foundation?"

Her skin was a beautiful walnut color, but Blake saw her face turn darker under her makeup.

"No, Mr. Thorn. It wouldn't."

"Why not? Weren't any of the major hotels available?"

"I'm sure they were."

"Yet you opted for the most expensive place in the city?" He looked around again. Laughter came from the brightly dressed women and the tuxedo-clad men. It was a beautiful function, in a gorgeous setting. "What's this cost? Without catering, this place alone must go for a cool hundred grand."

Ellie stepped back. Her body language was just short of her putting her hands on her hips and giving him the stare. "All the numbers aren't in yet," she said with controlled calmness, "but from what we calculated, that figure is three to four times larger than your estimate."

He whistled in amazement. "Is there going to be anything left over for the fund when all this is accounted for?"

This time Ellie took two steps closer to him. She leaned in until he could smell the tantalizing perfume she wore. Her voice was menacingly low when she spoke. "Mr. Thorn, it's nearly time to announcc dinncr. However, you seem very interested in the cost of this event and how much funds we raise. I assure you that, unlike your office, mine is always open. I go over the expenses of operations with your mother four times a year, including this weekend. If she has any issues with this event or any other financial considerations, I'm sure she'll bring it to my attention. Now, please excuse me. I have other guests who need my attention."

She left him then. Blake swung around and watched her move through the crowd. Even in anger, she walked with the grace of a queen. Few people, other than his brothers, ever talked to him the way she had. He was the head of the Thorns' San Francisco store, and his family's money gave him a certain amount of power. Elliana Hamilton didn't seem to care about that. He smiled. He liked her, yet he'd challenged her. He didn't have to ask himself why.

He knew why.

Ellie smiled, stopped and spoke to several people as she got as far from Blake as possible. She needed to be alone for a few minutes. Just before she reached the staircase, Judi, her best friend, stopped her.

"Hey, who is that guy?" Judi asked.

"What guy?"

"That gorgeous, super delicious, crystal glass of red wine."

She was looking directly at Blake Thorn. "Judi, remember, you have a date."

"Yeah, but I'm not married to him, and having a date doesn't mean I can't look…and admire." Her last two words were a growl. Normally, Ellie would have laughed.

"I take it you want to meet him?"

"Of course I want to meet him. Is he a new sponsor? I've never seen him before."

Judi came to the gala every year as Ellie's guest.

"What's his name?"

"Blake Thorn." Ellie felt an undefinable string that seemed to pull her insides.

"I guess it'll have to wait," Judi said. "Here comes my date."

Judi walked away with a false smile on her face, and Ellie made it to the stairs. She rushed up them and went into the makeshift office, closing the door. Thankfully, the room was empty. She took a deep breath.

She'd rarely set eyes on him before, and not for lack of trying. She'd gone to see him in the past, but he'd been unavailable. To think, he practically accused her of mismanagement when he'd never seen a book or knew anything about how she coordinated and obtained funding for the gala. Ellie had never met someone so condescending, so ready to jump to conclusions. She thanked the powers that controlled the universe that he hadn't been someone who was continually coming around to check on the foundation.

She thought it was unusual that Ellie had been with the foundation for three years and hadn't met Blake Thorn, when the store he managed was within walking distance of her office. She'd organized and managed three fund-raising galas, and this was the first one he chose to attend. For some reason, Ellie thought Katherine Thorn had something to do with his presence there tonight.

Ellie could have done without him upsetting her evening.

Her watch vibrated against her arm. She checked it and saw the reminder that it was time for dinner. Simultaneously, a message appeared on the small screen. It was from the catering manager. Dinner was ready to be served.

Taking a deep breath, Ellie left the office, hoping she could reach the dining room without encountering Blake again. Unfortunately she didn't get to completely ignore him. She was sitting with the Thorns.

Outside the ballroom, the crowd had begun to assemble. Soft bells chimed as the floor-to-ceiling doors automatically pivoted open on silent motorized hinges. The entire process was like a choreographed dance, and people flocked to see the dance of the doors as one patron labeled them. Ellie stood aside as the crowd surged in to find their assigned tables.

Surveying the corridor outside the ballroom, Ellie

checked that everyone was inside. Going to the door, she watched as friends greeted each other and found their seats. Actually, she was delaying her own trek to the head table. Blake would invariably be there. She only hoped he was already seated between two members of his family and she would be free to direct her conversation to one of the others. She didn't want a confrontation, and vowed to be civil and provide any of them with whatever information they needed.

As Ellie pushed herself away from the open door, someone came around beside her.

"I guess we're the last to go in," Blake Thorn said.

Her heart dropped.

"From the diagram, I see we're at table number one." He offered his arm as if she were his date and had been waiting for him.

Ellie knew she had no choice. If she refused to accept his offer, someone influential would surely be watching. She didn't need any unwarranted rumors. And Blake *was* a blood member of the Thorn family.

She slipped her hand through his bent arm, closing it around his biceps. She refused to totally link herself to him. Her body had taken on a heat level of its own, and she knew it had to do with him. He didn't know her and she didn't know him, but she was reacting as if there was something between them.

And there wasn't. There couldn't be—now or ever.

He led her around the perimeter, where there was ample room for the two of them, giving her no need to extract her hand from his arm. At the table, the two seats waiting for them were side by side. Ellie somehow knew they would be, but she hoped someone had wanted him closer and saved a place for him.

Pulling her chair out, Blake acted the gentleman and helped her settle before taking the place next to her.

She acknowledged everyone and apologized, “I’m afraid I’ll have to be up and down several times to handle the program, so don’t wait for me to eat.”

Several heads nodded at her as they began with their salads.

“Ellie, you look sensational,” Rose said. She sat on Ellie’s left. “I’ve done some buying for the Logan Beach store, and I’ve never seen anything as fabulous as that dress.”

Ellie looked down. The dress was white with a rounded neckline that extended to her shoulders, showing only a hint of her upper arms. What made it stand out was it was dripping with Swarovski crystals. From the neckline to the hem, the crystals caught the light at every angle. When Ellie first put the heavily weighted gown on, she felt like a walking light beam, but the beauty of it made any drawbacks worth it.

“You’re tall,” Mrs. Thorn added. “You can wear something like that.”

“Like a queen,” Blake commented. “Did you find it in our store?”

Naturally, they all assumed she shopped at the House of Thorn. Ellie did on occasion, but she hadn’t in a while, at least not in person.

She glanced at him, shaking her head. “My sister is a designer. She designed and made it for me.”

"She's extremely talented," Rose said. "Who does she design for?"

"She has her own firm, but she's always looking for more outlets for her clothes."

"A dress like this is a one of a kind," Blake said. "It would need to retail for..." He stopped and looked at her with keen eyes. "I'd say upward of ten grand. It's got to have a couple of hundred crystals." He lifted one on the arm of the gown. "And these aren't your one-carat variety."

Ellie wanted to pull her arm free, but that would damage the dress. She wondered if Blake always quantified things into dollars and cents. The dress would cost thousands of dollars. Her sister had spent a couple of weeks sewing the crystals on by hand. However, it hadn't been the only thing she did in a day. Yet for someone to hand sew them on would increase the price dramatically, and then there was the designer's rate. And she was happy to see her sister was a success.

"I'd still like to talk to her," Rose said.

"I'll get you her card," Ellie offered.

"That's it for business tonight," Andrew Thorn, Blake's father, said. Mr. Thorn rarely spoke, but when he did they all listened.

Dinner was served, and for a moment the conversation ceased. Ellie hadn't eaten her salad, and when the plates were set, she was not served.

"Are you eating?" Blake asked.

"She never eats at these things." Katherine spoke up. Her explanation seemed to tell Blake if he'd attended in the past, he'd understand these things.

"Dieting?" His brows rose.

"I'll eat later," she said without further explanation.

She then turned her attention to Rose and David, learning about their meeting and marriage. When dessert and coffee were served, Darlene signaled her from the side of the stage.

"I have to go now," she apologized. "It's time to begin the program."

Smiles followed her as she rose and moved toward the raised podium. The crystals clinked together, making the musical sound of someone running their hands through a chandelier. Her sister had done a far better job than Ellie dreamed when she asked about covering the dress with them.

Moments later Ellie looked out on the crowd. Her gaze went to Blake immediately, as if he was the person to focus her speech on. Nervousness accosted her, in a way it had never done before. Moving her head away from the microphone, she cleared her throat and turned back. He was front and center, so she couldn't avoid his gaze or his scrutiny.

Ellie rarely prepared speeches. She had a good memory and felt that speaking from the heart was better than anything she could write out beforehand. She began her welcome and forced her attention to move over more of the audience than just the Thorns' table. She must have spoken coherently since she heard laughter and surprise at several places. The laughter had her relaxing and seeing an almost smile on Blake's face, which took away some of the tension. She introduced several of the girls sitting on the side, who were recipients of the Give It to the Girl Foundation.

"The girls and the foundation are lucky to have such a wonderful program chairperson. Vera Gordon, please stand."

A redhead with a bright smile, sitting with the girls, stood up and waved a hand.

"Many of our programs have been suggested and developed by Vera. She's committed to the foundation and committed to seeing that the girls have as many opportunities as possible."

The room applauded and Vera resumed her seat. Ellie waited until the applause died down.

"I introduced the other board members earlier and the staff of Give It to the Girl. I held back on Vera because she was so instrumental in our surprise. But…" Ellie paused. "Before I reveal that very special surprise, I have one last appeal." She smiled at the crowd. "I've given you a few statistics about our work and how important it is to girls. Many of you are our contributors and we thank you. However…" She paused with her hand in the air. A ripple of laughter went through the room. Obviously her next words were anticipated. "There is always more to be done. So if you want to stop by one of the volunteers in the back of the room…" Ellie pointed. Several men and women stood with their hands up, and the crowd shifted to see them. "They're willing to accept your checks, credit cards or cash, if you carry that sort of thing."

General laughter continued. When it died down,

she added, "We'll wait for you before we introduce our surprise."

A buzz sounded throughout the room as people speculated on what she meant. Darlene and Ellie were the only people who had known the secret until this morning, when it was necessary to tell a few key people.

"Speaking of surprises," Ellie said. The room quieted. "We have a very special guest to entertain you tonight. One of the graduates, one who came to us and we gave it to the girl, has volunteered—" Ellie didn't have to finish. The applause started and then escalated until it drowned her out. Everyone knew whose name she was about to say.

Using her hands to gesture a lowering manner, she got them to quiet down. "Obviously, this lady needs no introduction. She said she wants to give back because Give It to the Girl changed her life. So, ladies and gentlemen, if you would move to the dance floor." The pivoting doors to the left swung open. "Please join me and give it to the girl—Chantelle."

The applause was deafening as the entire body rose to its feet. The adjoining room had been set up with both tables along the perimeter and a dance floor in the center. Chantelle's signature song began to play, and the room emptied quickly.

Ellie left the stage. Blake stood at the bottom, offering his hand to prevent her from falling.

"Thank you," she said.

"Good speech," he responded. "I'm tempted to donate myself."

She was unsure how to take that. Was he being serious or facetious? She didn't know.

"It's allowed," she told him. Glancing at the back of the room, she saw a small crowd with the volunteer cashiers. "Those people are ready and willing to accept your contribution."

Blake followed her glance, but when he turned back to her, he changed the subject. "You know, this event gets better and better," he said.

Ellie braced herself for another comment on the cost. Cutting him off, she spoke first. "You haven't been here in the past three years. How would you know?"

"I mean from what I've seen tonight. At every turn, there's something new and unexpected."

"Don't bring up what Chantelle cost," Ellie said. "I can assure you, she's volunteering her talent. Her intent is true. She wants to give back."

Ellie turned to walk away. She no longer wanted to talk to Blake, even if he was a Thorn. But Vera Gordon hampered her escape. Vera caught Ellie in a bear hug, smiling and talking enthusiastically, telling her how wonderful the event was going. Ellie smiled and nodded, concealing her true feelings for the man behind her.

"Hello," Vera said, relinquishing her hold on Ellie and offering her hand to Blake. "I'm Vera Gordon."

"Blake Thorn," he said. "I hear we have you to thank for the entertainment."

Vera grinned, glancing over her shoulder at where the crowd had gathered to listen to Chantelle's concert. "We have seats reserved for you."

"Thank you," Blake acknowledged.

As Ellie tried to move around to let Vera take her place, Blake captured her arm and steered her to the seats Vera pointed out.

Ellie needed to be available to join Chantelle on the stage when she finished. Vera had abdicated that responsibility. While Vera was an outgoing person, she totally froze when she had to speak to a crowd this size. Speaking to the girls and presenting projects in a conference room was something she could handle, but not a crowd this size.

With a seat in the front row, Ellie was close enough. She kept her face trained on the woman onstage, but her attention was ten years back, on a lonely stretch of road that had collided with her present a few hours earlier, when Blake Thorn had entered Riverton Mansion.

She'd relegated him and that day to the past and hoped it would stay there. But sitting in the darkened room, with his arm only a few inches from hers, she doubted she'd ever be able to do that again.

# *Chapter 2*

Blake's brother André seemed to be having a wonderful time. He was dancing with Ellie, and she appeared to enjoy his company. She threw her head back and laughed at something André said. An emotion Blake hadn't felt in years, and thought was dead to him, emerged. He lifted the goblet in his hand and took a sip of his wine.

"What's up, Blake?" David came to him, clasping him on the shoulder. "Are you enjoying the night?"

Blake looked around for Rose. Since David met her a little more than a year ago, the two had rarely been apart.

"It's a party," he responded.

"You like parties," David said. The wonder of him standing alone was evident to Blake.

"Not charity events. Not even our own."

"You didn't appear to dislike it during dinner," David said.

"Or before." Carter, one of the twins, joined in.

Blake turned and looked at his brothers.

"Don't give me that look," Carter said. "The sizzle between you two was practically visible." He indicated Ellie. "However, you better get in there. André looks like he wants to replace you."

Blake took a sip of his drink to buy time. His heart had kicked up a beat and his mouth was dry. "Not interested," he said.

"I'd be interested," Carter replied. "That dress alone is enough to get my attention."

Blake suddenly wanted to hit his brother, or rather his cousin. Carter and Christian were twins, but they had grown up with him and his brothers after their parents died. They were more brothers than cousins, so none of the Thorn boys ever thought of them as anything other than brothers.

He looked back at André and Ellie. The music ended, and the two of them began to walk away. André cupped her arm and Ellie leaned into him. Blake's teeth clenched. He made an effort to relax his jaw. What was happening here? He rationalized it was his brothers' comments, especially David's. Since he'd found Rose, he was a completely different man. Love had done that to him. But Blake wasn't David, and love had not entered his life.

His glance went toward Ellie.

"Go on, Blake," David said. "Go ask her to dance."

"Yeah, man. Short of a full-on kiss, holding a woman in your arms for a dance is the next best thing for gauging her attraction to you."

"And you do want to know about that, right?" David asked.

"I will go," Blake replied. "Not because I want to dance with her, or that anything you have said or thought is true. I just want to get away from you two."

Blake knew that was a lie as the words fell from his mouth. He set his glass on the table and then heard David and Carter's laughter as he headed to the place where Ellie and André were standing. When he was ten feet from them, André saw him and turned in a welcoming stance. Ellie's face turned to stone when she saw him. The smile didn't move; her features remained unchanged. It was like the Botox had suddenly set, and she couldn't move if she wanted to. Of course, there was no all-body Botox, yet her entire body could be compared to a statue.

"Blake," André said, opening his arm to invite him into the conversation. Blake stopped in front of his brother. Ellie gave him a bright smile that never reached her eyes. "Ellie and I were just catching up since we haven't seen each other since last year." He laughed and so did Ellie, obviously at something that had been said before Blake joined them.

André leaned back and looked behind Blake. He followed his brother's gaze to see Carter gesturing at him.

"Excuse me," he said. "We'll talk more before I leave."

Both Ellie and Blake watched. Only Blake knew

what was going on. "Why don't we dance?" he asked. "I believe they're playing our song."

He glanced at André and led Ellie to the floor. Pulling her into his arms, he heard the musical sounds of the crystals on her dress.

"Tell me, Blake, do you have any musical training?" Ellie asked as he whirled her around the room.

"I played piano when I was younger. Quit it when I went to college. Why do you ask?"

"Because the song playing is called 'Even Now.' It was written and recorded back in the seventies. There have been other songs with that title, even a book by a very popular author, but this song is about a man who had a history with a woman whom he is no longer with. He's with someone else now and still thinks of his old love."

Blake stared at her, raising one eyebrow.

"What I'm saying is we have no history. We are not current lovers or old lovers. So this cannot be *our* song."

He couldn't tell her he just wanted to get her away from his brother. He didn't even tell himself that, even though he knew it. Blake didn't reply to her comment. Instead he said, "This is the first time I've danced with someone who creates her own music as she moves."

Ellie lowered her head so he couldn't see her expression, but he felt her relax in his arms. He pulled her tighter. She didn't resist. Carter had been right. He listened to the tinkle of the crystals as they mingled with the song. They had no history together, and at the moment, Blake wondered if he wanted one. It had been years since he'd been serious about anyone.

Getting serious was something he'd avoided and finally removed from his plate altogether. He'd done it once, and it had ended in disaster. He wouldn't go that route again, no matter how good she felt and smelled. He nudged her hair aside and dropped his head. He would have kissed her naked shoulder if he hadn't remembered he was on a public dance floor and there were at least three pairs of eyes trained on him. It could be more if he included Rose, his parents and Christian in the mix. He wasn't about to give his brothers food for thought or fodder for future ribbing.

He didn't push Ellie back. He kept her close to him as the music continued and the story of lost love was played out. When it ended, he felt it was all too soon, especially when Ellie stepped back and lifted her head. Her face was flushed and her eyes bright, not with tears, but with something else, something he'd seen a long time ago and never thought he'd see again.

"Thank you," she said, stepping away from him. Her voice was strained. "I have to go and check on the other guests."

Blake said nothing. He inclined his head slightly and gave her room to pass him. She melted into the crowd, leaving the dance floor. Even after she was gone, he could smell her perfume, and the faint tinkle of the crystals played like a song in his ears. While that seventies' song might not be theirs, the clear bell sounds of those crystals would forever define their introduction.

* * *

The party went on until one o'clock. Thankfully Ellie didn't have to drive home. As hostess of the event, she was the last to leave the ballroom, but there was still work to be done before she could fall into her bed on the eighth floor of the hotel where most of the out-of-town guests were staying. She met with several staff members, made sure all the foundation's decorations had been removed from the ballroom and tallied the night's contributions. By the time she stepped out of her heels in her room, she was exhausted.

And hungry. She hadn't eaten anything except a few crackers, and that was just so the champagne toasts she participated in wouldn't leave her head reeling. She glanced at the cart that had been left for her. Her mouth watered.

The night had been wonderful, she thought. Except for Blake shadowing her, everything else had gone as planned. Nothing, however, could cure her encounter with the manager of the House of Thorn San Francisco.

An hour later, Ellie glanced at the clock on the side of the desk. It was after two. Just one more email, she thought, and then she'd go to bed. The crystals on her dress either clunked against the desk or the computer with each letter she typed.

It would only take a moment. She didn't have to work in the morning, and she wouldn't meet with Katherine Thorn until Tuesday, giving her plenty of time to have all the papers ready for their quarterly meeting.

She hit Send at the same time a soft tap came on her door. Glancing at the clock again, she wondered who that could be. Then she figured it was Darlene. Her assistant was fastidious and always prepared.

Ellie slid out of her chair and, holding the train of her gown, walked barefoot to the door. Recoiling at the distorted image she saw through the peephole, she took in a ragged breath.

What did he want?

She hesitated so long he knocked again. Ellie took in a long breath and opened the door a foot or so, wide enough for her to look out.

He still wore his tux, but his bow tie hung around his neck like twin silhouettes of Aphrodite. If anything, he was even sexier looking than he had been when he was fresh and pressed.

"Mr. Thorn," she said. "What are you doing here at this hour?" She added the last as a reprimand. Of all the Thorns, he was the last one she wanted to see.

"You refer to all the rest of my family by their first names. I'm sure you can manage Blake," he said.

"Well, Blake. Why are you here?"

"You didn't eat before the dance, and you had nothing afterward. I thought you might be hungry." He lifted the covered tray he was holding.

Ellie felt pleasure seep through her. It was rare for anyone to think of her needs.

"That was very nice of you," she said. "And I appreciate your thoughtfulness, but..." She pulled the door farther inward, opening it wide enough for Blake to take in the suite's living room, from threshold to windows.

The room service table, along with a crumpled napkin and the remains of her meal, stood like a sentinel awaiting redemption.

"Oh," he said.

Ellie laughed, relaxing from the surprise of his presence and the look on his face.

"I didn't know," he said.

"I know. And thank you."

"What should I do with this?" Again he lifted the tray.

"Why don't you bring it in? We can at least drink whatever you have there."

Blake passed her close enough for her to feel his body heat. Setting the tray on the coffee table, he removed the large napkin covering her food.

"Coffee or tea?" he asked.

"Tea."

"Iced or hot?" His voice sounded like that of a waiter.

"Iced," she said, again surprised that he'd covered all the options.

Taking a seat, he added ice to one of the empty glasses and poured the cold liquid into it. The ice crackled, making the only sound in the room.

Ellie sank down into the sofa, accepting the tall glass and drinking. The liquid was cold and sweet, exactly the way she liked it. She wondered how he knew, or if this was just an experiment that worked.

Joining her with his own glass, he asked, "Did you enjoy the party?"

"After a while. It's always stressful when you're the hostess."

"And the Thorns are in attendance."

"That, too," she agreed, sipping the liquid to avoid his scrutiny. "How about you? You didn't look as if you wanted to be here when you first came in."

"I didn't, but how did you know?"

"I was on the stairs when your family arrived."

"My mother insisted that I change any plans I had and attend this year."

She chuckled, hiding behind her hand.

"What?" he asked at the look she gave him.

"Are you trying to tell me your mother made you come?"

Blake looked at the ceiling for a moment, probably realizing what he'd said. "Yeah, I guess there is truth in that. But it was rather pleasant being here."

The way he looked at her made her feel exposed. His tone changed, and his words made her insides melt.

Ellie yawned and Blake took it as an indicator that he should leave. He'd like to remain in her room for the rest of the night, but she had to be completely out of energy by now. He didn't know everything about holding events. His store had events every month, but he had a staff that handled it.

"You should get some sleep," he said, standing.

Ellie stood, too, stifling another yawn.

"I'm sorry I kept you up."

"I appreciate the food and your thoughtfulness."

They started for the door. The grandfather clock in the suite hall chimed, punctuating the early-morning hour.

Blake turned. The light here was subdued, and while Ellie looked sleepy and drained, she was also beautiful. "Well, good morning." He smiled.

"Thank you again."

For a moment, neither of them moved. Blake didn't want to go. He wanted to take her in his arms, but he stopped himself by opening the door and stepping outside.

He'd taken two steps when the door opened and Ellie called him back. Blake found it impossible to describe how he felt at the sound of his name.

"This is awkward," she said.

"What?" He frowned, his elation plummeting.

"I need your help."

He took the two steps back to the door. "What is it?"

"The dress," she said. "Judi helped me zip it up, but I can't get the zipper down alone."

Blake wanted to grin, not just smile. He wanted to show a big, teeth-baring grin. But he resisted.

"No problem," he said. His voice was deeper than it had ever been, and he hoped she didn't notice.

She opened the door wider and he came back inside.

*This is not a difficult job*, Blake told himself as the door to Ellie's suite closed. He took a deep breath and let it out slowly. He'd done this before, not quite in the same situation, but close. Why did he feel all clumsy now? He hadn't even touched her yet, but his fingers felt like fat sausages. He checked them to make sure they weren't.

Ellie turned around.

Blake checked her, but didn't move. The space in the vestibule was more intimate with a low ceiling and the only light coming from the two lamps in the distant living room. He felt surrounded by a soft current that flowed around them. He knew he needed to keep that electric buzz quiet, not allow it to gain any strength. He was unsure what would happen if even a tiny spark ignited between them.

Ellie pulled her hair aside. At the ball, it had been piled in an amazing twist on her head. The style gave a clear view of her face, but with it falling past her shoulders, her look changed to sexy—not just sexy, and not modern sexy, either; more like film noir sexy. The dress contributed to the look. It was long, angled to the curves of her body and dripping with facets that caught the light, promising more.

"Anything wrong?" Ellie asked.

Blake tried to speak, but cleared his throat instead. He reached for the zipper. His other hand held on to the fabric between her shoulder blades, and he pulled the small instrument down. He hadn't intended to touch her skin, but his fingers had a mind of their own. Her back was smooth, warm, and she arched slightly on contact.

"I think I can do the rest," she said, pulling away from him and turning around. She held the bodice up. He could see the sides fall open and lie about her shoulders like angel wings. Blake's hands went cold when he was no longer holding the zipper, when his fingers were no longer brushing the crystals, but skimming over smooth, dark skin.

Ellie wasn't a foot from him. If he took half a step, they would be only a breath apart. And everything in his psyche told him to take it, take the chance, let it happen. But Blake stood his ground with effort. Taking that step would be like crossing a gulf.

And he wasn't up for that.

"Good night," he said, not even recognizing the emotion in his voice. He thought he heard Ellie say thank you, but he'd already opened and closed the door. He walked down the hall, feeling as if vertigo had attacked him. The hall yo-yoed in front of him, the walls moving closer, then receding, as if he'd had too much to drink. Except it wasn't drink that did this.

It was memory.

Blake had suppressed it, put it aside, relegated it to the back of his mind, but he'd wanted Ellie the moment he saw her, and that memory was looking for a get-out-of-jail card.

He couldn't…wouldn't let himself find it.

Sleep must have claimed Ellie as the morning sun tinted the horizon. She couldn't remember getting into bed or going to sleep. Blake's exit, however, was clear in her mind.

Ellie had yawned and Blake took it as a cue to leave. She was exhausted and sleep was a top priority. She loved the gown her sister had designed, but there was one drawback. Judi had been there to help her into it, but she was alone in the suite and had no way to get the zipper down. As tired as she was, she knew she couldn't sleep on the crystals.

There was no choice. She had to ask the only other person in the room for help. And it was his hands that were keeping her awake. He hadn't taken a long time to pull the zipper down. He hadn't spent an inordinate amount of time with his skin next to hers. It wasn't time that was an issue. It was the hot zing of emotion that went through her.

She thought he appeared at her door because he suddenly remembered where he'd seen her before. But that wasn't it. He was only there to bring her something to eat.

Ellie found that hard to believe. It was so out of character for the man she believed she'd known.

But had it been? Or could he be leading her toward a false reality? Ellie knew Blake Thorn. She'd known him for ten years, but tonight she'd come face-to-face with him, danced with him, had him unzip her gown, and yet he showed no indication that he knew anything at all about their previous encounter.

What would it mean to her future, when he did remember? It was inevitable if he continued to attend the same events she frequented. Hopefully, that wouldn't be the case.

He'd said he didn't like charity balls. Since their event only happened once a year, she could avoid him. The thought should have made her happy.

Yet for some reason, it didn't.

# *Chapter 3*

"*What a difference a day makes.*" The unmistakable sound of Dinah Washington's voice came across the radio waves. Ellie immediately found the button on her steering wheel and silenced the song. She couldn't listen to it. And it had been more than one day since her world had begun to crumble. There was a time she loved hearing that version. She'd even sung it herself in a recital when she was in high school. Her mother loved it, so Ellie learned it. That was until ten years ago, when the full and true meaning of the words defined Ellie's world.

Her old one was gone, blotted out in a single second. Nothing would ever be the same after that. In twenty-four hours, everything she knew had changed. There was no going back, no do-over, no way to correct the outcome.

It was what it was.

She had to live with it. And she was doing well, until Saturday night, until one man walked through the door of the Riverton Mansion and her worlds collided. There was no explosion, at least none that could be seen. There could be an explosion if Ellie had let things go on, things like Blake running his finger down her back.

But she wouldn't.

Their one night had been the twenty-four hours that made a difference. And it wouldn't happen again.

Ellie pulled into the office parking lot and cut the engine. She also cut all thoughts of the past, at least the long-ago past. She remembered the dinner dance and the events that had happened in her suite with Blake.

But today things would go back to normal. Blake Thorn would return to his store, and she would prepare for her meeting with Katherine Thorn.

She could put Blake out of her mind. She'd done it for ten years. She wondered if he was doing the same. Did he need to think about her the way she thought about him? What had his twenty-four hours been like?

She remembered what happened to them. He didn't.

And she hoped he never would.

At ten o'clock on Tuesday morning, twenty-four hours later, Darlene entered Ellie's office with a cup of coffee in each hand. She offered one to Ellie, who stood and accepted it, but looked at her quizzically.

"What's this?" she asked. Darlene never brought her coffee. She was her assistant, not her maid.

"Coffee," Darlene said. "But if I had tequila, I'd have brought that."

"What are you talking about?"

Darlene was a logical woman. She never brought coffee and she wasn't one to beat around the bush. She was levelheaded and efficient, and Ellie was lucky to have her on the team.

"You know that guy from Saturday night, the one you were drooling all over?"

"I was not drooling." Ellie turned and walked around her desk. Her face had suddenly gone hot, and she didn't want her assistant to see the flush of heat under her skin.

"Okay, maybe it was him drooling over you."

Darlene was fishing. That was why she'd shown up with a cup of coffee. Ellie should have known.

"Darlene, there's something you're not saying."

"He's in reception," she blurted out.

Ellie's heart leaped in her chest. "What's he doing there?"

"Apparently, he came for the meeting with Mrs. Thorn." She gave Ellie a sideways glance. "Or you were so appealing Saturday night that he just had to see you again."

Ellie ignored her assistant's facetious remark. What went through Ellie's mind was Blake's fingers sliding down her back. Heat infused her from the inside. She tried to keep her features as bland as she could. But Darlene was perceptive.

"Is Katherine with him?"

She nodded. “Do you want me to show them to the conference room?”

It was on the tip of her tongue to take Darlene up on her offer, but Katherine deserved her attention. She’d deal with Blake in her own way. Unfortunately she didn’t know what that was at the moment. She’d have to take her cue from him.

“I’ll do it,” she told Darlene. “Is everything set up?”

“I checked it three times.”

Ellie got up and smoothed the skirt of her suit down. She took her portfolio with the foundation logo on it and, squaring her shoulders, headed for reception.

“Katherine.” She smiled. “Good to see you again.”

Both Katherine and her son stood. Katherine kissed her on the cheek.

“Blake, I wasn’t expecting you, but it’s good to see you again.” She offered her hand and he took it. His was larger and warm. Ellie felt as if she was being overly formal. When Katherine had come in previous years, Ellie had never felt anything but a little nervous. “We have everything set up in the conference room.”

Katherine had been there before and followed as Ellie led them back into the office. Blake looked around, taking in everything. Ellie wondered what he was thinking, and whether he was viewing the desk, chairs and artwork in dollars and cents.

“There are folders on the table with all the information for your review.”

As the assembly moved to chairs and took seats, Ellie pushed a button on the conference table and a screen dropped from the ceiling. At the same time, the lights lowered and Ellie began her presentation. She went over the current programs and their statuses, gave the financial standing of the foundation and then put up a display of the new programs they planned to begin in the next year.

Katherine asked a few questions, but Blake remained attentive and quiet. His lack of response unnerved Ellie, but she went on.

"The last thing is the fund-raiser from Saturday night," she started. The foundation staff had spent all day Monday making sure everything had been accounted for, and they were ready for the meeting. Ellie pressed a button in her hand and the computer image on the screen changed.

A single page came up. The background matched the other slides of the presentation. This one showed the cost of the gala, along with the services donated by the various vendors.

"Wait a minute," Blake said, speaking for the first time. He nearly rose out of his seat as she pointed to the screen. "You mean all the services were donated?"

"The mansion did not charge us for the use of the facility or their catering services. They donated that." She used a laser pointer to highlight the item he questioned.

"Usually Ellie convinces a facility to donate their services," Katherine explained. "They benefit from new clients who see what they can do at our gala."

Blake glanced at Ellie, and she knew exactly what he was thinking. His look said, *You could have told me.*

Ellie turned back to the presentations. "These are the other vendors who donated products or services."

"Was there anything that wasn't donated?" Blake asked.

Ellie pressed her button again. "These are the expenses we had to pay for. Mind you, these numbers do not include any staff salaries or administrative costs."

"You'd have those even if we had no gala," Blake pointed out.

"Exactly," Ellie agreed.

"Twelve hundred fifty-seven dollars and thirty-eight cents." Blake's voice showed his incredulity. "That was the only expense? What about Chantelle?"

"She's on the donation list." Ellie went backward and pointed out her donation to the foundation.

"I am impressed you could do all this for practically nothing," Blake said.

"That's one of the reasons I hired her," Katherine chimed in. She smiled at Ellie.

"There's one more slide," Ellie said, pressing a button. "You saw the list of donations when I went over the financial information. These are the new donors and donations we took in on Saturday night."

Blake whistled.

Blake stared at the phone on his desk. He should call Ellie and apologize. He'd misread her completely. From the presentation she made the previous day, she was clearly a wizard, and his family and the foundation were lucky to have her. Blake didn't like charity events—too many people with their hands out. That was one of the reasons he avoided his own. However, he did sit on the board of several nonprofit organizations. On a whim, he'd gotten up in the middle of the night and looked at the finances of their events.

None of them held expenses down to any level close to what Ellie had done. He wondered how she could get so many businesses to totally donate their services. He remembered his brothers and how much fun they appeared to have at the gala. The other guests had clearly done the same, given the amount of donations Ellie collected that night alone.

A knock on the door brought Blake back to the present. Looking up, he saw his brother André pop his head through the door.

"Lunch?"

Blake looked at his watch. Had he been sitting there all morning, doing nothing? It was unlike him. It was rare for him to lose time while doing nothing but thinking about a woman. Especially a woman he'd met less than a week ago.

André stepped farther into the office. "Lunch?" he questioned again.

"Yeah," Blake said, standing up.

"You appeared to be lost in thought," André said when they'd walked the short distance to one of Blake's favorite sandwich shops. "Who was on your mind?"

"Why do you think it was someone? I was working and thinking about a new program that one of the department managers suggested."

André laughed, "No, you weren't." He gave Blake a knowing look. "Did it have anything to do with the beautiful executive director?"

Did the entire family see something that wasn't

there? He had no feelings for Ellie Hamilton beyond her work with the foundation. Even if she was a beautiful woman. There was no doubt about that.

Blake took a bite of his roast-beef sandwich before answering his brother. “It was the first time I met her.”

André glanced at him. “The first year I met her, I was attracted to her. I tried to get a date with her.”

Blake’s head came up and he stared at his brother.

“No go,” he went on. “She shut me down. Her voice was soft and she didn’t say anything that made me dislike her, but she was not interested.”

“I suppose that was a good thing,” Blake said, hiding the fact that he was glad she hadn’t dated his brother. “You hate the type who strings you along for what she can get from you.”

That had happened to André before, and while he dated a lot, he also scrutinized women to see if they were more interested in his money than him. So far he hadn’t found anyone who passed his test.

“We’re not talking about me,” André said, deflecting the conversation back to Blake.

“We both are in the same city. It stands to reason we’ll meet sometime. I wouldn’t want to be a stranger, but as for any attraction…” Blake shook his head, yet he knew there was more to his feelings than he was willing to admit.

“That’s your story and you’re sticking to it,” André teased.

“It’s not a story.”

André laughed again, giving Blake a Cheshire cat

grin. “Maybe you should try to see if she’s attracted to you?”

“Can we get off this discussion? If I were interested, I know how to go about pursuing a woman.”

André put his hand up in defeat. “Just checking. I watched David and Rose this past weekend, and the love between them is palpable. Maybe seeing them has brought out something in your subconscious, and you’ll finally be giving up on pushing every female away before they can get to your heart.”

Blake didn’t like the assessment of his character, but he couldn’t deny it, either. He kept most women at bay, breaking off any relationship before it progressed to an imaginary point he’d set.

“Believe me, there’s nothing between Elliana Hamilton and me.” As Blake said the words, he remembered how he had felt pulling that zipper down her back.

“All I’m saying is give it a chance. If it’s not Ellie, maybe it’s someone else. Just be open.”

André was perceptive, even if he did appear to be bulletproof, with comments and relationships easily bouncing off him. Blake knew that was false. His own experience had taught him that people kept secrets inside. They talked about them to no one. Good secrets were shared. They practically burst out of you. But the dark ones were suffered alone. Blake had his dark secrets, and because of it, he kept women at bay.

Ellie had gotten past the entrance, pulled his thoughts and emotions out of the jail where he kept them, but he’d wrangled them back in place, and there they would stay.

"I'll give it some thought," he told André, knowing he didn't plan to think about it at all.

But Blake did give it some thought. In fact, he seemed unable to think about anything else.

Ellie had been born in San Francisco and lived in California most of her life. There was a short span of time when her family lived in New York State, but once her father died, she'd returned to California. Ellie was aware of the changeable weather patterns, the fog, the rain and the cold. But as she and Judi, who convinced her to go, walked into the House of Thorn's restaurant, Ellie understood the true meaning of the cliché "skating on thin ice."

The store was huge, its footprint taking up an entire block of the shopping district, and that didn't include the parking garage across the street, with underground access to the store. Yet with all that square footage, Ellie felt she was only a step from running into Blake Thorn.

They were led to a table overlooking the huge windows, although Judi seemed to know where she wanted to sit. The windows were at the farthest point from the entrance, and that gave Ellie a slight bit of relaxation.

"You've got to try one of the desserts. The chocolate cake is to die for," Judi said.

"Judi, you do know I've been here before."

"Not in a while, and this cake is new to the menu."

Judi was a shopaholic, and while Ellie liked clothes, she knew what she wanted and often found it fast and left the store. Except for special occasions like the gala, when she would shop for days before going to her sister and telling her she had nothing suitable. This was something she did sparingly. Whitney Hamilton was in high demand, and day by day, her star was rising higher.

Both Judi and Ellie bypassed food and went straight for the chocolate cake.

"I know I'm going to have to pay for this," Judi said. "Chocolate goes straight to my hips."

"We'll spend more time in the gym tonight," Ellie said. The waiter placed the hunk of chocolate cake in front of them. Her first taste of the confection had her eyes closing in ecstasy. "This is sooo good."

"Told ya," Judi said.

"Oh God, this is too good. I never want another slice." She knew Judi would know what she meant. "And I definitely cannot take any of this home. It's a good thing I do most of my shopping online."

"I'm sure they'll deliver it to you if you order it. Maybe you'll luck out and find handsome Blake Thorn as your deliveryman."

Could Ellie get away from people constantly bringing Blake's name into conversations with her?

"Why do you think he would deliver something to me?"

Ellie spoke before she realized what the answer to that question could yield. And true to the conversation, Judi provided the expected response. "I saw the way he looked at you and the way you looked at him."

"I did not look at him any differently than I did his brothers."

Judi didn't say anything, only took her time pulling the fork out of her mouth. She cut another forkful of cake and lifted it to eye level. She did not eat it, but rather scrutinized it. "Do you think that chocolate and men really have the same sexual effect on women?"

Judi might have spoken to the cake, but her question was double-edged.

"How do you feel about it?" Ellie tried deflection again.

"Oh, I believe they are one and the same." She ate the bite on her fork.

"Does that mean you met someone Saturday night and you haven't told me about him?"

"No, it doesn't. I spent some time with André Thorn, but he lives a continent away. And he really isn't my type." She hunched closer to the table, as if the two of them were conspirators. To make matters even more intriguing, she whispered, "Not like you and that beautiful man who squired you around the dance floor."

Ellie couldn't help laughing. "Not my type, either," she whispered back.

"Too bad," Judi said.

"Why is that?"

"Because he's on his way over."

She sat back and Ellie froze. She didn't look over her shoulder, so Judi looked for her, smiling so brightly, she could be in a toothpaste advertisement.

"Please tell me you're kidding," Ellie said, hoping her voice didn't sound as if she were pleading.

Judi didn't have time to reply. A shadow hovered over their table, and as Ellie raised her head, she looked into the handsome eyes of the manager of the House of Thorn. He was everything people had been telling her about over the past few days. Wearing a gray business suit that hugged his shoulders the way her arms had done when they danced, called to her for a repeat performance. Ellie placed her hands in her lap.

"Ladies," he greeted.

Judi smiled up adoringly.

"Judi, right?" he asked.

"Good memory," she said.

"Nice to see you both." He included Ellie.

Judi slipped out of her chair and stood. "Ellie has to finish her cake. I'm off to the shoe department. They're having a sale."

"Judi," Ellie said with a warning in her voice. "I'll go with you."

"Could you wait a moment? I'd like to talk to you." Blake's comment stopped her from rising. Judi's thumbs-up was only seen by Ellie as her friend slipped behind Blake and headed out.

"Meet me in the shoe department," she called.

Blake took the seat Judi had vacated and pushed the remnants of her cake aside. A waitress, not the waiter who was serving them, appeared and placed a cup of coffee in front of Blake.

"More coffee?" she asked Ellie.

Ellie's throat had gone dry and she nodded.

When the woman left after refilling her cup, Ellie took a sip of the coffee. "You said you wanted to talk to me."

"Something you said Saturday night has been bothering me."

"I said a lot of things. Could you narrow it down?"

He looked down at the cup, then back at her. Ellie couldn't help noticing that he had the most beautiful eyes she'd ever seen. Her heart was beating a little faster than normal. What could he want to talk to her about?

"Have you been to my office today?"

That was a strange question. "We came to shop," she said.

"So you came for the sale?"

"Not especially. Judi is the shopaholic. She brought me along." She didn't know where he was going with this, but decided to be straight. "Is this what you wanted to talk to me about?"

"You said, unlike you, my office door was closed, or something to that effect."

She remembered the comment. "And?"

"What did you mean?"

She looked him straight in the eye. "I was hired three years ago. Since there was a Thorn store here in San Francisco, I thought it was courteous to come by and introduce myself. Unfortunately you were always conveniently out of town or in a meeting that wouldn't break for hours. I left a message, but never received a return call." She paused, continuing to look at him. His face didn't change. "After a while I got the message." She raised and dropped her shoulders. "You weren't interested in meeting me. Your absence at the galas drove home that conclusion. If your mother hadn't insisted you come, we'd still have yet to meet."

She waited for some reaction.

Blake raised his cup and took a drink. "I apologize," he said.

Ellie waited for him to continue, but he said nothing. "That's it? That's all you have to say."

"It appears I have no argument, no excuse."

"Were you avoiding me?"

"I didn't know you. I run a very difficult business here, and I was always legitimately away or in a meeting."

"Why aren't you in one now?"

"It's my lunch hour."

"And you regularly have lunch in the public restaurant?" She knew it was a rhetorical question. Blake did not answer it.

He leaned forward. Ellie felt as if she should move farther back, but she remained where she was.

"The real reason is I'm not a charity fund-raiser person." He put his hand out to stop her from responding. "Don't think I don't believe in charities. I usually just write a check."

"No, you don't," she disagreed.

"What?"

"The store donates. You have a department that handles community projects, and they make the decisions. I doubt you even see the amount as a budget item."

Blake took a moment to rub his eyes, and Ellie knew she'd struck home.

"Why should I take an interest?" he asked.

"It depends on your personal feelings, but charities help people. Sometimes the people are in need, maybe even dire need. For others, it could mean jobs, self-esteem or just providing them with the skills for a better future."

"You're obviously very passionate about charities. How did you get into this?"

"I'm not passionate about all of them. Some are better than others, but I happen to think girls and women don't get enough credit for what they contribute. They're taught to be beautiful dolls. Even with educational degrees, they're shortchanged by insurance companies, the media, corporations, you name it." She spread her hands, encompassing the world.

"Are you getting personal? Did one of those somehow happen to you?"

Ellie realized she had become passionate. Her voice rose and she leaned closer across the table, driving home her point. She relaxed. "It's happened to every woman, whether she knows it or not."

"And your plan is to change the world."

"One girl at a time." Ellie was serious. She regularly participated in workshops and programs to help girls realize their potential and to act on accomplishing whatever they strove to do. "Maybe you should get involved with a charity or two and see what they do and why they do it."

She offered it as a challenge, fully expecting him to make some excuse about how busy he was at the store.

"All right," he said, sitting up straight. "Where do we start?"

"We?"

# Chapter 4

"What do you mean *we*?" Ellie asked.

Blake didn't even recognize himself. He shouldn't have said it, but the word was out of his mouth before he knew it was coming. Her question had given him the perfect opportunity to retract it. So why wasn't he doing that? Why hadn't he done it already?

Why was he letting ten years of practice be undermined by a pair of brown eyes connected to a figure he'd like to draw his hands down? Why was he even sitting at this table? There was no need for him to be here. He'd seen Ellie through the glass doors that led to the restaurant, but he hadn't needed to come through those doors. He could have—should have—continued to the elevator and returned to his office.

Yet his feet had led him inside with the flimsy excuse

of something she'd said Saturday night, which she probably didn't remember. Blake had been on dates. And they all knew he wasn't a "get involved" person. When he met someone new, he sized them up, categorized them as to their future expectations. If they didn't coincide with his, he ended the relationship before it could start.

He had no relationship with Ellie. But somewhere down deep, in a place Blake didn't know or thought was hidden, there was a tiny voice screaming over an ocean, trying to be heard. He wouldn't listen.

"Blake?" Ellie called his name.

"According to you, I'm a novice, so I'm going to need some instruction on where to start and what to do."

She gave him a sideways look. Obviously the words sounded as false to her as they did to his own ears.

"All right," she said, her grin saying she knew something he didn't. She grabbed a pen and a business card from her purse and started to write. "Meet me Saturday morning—"

"I have plans for Saturday," he interrupted.

"Cancel them," Ellie said in a clipped voice. It was an order. She didn't even look up when she delivered it. Continuing to write, she finished and pushed it across the table, toward him. "Here's the address. Be there at six o'clock in the morning."

"What happens here?"

Ignoring him, she went on, "Change out of that suit and wear something you can get dirty."

"Anything else?"

"Yes, the next charity is yours. So do some research

and find a group you want to support. It helps if you're passionate about their cause."

She stood up, dismissing him and any further conversation. "I'm going to meet Judi in the shoe department. Pay the tab. Consider it a charitable contribution."

Blake watched as she walked away. He couldn't help appreciating the sway of her hips as she put one foot in front of the other like a model. He wondered if she'd ever been a model. Then a thought came to him of someone else who'd at one time thought she wanted to be a model.

He turned back to the table and blinked several times, trying to dislodge the image of Ellie's walk from his brain. The waiter presented him with the check and he signed it, grateful to have something to do. The feeling that he'd been set up settled over him. His principles had been compromised, and he hadn't even realized it.

He admitted Elliana Hamilton was a force of her own. And he wanted to learn about that force, but he knew pursuing that avenue was like sticking his hands in fire.

The address was only a few miles outside the city, in beautiful country. Blake spent a lot of his time in the office and did all of his entertaining there. He used to come up to the hills more often, but it had been several years since he could look back and see the skyline. The air was fresh and slightly cooler.

He parked his Jeep between a van and a sporty Mercedes and saw Ellie the moment he got out of the car. She was leaning against a wooden fence by the entrance to a horse farm. The sign read Purple Cloud Horse Farm. She smiled at him as he approached, and his body reacted to her as if he'd been anticipating her smile all morning. She wore black formfitting exercise pants that showed every curve of her legs. The pants were covered by a long T-shirt that stopped halfway to her knees. Blake looked at it as a tease. The clothes were begging him to lift them and see what surprises were in store for him beneath the cloth.

"Horseback riding," he said. "I haven't been horseback riding in years."

"You're not here to ride," Ellie replied. "You've got work to do. Come on."

She led him to a small building. He could hear the noise of conversations coming from it long before they stepped through the door.

"Ah, Ellie," a short fiftysomething man greeted her. "We're nearly ready to go out."

"Everyone, meet Blake Thorn. He's never worked on a horse farm, so we'll have to show him the ropes."

"I'll show him," a ponytailed teenage girl spoke as if she were submitting a bid. The room laughed. Blake did, too.

"You all know what to do. Let's get out and do it."

The group dispersed. The short man came over to them and Ellie introduced him to Jim Nolan, area director of the horse-farm project, an organization that takes first-offender teens and gives them community service to show them a different way of life.

"How long have you been doing this kind of work?" Blake asked Jim.

"Twenty-three years," he answered. "And many of the kids have gone on to lead productive lives."

"I'll show Blake around and give him a partner to work with," Ellie said.

The two left and headed toward the barn.

"Why is it called Purple Cloud? There are no purple clouds here," Blake said, checking the sky for confirmation.

"The owners are Edna and Claude Eastwood. Edna's ridden all her life. Her first horse was named Purple Cloud."

Blake nodded. He liked the way Ellie told the story, as if it were a Hallmark movie and there was more behind the horse and rider than had yet been revealed. Blake had no stories like that. Growing up had its ups and downs for him, as it did for any normal kid. He and his brothers had tried and discarded many projects. Their parents believed they should try whatever interested them and rule it out if they discovered they had no taste for it. However, they had to stay in it long enough to make that decision. And their parents had to concur.

He'd tried the trumpet, ice-skating, mountain climbing and a myriad of other things, keeping up with his brothers. But other than his interest in the store, he'd hung in there with swimming and the piano.

They rounded a corner, and Blake saw a horse barn in front of them. "Please don't tell me we have to clean out the barn," he said.

The look she gave him said that was exactly what they were going to do. She showed him around the place, going in and out of several barns and riding a golf cart around the grounds.

"Who's that kid?" Blake asked, glancing over his shoulder.

"What kid?"

Ellie looked around, but the kid was gone. "He was tall and lanky, with brown hair, and he's been following us around since we left the entrance."

"I haven't noticed anyone. But I'll be more observant from now on."

Back at the barn, she introduced him to Aaron Knight, a fourteen-year-old with dirty-blond hair, bright red cheeks and one crooked tooth.

Blake offered his hand.

"Call me Apple," he said, shaking hands. He had a surprisingly strong grip.

"Apple?" Blake questioned.

"It's because of the rosacea, the red cheeks. And it's better than being called Aaron." His smile was friendly and welcoming.

"Well, Apple it is."

"Follow me and I'll show you what we do."

As they walked, Apple gave him the fundamentals of where they were going and how to clean the stalls. They worked together, but in different stalls, cleaning out the horse residue. Blake hated the smell, but he was the only one who seemed bothered by it. On the other side of the farm were horseback-riding lessons and people coming out for a day of fun with the animals.

"Here. I almost forgot to give you this," Apple said. He handed Blake a cloth that looked like a surgical mask. "Most of us are so used to the smell that we don't notice it, but I see it's getting to you."

Blake could smell it and taste it in the back of his throat. It wasn't pleasant. He wondered if Ellie had gotten him assigned here because it was the worst place to be. Then he saw she was doing the same task but at a different barn, and he felt ashamed of himself.

The job took two hours, including hosing down the place, before Apple said they were done. Blake's sneakers were soaked, and he needed a shower. He couldn't imagine getting into his car with its soft, buttery seats and leaving it smelling like horse manure.

"Next time, wear rubber boots," Apple told him as they walked back toward the original building. Blake's shoes squelched with each step. "Hungry?"

"Thirsty," Blake said. He couldn't imagine eating anything in his present state. The smell was bad enough, and the back of his throat itched with the sensation. Apple grabbed a bottle of cold water from a cooler when they entered the building and handed it to Blake. He drank the entire bottle in one long gulp, then took a second one and downed half of that.

The same kid he'd seen staring at him earlier sat in a corner, his back to the room. Yet, surreptitiously, he glanced at Blake. Blake wondered why. He didn't recognize the kid—at least what he'd seen of him. He hadn't seen his full face yet.

Apple waved at a young girl sitting near the front. He bobbed his head. Blake had only seen her use her hand, but apparently there was some silent communication between them. He remembered those days, when life was both easy and hard. Girls were new to him and he was afraid of being rebuffed by them, but he was also grateful that he attracted so many of them.

"Is she someone special?" Blake asked.

Apple smiled and hunched one shoulder in a shy "I like her" gesture.

"Ellie—Ms. Hamilton—told me that all these kids are here doing community service," Blake said.

"Most of them," Apple agreed.

"You seem like a very nice kid. And you obviously love horses. How'd you end up doing community service?"

Apple looked uncomfortable. He turned his face away and stared at the floor.

"You don't have to answer that," Blake said. "I apologize. It's none of my business."

"I fell in with some guys who were committing robberies. I got caught," Apple said after a moment.

"I feel like saying I'm sorry."

"Don't be. It was a good thing."

"Good that you got caught?"

Apple nodded. "If I hadn't, I might be on my way to juvie or worse. When I got sent here, I hated the place, but eventually I discovered a love of horses and that I could make a living caring for them."

"But you're only fourteen."

"And if I continue to work, I can get a job soon."

"Two years from now."

"I can wait. I'll work here until then."

"Apple, how long is your community service?"

"Oh, it ended six months ago." He smiled widely.

"Now I volunteer. And when my work is done, I get to ride the horses. You wanna ride with us?"

Blake smiled at the enthusiasm of youth. His back and legs were already protesting from only two hours of work. "Us?"

"Yeah, Ms. Hamilton always rides."

Blake looked across the room. Ellie looked as fresh and clean as she had standing at the fence when Blake arrived. He, on the other hand, looked as if he'd been wallowing in mud.

She flashed him a smile and everything changed. He no longer thought of the pain or the dirt.

"Shall I saddle you a horse?" Apple asked.

Blake was surprised to hear himself agreeing. "I'll come with you and saddle my own."

"So, you ride?" Apple appeared surprised.

"I haven't done it in years, but I hear it's like riding a bicycle. Once you learn how, you never forget."

"Guess we'll find out today," Apple laughed.

The air in the room seemed to change the moment Blake and Apple came in. And Ellie wasn't thinking of the smell of horseflesh. She smiled at her group and detached herself, going to meet the two men.

"Hi, Ms. Hamilton," Apple said.

"How'd Mr. Thorn do?" she asked.

Apple turned to Blake and put his hand on his shoulder. Despite Apple being only fourteen, he was just a head shorter than Blake.

"He's a natural," Apple said. "And he's up for the ride."

"Really?" Ellie raised her eyebrows.

"I'll go get the horses ready," Apple said. "I'll saddle yours, too," he told Blake.

"How was your day?" Ellie asked when they were alone.

"I don't see how mucking out stalls helped a charity," Blake said, but there was no hint of complaint in his voice. Ellie still wondered if he thought she'd brought him here to challenge his beliefs on how well charities worked.

"Come with me," she said.

Blake followed her. They walked around the barns and across the field to a pony track. Ellie propped her arms up on the rural fence. "Look," she said, using her hand to encompass the kids riding ponies. There were ten of them, and each one had an adult walking beside the small horse.

Blake took in the scene, then homed in on individual kids. All were smiling or concentrating hard on the task.

"They're special kids," Ellie said. "This is not only a farm. It's a training camp for special-needs children. They learn daily tasks by taking care of animals. Not full-grown horses, but gentle ponies or smaller animals. As a reward, they get to ride."

Blake sighed at his lack of understanding. "Lifting hay and cleaning out the stalls is too heavy for them," he said.

"In most cases. Some of them are able-bodied, but maybe not mentally ready."

"Hi, Ms. Hammy." A small child mounted on a pony waved vigorously.

Ellie waved back.

"You must come here often," Blake commented.

"I used to work here," she said, looking at the building ahead. "I was one of them."

Ellie wanted to laugh at the expression on Blake's face.

"You have a juvie record?" he asked.

"Did my esteem just plummet in your eyes?" Ellie tried hard not to let the smile she felt inside blossom on her face.

"No, but you can't just drop a comment like that and stop."

"I didn't stop."

"All right. Tell me the story."

They were back in the main building. Half the group was outside, so there were plenty of places to sit and talk. Ellie took a seat on one of the benches and Blake straddled it. He looked to her for an explanation.

"First, I have no record. It was expunged when they discovered the mistake."

"Mistake?"

"I was fifteen, and as with a lot of teenagers, I traveled in groups."

"Safety factor."

"Are you going to let me tell this story?"

He shrugged, opening his hand and gesturing for her to go on.

"We were shopping that day, looking for anything we could find. We'd been in costume jewelry stores, makeup stores, dress shops—all over the mall. When I got home that night, the police came and arrested me."

"For what?"

"Stealing. They said I took several necklaces from one of the stores." She waited for him to interrupt again, but he only looked at her. "No, I didn't take anything, but they searched the house and found jewelry in my room. It was legitimate. I'd bought and paid for it weeks earlier, but I hadn't worn it."

"Didn't you have receipts?"

"I threw them away. Two of the necklaces were going to be gifts for a friend's birthday. I didn't want the price tag on it. I knew she wanted them. She'd admired them several times, dropping gentle hints that she'd love those for her birthday."

"What happened next?"

"No one believed me. I was sentenced to do community service and brought here." She took a moment to look around the hall. It had been years, but Ellie remembered her first day here. She was so angry. She was innocent, and she had to do community service for something she hadn't been guilty of.

"How long did you have to come here for?" Blake prompted her back to the present.

"Every Saturday, for a couple of months. My father finally began to believe my continued pleas of innocence. He started checking into things. We discovered that a few of the kids had cell phone video footage. He found it online when someone posted about their friend who was also in the mall. I didn't know her. But the video showed the person taking the jewelry and hiding it in her purse."

Blake leaned forward. Ellie hadn't told this story in years, and it no longer carried the anger it once had.

She hated the injustice of the system, but had learned about horses in the time she spent with them.

"To be fair, the girl did look like me. She even had on the same color shirt I was wearing that day. My father hired a lawyer, and we got the kids at school to watch the video and see if anyone recognized it or the girl. She was identified and I was released. My record was expunged, and I loved my father even more for what he'd done."

"What about the other girl? What happened to her?"

"You're concerned about the other girl?" Ellie had no censure in her voice. She even admired Blake for thinking of someone else. "You met her Saturday night."

He frowned.

"Vera Gordon, the perky redhead with the big smile who stood with the girls I introduced."

Comprehension came over Blake, and she saw the recognition in his face. Ellie also understood he was remembering not only her perkiness, but the fact that her smile and cup size were both large.

"You two are friends?"

"Not exactly. We're not enemies, though. Vera never stole anything again. She apologized to me, and after her community service was done, she went on to teacher's college. She now teaches high school English, and at night she has an English-as-a-second-language class."

"It seems like community service works out for some kids," Blake said.

"Some, but not all."

"Like that kid over there?" He indicated a boy sitting alone. He was about seventeen, with torn jeans, a

T-shirt too large for his lanky frame and hair that could stand a good barber.

"What's his story? He's been following me around all day with his eyes, the kind that look at you and avoid you at the same time."

"I don't know. Why don't you go ask him?" Ellie said.

"I think I will."

Blake was ready to go to the kid when he rose from the table, but Ellie stopped him. She pointed out that the showers were free if he wanted one and asked if he had brought a change of clothes. Blake had his gym bag in the car, and he always kept two sets of exercise clothes and a pair of slacks in it. Often he needed to drop into a store or pick something up on his way to his condo. And if he just happened to run into an impromptu game, he wouldn't ruin his clothes.

Freshly laundered, with his hair still wet, Blake returned to the central hall. The boy was in the same place, as if he was waiting for something to begin or for someone to give him the next instruction. His body language said he was ready to argue over why he should do anything they asked him.

Blake put his boxed lunch down on a wooden table next to the kid. As usual, the kid glanced away, refusing to make eye contact.

"Hello," Blake greeted him. "Mind if I join you?"

The kid said nothing, only pulled his baseball cap with the San Francisco Giants logo stitched above the lid down lower on his head, blocking half his face.

"Is that your favorite team—the Giants? Ever been to a game?"

The kid threw him a glance that, even though it didn't connect, said he had to be joking.

"My company occasionally gets tickets. Maybe when the season begins, I'll send you a couple."

At that, the young man turned his full attention to Blake. "Why would you do that?" His voice was deep, gruff and challenging.

"No reason other than giving you a chance to do something you'd enjoy."

"You don't know me or what I enjoy. And nobody does nothing for nothing." The kid rolled his eyes, coming short of sucking his teeth in that dangerous leave-me-alone manner. Blake recognized it. Even though his parents owned a chain of department stores and money was never an issue in his family, they were not granted carte blanch. Blake had had his share of playground fights, heard the taunts and insults because someone else's perception of him was lacking, or because they were jealous of something he had.

Blake nodded. "You're right, nobody does nothing for nothing." He refused to correct the young man's grammar. He thought that was a front, too. "It's usually true, but sometimes people are just being nice. There are times when we get more than we can use, and someone who'd love to go has a conflict. Rather than waste the ticket, we give it to someone who will enjoy the game. Don't you agree that's better than letting the seat go empty?"

Blake waited for an answer. The young man repositioned himself in his seat, but to Blake, it was a squirm.

"I guess," he finally said. He hunched one shoulder as if he didn't care. Blake knew that was a defense mechanism. He'd done it himself when he was trying to hide the importance of something.

"I'll tell you what—if we have extra tickets, I'll contact Ms. Hamilton, and maybe we can get you to a game. Deal?"

"Man, you sure you want to do that?"

"Is there a reason I shouldn't?" Blake asked.

Again he dropped his eyes. He sat like that for a long moment. Then he looked up. "You know why we're all here, right?" His voice held less volume, but no less strength.

"Ms. Hamilton told me most of you have had some trouble with the law and you're doing community service to satisfy your punishment."

"Did they tell you what I did?"

Blake shook his head.

"I shoplifted."

"Apple told me he did the same. I don't condone it, but doing community service in this environment seems like a pretty good way of changing—"

"I stole from you," he interrupted. They stared at each other for several seconds.

"From me?"

"From your store."

"You know who I am?" Blake asked.

He nodded.

Now Blake understood why he didn't want him to

see his face. He thought Blake would recognize him. Little did he know, few security issues ever reached him.

"I picked up a pair of tennis shoes on my way out the door," the young man continued. "The sign said they were over three hundred dollars."

"And you were caught," Blake stated.

"On camera. Security guards stopped me as I rounded the outside corner, and I ended up here." He looked around the room.

"Why are you telling me this?"

"So you know who I am and who you offered Giants tickets to."

Blake smiled. The kid had character hidden inside him. Blake knew it. He'd interviewed countless people over the years, and thanks to his dad, he'd learned to determine the important things about a man. It wasn't his skills or what his résumé said, it was who he was deep down inside, and despite the theft and what had led this young man to this horse farm, he was the kind of person Blake liked to work with.

"Now that I know what I'm getting, do we have a deal?"

The kid smiled. "Deal."

Blake offered his hand and they shook. "There's just one thing you haven't told me," Blake said.

"What's that?"

"Your name."

Another smile from the young man. "William Jerome," he said. "My friends call me Will."

"My friends call me Blake."

# *Chapter 5*

Those hills seemed to call to Ellie as she drove back toward the busy parts of San Francisco. The day had been satisfying and inspiring. She hoped Blake had enjoyed himself. He appeared to. And he'd connected with one of the boys. Blake might not know it, but his few minutes today could have an impact on that kid's future. She hoped so. It wasn't often they got to see the results of their efforts. Edna and Claude kept in touch as much as they could with some of them, but there were many others who left and went on with their lives in other directions.

The skyline of San Francisco came into view. Ellie took in a breath at its beauty. It was a perfect way to end the day. The sun was still high in the sky, and the air was clear for miles.

Ellie pulled into a visitor's spot, where photos were often taken by tourists who ventured this far, and got out of her car. Like the tourists, she took her cell phone out and captured a few photos. She wanted to be reminded of this day. It was one for the memory book. Of course, she had no real memory book, only her head, with days she collected to bring out and remember in the future.

Today had been one with Blake. She knew days with him were limited. She couldn't see him for anything other than an occasional charity event once their challenge was over. He had to take her to a charity event next, and then it would be over.

She snapped another photo, but the camera moved and the image was blurry. As she deleted it, she heard another car and turned around.

It was Blake's Jeep. He unfolded his long frame from the cab and came toward her.

"Are you all right?" he asked, concern on his face.

"Yes."

"I saw your car." He looked back at the sporty Mercedes. "I thought you might be having car trouble."

He was right in front of her now. Ellie wondered why the air seemed to change whenever he was near her.

"There's nothing wrong. I stopped to admire the view." She glanced at it. "This is a really beautiful spot." Ellie breathed the words as she surveyed the city in the distance. It was windy, and all of San Francisco basked in the summer sun before her.

"You've been up here before?" Blake seemed surprised.

"It's not on the tourist route." She smiled. "I have been up here, but usually behind the wheel of a car. It was necessary to look out for other cars or kids instead of the view. This is the first time I've stopped. Look at how the light changes the color of the buildings."

Some of them were golden, and others took on a copper hue. The water in the bay was a brilliant gray.

Blake came to stand next to her. They watched the sweeping panorama of high-rise buildings and several shades of grass and trees that seemed to run over the hills to reach the concrete jungle before them.

Ellie turned and perched on the fence. It was several yards from the edge of the hill, so even if she fell, she wasn't in danger.

"I want to thank you for today," she told Blake, who now wore comfortable-looking shorts, a T-shirt and flip-flops. He looked nothing like the man she'd seen at the gala or the one who arrived at the farm earlier today. But the outfit hugged his broad shoulders and arms. His legs were powerfully built. Obviously, working out was part of his agenda. And the sex factor couldn't be ignored. Ellie could feel her nipples hardening from the thought of how his arms would feel around her.

"I enjoyed it in the end. Of course, I can do without cleaning out another horse stall for a long time—like *forever*." He emphasized the single word as if it were two words.

She laughed, "We didn't really give you the worst job there was."

"There's something worse?" His brows went up.

"Don't ask what."

He gazed at her until it became a stare. Ellie's throat closed, and even if she could think of something to say, she wouldn't have been able to utter a word.

The wind blew Ellie's hair. Both she and Blake reached to push it out of her eyes. Their hands touched. Blake didn't let go, and Ellie's eyes locked onto his. The air between them crackled with electricity.

Using one finger, Blake brushed her hair behind her ear. Then he pulled her hand down, and released it as both of his slipped around her waist, pulling her down from the fence and into contact with him. All the air seemed to leave Ellie's body. She wet her lips. Blake's focus moved to her mouth. Her knees felt like melted ice cream. She was sure she'd fall without his support. She liked the strength of his arms, the way he held her, even the smell of the soap he'd used in the shower.

"I've dreamed of holding you like this since the gala," he said, his voice thick with emotion.

They had danced together, but Ellie didn't think this was the time to remind him of that.

Then his face blurred as it came closer to hers. Her eyelids fluttered closed as Blake's mouth touched hers. His lips were soft, seeking, teasing. He moved his head from one side to the other, kissing her on the left and right sides of her mouth. Ellie could feel the heat rising in her face, feel the pounding of her heart. Her neck and ears were hot enough to melt. And the wind must have picked up, because she suddenly heard it roaring.

Her arms circled Blake's neck, and her body melted into his. His arms banded her waist, then traveled smoothly up her back. His mouth crushed hers as if it were hungry for the sweetness only she could provide. Desire and wonder flooded through her as something so elemental, so right, pulsed within her. She'd been kissed before. But she'd wanted Blake to kiss her. It was their first, although she was unsure if there would ever be a second. But this was not a first kiss, not an initiation or a getting-to-know-you sampling of need. This was an elemental consummation of a brand. Blake was claiming her, making her his, speaking only to her, and his message was clear. She might never see him again, but she would from now on compare every other man to him and find them wanting.

Ellie tried to breathe, but Blake held her captive. Finally, she had enough room to open her mouth and take in a gulp of air. He allowed it only for a second, before his tongue rushed in to capture the opening. She felt the wetness of it as it filled her, as it dragged her to a place she had yet to visit. She wanted to go there, wanted to know where this would lead, and if the promise of his mouth was as good as it felt.

He shifted, and his legs, which she'd thought of as powerful, molded themselves against hers. Her pants were little protection against the heat they generated. The sensation was erotic and brought his tight erection into contact with the vortex of her legs. His arms moved down her back, taking her hips and grinding them into his.

Ellie would have cried out if she had the breath. The wind twisted about them, pulled her hair out toward its edges, while leaving the two of them at the center of their world.

*Let it continue*, Ellie begged the universe. For just a moment or a lifetime longer, she didn't want to break contact. This small piece of land was their entire universe, and she wasn't ready to return to the world at large. Apparently, neither was Blake. He gathered her closer—if that were possible. The kiss went on until they had to stop for breath or pass out.

When he lifted his mouth, Ellie's head fell onto his shoulder. Her chest heaved as she forced breath in and out of her lungs. Blake did the same thing. They held each other, supporting themselves until strength returned to their arms and legs. Minutes ticked by. Finally, Ellie pushed herself free. She wobbled for a second, disoriented. Blake didn't move. They faced each other, neither apparently able to confront what had just happened to them.

They didn't know each other, didn't even like each other, but they'd kissed as if they had to, as if they needed each other to go on living, as if it were the last thing they would ever do in this life.

Blake reached for her hand. Without a word, they walked to their cars. Silence accompanied them. He opened her car door and she slipped inside. He followed her down the hills until she turned left to go to her house, and he went in the opposite direction, toward his condo.

They'd parted, Ellie thought, but somehow she had left part of herself with him.

And she carried the feel of his hands and the taste of his mouth with her.

Ellie could not let that happen again. Getting out of her car, she nearly ran into her house and slammed the door shut. Blake wasn't behind her, but she felt his presence on every inch of her body. How could she let him kiss her like that? How could she kiss him back? This couldn't happen. She closed her eyes against the moisture that had gathered there.

This could not happen, she told herself again. She needed to stay away from Blake Thorn. She could go with any of the others, with reservations of course, but she could do it. The weight of everything she knew about their past didn't exist for Blake, yet it was as heavy as a boulder on her shoulders.

Suddenly she wondered if he'd been acting. Did Blake really know who she was? Ellie dropped her head. Of course he didn't. If he had, he was in the wrong city in California. Hollywood should have his name. Ellie stepped away from the door, confident that there were no ghosts on the opposite side. The ghosts were already here, and had been for ten years.

She was putting problems where none existed. At least for the moment, they didn't exist. But as time went by, as she spent more of it in Blake's company, he was bound to remember something. And it was her fault.

She'd goaded him into these tests of charity work, and look who was the fool. Blake had excelled in the work they had assigned him. He'd spent time with a troubled youth and got him to talk and accept the work he had to do to complete his service.

There was more, Ellie reminded herself. She had to go with him to the next charitable function. It was his choice as to what they did next. It meant she had to be with him, close to him and do whatever job he chose for her. One thing she wouldn't do again was stop on the way home. Seeing that view was like looking at a painting. And the parking lot was right there. If she hadn't pulled into it… If Blake hadn't recognized her car… *Too late for ifs*, she told herself. She had, he had and the result was a kiss. A ravaging connection between two human begins. It was almost life changing. She wouldn't allow that again.

Not with him.

Before he'd appeared at the gala, the last time she'd seen him, he'd been on a stretcher, being wheeled into an ambulance. His spine had been stabilized with a cervical neck collar and an orange head-brace restraint. His face was smeared with blood, and the EMTs were working feverishly over his girlfriend.

Ellie's eyes were blurred with tears. Her father's lifeless body lay against her. Blake never saw her, never knew she was there. She'd thought about telling him when she tried to see him at his office, but she knew she'd chicken out. How do you walk into a total stranger's office and say, *I'm responsible for your girlfriend's death*?

The official report said it was an accident, but Ellie

knew better what had happened. She was the cause. She should have tried harder, but she had her father to save. And she couldn't even do that.

On some level, Ellie was glad Blake wasn't there to see her. Had he been, the two would greet each other as friends, and they could never be friends. Despite today. Despite the mood and the scenery and despite her attraction for him and his, if there was one for her, their lives were on different planes, different timelines. They had a past, but no present, and definitely no future together.

That thought saddened Ellie. She hadn't been involved seriously with anyone in a long time. She hadn't felt an attraction this fast and fierce in forever—more like never. But it was wrong. She'd been responsible for Alexis Ferrell's death. She couldn't control the car. And a woman, along with Ellie's father, had died in that accident. Blake had been seriously hurt, and several lives had collided, tangentially smacking them like billiard balls in different directions.

Blake rolled over in bed that night and looked at the digital dial on his clock radio. It was nearly two o'clock. He'd been dead tired when he got home, but unable to go to sleep. His mind was working a mile a minute, and it wasn't about the store. That was where his usual thought processes were, but rarely did anything at the store keep him awake. This insomnia had to do with Elliana Hamilton.

Why?

Why couldn't he put her in the same basket with the

other women he'd dated? But he'd never dated Ellie. He'd only seen her twice and kissed her once.

Blake sat up and swung his feet to the floor. He held his head in both hands. What had come over him? Why didn't she resist? Why didn't she turn her head or push his hand away? Why did she smell so good? She'd had a shower and wore fresh clothing. He would smell the lemony soap she'd used.

He could still feel her softness, the texture of her mouth on his, the sweetness of her tongue tangling with his own. He could recall everything about her, as if the day had been imprinted on a section of his brain that was at the forefront of memory. And try as he might, he couldn't push it away.

Blake stood up, walked to the window and pushed the curtains aside. The city lay before him in all its colorful splendor. Where was she? Was one of those lights out there in the dark illuminating a room in her house or condo? He didn't know which one she lived in, or even if she lived alone.

Blake dropped the curtain and moved to the kitchen. He turned on a light and flipped the coffee pot switch almost simultaneously. Ellie was a diversion. He'd get over her, the same as he'd done—he stopped. He wasn't going to allow that memory to take root. Ellie was the issue, not his past.

His usual reaction would be to forget things, break it off, stop anything before it could begin. That was where he was with Ellie. Nothing had begun. Only one devastating kiss.

But he had to see her again. He'd committed to the

charities and he had to hold up his end—at least for one more time.

Then it would be over.

The buzz of Ellie's cell phone had her jumping. She'd been doing it for a week, ever since she gave Blake her number. They'd agreed to a plan, yet if he never contacted her for the next segment of it, she would gladly let it die from nonuse. Apparently that was not to be the case. The message indicator flashed on the screen. A second later, it disappeared and she saw the number one on the small icon. She clicked on it and read.

Saturday morning, 6:00 a.m. Wear pants and bring a jacket.

The message was cryptic and gave her no information of where they were going or what they would be doing.

She nearly smiled. "Payback," she said aloud to herself.

Ellie thought about the message. She waited twenty minutes before replying that she would be there.

She was still thinking about Blake when she left the office that night. She and Judi were meeting for dinner. Ellie arrived first and was led to a table. After ordering drinks for both of them, she took the offered menu and looked at it, but saw no words. Everything was a blur. Putting it down, she stared at the room, glancing once at the door to see if Judi had arrived.

The date had been set, she thought. "Not a date." She again spoke out loud.

"What do you mean, not a date? Not a date with whom?" Judi asked.

Ellie looked up. Judi was taking the seat in front of her. Ellie had been concentrating so hard that she hadn't heard her friend approach.

Judi waited, her face clear but expecting an answer. "It's him, right?"

Judi didn't have to identify who she meant by *him*. Both of them knew.

"He sent me a text. We're going to the second function on Saturday."

Judi smiled. She was all for Ellie finding a relationship, but Judi didn't know about the past that Ellie and Blake shared.

"Where are you going?"

"I don't know." She told her the details of Blake's message.

"And you didn't ask?" Judi said in surprise.

"It was payback."

The waiter arrived and they gave their orders.

"What does that mean?" Judi continued when they were alone again.

"When we first agreed on this, I challenged him by giving him an address to come to and telling him what to wear. He's paying me back."

"So, you're going on a date—"

"It's not a date." Ellie was determined to get her point across to both her friend and herself that this was a lesson she was teaching Blake. Unfortunately *she* had to participate in it, too.

"Even if it's not, what's so hard about spending time with a good-looking man? And it won't hurt you if you develop feelings for him."

It would hurt. For a moment, Ellie wavered between telling Judi the truth, the whole truth about when and how she'd met Blake. Just before she spoke, however, she changed her mind. She'd held on to her secret for ten years. There was at least one person who knew about it, and Ellie didn't believe she was totally on her side, but she wasn't going to confide in Judi yet.

"I'm not looking for a relationship," she said. The words sounded false even to her ears.

"Then you're dead, honey. Crawl in the grave and pull the grass over you."

After a moment, Judi shifted in her chair and leaned forward. She whispered, "Ellie, tell me the truth. Do you have feelings for Blake Thorn that you're hiding, even from yourself?"

"I—"

Judi raised her hand to stop Ellie from speaking. "Don't answer too quickly. Take your time and tell me the truth."

Ellie waited a beat and then spoke. "I suppose there is something about him that attracts me."

"But…" Judi prompted.

Ellie knew she couldn't answer that. Not with the whole truth. "But I work for his family. I don't want to have any crossover or interaction that might result in a conflict of interest."

Judi frowned, knowing that was another weak argument. She wasn't sure if Judi understood conflict of interest between herself and the Thorns. She hoped she didn't.

The waiter returned, setting two hot plates with sizzling steaks in front of them. The smell was wonderful, and Ellie's stomach growled at her for keeping it so long at bay.

"I don't think a date will result in anything other than maybe a second date," Judi said, cutting the tender meat.

"We're not dating," Ellie said, a little stronger than she intended.

"Well, I guess that's a good thing."

Ellie stared at her friend. Why had Judi changed her tactics so abruptly?

"Why?" she asked.

"Because he's obviously dating someone else."

Ellie saw that Judi's attention wasn't on her, and it wasn't on her food or drink. Turning to look, she saw Blake Thorn had just entered the restaurant. On his arm was the beautiful woman from the gala. A fizzle of something undefinable went through Ellie. For a man she hadn't seen in ten years, he seemed to constantly be running into her. Their businesses weren't that far apart, but she and Judi ate here enough to be semiregulars. She'd never run into Blake before. Yet there he was.

And with a date.

Ellie followed the two as they were shown to a table in another part of the restaurant. He never even looked in her direction. His attention was on the woman at his side. *As it should be*, she reminded herself. Yet that feeling inside her refused to find a place to hide. She wanted to leave immediately, but if she suggested they go just after the waiter had set plates in front of them, it would be like giving Judi a trump card. Every argument she'd given tonight would be in question.

Surreptitiously, Ellie tried to eat and see what was going on at Blake's table at the same time. She and Judi were sitting where he could not see them, but she had a clear view of his back. She failed at eating the food. For several minutes she pushed it around on her plate but ate nothing.

"You know you're wasting a perfectly good piece of meat." Judi broke into her thoughts.

Ellie looked at her friend, but Judi was looking at Blake. Suddenly her words rang home.

Last date. It was ironic that Blake thought of this as their last date when they hadn't had a first date or any dates in between. He parked the Jeep in front of a small house on Mulberry Street and got out. He didn't immediately go to the door, feeling he needed a moment to think about the coming day. He laughed at himself. This was something he'd never done before. Dates were easy. You went out. You had fun. You came back.

Meet. Enjoy. Repeat.

Only there was no repeat planned. This was the last time. He was sure she'd agree.

He knew from the moment they ended the kiss on the hill overlooking the city that the move had been a mistake. And not on his part alone. They had both participated in it, but it had been the death knell to any future encounters. Today he would complete the promise he'd made, but after that… He didn't think any further.

Pushing himself away from the Jeep, he headed for the door. Ellie opened it and stepped out before he could ring the bell.

"Good morning," she said as cheerily as a cereal-commercial model. And she looked like a model. Blake's body began to respond, and he quickly changed positions to stop its progress.

"Ready?" he asked, his voice slightly deeper than normal. He felt like a teenager, nervous for a first date. He knew it was the kiss they'd shared the last time. Was she remembering it, too?

He certainly was.

He'd hardly been able to think of anything else since they'd left that breezy hill.

"I hope this works, since I don't know where we're going or what we're doing." She turned in a full circle to show him her jeans, sweater and a short jacket over her arm. The jeans were formfitting to every curve of her tight bottom and long legs. Blake cleared his throat, which seemed to clog even at the thought of her. The full, three-dimensional package was a challenge to his entire bronchial system.

Blake led her to the Jeep and opened the door without supplying any information about their upcoming day.

"You're paying me back, right?" she asked when he'd gotten in and pulled away from the curb.

"Payback?"

"For the way I gave you the address to the Purple Cloud Horse Farm?"

"Why, Ms. Hamilton, I have no idea what you're talking about," he drawled, impersonating a Texan.

"That was terrible," she said. "You're from New York. I might believe a New York accent."

"You mean I don't have one? I've lost it?" he asked in mock surprise.

"Not lost. I'm sure you know where it is, and you'll find it when you need to."

They'd become playful. It was all he could do to keep from pulling her into his arms. Those tight jeans and the sweater-girl look would make any red-blooded man look for an alternative to acting like a pubescent teenager at the sight of a pretty girl.

And Ellie was more than a pretty girl. She had a beauty that seemed to glow, even if only in his eyes. He wove the Jeep through the streets of San Francisco until they were on the highway. As he took the exit that only led one place, Ellie spoke again.

"The airport. What airport is this?"

It wasn't SFO, San Francisco International. There were no runways where they were going capable of taking off or landing a 747. Not even a 727, if they were still in service, would find this place amenable to its needs.

Continuing down the road, Blake turned left and right three times before the road ended at a small airport.

"'Fifteenth Annual Diabetes Jump.'" Ellie read from the sign as they passed it. "Jump? What's a jump?"

They were at an airport. He wasn't sure if Ellie's question was rhetorical.

She turned in her seat as much as the seat belt would allow. "We're not going up in an airplane, are we?"

"Yep," Blake said. "This is the charity event I've chosen."

"I didn't get a chance to read the entire sign. What does it say?"

"It says this is the fifteenth annual diabetes jump."

"What diabetes charity does it benefit?"

"The money goes to research, and its major benefit is to support Western Indian reservations."

Blake parked and cut the engine. Releasing his seat belt, he didn't get out of the car, but faced Ellie. She was close in the small cab of the Jeep. If he slipped his hand along the back of the seat, he could caress her neck or thread his fingers through her hair. He curled his hands.

Ellie nodded, giving both support and approval of his choice.

"Who's doing the jump?" she asked.

"We are." Blake opened the door and got out before she could say anything.

"More payback," Ellie whispered when he helped her out of the cab. He was unsure if she was talking to herself or if she intended for him to hear.

"Have you ever been skydiving before?"

She shook her head. "Somehow I think you already knew that."

"How about heights? Do you have a fear of heights?"

"Too late to ask that, don't you think?"

He smiled, taking her arm and leading her toward the one-story airport building. Inside he saw Chase Locklear break away from a group and come to meet them. Chase was one of the first people Blake had met when he moved to San Francisco. They'd become friends, and Chase had introduced him to skydiving. Blake refused more of his invitations to fly than he accepted, but he did like the sport.

"Blake, you made it." Chase offered his hand as he came toward him. They shook, and Blake introduced Ellie. Chase looked every bit like the cover model he was. He had long black hair that passed his shoulders. Today he'd pulled it back and bound it with a leather strap. He reminded Blake of the first time he'd seen Chase. It wasn't in person, but as a life-size cardboard cutout, standing on the edge of the book department in the store. Women stopped and admired the poster before going into the department. He was pleased to discover the real man was a friendly person whom he immediately connected with. It didn't take more than a couple of meetings for Blake to feel as if he'd known Chase since childhood.

And that friendship had brought him to skydiving.

"You're flying with us today." Chase gazed at Ellie.

It was a statement, but Ellie answered it confidently. "Yes," she said.

"First timer?" Chase asked.

"First timer," she confirmed.

"Hey, guys." Chase spoke to the group of men in the corner. They all turned to look at Blake and Ellie. "We've got a virgin in our midst."

Blake felt heat steal up his face. He'd forgotten how

base the guys could be and how much Ellie reminded him of someone who should be treated with utmost respect.

Ellie laughed at the taunt.

"Since Blake doesn't have a license, I volunteer to do the tandem with Ellie," one of them said.

"Not on your life," Blake said.

"Sorry, guys. Blake already asked me," Chase stated.

A collective "aah" rang through the small building.

The crowds had arrived, and it was time to get ready for the jump. Blake explained to Ellie what a tandem jump was and that she'd be in good hands with Chase.

"Is he a good jumper?" she asked.

Blake could hear the apprehension in her voice. "No need to worry. He's the best. He took me on my first jump."

"And how many times have you jumped?"

"Not as many as I should have. I have enough to go solo." He wasn't certified to teach, but that hadn't been part of his needs. Not until today. He wished he could strap the tandem harness on Ellie and fly with her. Blake usually went flying when Chase called and cajoled him into a day away from the store.

Chase came forward with the harness the two of them would fly in.

"You're up for this, right?" he asked, confirming that Ellie was there to jump.

She looked at Blake. "Tell me again why I'm doing this."

Chase answered before Blake had a chance to. "Everyone who participates is backed by several corporations across the West. Many of them donate over a thousand dollars per participant. Last year we raised half a million dollars. We stand to break that record today."

Ellie smiled. "Good luck."

"Blake tells me you work for a foundation that raises money for girls," Chase said.

"That's the gist of it," Ellie said, nodding. "We do a lot more than raise the money."

"How many people are participating today?" Blake asked.

"Including the two last-minute entrants—" he shot glances between him and Ellie "—the count is six hundred."

"There are six hundred people going up today?" Ellie's voice showed surprise.

"Not all at once," Chase said. "The event goes on all day and into the night. It's beautiful at night. I hope you guys are planning to make a day of it."

Blake's look to Ellie was questioning. She gave him no clue to her desires. He'd brought her for the jump, not to spend the entire day and night together. He supposed this was one of the times that playing things by ear was the appropriate action.

"Well, let's get dressed. Our ride is ready and waiting," Chase said.

Blake moved with Ellie toward the airfield behind the building. If this was to be their last date, it was certainly going to be memorable.

# *Chapter 6*

They didn't immediately dress and walk to a plane, although the day had already started. There were planes taking off and parachutists going up. Ellie had to take a short class before the jump, and she wanted to find out what to expect before it happened. An hour later, Chase strapped the two of them into the harnesses. He wore a parachute, but Ellie didn't. He also put on a helmet.

"Don't I get a helmet?" she asked. Her stomach was already feeling the strong pressure of fear.

"You don't wear one for the tandem jump," Chase explained.

"If you did," Blake said, coming up behind her and standing so close that his body heat merged with hers, and the heated air between them could not escape. He put his arm around her upper shoulders and pulled her back. Her head tapped his chin. “If you were wearing a helmet, you could knock the pilot out and both of you would free-fall.”

He didn’t say free-fall into the ground, but Ellie understood that would be the result. She also understood that Blake was again pressed so close to her that there was little if any separation between them. He released her after his demonstration, and she took in a long breath. Her heart thudded so hard, she was sure it could be seen in the rising and falling of her chest.

“The ride is going to be thrilling,” Chase was saying when her world righted itself and the rushing hum in her ears subsided to normal decibel levels.

Ellie said nothing as the three of them joined a group of thirteen others heading for a plane sitting on the tarmac.

“How many people are doing this?” she shouted over the noise of the wind and engines.

“On our plane, sixteen. It’s a Cessna C208B Grand Caravan—perfect skydiving plane. On other planes there are more, some less. Depends on how many are ready.”

Ready or not, Ellie thought, she was heading for the sky. The event she’d taken Blake to might have had him twist an ankle or fall from a horse. There were dangers in just getting out of bed in the morning, but skydiving held a greater amount of risk than anything else she could think of, short of falling in love.

Ellie coughed at the thought. Where had that come from? she wondered.

She tried to send the thought back.

Chase got in front of her and boarded. She followed and found two bench seats on either side of the plane. He straddled the seat and motioned for her to sit with her back to him in the same straddled fashion. Blake sat in front of her. The aircraft quickly filled with skydivers, all of them seated toward the back of the plane, the way she was. Even though it took fifteen minutes for the four-ton plane to reach the skydiving height of thirteen thousand feet, it seemed faster than that.

Chase connected her straps to his, and soon they were scooting along the seat. At the huge open door, she saw Blake fall out. Her heart shuddered. Then it was their turn. The wind caught her as she looked out on nothing but air.

"Here we go," Chase said. He grabbed her head and pulled it back. "Scream," he said and they fell out into space.

Ellie didn't need prompting. She screamed, and then she was falling and floating. The wind whipped her hair back. Her arms spread and her legs were pushed up, bent at the knees, by the currents. *Wow*, she thought. It was amazing. She loved the rush of air, thc speed of the wind on her skin.

Several planeloads of skydivers were at various levels below her. She searched for Blake, wondering whether she could find him in the colorful array of floating suits. Chase must have understood what she was doing. He pointed to a flyer to their right, and she saw Blake below them. Chase spun her around and did a complete circle in the air. Ellie gave him the two-thumbs-up signal, since speaking in the wind was out of the question.

At her acceptance, he went through several other arcs before the one-minute mark had been reached. Then he reached for the "hackey," or what most people think of as the rip cord, and deployed the chute. Ellie had never felt so free. They were floating. She looked at the landscape below, seeing it from an angle that resembled a photograph, but there was nothing like the real deal.

Five minutes later, Chase brought them safely and smoothly to the ground. He released her tether, and she pulled her goggles off.

"That was wonderful."

Blake came up behind them, dragging his chute. "I guess you liked it," he said.

"Can we do it again?" Ellie couldn't contain the excitement in her voice. "I've never done anything like that before."

"It's up to Chase," Blake told her.

They both turned expectantly to the black-haired man. Chase smiled. "Give me a couple of hours. I have several other jumps to do."

"We'll get something to eat," Blake said.

Ellie thanked Chase before they walked away. They got something from the snack bar and found seats at picnic tables that had a view of the skydivers. Watching them was a totally different experience now that Ellie knew what they were doing, seeing and feeling.

"I get that you liked the diving," Blake said. "And are you enjoying yourself otherwise?"

"You mean now that I'm no longer scared to death?"

He smiled. "Something like that."

"I am. Everyone is very friendly, and they all seem to be interested in donating to the cause."

Blake nodded.

"That doesn't include you," she said. "Today doesn't count as fulfilling your obligation."

Ellie was sorry the moment she said it. Today was the end of their time together. She expected to spend the entire day with him. He'd done it at the horse farm. She had nothing else planned for the day or evening.

Her enthusiasm when she and Chase had completed the jump was overwhelming, and her request to repeat it came out before she thought about it, just as the words that this day and this event did not qualify came out without her realizing the goal she'd set for herself to finish anytime with Blake was out. She couldn't pull it back.

"What do you mean it doesn't count? It benefits the diabetes foundation. We raised a lot of research dollars already, and by the end of the night, they'll be well over the set goal."

"They, not you?" Ellie countered. She'd started down this road. She had to go on now.

"What?"

"*They* raised money." She pointed to the group of skydivers who'd jumped with them. "They are passionate about helping people with the disease, about finding a cure. You did it for fun."

"I made a sizable donation."

"That's what you always do. You write a check, and that closes the books, so to speak."

Blake opened his mouth, then closed it without saying anything.

The day should have ended there, Ellie thought. She'd challenged Blake's choice, accused him of only being at the event for the fun of it. He wasn't here to support the group as anything other than a patron. Ellie wondered why she hadn't let it go. Her action had inadvertently set them up for another day together. Pushing the thought away, she turned to him.

"I hope I didn't spoil the day."

"No." He shook his head. In an instant, he'd regrouped. "We'll go on the next jump." His smile was as charming and intoxicating as always. "We'll have dinner and attend the dance afterward."

"Dance? Dinner?"

"It was part of the deal," he said.

"This is the first I've heard of it."

"You like surprises," he said. "I could tell that by the way you invited me to the horse farm."

"You're still paying me back," she said. Then she nodded. "I do like surprises, although I hope you give me enough notice to get properly dressed."

"There will be plenty of time for that."

He grinned and Ellie relaxed. "It was a joke," she said.

He nodded, his smile still in place. "Sorry."

"No need to apologize. I understand payback." She said it in a manner that meant this was not over. There was more to come, and he wouldn't see it before it blindsided him.

Ellie didn't want to fight with Blake. She wanted their last hours to be ones she could add to her memory box, something she could take out and revisit with pleasant thoughts.

They left the table and went to watch the skydivers forming patterns in the sky. Ellie was in awe of them flying out of planes and grouping up in the sky. Her fall had been nothing like that. Chase had given them a few somersaults and a couple of twists, but it was the two of them all the way to the ground. She marveled at what she saw, taking her cell phone out many times to record the beauty of what she could only call poetry in motion.

"I can't wait to see this at night," she commented.

"It'll be dark in a couple of hours."

"When do we go up again?"

The question was like a summons for Chase. He appeared almost as soon as she finished speaking.

"We're up in about fifteen minutes. Better suit up," he said.

Ellie jumped up as if she were a kid about to go on a roller coaster for the fifth time. She got into her harness and looked at Blake. "Aren't you going again?"

"I'm going to watch you from the ground. I'll get a lot of footage as you come down. Besides, Chase has to go in tandem with you."

"Your loss, my friend," he said. "If you'd finished that certification, you could be in my place."

"Don't taunt me. I feel bad enough."

Ellie felt herself go warm. She felt heat rise in her face at the tenderness of his words. With a short wave, she followed Chase to the waiting plane. It was the same Cessna they had flown in earlier. This time she wasn't as frightened as she'd been before.

Her second jump was just as thrilling as the first. She looked at the landscape and felt the wind, which had changed in the passing hours. It was slightly colder, but she didn't mind. Her hair slanted back from her face. The goggles kept her eyes from smarting as they fell through space and time. For a moment, Ellie heard nothing. She was alone with the universe, floating on the air currents, a feather pushed about by air and drawn to the surface by gravity. None of these constructs of physics entered her mind as she spread her arms and allowed the invisible lace to support and carry her.

When Chase deployed the chute, she looked to the ground, watching the green surfaces turn to trees and grass and houses in the distance. She searched for Blake, wondering where he was among the crowds of people no larger than ants gazing up at the falling bodies.

Ellie would never have gone skydiving, never thought of it on her own. It wasn't something on her bucket list. Blake wasn't on that list, either, but falling in love was.

And her free fall was bringing her closer and closer to Blake, a man she had no business even thinking of or completing a sentence that used his name and the word *love* together.

The moment she and Chase touched Mother Earth, Blake was there, helping them up and unharnessing her from his friend.

"Was it just as much fun?"

"Without a doubt," she said.

"Maybe you'll come back again," Chase said. "Even though this event only takes place once a year, we're here at least once a month. Maybe you can convince Blake here to finish his certification."

She glanced at Blake. "That would be up to him, but I thought you owned this place. You look so comfortable here."

Chase laughed.

"Chase is the CEO of an investment company," Blake supplied. "But I met him when he was a cover model."

Chase frowned.

"I'm intrigued," Ellie said.

"A story for another time and after many drinks," Chase returned. "Other than investments, I'm also very active with the diabetes foundation. Both my parents have the disease. My mother has lost her sight and my father died because of it."

"Oh, I'm so sorry."

He nodded, rather than saying anything in response. "You see why I'm involved in finding a cure?"

Ellie glanced at Blake. She could tell he knew why. Chase was engaged, vested in his cause. Blake was only an observer.

The air in the Jeep on the way back to Ellie's was heavy. The sun had set, and it was dark in the cab. The road had few lights, too, making it even more ominous.

Blake didn't know how to lighten the mood. He was the main reason for it having a size and weight of its own.

"Blake, let's not end the day on a low note," Ellie said in the darkness. "It was a wonderful outing. I had a great time."

"How about we stop for some dinner?" he said without answering her.

"I'd like that."

Her voice was soft, dissipating some of the heaviness between them.

"Any suggestions for a good place to eat?"

Ellie looked around. They had reentered the city and were driving along one of the major thoroughfares.

"Turn right at the light," she said. "Do you like Italian food?"

"My middle name is pasta."

She laughed and Blake felt all the heaviness depart. The tension he'd been holding in his body left him, and he relaxed. With her directions, Blake found a small independent restaurant called Mama's Table. Inside, every seat seemed to be filled with people. The smells had his mouth watering.

"Miss Ellie, good to see you again." A large man in a white apron opened his arms and folded Ellie inside them. They kissed on both cheeks and then he stepped back. "So good to see you."

"You, too, Connie," she said. "This is Blake Thorn. Blake, meet Constantine. He's the owner and major cook." Then she looked up at him again. "Do you have a table for us?"

"For you, I'd build a table."

He led them to a small table for two in the back of the restaurant. It was hard to see from the entrance. Blake was surprised to find anything available.

Connie produced a lighter and lit the candle in the middle of the table. Small white lights in the ceiling above gave the area a romantic mood. Italian paintings on the walls and people enjoying their food added to the ambiance of the restaurant.

"You're well-known here," Blake stated.

"I've been known to eat here a time or two."

They took seats. "What's good tonight?" Ellie asked.

"Great lasagna. We have the fettuccini you love."

Ellie's smile brightened and she ordered it. Blake settled on the lasagna. After the waiter brought their drinks, Blake lifted his glass and looked directly at Ellie. He'd seen her all day, but in this amber-lit alcove, with a candle between them, the glow on her face rivaled the lights on the nighttime skydivers falling from the heavens.

Ellie raised her glass and looked at the golden liquid. "Blake," she said. "I've been thinking about our charity arrangement."

"What about it?"

"Well, it seems a little childish on my part to continue these, for want of a better word, exercises. I know I practically goaded you into accepting the challenge, but now that we've gone to two events, I think we should call a halt to it. You've got a store to run, and I've got programs for girls to fund and administer."

"Are you saying that you don't want to go on?"

"Not exactly. And you don't have to say it like I'll be losing a bet. This was not a bet."

"No, it was a challenge and you held up your part. By your own words, I didn't do mine."

"You don't have to. We can let it all drop. There's no one to know we even started this but us."

"A very important person," he said. "I will know."

"And you're a man who never quits, I take it."

"Not until I know defeat is the only ending," he said.

Ellie had the feeling he was saying more than his words revealed. And there was an undertone of teasing present in his voice. That was all right. She could take a little cajoling. In the end, things would work out for the best.

"There's no need for that. We can stop a process anytime we want. Isn't that something you do in the store when a program is not working?"

"Absolutely, but this one is working. So why would I… We," he corrected himself, "stop it?"

"Lack of need. A goal that has no purpose." She gave him two reasons for gracefully ending the challenge.

"As I remember it, Ms. Hamilton, you pointed out several reasons for me participating in charity work. The fact that you want to cancel it leads me to believe that you are the one who has an alternative reason for this suggestion." He gave her a knowing look. "What is it?"

"Nothing in particular. I thought you might want to make better use of your time."

"Better than being with you?" he teased. "What could be better than that?"

Ellie didn't smile. She couldn't tell if he was being facetious or serious. Whichever one it was, she didn't want to be part of it.

"We're not doing this to be with each other," she said.

"Our purpose was to see that I understand what a charity is and does. And since today did not qualify, by your standards, I guess we'll have to keep doing it until we get it right."

The last was delivered in a serious tone. Ellie wondered what his real goal was.

"Why?" she asked.

He frowned. "Why what?"

"Why do you want to continue? If you didn't like charity work before, you couldn't have changed your mind in the last couple of weeks. So why not cut your losses? Go back to your life and let this go?"

He looked at her for a long time. Ellie accepted his stare until his eyes changed. They became darker, even in the subdued light. Need was the only way she could describe them. He didn't bother to try to hide the fact that he wanted her. The thought hit her like the sun exploding. The fact that she wanted him, too, only added to the nuclear fusion that rioted inside her.

*Put the brakes on*, she told herself. She needed to find some excuse to leave the restaurant and get as far from Blake as she could. Why would he want her? They hadn't met that long ago. He couldn't want her, and if he did and then found out their past, where would that leave her? Ellie knew the right thing to do. She knew she had to control the situation. It was important that she keep her head on the side of logic and not be swayed by the emotions banging at the door and fighting her to abandon it and go with her heart.

"We need to think more about this," she said, not defining what she meant by *this*.

"I don't," he said, again keeping his voice and gaze steady on her.

"I think we should leave."

"I see I've made you uncomfortable. It wasn't my intention to do so," Blake said.

"I do have some reservations," Ellie said.

"What are they?"

# *Chapter 7*

The night was warm when they left the restaurant. Ellie had enjoyed herself. The day had proved to be fun, and she wished they could do it again. But the longer she stayed in Blake's company, the more apt he was to remember that her name and his together had a significance.

Ellie knew Blake was waiting for her to answer his question. The waiter had come before she could reply, and after they'd settled the bill, she'd stood to leave.

"Tired?" Blake asked as they headed for the car in the parking lot.

"I should be, but I feel excited and exhilarated."

"That's the way Chase would want us all to feel."

"I like him," she said, but Ellie wondered if he was really talking about his friend.

"He has that effect on most people. He's invited us to join him anytime for more flights."

Ellie stopped, then started walking again.

"He can't be one of your reservations," Blake stated. "Just because we're not going to charity events at the airport doesn't mean we can't return."

"It's not Chase."

"What is it, then?"

"Aren't you…" She hesitated.

"Aren't I what," he prompted.

"In a relationship? Don't you have a girlfriend?"

They'd reached the lot and were passing one of the huge lights mounted on the building. Blake stopped and stared at her, unsure of what she meant.

"I saw you at the gala and a few nights ago in a restaurant with the same woman. The two of you looked like more than friends."

He grinned. "That's it? That's your reservation?" He was almost laughing, but seeing the set of Ellie's jaw stopped him. "I don't mean to make it sound trivial."

"It has been known that people, both men and women, have more than one relationship at a time. Not that we have a relationship," she stated. "But I wouldn't want there to be any complications between you and the lady painted on your arm."

"Despite what it looks like, Wilson Mathison and I are friends—the best of friends."

"I doubt that's how she sees it," Ellie said. "Not from the way she looks at you."

"We've known each other for years," he said in defense.

Ellie was shaking her head as he spoke. "You're wrong."

"What do you mean?"

"I'll show you," she said. "Walk with me."

The two of them began walking side by side.

"This is how two friends walk. They talk to each other, occasionally look at one another and comfortably debate whatever the conversation may be."

He nodded. Then Ellie took his arm. She wrapped one of hers around his and snaked it toward his shoulder. Blake liked where she was going. With her other hand, she secured his arm to her. His biceps touched her breast. Instantly, he went into overdrive. Shifting her body a third of the way toward him so their legs were almost tied together, she was practically restraining his ability to think or walk.

Blake would have stopped if she hadn't pulled him along. He wasn't expecting this close contact. He could smell her shampoo and the faint scent of the wine she'd drank with her meal.

Blake's body reacted. He felt himself grow hard, and the need he felt for Ellie increased to an almost-painful level.

"This is the way lovers walk," she said.

He had to strain to hear her. Her proximity to his emotions affected his hearing. All he wanted was to turn to her and kiss her until neither of them could breathe.

"This is how I saw the two of you at the gala and when you walked into the restaurant a few nights ago."

Blake barely heard her. He felt her, and she felt better than anything he could remember. Turning his head, he gazed at her. Ellie opened her mouth to speak, then closed it. She dropped her eyes to his chest. He waited in silence. When she gazed up at him, something dark and alluring reached out. In less than a second, he faced her head-on. Using his free arm, he circled her waist and pulled her into full contact with him. His mouth clamped down on hers as if he were a dying man.

Hunger and lust might have instigated his actions, but he felt he needed her kiss as much as he needed to keep breathing. Their arms untwined and he opened his legs, tightening his arms and reducing the circle of space between them.

Her mouth was firm, yet her hunger matched his own. Their heads bobbed back and forth as if the need to touch, taste and devour the other was a goal that could crush them if they didn't reach for a place that had eluded them until now. After a moment, Blake raised his head and took a breath. He wasn't ready to end the kiss. This time, his hunger hadn't abated, but he wanted to be tender. He wanted to talk to her with his mouth. He kissed one side of her lips and then the other before covering her mouth again. She opened to him, allowing him in. Blake felt as if he could stay there forever, that he could go on kissing Ellie until the sun rose and set again.

The pressure between them was building, although his hold on her was light enough for her to move if she wished. Still, the touch of her sent a jolt of passion through him that made him want her more. He wanted to be closer, feel her naked skin, listen to her lovemaking sounds. He wanted everything.

He wanted to run his fingers through her hair and see her half-closed eyes when they woke in the morning. He wanted to explore her neck and the hot erotic place behind her ear. He wanted to create fire with her, to savor their consummation with the age-old and timeless ritual.

Ellie finally slumped against him. He held her, breathing hard in the night air. The two of them stood still, each keeping the other upright. He couldn't say how long they stayed that way, whether for a second or a lifetime. Finally, Ellie pushed herself upright. Blake didn't know what to expect when he looked at her. It hadn't been his intention to repeat the kiss they'd shared outside San Francisco. It hadn't been his intention to see her again or touch her, but her act of showing him how lovers walk had changed that.

When her body wound around his, he was lost. Feelings he'd buried sprang to life, overwhelmed him, climbed out of the small box he'd put them in and exploded into being like some big bang that needed only a spark to ignite the world.

"We'd better go," Ellie said. Her voice was deeper than usual. Sexy and sultry. The darkness helped. They'd walked out of the light when she began the journey that led them to this place in their lives. Her voice took hold of him and pushed the small hedonistic buttons that left him in no doubt that he wanted a lot more from Elliana Hamilton than a kiss in a dark parking lot.

"Any more reservations, or have I cleared them up?" Blake's chest was tight and his voice was a note or two deeper than usual. He didn't know why it was important that she believe him, but Blake was discovering many things had an importance where Ellie was concerned.

"So, who is she?" Ellie whispered.

"Who?" Blake frowned.

"The woman attached to your arm."

"You mean other than you?" he said. His joke didn't come off very well, though. Ellie's eyes were serious and didn't change. "She's a friend. That night she was doing me a favor. In the restaurant, I was doing one for her."

"Is she a friend with benefits?"

He frowned, anger rushing to him so quickly, he felt it could knock him over. "I'm not going to answer that."

"That's fair. I should never have asked it. Since it's unlikely we'll see each other except at charity events, I have no right to ask any of these questions. She's your business, not mine."

Blake agreed with her to a point. Wilson was his business. And Ellie deserved an answer. That kiss told him she did.

Ellie started for the Jeep. Blake used his car remote to unlock the doors. She didn't wait for him to help her, but pulled the door open and got inside. He took his seat behind the steering wheel and hit the lock button, but didn't start the engine.

"Her name is Wilson Mathison. She's a model. I've known her since I took over the store. We are friends and *only* friends."

Blake waited to see if there was a reaction from Ellie. He wanted her to smile or show that she was relieved there was nothing between him and Wilson. But she gave him nothing. She faced the front window, wearing an unreadable mask.

"The reason she was holding on to me was that her ex-boyfriend was there, and she didn't want him to think she still had feelings for him."

"Or that she was alone. Or that he was a better date than you," Ellie said. "Don't give it another thought. It doesn't matter anymore."

Blake nodded and waited for more. The subject was obviously closed. But only on her part. She was wrong about one thing, though. It did matter. It mattered greatly. While her face was unreadable, her kiss spoke louder than a shout.

The morning mist was heavy. Blake fought to see through it. Using his hands, he pushed it aside, his arms moving in swimming motions as they tried to clear the fog. Then the lights came—bright, brilliantly white and stabbing his vision.

Blake jerked awake, sitting up in bed with a loud shout. His body was flush with sweat, the bed sheets wet, soaked with the heart-pounding exertion of the dream. Flopping back against the pillows, Blake wiped the moisture from his face with his hand.

Taking deep breaths, he closed his eyes. He hadn't had that nightmare in years. But it was back. It never truly went away, only lurked at the base of his brain, waiting to spring on him at the oddest moment. What had caused it this time? Was it the fact that his ideas of a future were changing? Blake stared at the ceiling as if that thought had sprung from someplace he'd never visited.

It had been ten years since the accident that put him in a coma for four days and had killed his girlfriend, Alexis Ferrell. It had been seven years since he had dreamed of the accident. He tried to change the events in that dream, tried to swerve the car, get it out of the way of the oncoming vehicle, but the results were always the same. The impact happened. Blake could still hear the crash of metal, the sound of breaking glass, Alexis's scream as the protective shell around her folded into a ball of tangled steel.

Blake had woken up four days later with no memory of the accident. The doctors said it was normal, that his memory could return, and it had…in the form of nightmares. But they had long since ceased, until a few moments ago, when he was nearly propelled from the bed.

He got up, went to the kitchen and drank a bottle of water, feeling as if the fire in his dream was real enough to parch his throat. It was the feeling he had had when he woke from the accident, the need for water. And Alexis—where was she?

Blake left the kitchen and went to the guest bedroom. He was determined, searching for something specific, and nothing would deter him. In the second box he found it, the newspaper clippings from the accident. Alexis stared back at him from a grainy photo. It was her high school yearbook picture. She would have graduated that June, in the same class as Blake, but because of him, she was gone.

Would he ever be free of the dreams, or was this to be his endless penance? Why were they fighting? Why didn't he take better care to watch where they were going? Where had that other car come from? So many whys. So few answers.

He looked at the photo again. Time had changed him. There was a gap, a detachment between this time and that. He could look at her photo and not relive the emotions or the feelings he'd once had for her. They hadn't progressed to the point of being in love. Although Blake had been heading in that direction. He couldn't help but wonder what their lives would be like today if it weren't for that one awful night. Would their argument force them apart or grow them closer together? Could they be married now, with a mortgage and their second kid on the way? Would he look at Alexis the way his brother David looked at his wife, Rose?

Would he be happy?

He'd never know. Fate had taken that decision from him. Although fate had not left him with something better. He was worse for the wear, and he knew it. Until Ellie had entered his life less than a month ago, he'd been content to keep everything and everyone at bay. She was defying that oath. She was getting under his skin. No matter how much he told himself that the two of them should stay away from each other, he wanted her.

And by the way she'd responded in his arms, the

way her body molded to his, fitted into the grooves and contours of his physical structure, she wanted him, too. It didn't matter what her mouth said. Her kiss told him more, told him what he wanted to hear.

Blake dressed and got to the store an hour ahead of his normal time. The place was empty and quiet. He knew the House of Thorn was his refuge. It had been like that since he was a boy. He loved running through the floors, hiding between the racks of clothes before he was tall enough to be seen by his parents.

He spent several minutes walking through the darkened departments, checking that everything was in order. As usual, it was. He could count on the store the way other people counted on family to soothe their hurts. Blake knew his family would always be there to back him, but this was not one of the situations where he could go to them. At least not one where he wanted to go to them. Why hadn't he taken Ellie's offer to end this? Why did he refuse, even attack her for merely suggesting that they let the charity thing go? He didn't have an answer for that.

After going to his office and pulling up reports on his computer screen, he scanned several pages of financial statements and requests for major acquisitions. Then he saw the email with an attachment he'd requested. Although her name wasn't there, it shouted Ellie. He'd asked for a report on how many charities the store supported and how many employees took advantage of the day off to do charity work. Blake scanned screen after screen until he came to a statistic that stopped him.

The list was adequate. He had no problem with it. He noticed that the Purple Cloud Farm was not on the list, and that his family's charity received a far greater proportion of support than any of the others. He supposed that should be expected if there was no direction to treat it the same as the others. The most appalling statistic was the comparison of the House of Thorn's employee rates to other businesses in the area. And even worse when compared to competitive businesses.

Blake leaned back. Ellie had been right. Since he didn't give community service a priority, neither did his staff and employees. Only 40 percent of the people who worked at the store took the day option. Compared to other area businesses, they were almost at the bottom of the list. Compared to his biggest competitors, they were at the bottom.

Words his parents had said more than once came back to Blake. *The House of Thorn stores need to be part of the community.* How could he have forgotten that? He was surprised his mother hadn't reviewed this area and noticed how poor a showing they had. He was going to have to rectify that. Like Ellie said, the direction came from the top. He would have to lead by example.

The cell phone lying on his desk buzzed, and Blake glanced at it. For a short moment he hoped it was Ellie, but his brother André's photo appeared on the screen. Blake answered on the first ring.

"What's up?" he asked by way of greeting.

"You know that friend of yours, Ellie?"

Blake tensed. "Yes." He drew out the single word as if it had three or four syllables.

"She said she has a sister who designs."

Blake nodded while confirming the statement. "You need something designed for the store?"

"Not for the store. I have a friend who's getting married and she wants something spectacular to wear. I told her about that dress Ellie was wearing. It was hard to forget, especially for someone raised in retail."

Blake conceded the point. He just didn't want his brother anywhere near Ellie. He loved André. They were more than brothers; they were partners, confidants, the holder of each other's secrets. All except one. There was one secret Blake kept to himself.

"You want Ellie's sister's contact information?"

"I would have called the foundation and gotten the information myself, but you two seemed to have eyes for each other, so I thought I'd go through you."

Blake's body stiffened again. "There is nothing between us," he said.

"Yeah," André said. "Tell that to the judge."

"It's true." Blake realized his voice was a little stronger than he intended. He hoped André didn't notice it, but he knew his brother well, and the two of them were in tune with each other like telepaths. They often knew what the other was thinking even before they said it. "I'll get the information. From a retail point of view, I hope your friend can afford something like the dress Ellie was wearing."

A vision of her in the white dress with all the crystals formed in Blake's mind. He couldn't help reacting to it. She looked like a man's wet dream, and he spoke from experience.

"She can."

"Who is this?" Blake asked. "Someone I've met?"

"You haven't met her, and before you jump to conclusions, we're not involved."

"Yet?" Blake questioned.

"She's getting married," André said. "But even if she wasn't, there's no chemistry between us. When I look at her, there are no stars in my eyes, the way there were in yours when you looked at Ellie."

Blake tried to deflect the conversation to André, but he steered it right back to Blake and Ellie.

"I'll text you her sister's contact info," Blake said.

They hung up and Blake stared at his phone. His finger ached to call Ellie's number. He wanted to hear her voice. If he couldn't see her, he wanted to hear the cadence of her tones in his ear.

He'd dialed her number before he knew he'd done it. Ellie answered on the third ring. This told him she'd stared at her phone, deciding whether she should answer or let the call go to voice mail. At the last minute, she spoke.

"Blake, I didn't expect to hear from you so soon. Have you decided on another charity event for us to attend?"

"Not yet. In fact, I'm calling for one of my brothers."

"Oh."

Blake wondered what the inflection in her voice meant. "Apparently the dress your sister designed, the one you wore the night we met, has made a hit with more than one member of my family."

"Which brother?"

"André," he replied. "Apparently he has a friend who wants to contact your sister and have her design a wedding gown."

"Oh," she repeated, and Blake wondered again about the inflection in her tone. "Her name is Whitney. I told her how much people liked the dress she designed for me."

"It was stunning," Blake said honestly. Ellie was stunning, too, but he'd keep that to himself.

"I'll send you her contact info and tell her to expect a call. What's the woman's name?"

Blake started to speak, then realized he didn't know the answer. "I forgot to ask him."

Ellie laughed. Blake loved the sound of it. He'd been so focused on talking to Ellie that he'd forgotten to ask his brother who wanted the dress.

"I'll find out and—"

"It doesn't matter. I'll let Whitney know the woman wants a wedding gown, and she'll talk to her when she calls."

For a moment there was silence. He felt the purpose of the call was over, but neither of them said goodbye. Blake was about to do it when Ellie spoke.

"Do you know if Rose contacted my sister yet? She hadn't the last time I talked to Whitney."

"I don't know." Blake hadn't spoken to any of his brothers since they had left after the gala. He'd been fixated on all things Ellie. He had to get his life back on track. There was more than one reason for him to make sure the two of them stayed apart. It wasn't her. She knew nothing about his past or his reason for living the bachelor lifestyle. Yet here she was on the phone, and Blake was reluctant to end the call.

"She might have reconsidered," Ellie said.

It took Blake a moment to realize she was continuing the conversation about her sister and Rose.

"Whitney's designs are very expensive. If Rose wanted to include her designs in the store, they would probably be cost prohibitive to their clientele. And Whitney has yet to allow her designs in department stores. They were usually sold in exclusive boutiques or by appointment."

Blake interpreted that to mean the designs were sold to well-heeled, money-crusted clients.

"The store has a series of small boutiques that cater to those clients. It's part of the House of Thorn, but it has a different brand. Most people don't know the two are associated. So Rose has a place to sell the designs if your sister agrees."

He didn't want to sound condescending or as if he were reprimanding her, yet that was how it came out.

"I stand corrected," Ellie said. "I shouldn't have made the assumption."

She didn't ask for the name of the boutiques.

"I'll send you the information you need," Ellie said, obviously wrapping up the call.

"Ellie," Blake called before she could hang up.

"Yes."

"Would you like to go to dinner?" The question

came from nowhere. He wanted to see her, and his mouth and brain connected, even if it was without his consent.

"Tonight?"

"Tonight," he agreed. "I'll pick you up at your office at six."

"Six will be fine."

He could almost hear her smile through the phone. Blake smiled, too. Thoughts of the accident tried to intrude, but he pushed them away. His heart was happy and he refused to allow that to change right now. Later it would come back to him. He knew that, but for today, for this moment in time, he would allow himself to be happy about a woman without the intrusion of the ghost of another.

The office doors were still unlocked when Blake arrived at the Give It to the Girl entrance. Practically everyone had left for the day, and Ellie tried to keep her excitement down, but since Blake had asked her out, asked her on a date that wasn't part of a deal, she felt lighthearted and giddy. She reminded herself that they weren't going to have a relationship, but her brain missed that when his invitation to dinner came.

She wished she'd worn something that would go from day to night, but her suit would have to do. She'd removed the jacket and opened the first two buttons on her blouse. In the bathroom mirror at her office, Ellie pulled her hair around to one side of her head and anchored it with a rhinestone comb that she'd forgotten to take home. Doing a little repair to her makeup made her feel like she was ready for dinner.

When he walked into her office, he looked as if he'd stepped out of *GQ* magazine, but his eyes told her he approved of the way she looked. Ellie stood up. Blake came to her. He put his hands on her waist and kissed her on the cheek. He didn't hold her long, but stepped back.

"You look great," he said.

"Better than I did the last time we were together."

She thought of herself at the airfield, dressed in the bulky flight suit and wearing a tandem harness.

"The jeans and T-shirt looked good to me," Blake said.

Ellie laughed. She'd forgotten that, along with attempting to push thoughts of what happened after dinner in the parking lot in the back to her mind. "Where are we going?"

He helped her with her jacket. "A small little inn that's not far from here."

Ellie discovered the small little inn was a tavern. It was a loud, happy place, where everyone seemed to know each other and everyone knew Blake. He shook hands and greeted the crowd as if he were a bridegroom doing a reverse reception line. Ellie found it fun. The group seemed to accept and greet her with the same enthusiasm they gave to Blake. Conversations were shouted across tables and across the floor to other tables. Laughter reigned, along with the delicious aroma of foods. Ellie felt right at home.

"Wow," she said as she dropped into a seat. "It goes without saying that you've been here before."

"You got it," he said.

"I'll have to be careful with what I say from now on. Some of my thoughts might not need to be acted upon."

"What would some of those be?" he asked.

Things like making love to him or being held and kissed the way she was in an outside parking lot defied her resolve and shot into her mind, heating every part of her and turning her ears to liquid. Using her hand, she made sure her hair covered one of her ears. She clamped her teeth together to prevent the words from spilling out.

Covering her face with the menu, Ellie felt like using it to fan herself. She heard Blake's chuckle and wondered if he had the same visions as she did.

"I guess I'll just have to wait and see what we uncover."

She lowered the menu and gazed into his eyes. That comment had a second meaning, and she knew that was what he meant. Ellie let the moment go on for several seconds before she spoke.

"My sister called to thank you for a client. In case you didn't know, the woman André referred to was Anna Kingsley."

"Senator Keith Kingsley's daughter? That Anna Kingsley?"

"One and the same," Ellie said. "Whitney called me this afternoon. She and Anna Skyped, and they have an appointment for next week. She said she sent a photo of my dress, and Anna was impressed enough to tentatively hire her."

"Great news. We should drink to that."

"We didn't do anything but pass along a phone number."

Blake was already raising a glass of wine. Ellie picked hers up, and the two clinked the rims and drank. Ellie laughed as she set her glass down.

"What's so funny?"

"We are," she told him. "We're celebrating someone else's victory. Someone you've never met or seen."

Blake started to laugh, too. The sound they made only blended with the noise already in the room. They ordered, and the food arrived in record time. The plate of bangers and mash looked and smelled so delicious, she dug her knife and fork into the food, and the first taste was like pure heaven to the taste buds.

"Have you been to England or Ireland?"

"Junior year abroad," she said between bites. "I stayed with a family who owned a small restaurant. These were a specialty of the house."

"Is that why you like small, homey-type restaurants?"

Ellie cocked her head. She'd never thought about it before. "It might have some bearing, but I like huge dining rooms and gourmet food, too."

"From the people who donated product and services to the gala, I agree with you."

"I got that from the Irish family, too. They catered to some really fancy affairs. As a college student, I was thrilled to see some of the castles and halls that weren't open to the public. I asked to tag along, and in doing so, they taught me how to cook some wonderful food served in both Ireland and England."

"You cook, too?" he said.

"At one time I considered opening a restaurant. And that's where I met all those people who are not only my friends, but help me out with the gala."

"My mother must have thought you were a saint when she came across your résumé."

Ellie tried not to react. She kept her face still. "I hope so," she whispered and took a bite of her sausage.

"With your experience in food, how did you get into charities?"

Ellie was relieved that he asked that question. It took her away from thoughts about his mother and how she'd gotten the job at the foundation.

"I was one of those girls. I told you that." She paused. "During the time before my record was cleared, I became friends with some of the girls. I listened to them and commiserated with their issues. When I went home to my family, I remembered that many of them had no family. The strikes were against them, and I wanted to do something about that."

Ellie thought about the girls. Some went on to become complete successes, but many didn't.

"When I started working in social services, I found my calling, the place that gave me the most satisfaction."

"And it keeps these girls out of juvenile hall."

"That's the main goal. All of the programs aren't for troubled girls. There are some who find opportunities or interests that they might not have been exposed to otherwise. I never would have learned to ride or take care of horses if not for Edna and Claude Eastwood at the Purple Cloud."

Blake dropped his head. Ellie felt that he must have found some fault in her story or remembered something from his own past that wasn't pleasant. Someone shouted Blake's name, and he raised his head. Both of them looked in the direction of sound. A man dressed in a business suit and carrying a case was coming toward them.

Blake's grin widened, and he stood up. His hand was already extended as the two men shook, then embraced.

"Averal…Averal Ballantine, what a surprise." They embraced again, obviously friends who hadn't seen each other in a long time. "What are you doing here? Where's Never? Come join us."

He pushed back and slid into the booth where Ellie was sitting. She was sure he'd forgotten about her until his hip bumped up again hers. He introduced her to Averal Ballantine, an old friend.

"Never is my wife," Averal explained. "Her full name is Nefertiti, and it took a while to get used to calling her Never." He looked at Blake. "She's holding down the fort in New Jersey."

"Is she still into video games?" He explained that Never was a game designer.

"She still writes an occasional game for the kids, but she's moved up from the ones you find on the shelves of game stores to games theory and computer simulations."

"Government contracts?" Ellie asked.

Averal shook his head. "She refused those. The simulations are mainly corporate. With the leaps and bounds of technology in the last decade or so, games are used in more places than you can believe. There are times I have to stop her from accepting everything that comes across her computer screen."

The waiter placed a plate in front of Averal. Ellie hadn't seen him place an order, though he was obviously known here, too.

"Thanks," Averal said.

"Are you playing tonight?" Again, Blake included her in the conversation. "Averal plays saxophone. He learned during his stay in Paris."

"I am. Going home tomorrow, so I thought I'd see what was happening here."

Ellie glanced at the bandstand. It was empty at the moment. "There's live music?"

"It's impromptu," Blake explained. "Several businessmen and women who work in the area drop in from time to time and play."

"Do you play?" she asked, remembering he'd studied piano.

Blake shook his head. "My mom made us all learn an instrument, but I haven't practiced in years. I'm purely an audience member."

"Don't let him fool you," Averal said. "He plays a wicked piano and occasionally he joins us."

"But only when they have no one else." Turning

to Ellie, he added, "I need more practice to be able to keep up with these guys."

Ellie nodded, but didn't think Blake needed practice for anything he put his mind to.

Several minutes later the group began to play. Ellie enjoyed listening, but more than the music, she enjoyed sitting in the booth with Blake, his body pressed tightly against hers.

# *Chapter 8*

Ellie was a little tipsy when they walked out into the night air. It was warm, although not as hot as the space inside the tavern. She sidestepped someone on the street, and Blake's hands came out protectively. When they were again side by side, Blake took her hand. Her fingers entwined with his and they continued walking together. His hand was warm and she liked the feel of the solid, but smooth, surface against her own. Ellie had never encountered anyone whose touch arrested every feeling she had.

They passed one block in silence, then a second. As they crossed with the light on the third block, she noticed the street had more pedestrians, and Blake pulled her hand up and her arm through his. This brought her closer to him, their steps in unison.

Without discussion, the companionable silence continued. The two walked back to the House of Thorn store and the parking lot, where Blake kept his car. Ellie didn't object when he opened the door and helped her inside. She didn't trust herself to drive, and secretly she wanted a few more minutes with Blake.

"I had a really good time tonight," she said as Blake negotiated the streets leading away from the busy area and out to more residential streets. "I liked your friends."

"That place is like that all the time. If you go in there alone, you'll meet everyone before you leave."

Ellie heard the pride in his voice. He wanted her to like them. She wondered if he'd taken her there for that reason. And why? She reminded herself that they weren't entering a relationship. Approval or dislike shouldn't matter to either of them. Yet at least for her, it did. Judi already liked him. Ellie hadn't introduced him to anyone else. The women in her office reacted to his good looks. She understood that. The kids at the Purple Cloud liked him. On the other hand, he'd introduced her to Chase at the airfield, and tonight to an entire complement of friends, including Averal Ballantine. Obviously those two had known each other for eons.

Blake stopped the car in front of her small Colonial. It was barely fifty feet across, but ran back almost three hundred feet. The outside was painted yellow with white trimmings and a large front porch, where she often sat reading or enjoying the weather.

Ellie didn't immediately get out of the car. She hadn't had that much to drink, although her brain was still in the twilight area. This had more to do with her companion than the amount of wine she'd consumed. Blake rounded the back of the car and opened the door for her. She put her hand in his and stood up. This time he put his arm around her waist, and the two mounted the five steps that led to the front door.

Ellie opened it and turned to thank him for dinner. The words caught in her throat, and before she knew it, Blake had his arms around her and he was inside, with the door closed. His mouth descended on hers, and she could think of nothing except she didn't want him to stop. The kiss began hard, the clamping of two mouths that needed to touch. Then it changed to hunger, something animalistic and raw. She had to have him, and he her. Ellie, pressed against the wall between door and window, moved one leg and Blake immediately found the space with his hard body.

His mouth ground against hers, his tongue seeking and finding the erotic crevices hidden inside. Ellie gave up any pretense of not wanting everything from Blake. She wound her body around his, pressed into him, kissed and accepted his kisses. Their heads bobbed from side to side. Blake's hands caressed her back as he embraced her, pulling her closer and closer to him. Together they drank of each other, savoring the taste and smell of the other.

Hands ran around her waist. He cupped her breasts. Ellie's knees melted and she slumped. Blake held her in place, his hands and mouth dancing over her skin, burning his touch into her.

"Where's the bedroom?" he asked, lifting his mouth

only long enough to make the request. "If we can't get there, I'll take you right here on the floor."

Ellie didn't say a word. She was incapable of speech. Pointing, she indicated the stairs. Blake grabbed her hand and started to run, dragging her behind him. Her bedroom had double doors and was at the top of the staircase. The doors were open, but Ellie thought Blake would have barreled right through them if they were shut.

With frantic hands, they undressed each other, keeping their mouths pressed together, only separating their bodies to push a shirt or blouse or other item of clothing away. They took little care with their garments, throwing them haphazardly away from the body heat surrounding them.

Blake's hands touched her skin. Fire burned her, but it was a fire she craved. Her mind spun as Blake massaged her skin. Flames sparked from his fingertips, igniting the flesh beneath. Ellie's head fell back and she breathed in. Blake kissed her neck. Her heart exploded. She felt it hammering against her chest.

Ellie turned fully toward Blake, one naked body pressed against another. She felt everything about him—the roughness of his legs, the hard ridges of his stomach muscles, the smooth hands that caressed her. She could define the indentations of his arms, the bulge of blood that coursed through his veins, the way he could set her on fire, the way her body pulsed as if it knew it was making itself ready for him.

Blake kissed her until she could no longer stand. Bare hands brushed across her nipples. Had she seen sparks before Blake's mouth ventured down her neck and closed over the straining nipples? Ellie moaned at the pleasure she'd never felt, but had every right to want. And she wanted more. She wanted it all.

"Blake," she moaned into his hair. Her voice was low and hoarse. His arms circled her back, his hands cupping her and drawing the core of her toward the core of him. Contact was a small explosion, one that said this was not the last. This was only the first of many. The mother lode was yet to come, but here was a promise.

And he delivered.

Blake took her to the bed. He flung the comforter off it, and it followed the same plight as their clothes.

"Do you know you drive me crazy?" He performed a dance. "And it's been happening since the crystals on that dress decided to speak to me. And you." He nibbled on her shoulder. "The sexy body carrying them around." Another kiss. Each time his wet tongue brushed her skin, Ellie drew in a breath. "That sexy body homed in on mine."

Pushing her down, he straddled her and pushed himself inside her. Ellie thought she was ready, but the initial contact, the first brush of his sex against hers, the primary joining, was more than she thought possible. Passion, as liquid as a column of superheated steam, raced through her like a hot geyser, building pressure and searching for release. Ellie had to have it soon, or she would explode.

Blake took her hips and lifted her. His strokes began hard and fast and got harder and faster as he went deep inside her. Ellie gasped at the pleasure bursting through her. Raising her legs, she circled Blake's back and joined him in the primal dance. Everything around them seemed to build. Sound reduced to nothing, except the heated exchange of breath. Her heart pounded and her body writhed as the rhythm between them built, increasing a step higher and then one more and one more. Ellie was unsure she could sustain the feelings that elevated her, drove them up a mountain, where the inevitable had to happen.

She went with him, taking his body into hers time and again, pushing and pulling, unaware of the moans that came from her throat. She pushed on, climbing, reaching upward until she heard the scream of pleasure as a rapture so replete took her over the edge and flung her into a place she'd never been before. Blake was with her, his voice joining hers as the two of them climaxed together.

The float back to earth had never been so satisfying, Blake thought, cradling Ellie to his side and pulling the covers up. He wanted to keep holding her for the rest of the day and tomorrow as he envisioned it. What had happened to him? He'd never been this mesmerized, this intense in a relationship. Not even with… He stopped. He wouldn't let his mind go back ten years.

Ellie moved against him as if she knew his thoughts were wandering, and she could bring them back to her. Blake kissed the top of her head. Her eyes were closed and her breathing even, yet he knew she wasn't asleep. Words were not necessary now. They had spoken. With their bodies and their minds. With the touch of fingers and the deep-throated moans of time, they had found a place that only existed for them.

Blake would have previously denied there was such a place. It was women who manufactured these invisible places they reached during lovemaking. But he'd just found one. Maybe there was only one. Maybe he would never find it again. The thought produced a physical pain in his chest. He heaved a breath. He had to go there. He had to know that this night wasn't a onetime deal. He wanted to go, and he wanted to go with Ellie.

She was still hot next to him. Blake ran his hands over her smooth skin. He loved the feel of her, the softness of her belly, the erotic smell of sex. Pushing her hair back, he kissed her temple, then her ear. She lifted her head and he found her mouth, open, seeking. Pushing her onto her back, he once again straddled her.

"So soon," she stated, her voice low and husky, her hands running over him, surrounding him and brushing her thumb teasingly over the tip of his penis.

"It's not soon." Blake's voice was barely louder than a croak. "At least a millennium has passed since the last time."

She continued the pleasure pain she was subjecting him to, yet he didn't stop her. His erection was rock hard. He'd withstand it, allow it to go on until the need within him was so great, he had to release it. Did Ellie know that?

She placed him at the entrance of her sex. Her body didn't open to grant him access, but he played at the entrance, gently brushing him against her like a gentle fan swinging back and forth. The action was so slow, so methodical that it could have been a game if she wasn't driving him toward complete satisfaction.

Blake reached the breaking point. Taking Ellie's hands, he jammed them above her head and pinned her to the bed with his body. His mouth clamped over hers as if some demon drove him. In seconds, he'd joined them, and just as before, Blake found he could not control himself. He wanted her, all of her.

And he was determined to go all the way. He sank into her heat. She closed around him, taking him in and pushing him out to the brink before pulling him back inside. *Heaven* was the only word he could use to describe what her body was doing to his. He felt the wave that rose inside him each time her legs crunched his sides. Then she would push him back, holding him until he was on the edge of release. But she wouldn't let it happen. Need rose with the heightened race of his blood and flexing of his body. He reached inside himself, forcing their rhythmic beat to step up a notch, then a notch higher.

Blake couldn't say when the explosion came. The rush of need within him was lightning fast. All at once, he couldn't stop the coming climax. Ellie couldn't stop him this time, either. It overcame him, took the two of them higher than he knew the boundaries to be. The shout that was thrust from his throat released the pent-up emotions he'd held back. Ellie's scream coupled with his as they both shot over the earth and climbed, their climaxes reverberating into the electricity as release satiated them.

* * *

The kitchen table was set for two. Orange juice, toast and marmalade were already waiting. Ellie turned an omelet in the pan and pulled a tray of bacon from the microwave.

Blake grabbed a piece over her shoulder and played hot potato with it before putting the whole thing in his mouth.

"I love breakfast," he said between bites. "Especially when someone else cooks it."

"Don't you cook?" she asked, her voice a little flat.

He shook his head. "I can do spaghetti and eggs, but that's it for cooking. Now, baking—that's something I excel at."

Ellie looked at him. She placed the omelet on his plate and took her own seat.

"Tell me the kinds of things you bake."

"Anything you find in the store bakery, I can reproduce almost exactly."

"*Almost* covers a lot of territory."

"Mine are better."

Ellie smiled. "Maybe we could put that to the test one day."

"Another challenge?" he asked.

"I'm sure I'd lose."

"Just as we all learned the retail business, we had to have a stint in the kitchen, too," he explained. "My mother insisted that if we were going to manage stores, we needed to know about everything the store sold."

"So you know clothes, gowns, jewelry, shoes and cooking."

"Appliances, books, exercise equipment, furniture, to name a few," he said. "We have experts in each department, but she wanted us to be able to discuss intelligently all aspects of products."

Ellie nodded. "I knew your mother was a great businesswoman. I guess she taught you well."

Blake was talking about cooking, but Ellie's comments had a different interpretation. She waited until after they'd finished eating. Piling the dishes in the sink, both of them got a cup of coffee and walked to the living room.

Ellie found it difficult to keep up the facade she was presenting. It had nothing to do with their lovemaking. That had been beyond words. Blake was a perfect lover. Ellie could find no fault with him. She wasn't looking for any, either.

It was after their loving that Blake had fallen asleep and talked. Ellie took a sip of her coffee.

"You seem distracted," Blake said. "Is something wrong?"

"You talk in your sleep," she said, not bothering to ease into the discussion.

"I do? What did I say?"

"You called Alexis."

Blake sighed. "Did I call you by her name?" he asked.

"No."

He seemed relieved.

"Who is she?" Ellie asked the question, but she already knew who Alexis was. She should have let the subject go. Blake hadn't called her Alexis. He was obviously dreaming, and he'd called the name in his sleep. Ellie was already out of the bed. She'd planned to go to the kitchen and make him breakfast, which they would share, among the rumpled sheets and in the morning-after glow. But the name paralyzed her for a moment and she was in no mood to go back to bed.

"Come here," Blake said. He put his cup down and opened his arms, inviting her in.

Ellie hesitated before going to him. He took her hand and pulled her down next to him on the sofa and put his arm around her.

"Ten years ago I was in an accident," he began.

His voice was low and seemed to be coming from ten years back.

"Alexis was my girlfriend. She died in that accident."

Ellie swallowed hard and leaned against him.

"It was raining and we were coming back from a movie. She was driving. Things hadn't been going well for weeks. That night we were arguing. And then there was a truck on the same side of the road. Between the rain, the headlights and Alexis crying, we were hit head-on. The other car didn't even try to return to the other side of the road. Not until it was too late."

"What were you arguing about?"

Blake was quiet for so long, Ellie didn't think he was going to tell her.

"She'd found someone else. She was breaking up with me."

"And you didn't want that?"

"I'm not really sure. It was more the other thing she said that had me so angry."

This was something Ellie didn't already know.

"What was that?" She made her voice low and slow.

"She was pregnant."

Ellie sat up straight and turned to look at Blake.

"It wasn't my baby. It was the man she was dumping me for."

Ellie wouldn't ask who that was. She wouldn't know him anyway. They didn't live in the same town or go to the same schools.

"I was taken to the hospital. Four days later, I woke up and was told I'd been in a coma."

Ellie's father was pronounced dead, but she'd walked away with practically no injuries. She had a few cuts from the broken glass and several bruises on her legs, but nothing serious. The only serious thing was the fact that she had lost her father. If he'd let her drive, the outcome might have been different.

A tear fell from her eye and rolled down her cheek. She brushed it away. Blake gathered her in his arms and held her there. She knew he misinterpreted her emotion. She felt compassion for him and for Alexis, but her tears were more for herself and the loss of her father. One single decision, and the outcome of their lives had changed in a split second.

Alexis might still be alive. She and her mother might never have moved back to San Francisco. She and Blake would never have met.

"When I woke up, Alexis had been buried and I didn't remember the accident," Blake said.

"That's pretty normal for a head injury." The trace of tears was still in her voice. "Your memory returned, right?" She was afraid of this answer. If his memory had come back, then he should know who she was.

"It took months for everything to fall into place, but it did return."

Ellie stiffened, then forced herself to relax. What did he remember? Did he know who she was? If so, why hadn't he said anything? They'd been seeing each other for at least a month. Blake hadn't dropped any hints that he and Ellie knew each other before the gala.

Heat burned her skin.

This was the perfect time to confess. Ellie wanted to. She wanted the weight of knowledge she'd lived with for the three years since she discovered he was the manager of the San Francisco House of Thorn lifted from her shoulders. She wanted to clear the air, tell him that she was the young girl in the truck. That her father was at the wheel and had suffered a heart attack and died.

She wanted to expunge the guilt she felt at the loss of life and the way it had changed them all, but she also wanted a repeat to the way he made her feel. Giving up one for the other was something that she needed more time to decide on. She wanted to be alone, without the need for his warm body to connect with hers.

Ellie needed to come to terms that if she spoke up, if she told the truth, Blake would be gone from her life. This, too, was like that decision of her father's to drive—a life-changing moment. And she didn't want it to happen. She wanted to hold on to what they had, even if it was temporary. Even if eventually she had to tell him. She didn't want to do it today.

She didn't want their lives to move from the track they were on. They would, sometime in the future. It was inevitable.

But not today.

*There should be a song called "Ellie On My Mind,"* Blake thought. Because she was always on his mind. He spent more time walking the floors of the store or sitting at his desk and staring into space, wondering where Ellie was and what she was doing, than getting his own work done. Was she out with one of the girls' programs? Even though she was the executive director, she was a hands-on person, someone who loved interacting with the girls and not just making sure the office ran efficiently and costs were within budget.

He knew she had a positive effect on people, and he was one of them. If not for her, he wouldn't be getting past Alexis and the effect her death had on his life. She knew nothing about that, but Ellie was the one person in the last ten years who had caused him to greet the day with a greater enthusiasm. He loved the store. Going there was fulfilling, but it didn't hold his hand or wrap its body around him in a way that gave him a glimpse of heaven. It didn't run its legs up and down his and caress him in the most intimate way.

She did.

The store was an entity, while Ellie was a living, breathing woman.

And she was his, even if she didn't know it—yet.

He thought about their morning after. Not a morning typical of that connotation. But then again, Ellie was often not what he expected. He hadn't thought of telling her about Alexis, especially after the night before, after the way they had made love, but it seemed natural to talk to her, to tell her the details of a life that was so much a part of his own that it seeped into all aspects of his days.

Ellie's tears had moved him. She understood how he felt as no one else could have. He smiled at the thought of her. She truly completed him. He could hardly wait to see her again. When one of the employees caught him and returned his smile, Blake knew he had to get back to work.

He was in the men's department when his watch buzzed, and he checked the time. It was nearly four o'clock and he had an appointment. At the elevator, he met Will Jerome, the person he was expecting.

"Will, good to see you again. Thanks for coming." The two shook hands.

"I don't know why I'm here, really." He paused. "Did Ms. Hamilton ask you to talk to me?"

"She did not. She doesn't even know you're here."

Blake noticed he relaxed a little. Obviously Ellie kept in touch with him. She probably kept in touch with everyone at the farm.

The elevator doors opened, and they exited on the office floor. Blake led the way, past glass walls that let in the natural light, to his office. Will looked around at places the public never saw.

In the small reception area, two girls Blake had met

at the farm were coming out. Both smiled and gave a short wave, then giggled as they continued down the hall.

"Hi, Will," they said in unison.

"Patty, Gloria?" He made their names a question. "What are they doing here?" Will turned to Blake when the girls were no longer within hearing distance.

"The same thing as you."

Will looked confused. "And what is that?" His tone was challenging. Blake knew they were back at the farm, untrusting and unknowing what the other was about.

"In due time, but don't worry. It's all good."

In his office, Blake took the seat behind his desk and offered Will one of the guest chairs. The young man dropped his backpack to the floor and took a seat. He glanced over his shoulder, checking to see if the two girls were still in the hallway.

Blake looked through the glass enclosure.

"I'm waiting," Will said.

"Are you always this impatient?"

"Sometimes I'm intense," he said.

Blake sighed. "I thought we agreed to be friends."

"Why did you ask me here?" He emphasized the last word. It took Blake a second to understand what the young man was thinking.

"I said it was all good. I didn't ask you here to reprimand you on our previous discussion. That's all in the past."

"And not to be repeated." The kid appeared to finish a sentence Blake had not started.

"That's not it," Blake said. "But I hope it will not be repeated."

"Okay, if it's not about me stealing, then what is it?"

"I have a job to offer you, if you want it."

The look on Will's face was pure surprise. His eyes opened wide and his jaw dropped. "Where?" he asked after a moment.

"Here at the store."

Will appeared stunned for a moment, then he burst into laughter. Blake waited while the sound reverberated around the room. He kept his expression steady, letting Will know he was serious.

"Here? Are you kidding me?"

Blake understood that *kidding* wasn't the word he wanted to use. He took it as the young man's show of respect for Blake. Instinct told him there was a good kid inside this almost man's body, and that with a little guidance, he'd turn into a solid citizen.

"Where?" Will asked. "In the basement, janitor or—let me think… In the shoe department, specifically the area that sells sneakers."

Blake shook his head. "Security," he said, his voice nearly a whisper.

"Security!" Will's shout was loud. "Come on, man. Why are you putting me on?"

"I'm as serious as cancer," Blake said. He waited a beat or two to let Will take it in or contradict him. The young man said nothing. "The job is in Security." Blake held up a hand to stop Will from speaking. "Yes, I based it on your previous experience. I hope that was just a one-shot deal, but we're not going to rehash it. If you understand how people shoplift, you're perfect for the job of making sure it doesn't happen."

"You mean like giving the guy who hacked into your website the job of securing it?"

Blake smiled. "Exactly."

Will sat back in his chair. Blake knew enough about selling and closing the deal to tell Will was more than interested in his proposal.

"What would I have to do?"

"First, keep your grades up in school." Blake lowered his chin and waited for Will to agree. It took a moment, but he nodded.

"What's next?"

"Three days a week, you come to the store, report to the security office and work for three hours."

"Do I get paid?"

"Initially, no," Blake said. Will's face fell. "After you cover the cost of the stolen sneakers, you'll earn a salary. Human Resources will give you all the details."

"They took the sneakers back. Why do I gotta pay for them?"

"Because you're going to donate them to a kid who needs them." Blake kept his face serious.

Will smiled for the first time since he'd entered the store. "When do I start?"

"Monday afternoon. If you have other activities, we can work around them. Just give your schedule to the counselor, put in the hours and I know you'll do a good job."

Blake offered his hand. Will stood up and took it.

"You have that much faith in me?"

"I have more faith in you than you do," he answered honestly. The young man suffered from self-esteem issues. Blake felt that trust and a little belief from adults that he could do a good job would help him do just that.

Will turned to leave, then turned back. "Where will Patty and Gloria be working?"

Blake smiled. "Patty is in the shoe department, and Gloria will be in the bakery."

Will smiled, then frowned. "Are they here because…" He didn't finish the sentence.

"I can't answer that," Blake said. "It would be a breach of confidentiality." The two men looked at each other for a long moment. "Just like if I told them why you were here, it would be a breach of *your* confidentiality."

Today wasn't one of the days Ellie spent at the Purple Cloud, but Edna was away and they were short a counselor. So Ellie had agreed to fill in. Since she was so busy, she didn't have a lot of time to talk to some of the kids who had been there awhile. Finally, when she was leaving, she saw Apple.

"Hey, Ms. Hamilton. How's it going?"

"Good." Ellie smiled. "You know I always feel good when I come here."

"Me, too," he said. "That's why they can't get rid of me."

Apple was a mainstay. His community service time had been fulfilled, but he'd rather spend time with the horses and the other teens than anything else. And the Eastwoods were grateful for his volunteering.

"Where's Will?" Ellie asked. "I didn't see him today."

"He's not here anymore. Neither are Patty and Gloria."

"They weren't sent back…?"

"Oh no," Apple interrupted.

Relief had her dropping her shoulders and expelling a long breath. For a moment, she thought they'd done something to get sent to juvenile hall.

"They were reassigned," Apple told her. "To your friend Mr. Thorn."

"What?" The relief was gone, and Ellie was tense now. Blake's name did that to her. It was like she needed to keep her guard up, yet when she was near him, she couldn't remember anything about keeping away. Truth be told, she didn't want to be away from him. She wanted to be around him all the time. It made no sense. Her brain told her that and she agreed with it, but her body had different things in mind when he was close.

"He got them transferred to his store," Apple said, bringing her back from the fantasy playing out in her mind's eye.

Ellie kept her mouth closed, although it was an effort.

"Will said Mr. Thorn gave them a job. And they'll get paid. Sounds like a sweet deal to me."

Too sweet, Ellie thought. And it sounded too good to be true, her brain engaging in the logical progressions it was designed for. What was Blake up to? He didn't do charity work. Maybe he didn't consider his hiring the students to be part of a charity. Or maybe he didn't understand what it meant to push and pull the kids around from place to place.

Ellie did.

Doing what Blake had done wasn't an easy trick. Getting a kid reassigned was a process. There were bureaucracy, forms, meetings with court officers, transfer forms and the obligatory psychology sessions. Had Blake done that for three students? And in so short a time? As far as Ellie knew, the House of Thorn had no program for community service. Had Blake added one in the last few days?

She had to find out.

It was Sunday, but retail establishments had only three holidays a year: Thanksgiving, Christmas and New Year's Day. It was likely Blake was at the store. Ellie entered the building through the main doors. The place conveyed the feeling that it had stood there for decades. It wasn't a modern glass-and-steel building, but one that blended into the hundred-year-old neighborhood. Its walls were designed to withstand an earthquake. So far, though, they hadn't suffered any damage due to Mother Nature's testing of the tectonic plates.

The store was crowded with people shopping and buying. Ellie went straight to the elevators, but before the doors opened, she saw Blake coming from the bakery area. He hadn't seen her yet. His attention was focused on negotiating the crowd. As the floors ascended, the number of customers thinned out. This was the first and busiest floor.

Blake stopped at the set of elevators farthest from Ellie, the private one that went straight to the top floor.

Using his key, he called it. The doors opened and he stepped inside. Just before they closed, Ellie slipped through an opening barely wide enough for her body.

*Ellie* was the only word he got out before she clasped her hands on both sides of his head and kissed him. At first Blake was stiff with surprise, but a second later, he was fully engaged in mouth-to-mouth resuscitation. Ellie hugged him, squeezed as hard as she could and aligned her form to his in a way that rendered them one and the same.

He understood that her kiss was for gratitude; at least it had begun that way. Yet somewhere between the first touch and the next nanosecond, the spark between them flared into a raging fire, and she forgot everything and everyone while clasped in Blake's arms.

The bells rang, indicating they had risen to the desired floor. The doors would open. Blake pushed her back.

"I'm not complaining, but what brought that on?" he asked.

Blake took her arm, led her to his office and closed the door. He looked at the glass walls. Ellie could almost read his mind. It didn't take a medium to know what he was thinking. She thought the same thing. If the walls were not made of glass, they could continue the kiss they had started in the elevator. She desperately wanted to kiss him again.

"Now that we're alone, what brings you here?"

Even though it was Sunday, there were people in the office. "I hear you have three new employees."

Blake dropped his head, then lifted it with a smile. “Who told you?”

“Apple. I went to the farm this morning, and the roll was down by three.”

“They’re doing fine here. I thought they could work out their service here and learn the retail business.”

“How’s it going?”

“It’s only been a few days, but I put them in places where they had an interest.”

“You’re taking responsibility for making sure they comply with the court order?”

He nodded. “I’ve been instructed on what to do. Don’t worry. We’ll be fine.”

Ellie wanted him to see what the work was like, but this was a wrinkle she hadn’t anticipated. She thought they’d do projects like the one at the farm, or even the support they’d lent to the diabetes fund-raiser. Taking responsibility for keeping kids in check was a completely different animal.

“Will is here today,” Blake said. “Do you want to see him?”

Ellie shook her head. “I don’t want him to think I’m checking up on him.”

“Maybe if you said you were concerned, it would save your face and pump up his self-esteem.”

Blake had discovered the young man’s need to believe more in himself. Ellie’s heart warmed. She nodded, indicating that she wouldn’t mind seeing him.

“Where does he work?”

“Security.”

Ellie nodded, although that was the last place she expected Blake would put him.

"I'll give him a call to let him know we're coming." Minutes later, they entered the control room for the store. Ellie was amazed at all the equipment.

"Hello, Will."

"Hi, Ms. Hamilton." Will came to her with a smile. He looked like a different person. His clothes were clean and pressed. His hair had been brushed and cut. His face was clean, although a little acne showed along his forehead.

"You look great, Will. Working here must agree with you."

He glanced at Blake. "Mr. Thorn trusts me, and I don't want to disappoint him." He paused. Ellie waited. She could tell he wanted to say something else. "My mom thinks the change is good, too."

"What do you do here?"

"I check the monitors, and if I see anything suspicious, I alert someone on the floor. Sometimes I'm the person on the floor."

"I'm glad you're happy. I was concerned that something had happened to you when you weren't at the farm. But I see you like this work a lot better than being around the horses."

He smiled. "And I get a store discount." He pulled his pant legs up and let her look at his new pair of sneakers.

"Nice." Ellie smiled, recognizing the brand.

"My mom got them, but I'm grateful to Mr. Thorn for choosing me."

"Enough," Blake said. Looking at Ellie, he explained, "He's said that at least five times today."

All three of them smiled.

"We're going now," Blake said.

"See you later, Ms. Hamilton."

Ellie smiled and they left the room. She wanted to hug Will, but that would be stepping over the line. She'd just have to settle for hugging Blake.

# *Chapter 9*

"You're awfully quiet," Blake said when they'd walked several yards and taken the steps back to the office floor.

The corridor was empty, and Ellie stopped and faced him. "On the surface, this looks ideal."

"On the surface," Blake repeated.

"Is this real? Or are you setting these kids up for something that will hurt them in the long run?"

"You think I would do that?"

"I don't know. I don't want to believe that."

"Then why do you?" He tried to keep the anger out of his voice, but speaking through clenched teeth didn't allow for that.

"You've met him once," Ellie said.

Her voice was controlled. At that moment, Blake

thought she would make a great social worker or 9-1-1 operator.

"He's been reassigned to your store. That involved a lot of work, transfers, the court, interviews, not to mention specialized training. It begs me to wonder if there is another reason behind all that."

Blake took a menacing step toward her and stopped. Ellie didn't move, didn't give up any ground or appear threatened.

"I'm only interested in their well-being. I thought they could profit from the experience they could learn here, and they wouldn't have to begin at the lowest level. But I can see clearly that, in your eyes, I've failed."

Blake walked away from her then. He headed for his office without looking back. He wanted to slam the door, give it all the force of his strong arms. But he resisted. As he softly closed it, he heard the muffled sound of the elevator bell ringing.

How could she think that? He paced back and forth. He'd been interested in Will after talking to him. The same with Patty and Gloria. He did feel he could help Will with some sort of rehabilitation that involved trust and not iron bars. Patty and Gloria had expressed an interest in retail.

Ellie worked with a charity all day. She participated in the development of programs to do exactly what he was doing. He didn't need her approval or sanction. He had the court's permission. The kids were doing all right. He monitored reports about them every day, and so far they were taking to their tasks with enthusiasm. Patty had even made a suggestion in the shoe department for a better way to display shoes that appealed to her demographic.

Blake wanted Ellie to approve. He hadn't had the kids reassigned to get her approval, but he thought that would be one of the outcomes. When she arrived, practically implanting her body onto his, he was sure she was onboard with him. The interview with Will was nothing but positive.

Then…

Then the truth came out. She didn't believe him for a second. Well, he didn't need her approval. He knew the truth, knew his reasons for doing what he did. And they were true. He wanted the kids to succeed. This was his small way of trying to do something that would give them dignity and a life skill. Why hadn't she seen that?

Blake dropped down in his chair. Nothing on his desk was visible to him. All he could see was the frozen expression on Ellie's face just before he'd walked away from her.

Judi grabbed her glass of wine and folded her legs under her as she sat in an oversize chair in Ellie's living room. "You know I could lose my shopping privileges for this?" she said. "They could take my credit card, and I'd be lost without it."

She was kidding and Ellie knew it. "Just tell me."

"I talked to Patty and Gloria. They love working in the store. They say they see Blake several times when they're there. Of course, he is a gorgeous man—makes my mouth water just looking at him."

Ellie's eyes flashed at her friend.

Judi laughed, "So he does get your juices running. You should see the way the girls look at him."

Ellie said nothing, but she felt the stab of jealousy that raised its head within her.

"They're teenagers, Ellie, often in love with a good-looking man. The fact that they don't know what love is is beside the point."

"I've seen the looks," Ellie said.

"Not coming from your own eyes," Judi finished for her.

"What?"

Ellie remembered not only the way Blake had looked at her, but the way she felt in his arms, the way they'd made love, the way the two of them fitted together like opposite sides of the same coin. Heat started working its way up her face.

Judi leaned forward, coming out of her relaxed position. She set her glass on the coffee table and looked Ellie right in the eye. "Elliana Hamilton, you're more than attracted to Blake Thorn. The two of you have passed step one."

"Don't be so antiquated." Ellie groped for something to refute her friend's claim.

"All right, you're beyond first base. You've rounded a corner and you can't undo what's been done. So, what's been done?"

Ellie waited a long moment. The two stared at each other. Ellie had been friends with Judi since they'd met in a wine-tasting class five years ago.

"He kissed me," Ellie finally said. She wouldn't share anything more, definitely not the fact that he'd produced a heaven within her that she knew no one would ever come close to duplicating.

"I knew it. I could tell by that expression on your face. You go all soft and gooey whenever we talk about him."

"Soft and gooey?" Ellie screwed up her face. Yet she didn't deny Judi's words.

"It's the only description I can think of." Judi picked up her glass and sipped the wine. "How do you really feel about him?"

Ellie ran her fingers through her hair. It was down and falling over her shoulders. She pushed it back behind her ear, remembering Blake doing that on the hill outside the Purple Cloud.

She mulled over answers she could give Judi. The two usually shared a lot of their lives, although Ellie had no doubt that Judi had secrets she kept to herself, just as Ellie did. She wasn't thinking of lying to her friend, only offering her the technical truth without the full and complete story.

"I think I'm falling in love with him," she said.

Judi's body came forward as if she were propelled off the chair.

Darlene appeared in Ellie's doorway. Ellie looked up from the monthly reports she was reviewing.

"I wanted to remind you that I'm leaving now."

Ellie nodded. Darlene had a doctor's appointment. "See you tomorrow."

"Before I go, you had a call from Mr. Thorn."

Ellie's heart lurched. "What did he want?"

"He asked if you'd call him back." Darlene handed her a notepad page with his name and number on it.

"Thanks," Ellie said.

Darlene waited a second too long before smiling and leaving Ellie's office.

Looking down at the paper, Ellie realized the number belonged to Blake's cell phone. Ellie wondered why he hadn't called her on her cell. He had the number. It had been two weeks since their encounter in his store. She'd had no reports about the camp kids being transferred and not liking it. She felt bad about her suspicions, although they were warranted.

What could he want now? Certainly not to talk to her. She felt their friendship had ended that day in the corridor of the House of Thorn. Ellie debated returning the call. But he had placed it to a business number. He could want something related to the foundation, and it would be both rude and unprofessional to ignore it.

She picked up the phone and punched in his number. It rang three times before he answered it. In the past, before the store confrontation, he'd answered on the first ring. Did he want to talk to her, or was he answering now simply because he *had* to talk to her?

None of these thoughts kept her body from reacting to the sound of his voice. Ellie never really knew things like this could happen. She'd read romance novels, watched Hallmark movies and enjoyed the company of men, but never had she had these wildly swinging emotions. But apparently her mood swings were only associated with one single man—Blake Thorn.

"I have a message that you called." Her voice was

stiffer than she wanted it to be. She knew if she didn't force herself, it would come out "all soft and gooey," as Judi had said.

Blake cleared his throat on the other end of the phone line.

"I called to remind you that we have a project to complete."

He made it sound as if they had a business arrangement. That might have been how it began, but they were well past that now. Their first kiss on that windswept hill had been a change to the path she expected to run. If that didn't change things, their night of lovemaking had solidly altered their trajectory. Ellie didn't know where they were headed. One minute she'd had her body wrapped around his like a candy cane, and the next she was berating him for having an ulterior motive.

And her determination to stay clear of Blake had long since been forgotten.

"I assumed we'd already done that."

"Why?" he asked.

"At the store." She stopped and cleared her own throat as images of them in the elevator flooded her senses. "When you demonstrated the hoops you'd gone through to help some of the teens—that was proof enough for me."

Did she hear a sigh through the phone? Was Blake relieved? Her heart sank.

"Blake?" Ellie lowered her voice. "I want to apologize."

"Not necessary," he said.

"I want to do it anyway. I jumped to a lot of conclusions the last time I saw you. Apparently the kids are doing fine. They love working in retail and are happier there than they were at the farm."

"Good to hear," he said. It was the type of comment you made when you had nothing else to say.

"Thank you for being able to see that and doing something about it. It proves how much of a foundation person you are."

"Thank you."

"So," she said, drawing the word out. "We've completed the project."

"Not yet," he said, stopping her. "There's one more event we have to attend."

"What's that?"

"The celebration."

"I don't understand." They had never discussed having a celebration when they finished a project.

"As a celebration to the end of our agreement, I have tickets to the Gladys Oberon Children's Cancer Hospital Ball. They invite me every year, but usually I have a conflict. So I send a check. This year I'm free. It's a fund-raiser, so I thought it was the perfect place to celebrate."

It was a wonderful organization. Ellie had attended several of their events, but she'd never gone to their ball. Gladys Oberon was a small hospital that was gaining a great reputation for innovative procedures and patient care.

"When is it?"

"Saturday."

"Is it all right to add this to my calendar?" he asked.

It sounded more like a business meeting than a date. It wasn't a date. She'd had her turn at dating Blake. This would only be the completion of an agreement that she regretted ever making. If she hadn't, her heart wouldn't be in such danger of breaking into pieces.

"I'll add it to mine, too," she agreed without giving the customary yes or no.

He agreed to pick her up on the night of the fundraiser. Ellie ended the call and placed her phone on her desk. She gazed at it as if it were alive and only acting dead. It could strike her at any moment. It was fire. Why was she playing with it? And why was her mind skipping to what she would wear? The pearl-encrusted shoes with stand-up butterfly clips on the front were on the shelf of her closet. She'd have to get them down. They would go with the red strapless gown her sister had given her for Christmas a year ago.

She wanted to look special. More and more, she thought of Blake and herself having a future together. She didn't know if that was possible. But when he saw her, she wanted his memory to be of her looking like a queen.

When she got home that evening, she went straight to her bedroom and pulled out the dresses, deciding on one and making a mental note to have it pressed.

Saturday night arrived with the slowness of a tortoise race. Ellie had anticipated it everyday since she'd spoken to Blake. She had everything ready, taking nearly an hour to get her makeup and hair perfect before donning her gown.

The box with her shoes was on the top shelf of her closet. She reached up and pushed aside several other boxes, looking for the one labeled Pearl-Encrusted Shoes. Seeing it, she went up on her toes and grabbed it. Down it came, knocking another box with it. Ellie used her hands to protect her head as both boxes crashed to the floor. The shoes fell out, along with the rhinestone butterfly clips that adorned the front of them.

Papers from the other box were strewn all over the bedroom floor. Quickly Ellie gathered them up and pushed them back onto the floor of the closet.

Standing up, she adjusted her gown and slipped her feet into the high heels. Taking a look in the mirror, she was pleased, but her hair needed a bit of fixing. The box had hit her and pulled her twist loose. Ellie put it back in place, anticipating Blake ringing the doorbell.

The computer's trill caught Blake's attention. He was sure it was one of his family members. They usually called when a conference was scheduled. There was nothing on his calendar, so it could only be one of his brothers. He grinned when he saw André's name highlighted on the screen.

"Hey, André, what's up?"

"I should ask what's up with you. Look at that room."

Blake glanced behind him, seeing the mess he'd made of his bedroom. He swung the computer around. André's camera was limited to the wall behind his desk. Taking a seat, Blake relaxed for a moment.

"We're on our way to a charity ball."

"You?" André said. "You hate balls."

"Not exactly. I hate all the pomp and circumstance that goes into balls where the money never reaches those in need."

"I know Wilson didn't convince you to go, so who is the lucky lady?"

"You're sure a woman convinced me?" Blake hedged.

"I'm looking directly at you."

"Is there a purpose for this call? Or did you just want to shoot the bull?"

"I was thinking of you and wondering how things were going," André said.

"They're fine," Blake told him, then shrugged. "Yep, I'm going out. I'm accompanying Ms. Hamilton to a ball."

"Ellie Hamilton, the exec at the foundation? That Ms. Hamilton?"

"One and the same." Blake tried to keep his voice even, yet just thinking about Ellie aroused him. Saying her name made his voice soft and gentle, the way she was.

André moved closer to the screen, as if the two were in the same room and he was getting close to prevent others from overhearing.

"Are you two seeing each other?" he asked. "Dating?"

"Not exactly." Blake couldn't call their time together dating.

"What exactly, then?"

"We've been attending a few events with each other."

"And you don't call them dates?"

"They're not dates."

"Okay. Have you had dinner together?"

"Twice."

"Then it's dating."

"André, with Ellie it's complicated," Blake said, his voice sounding hesitant and confused.

"I see, you've gone from Ms. Hamilton to Ellie in one lightning strike. Are we going to go from dinner to a wedding, or are you planning to leap tall buildings in a single bound first?"

Blake knew his brother was teasing, but he was closer to the truth than he knew. For a moment, Blake considered telling him everything.

"Blake," his brother said. "What's going on?"

"I am dating Ellie."

"You said that like it's serious."

Blake thought for a moment. "That's the complicated part."

"Unrequited?"

"I'm not sure."

"Blake, this is not like you. What happened to the end-it-on-the-third-date guy? You're acting more like David when he fell for Rose."

Blake agreed. "It doesn't feel that bad."

"Oh my God, you're in love with her." It was a statement of fact.

André flipped back in his chair, pushing himself away from the computer screen. Blake watched without comment as the perspective changed. He glanced at the bed. A blue velvet box lay there. André couldn't

see it. Blake had moved the computer screen away from a view of the bed.

"How does she feel about you?"

"It's complicated."

"Stop saying that." André smacked the desk with his hand. Blake blinked but didn't move. "Either she loves you or she doesn't."

Blake understood his brother more than André thought he did. He was protective. All of the Thorn boys were. They stood together as a family, and no one wanted any of them to be hurt, physically or emotionally.

André wasn't an emotional man. He didn't wear his feelings on his sleeve and he didn't jump to conclusions. He weighed things logically before making a decision. It was because it was family that his back was up. Fortunately attack mode was miles away from his current state.

"Let's just see where it goes," Blake said. He had a plan to move things along. Ellie had started this journey and she wanted to end it, but he wasn't about to let that happen. The two of them had something. Blake felt it, and he knew she did, too. As much as he fought against his feelings, she was fighting hers, as well.

Now she'd have to fight hers and try to deter him from his mission to make her his—in mind, body and soul.

Three tuxedos lay in various places about Blake's bedroom. He'd dressed and undressed several times after getting off the phone with his brother. Changing clothes multiple times was something he'd always believed only

women did. He'd never done it before. Usually he chose his clothes, showered and dressed. There were no Thorn girls except his mother, and he had never noticed her being so unsure of how she looked that she discarded one outfit for another three times before settling on one. He'd seen her change her jewelry once or twice, but never her clothes, unless she spilled something on herself.

Blake took the white jacket off and replaced it with the black one. Nodding to his reflection in the mirror, he needlessly pulled down his cuffs and slipped his feet into his shoes. His watch pinged. It was time to leave.

Ellie opened the door when he arrived, and Blake was speechless. The white gown she'd worn with the crystals was beautiful and drew the eye. Tonight, she was a lady in red. Her hair was up and red ribbons were braided through it. All he could think of was running his fingers through it and pulling it down.

The dress was strapless, formfitting in the front, and the back was gold, with a floor-length drape that pinched in at the waist and ended with a short train, which flowed when she walked toward him. For a moment, Blake was speechless and his throat was so dry, he had to pry his tongue from the roof of his mouth.

Blake was suddenly unsure how to act. They'd parted on terms that could have been better. Was Ellie the type to hold a grudge, or was she the forgiving?

"You look lovely," he said. She actually bowled him over.

Ellie looked him up and down. Finally she said, "I've always thought of you as a *GQ* model."

"Was that a compliment?" he teased. That was the first time she'd ever complimented him, and something inside him moved, clicked into place.

"Is this another creation by your sister?"

"It is." She turned fully around, allowing him to see the gown. On her feet were a pair of shoes that had butterflies on them and looked as if they were covered in pearls. They complemented her outfit perfectly.

"Very talented. I'd love to meet her one day," Blake said.

"She wants to meet you, too," Ellie replied.

"You told her about me?"

"We have no secrets." She winked.

"Everyone has secrets," Blake said. He knew he did.

Looking at Ellie, he felt a change in the mood. He didn't want anything to spoil tonight.

"We'd better go," she said.

"Before we leave, I want to say something."

She pursed her lips and took a stance where she placed her small purse under her arm. Blake wondered if she was expecting him to say something awful.

"I know we've had some words." He paused. "And our last meeting wasn't the best."

She nodded and appeared to soften a little.

"Tonight may be the last time we attend an event together. So I'd like us to attend the ball as two friends, with no strings, no overtones, no ulterior motives. How about it?"

She nodded. "I can do that."

They arrived at the hotel. The ballroom walls were decorated with huge gold ribbons that denotated childhood cancers. The tables were covered with white tablecloths boasting the same gold emblems. Hostesses at the entry doors gave out gold-colored metallic ribbon pins. Ellie placed hers on the left side of her strapless gown. Blake followed her movements. They found their table and went to the bar for drinks.

"Blake, we finally got you to come," a woman said from behind them. Blake turned to see Dr. Opal Calendar.

"Hello, Dr. Calendar. The timing works this year." The fiftyish woman had white hair and bleached teeth. Her dress was blue and a little too small for her figure. He introduced her to Ellie as the director of oncology at the children's hospital.

They shook hands. "I've heard of you," Dr. Calendar said. "You run a foundation for girls."

"I do," Ellie said with a smile.

"Good work," she said. Someone tapped her on the shoulder and she turned. Giving the couple a kiss on the cheek, she excused herself.

Blake slipped his arm into the small of Ellie's back and the two walked toward the dance floor.

"How does it compare?" he asked.

"What?"

He hadn't relinquished his hold on Ellie. With his free arm, he gestured to encompass the room.

"I don't do that," Ellie said.

"Don't do what?"

"I don't compare fund-raisers. Each one is different and based on too many factors. I like the colors in the room."

"Gold and white appeal to you?"

"They do here."

"Don't they remind you of a wedding reception?"

"A little, but I focus more on what the money will do for the charity's mission than how well-appointed the room is."

"Yet yours is decadent?"

"To the extreme," she said.

Blake decided not to continue this line of conversation. Ellie was very protective of the foundation. Her heart was in it all the way, and from what Blake had personally witnessed of the finances, she didn't spend a single penny on anything that wasn't absolutely necessary to maintain the business. Every other dollar went to programs for girls.

"How about a dance," Blake suggested. The band was playing, and a few couples were already on the dance floor.

Ellie nodded and they stepped onto the wooden parquet. Blake turned her into his arms and pulled her close. Their steps matched as if they'd been dancing together for years. She anticipated his movements, followed his steps, swayed to the music as if she were part of it, part of him.

He realized he wanted her to be.

During the next hour, Ellie was barely an arm's length away. They danced and laughed. He introduced her to some of the people he knew, and unlike a few of his other dates, Ellie seemed comfortable with everyone she met. Blake couldn't help taking a little pride in her, knowing that she was his date and that the other people knew it, too.

Finally, the meal was served and the speeches began. Blake wanted to leave. He wanted Ellie all to himself. But they had to stay at least until the dancing began again.

The executive director, Dr. Martin Pine, stepped to the podium and made his welcome speech.

"Ladies and gentlemen," he said, "before we return to the dancing, I'd like to introduce the newest member of our board. You may know him as the manager of the San Francisco House of Thorn department store chain. Blake Thorn, would you stand?"

Applause greeted Blake as he stood. He smiled, waved and returned to his seat. He so wanted to check the expression on Ellie's face, but kept his eyes on the speaker. Suppose she thought he only got on the board to prove he was serious about giving back to the community? Or worse, suppose she thought he paid his way onto the board?

Neither was the truth, but their history might not support that. The music began again, and as their table emptied, she propped her chin on her hand. "Got to you, didn't it?"

Blake smiled. Her tone told him all he needed to know.

She approved.

"So, tell me, Mr. Board Member, why this charity? What makes you want to be involved in an organization that works with children and the families of children with cancer?"

"After Will, Patty and Gloria began working at the store, I asked the employees to send me a list of charitable organizations that they supported."

"This one was on the list?"

Blake nodded. "And not just once, but over and over again. I decided to go talk to the directors and investigate the group. Will was very helpful in getting me information." Ellie's expression changed. Blake knew what she was thinking. "It was all legal. That kid's got a good brain. He interpreted all the information and presented me with a report that told me a lot of what I needed to know."

"That's good to hear. He just needed someone to believe in him. I'm glad it was you."

Now, why did she have to say that? Blake was talking about one of the kids and now his focus switched to her, to the feel of her and the way her body moved against his.

"Are you thinking of moving him out of Security?" Ellie asked.

The music ended and they walked to the edge of the dance floor. Blake had his arm around her waist. Other couples took their places, and the band started another song.

"I'm thinking of sending him to college."

Ellie threw her arms up and hugged him. She kissed him on both cheeks several times. Blake's hands came up and pushed her back, stopping her.

"It's not that I don't want your praise," he said. "But this is a public place, and I won't hesitate to kiss you silly once I start."

Ellie smiled. Blake wondered if he'd seen something else on her face. Was it the promise of something to come later tonight? He hoped so.

"Go on," Ellie said. "Tell me about Will."

"Since he's been at the store, his grades have improved. The guys in the office make sure he does his homework and understands it."

"All he needed was someone to care about him," Ellie said.

"That's all any of us need."

Midnight came and went, and the two of them were still on the dance floor. Blake wanted to hold her, and this was the only place he could do it without explanation. As the evening came to an end around one o'clock, she was humming a song.

"You didn't finish telling me how you came to support this particular group," Ellie said as she picked up her pearl-covered evening bag and they headed out. "We diverted to Will. So, what's the draw here?"

"A couple of employees have children with cancer. I didn't know that until I asked about people volunteering at community events. The ones who volunteered at the children's hospital did it often and are friends with the mothers of the kids. I thought it would be good to support them and do what I could. It will be more than writing a check."

Ellie leaned forward and kissed him. "I'm proud of you," she whispered.

Blake was smiling. How different they were tonight from the way they had been at the first ball. Had this been the way his brother met his wife? Had their parents had a rocky start, but eventually learned they couldn't live without each other?

Blake knew it had to be true. He couldn't imagine living without Ellie. Both had told each other they weren't dating, had no relationship. Blake said he didn't want one, but he knew now that that was a lie. He wanted Ellie more than breath, and she apparently felt the same.

He touched his jacket pocket. Inside it was a surprise for Ellie, for them both, really. He imagined what her face would look like later tonight when he dropped down on one knee and uttered the most famous phrase in the world.

Ellie was still dancing on air when they got back to her house after the party. Stepping out of her shoes, she hummed along to the last song that had played before they left the ballroom. Blake took her arm and matched his dance steps to hers. After several turns, Blake pulled her close. His arm encircled her waist and he pulled her tight. They danced to their own music, each of them humming and singing only the words they remembered.

Hearing Blake's deep voice warbling as he stumbled over several words had Ellie laughing.

"What are you laughing at?" he asked teasingly.

"I'm sure my singing is at least as bad as yours."

"Bad? I'm a regular Pavarotti."

"You mean you wear a big clown suit?"

Both of them burst into laughter again. As the laughter faded, their heads came up, gazing into each other's eyes. The air in the room seemed to change from normal to highly charged. Blake didn't try to hide the need in his. He wanted Ellie. He'd wanted her since he'd first seen her, even when he was fighting against his feelings, even when he was comparing her to every other woman he'd ever known and finding her better…wanting her more.

His need only grew after they kissed and made love. He wanted her near him, wanted her every day and every night. But this night was their last. It was part of the agreement, how they had set up the pact. And Blake wouldn't violate the pact, but he wouldn't go out without a flaming end, either. He wasn't planning to leave with a bang. What spurred him on was nothing less than detonation.

Blake moved. Both hands took Ellie's waist and he stepped in until they were close enough that their breaths mingled. He looked at her face, his gaze moving slowly from place to place, mapping her features, memorizing every detail of her eyes, the way the pupils grew and darkened, the way her lashes swept down in a lazy blink, the way the tip of her nose begged for a peck, and then her mouth, the perfect curve of her upper lip, the rounded bottom that together turned him on faster than lightning could strike an open field. He settled his gaze on her mouth, tempting himself to close the small distance and take it for his own.

Her lipstick flowed across the surface, red and inviting. Her tongue came out and she wet her mouth. Blake's body stiffened in all the right places. His erection strained against his clothes, pointing toward her, aching for her. Her head leaned toward him, her mouth slightly open. Blake knew she was as hungry for him as he was for her.

And she proved it.

Her arms clamped around his neck and she kissed him. Her mouth ground against his desperately. Something in Blake burst and he took control, drawing her closer, stepping between her legs, taking the comfort she offered. He felt her from shoulder to thigh, the softness of her, the length of her legs matching his, the feel of her mouth, aggressive and wanting. She wanted him. The knowledge excited him. He wanted her, too, wanted to be inside her, but he knew he'd have to wait. He wanted to show her his love, savor their time together, take it slowly, build the excitement until they were both at the point where they couldn't go another second without each other.

Except Blake was almost there now.

She did that to him. No woman had ever gotten him so ready for her that he could hardly contain himself.

This one did. Ellie did.

Blake found the zipper of her dress and slowly pulled it down. His fingers brushed across her smooth skin and she gasped in his ear, her body arching against his. Blake felt her breasts pressing into his chest. His fingers tingled with the need to find them and rub his hands across the small buds. He wanted to taste her, beginning with her mouth and working his way to the core of her. He wanted to know the taut muscles of her thighs, familiarize his mouth with the soft places behind her knees, listen to her quiet cries of satisfaction.

"Have I told you how good you smell?" Blake murmured, nuzzling her neck.

"Only as often as I've told you."

Blake felt Ellie's grin. It empowered him, pushed him onward.

The dress fell down to her waist, and Blake helped it to the floor. Ellie wore long red stockings that stopped at her thighs and a bra that concealed only half of her breasts. Half-moons of golden skin angled toward him. He wanted to release the bra, allow the weight of her to fall into his hands, but he held back. Ellie's breath rose, but he couldn't separate the sound of hers from his own.

He kissed her shoulders, following the natural curve of her neck to the small space between the moons. His fingers flicked the catch of her bra, and his mouth moved over one heavy breast to the dark nipple. She cried out in pleasure as his wet tongue closed over the hard nub. Tremors started in his loins. He gripped her tighter, using her to balance himself, keeping his mouth to her as if connected.

Blake moved from one erotic planet to the next, each providing its own landscape, its own unique properties that only increased his need to be inside her. Lifting her from the dress, he took her to the stairs. One sexy step at a time, they danced up, twisted around, kissed, felt, tasted each other until they'd reached the top. Ellie removed his clothes, one piece at a time, as they went. Behind them lay a trail of pants, a shirt, a jacket and shoes that followed them to the bedroom.

Not bothering with the bedclothes, Blake removed

the last of his clothing. Extracting a condom from his pocket, he quickly protected them and laid Ellie on the bed. He edged her legs apart at the knees and entered her. She was warm and wet and ready for him. He could hardly hold back. He wanted all of her. He wanted to sink into her, thrust with everything his body told him he needed to get the release.

Ellie was no help. Her hand kneaded his back, her legs spanning him, her body moving and pulling, asking him to take her, take her hard and fast, but Blake was determined to wait, to make her wait. He knew it would be worth it.

*She* was worth it.

Ellie's eyes opened and closed as their bodies melded together. Her face showed the pleasure only two people could create. He thrust into her, reading her renewed expressions. Her body took him, squeezed him tight and engorged around him until he was ready to shout.

"Blake, now!" she begged.

"Not yet," he groaned. He wasn't ready to end the pain-pleasure mix that shot through his blood like a ballistic missile.

Ellie's fingers dug into his skin as her body writhed beneath him, forcing their strokes to couple and release in an escalating rhythm. Blake must have been out of his mind to think he could pull off something like taking his time when he had Ellie in his arms. Everything about her was pushing his buttons. No—not pushing; they were stabbing them impatiently, like someone waiting for an elevator and thinking it would speed things up if they continually clicked the button.

In his case, it was working.

Her legs wrapped around him. She drew him in. Setting a new pace where the heat within them was fast enough to cause spontaneous combustion, she forced him to respond, to give her what she wanted. Blake needed to fulfill the promise his body made. To complete the vow he'd pledged to himself.

Taking her legs, he lifted them one at a time over his shoulders, joining the two of them in the most intimate way. He pushed into her, giving her everything he had. He held nothing back. All he felt for her, every ounce of feeling, poured from him as their bodies danced. His hips pumped up and down, in and out, from one side to the other. Each thrust produced a sound from her throat. Blake loved to hear them. They told him how she felt, forced him to confront the feelings he had. The runaway passion he felt and wanted to convey, not with words, but with the language only the two of them were privileged to know.

Ellie's hands reached for him, then grabbed the bedcover as she writhed in pleasure. Her head whipped from side to side. Her body dug into his.

"Blake," she cried. "Now!"

It was time, Blake thought. He couldn't hold back. He couldn't stop what was happening. A swirling tornado formed in his lower gut. It grew, taking him, then overtaking him. His body pushed with uncontrollable speed. He didn't fight the feeling, didn't try to prevent the sensation. He went with it, letting it grow in strength. Instead of bouncing him around, the wind was to his back, aiding him. His movements burned in the swirl of hot air.

"Now," he said, his voice so low he could barely hear it.

All sound ceased to exist. And then.

Detonation.

# Chapter 10

Blake didn't want to open his eyes. He knew the sun was up. It had been tinting the horizon by the time they pulled the sheets back and got between them. The brightness filtered through his closed lids, but Blake didn't want the night to end.

It had been more than perfect, and he remembered every moment of it. Even the most minute detail about last night was imprinted on his brain. He smiled, reaching for Ellie. Her naked body was warm and soft. He ran his hands over her hips and legs, down her belly and up to her breasts. She pushed her bottom into him, fitting perfectly in the spoon-style space.

Last night he'd said this was the last time. This morning he knew it couldn't be. Not after the way they'd made love. He needed her in the worst way, in the best way. He needed to be with her all the time. She was the air he breathed and the food he ate. Ellie complemented him, filled in all the dark and light spaces in his life. She completed him. He'd never understood what that meant before.

The dawn not only began the day, but it started his new life. He was in no doubt that the new life included the woman in his arms. He couldn't imagine a future any different from waking up, holding Ellie. He kissed her hair, sealing the turning point of his new reality.

Nuzzling Ellie against him, Blake fell into a contented sleep. When he woke, he was alone. The sound of the shower drew his attention. For a moment, Blake thought of joining her. He slid off the bed, naked and aroused. Only as a teenager had he ever wanted sex this often. The difference between him at seventeen and him at twenty-seven was he *only* wanted to have sex with Ellie now.

Finding his boxers on the floor, Blake picked them up. A piece of paper fluttered from beneath them and wafted through the air. He slipped into the underwear, listening to the shower water and imagining Ellie naked under the spray. If he got into the shower, he'd never get to the store today, and he had to at least check in. This meant going home, showering and changing. If Ellie came out of that bathroom, all steamy and fragrant and wrapped in only a towel, as his imagination portrayed her, he'd be lost.

Forcing himself to take a step toward the door, where his pants started a parade of clothes back to the front door, he saw the piece of paper that had fallen to the floor. The closet door was ajar and the paper lay partially under it. Reaching to pick it up, his body stopped in midbend, frozen, paralyzed as the image of Alexis Ferrell looked up at him from a ten-year hiatus.

Cold seeped through him, beginning at his bare feet and working its way up until he was all but shivering. Forcing his hand to move, he opened the door. The paper lay against a box of newspaper clippings.

*What...? How...?* he asked himself, searching for a reason for this paper to be in Ellie's bedroom. What did she know about Alexis? The paper was yellowed, old, too old for her to have copied it from someplace, and there was a handwritten date on a neatly trimmed edge. He glanced at the box. It was full of clippings, all of them having to do with the accident, *his* accident.

How could they be here? He tried to wrap his brain around the fact that she knew. Ellie knew about him and Alexis. But why? Why would she have a box full of clippings?

*Unless...*

Blake wanted to sit down. He wanted to understand what he was seeing, process everything that was hammering its way like a battering ram into his memory.

The bathroom door opened and Blake turned, the paper still in his hand. Bright lights backlit Ellie and seemed to flash through the mist that surrounded her. Blake didn't look at her with arousal. He'd been reading the words on the paper. His memory opened, and the accident played its way into the present. He saw the car coming, just as it had in his dream. He heard the impact of the crash, the sound of metal folding up like someone crushing paper into a ball.

Blake said nothing. He opened his mouth only to find he was incapable of uttering a word.

"I can explain," Ellie said, coming forward.

Blake backed away.

He remembered. The name of the driver of the other car was printed in the first paragraph. He'd forgotten the man was driving with his daughter. Blake had relegated that day and all its hurtful memories to a place deep in his brain. Yet something should have told him. The name *Elliana Hamilton* should be permanently imprinted in his mind. How could she see him time and time again and not reveal who she was? Even when he poured his heart out to her, after the tears that formed so quickly in his eyes, how could she keep this information concealed?

"Blake," she started.

He raised a hand, palm out, stopping her from any further speech.

"I remember," he said. "I remember I told you all about Alexis and the accident. And I remember your tears. The ones I thought were for me, for the loss of a life. But I know now they were for you and your part in killing a young girl."

He looked at the clipping as if it were a flesh-eating virus and threw it at her. The paper fluttered in the charged air. Blake turned and left the bedroom. Picking his clothes up as he went, pushing his arms into his shirt and legs into pants, he hopped through the house and out the front door, slamming it hard enough to shake the foundation.

Inside the car, he pushed the button and the engine roared to life. Blake threw the car into gear, but kept his foot on the brake. After a moment, he slammed his hand against the steering wheel and stared through the front glass at the tree-lined street.

Why hadn't he adhered to his policy? Why had he allowed Ellie, Elliana Hamilton of all people, to get into his blood? After last night, he was ready to ask her to marry him. Blake's head fell forward onto the top of the steering wheel. The hard plastic bit into his skin. He ignored it, needing the pain, the solidness of it, of anything, to get perspective on his life, on his next action.

He didn't know how long he stayed there. Ellie could be looking at him from an upstairs window. He didn't know and refused to look. Finally, he settled back, put the car in gear and let it slowly roll away from the curb.

The hurt squeezing his chest was incomparable to anything he'd ever felt before. He thought that losing Alexis had been painful. He knew now that he and Alexis hadn't been in love. What Blake felt for Ellie was life changing. His life had changed tonight, and it would never be the same again.

Blake laughed at himself. He'd wanted the night to end with a bang, a detonation. And it had happened. However, it hadn't ended. The chain reaction had started and continued without stopping. As long as there was fuel, it would never end. And he was at the center of the mushroom cloud.

* * *

*Day one*, Ellie thought when she got up that morning. She'd survived her first night after Blake left. All she wanted was to crawl back in bed and pull the covers over her head. But she couldn't. She had a scheduled lunch. The last thing Ellie needed today was to have to smile at people, but she'd promised the kids working at House of Thorn that she would take them to lunch. It wasn't something she could back out of. She called Judi for support and also to have another person to help carry on a conversation.

They were supposed to meet in the store's restaurant, but Ellie couldn't do it. She couldn't be that close to Blake and maintain the fragile facade that was barely holding her together, and she had no wish to run into him. Ellie was sure he didn't want to see her again, either—maybe never again. The thought caused her physical pain.

And it was her fault.

If she hadn't had to wear those pearl-encrusted shoes, she never would have pulled that box down, and she wouldn't have left it sitting on the floor of her closet. Being in a hurry, Ellie hadn't noticed that a page had slipped out and lay in plain view. Surely, she wasn't noticing scraps of paper when she and Blake entered her room. Her eyes, hands and attention had been solely on him.

"Hey." Judi slid into a chair next to Ellie. "I called your name three times and you didn't even look up. What's happening?"

"Blake and I had a fight."

"Oh?" Judi's tone had a lifting quality at the end of the word, turning it into a question. She waited for Ellie to go on. "Too bad you're expecting teenagers, since I get the feeling this should be a liquid lunch."

No sooner had she said the words than the three teenagers entered the restaurant. With cell phones in one hand and backpacks slung over one shoulder, each epitomized the American teenager uniform of their generation. Will pointed toward them and smiled. The three walked over and took the available seats. Backpacks thudded to the floor and cell phones were placed within easy reach.

"Hi," Judi said. "I'm Ellie's best friend, Judi Burns."

She shook hands with each as Will, Patty and Gloria introduced themselves.

"I hear you all work at House of Thorn. How's that going?" Judi had already commanded the conversation. Ellie knew her friend was giving her time to pull herself together.

"I love it," Patty said. "My mom is thrilled that I get a store discount."

They all laughed, including Ellie.

"Mr. Thorn is such a good person. He listens to us, lets us express ourselves and he follows through on his promises," Gloria said. "I wish my dad was more like him." Realizing how her comment sounded, she continued, "Oh no, my dad is great. He's just busy and doesn't always listen like Mr. Thorn does."

Ellie reacted to the mention of Blake's name. Memories of him smiling, of his telling her jokes and her leaning against him, came into her head.

"How about you, Will? Do you still like Security?" Ellie asked, needing to get her mind off Blake.

"It's really good working back there. It's like being backstage. At first I felt like a Peeping Tom, but now I know there is a real need for security."

Ellie wondered if he was thinking of his own experience with being caught shoplifting.

"There's also the trust Mr. Thorn puts in me. I never would have allowed someone who stole from me to come work in my store."

"And he cares about us," Gloria said.

"Wonderful," Judi chimed in. "Now that we've shared the greatest traits of your employer, what are you guys up to? How are things in school?"

Ellie listened to them talk. Will, who'd previously been sullen and uncommunicative, had cracked the shell he'd built around himself. Ellie felt she was working behind a wall, keeping hold of her emotions while smiling and listening.

After the meal, which for the kids was comprised of burgers and fries, came dessert. They opted for ice cream sundaes or chocolate cake. Ellie was surprised she could get anything down, while they seemed to be hollow inside. Ellie and Judi only ordered coffee to complement their meals.

"Do you miss the horse farm?" Ellie asked after the waiter set down plates large enough to be a full meal in front of each teenager.

"I miss some of the people I made friends with,"

Patty said, "but I felt like the farm was work. At the store, it's fun."

Gloria concurred with her. "I'm so glad Mr. Thorn chose me."

"Me, too," Will said. "I was so hostile to him, I figured he wanted to make an example of me, but he's not that kind of guy."

Ellie felt Judi grab her hand and squeeze it in assurance under the table.

"And I'm learning so much," Will continued. "The older guys tease me some, but they're behind me. Not only am I learning about security, but they're teaching me some computer programs."

"And I'm sure you're teaching them video games."

He smiled, confirming her suspicions.

When the last one finished dessert, they thanked Ellie and said goodbye.

"We'll have to do this again," she said.

The three of them stopped and looked at her.

"My mom says we should do something for you," Patty said.

"You're already doing it," Ellie told them.

When she and Judi were alone, Judi looked at her. "Time to dump the coffee and open the wine."

After leaving the restaurant, they went to Judi's. She lived alone in a condo overlooking the San Francisco Bay. Judi wanted none of the responsibility of home maintenance. Although she grew up on a farm and knew how to fix things, her usual comment was *been there, done that, not doing it again.*

Ellie didn't want to be in her house. Blake was imprinted everywhere she looked.

Judi handed Ellie a glass of white wine and placed a small wheel of cheese, fresh fruit and crackers on the coffee table, despite the fact that they'd already eaten.

"Now, start at the beginning," she said.

Ellie sipped the wine. It was her favorite. She took her time, mulling over where the right place to start was. Using Blake's arrival at her house as a jumping-off point, she related the story. Omitting only the segment of them making love, she told her everything, even the truth about the car accident that took the life of Alexis Farrell. Ellie expelled a long breath when she finished.

"It wasn't your fault," Judi said. "He can't blame you for something that wasn't your fault."

"He's blaming me for concealing that I had a part in the story and I kept it secret." Ellie took a moment to blink, forcing herself not to allow a single tear to escape her eyes. "And he's right."

"What?"

"He told me about the accident. He explained everything he knew, before he went into a coma. I listened, but I didn't tell him I was part of that story. I kept it to myself."

"Why?"

"I thought he'd leave, and I didn't want him to."

Judi's face changed to compassionate. Ellie didn't have to say she was in love with Blake. It was apparent in the crack of her voice. But now he was gone anyway. She knew that had to happen. It was the only outcome, the only resolution to the secret she held.

Ellie took a sip of her wine, then set the glass on the table. Wine wasn't the answer. Blake was a question that had no answer, a mathematical uncertainty. But wasn't that what love was? Something with no logic, no formula, no method of predicting an outcome?

Ellie had to face the truth. She was in love.

And love hurt.

A week later, Blake lay on the sofa of his condo. His drapes were closed, blocking the strong sunlight that glinted off the bay in the distance. He was still in his pajamas and had been for two days. He hadn't brushed his hair or his teeth.

This was the first time in ten years that he'd taken two days off in the middle of the week. When he got up, he knew he couldn't go in. It was too much of an effort. That newspaper clipping kept falling through his mind like some film set on repeat. Elliana Hamilton had been in the other car. And she hadn't told him. She knew, and she'd kept it a secret. The jarring headline stated it was her fault. Her fault, and she'd walked away with only a scratch, while Alexis had…

Blake blamed her. But she wasn't the driver. What had she done to distract the driver?

His phone rang. Blake jumped at the alien sound. Checking the display, he expected to see someone from the store calling. Instead, the gala photo of his mother filled the screen.

He didn't want to talk to her, but she would know something was wrong if he rejected her call.

"Mom, is anything wrong?" He didn't expect that

there was, but going that route was better than trying to be cheerful.

"Yes, something is wrong, and I want to talk to you."

He sat up, swinging his legs to the floor and giving her his full attention. Had something happened to his dad or one of his brothers?

"What happened?"

"I'm not going to tell you on the phone. I'm in the lobby."

*Lobby? Here?*

She was here, in San Francisco?

"You're here?"

"I just said that." Her voice was impatient.

Blake looked around. The cleaning crew had been here two days ago, and except for the mess he'd made since then, the place was presentable, even if he wasn't.

"Come on up."

While he calculated how long it would take for the elevator to reach the top floor, he rushed to brush his teeth and pull on a pair of pants. He got both of them done, but the shirt he already had on would have to do. It was gray, wrinkled and had a logo for an athletic gym on the front.

The doorbell rang, giving him no time to move the array of pages and clippings about the accident from the dining room table. He partially covered them with a dish towel.

He padded to the door on bare feet and he opened it. Katherine Thorn, dressed in royal blue, from the hat on her head to the heels on her feet, stepped inside.

"You're a vision," he said as he hugged her and closed the door.

She looked around the room and walked to the windows. "Mind if I open these? I love the view."

Blake picked up a remote control from the littered coffee table and pushed a button that retracted the curtains. Light flooded the room, emphasizing the concealed papers, at least to Blake's mind. The bay came into view, and for a long moment, his mother took it in. Then she walked to a chair facing the sofa and sat down.

Blake got a bottle of sparkling water from the kitchen, along with a glass for his mother. He'd drink his from the bottle. Returning to the living room, he sat in the chair opposite her.

"You said something was wrong. Is anyone sick?"

"I don't know. Are you?"

Blake was taken aback. "Me?" He stared at his mother for some sign as to the point of this conversation.

"Yes, Blake Thorn. It's you I'm here to talk about."

"Why? I'm fine."

"Not from what I hear."

"Mom, you're not making sense."

"All right, I'm here about Elliana Hamilton."

Thankfully, Blake was sitting down. *Elliana Hamilton* were the last two words he expected her to say, and the two he was most unprepared to hear.

"What about her?"

"You must have discovered who she is by now."

Realization dawned on Blake. He stared at his

mother. Unable to keep his seat, he stood up and walked around in a large circle.

"You know?" It was more an accusation than a question.

She nodded. "I know who she is."

"How long have you known?"

"Since I hired her. She told me who she was."

"And you still hired her?" He frowned, only keeping his voice a shade below a shout when his brain reminded him that it was his mother sitting there in blue.

Katherine nodded. "She was highly qualified, and at her interview, she told me who she was. She didn't want me to even consider her if I had an issue with her past."

"Why didn't you tell me?"

"Frankly, I didn't know what you would do. I know Alexis's death changed your life."

Blake didn't respond. Alexis's passing had had a profound effect on him, but he wasn't willing to discuss it with his mother.

"Once she was gone, you decided to give up on any long-term relationship. There hasn't been a single woman since whom you've shown any interest in for more than a couple of dates. Other than Wilson, who we know is a friend and you use her to keep other women at bay, to keep anyone away who might challenge your heart. She uses you, too, for maybe the same reason."

Her words were true, but that didn't make them easy to accept.

"Have you talked to her, Blake? Listened to her side of the story?" his mother asked.

"I don't need to hear her story. It's all there in those

pages." He pointed to the dining room table. He'd been hiding them from his mother, not knowing the subject was the very reason she'd flown four thousand miles to see him in person.

Katherine Thorn looked where he pointed. Blake yanked the towels back. Pages flew into the air, fluttering like broken memories sliding into place.

"We both know newspaper accounts don't tell the whole story," his mother said.

"They may not, but her note says it all." Blake lifted one sheet and dropped it in front of his mother.

"She was seventeen, Blake. And so were you. If you've read this, you'd know the headline is just sensationalism. It's not the whole story."

No one knew the whole story. Not the newspapers, not Ellie, not even his mother. Only he and Alexis knew what was going on, and Alexis could no longer tell her side.

"I think you should talk to Ellie."

"No," he stated. "If she wanted to talk, she could have told me. She had plenty of opportunities."

"Didn't she try to tell you and you walked out on her?"

"How do you know this? Did you talk to Ellie?"

She shook her head. "You're easy to read, Blake. I've known it since you were a child. But you're no longer a child. You're an adult, and you should act like one."

"What do you want me to do? I trusted her. I told her things I haven't told anyone. Yet she didn't tell me about something this important. She told you at the risk of not being considered for a job. Why would she keep this from me?"

"Would you have given her a chance?"

"No." He was emphatic.

His mother sat still. She didn't have to tell him that he had his reasons.

"But she did something for you that you should be grateful for regardless of whether you two have a future."

"Yeah," he said with a grunt. "What's that?"

"She taught you that you can feel again. Losing Alexis was an accident. Nothing more. It was a combination of wrong circumstances that resulted in an accident. You lost your girlfriend and Ellie lost her father."

Blake looked up. "She lost her father?"

"He was driving the car. He had a heart attack, and she couldn't get control in time to stop their truck from hitting yours."

Blake was stunned. "And we were fighting." He spoke under his breath, not realizing his mother would hear him.

"You and Ellie?"

Blake shook his head. "Alexis and me."

His mother didn't ask what they were fighting about. It was the other man. Alexis was pregnant. Not with his child, but with someone else's. She chose to tell him that night, in the dark, in the car. Tears had run down her face. And then the accident happened, and he knew nothing until he woke up in the hospital.

"Blake, it's your turn." She stood up. "You need to talk to Ellie—now."

“All right. I’ll talk to her,” he agreed, wanting this conversation to end.

“Now.” She looked at the door.

Blake glanced at it, too.

“I have some shopping to do,” she said. She kissed him on the cheek and started for the door.

“Mother.” Blake stopped her. “How did you find out? You flew all the way here to have this conversation with me?”

“Not exactly. I’m on my way to Seattle to see my sister. And I need a birthday gift for Helen.”

“But you decided to stop here?”

“It gave me a chance to see the store and the bay.” She glanced at the windows and the water in the distance. Blake knew there was a message between the lines. She was here to see him, and the bay had nothing to do with it. Even though she was on her way to his aunt Helen’s, San Francisco wasn’t a layover. There were direct flights from New York to Seattle.

“Did you and André have a discussion before you boarded the plane?”

“André and I speak regularly. He’s in New York. It would be strange not to talk.”

Blake didn’t ask anything else. He went to his mother and kissed her on the cheek.

“Say happy birthday to Aunt Helen for me.” His mother and aunt always spent their birthdays together. She went to Seattle for his aunt Helen’s, and in February his aunt would fly to New York so the two women could visit, shop, go to a Broadway show or take a long weekend together.

Katherine Thorn nodded and went through the door. Instead of closing it, she left it standing open. Blake expected Ellie, but she didn't appear. Grabbing the doorknob, he looked toward the elevator. The hall was empty except for his mother waiting for the doors to part. Blake let out a sigh of relief, his shoulders dropping. He wasn't ready to talk to Ellie. He wasn't sure he would ever be. His heart was hurting, and he needed time for the bruises to heal.

But his thoughts were cut short when he spotted Ellie sitting on the floor at the opposite end of the hall near the exit stairs. He'd know her anywhere, know the curve of her back, the shine of her hair, the tilt of her head and the hammering of blood that coursed through his system at the thought of her.

Ellie looked at him with huge eyes that said she hadn't slept in the same number of days he hadn't.

"Come in," he said.

"I'm probably the last person you want to see or talk to," Ellie said.

"You're at the top of the list," he replied.

Ellie felt a coldness go through her. She knew coming to Blake's condo with Katherine Thorn wasn't a good idea. First the owner of the foundation where Ellie worked showed up unannounced and wanted to meet with her. She didn't want to discuss Give It to the Girl. She was there to talk about Alexis Ferrell and Blake Thorn. Ellie didn't ask how she knew that she and Blake had been seeing each other.

Even though Ellie had explained that Blake was

aware of who she was and that he didn't want to see her, the older woman had insisted she accompany her. And now she stood in front of Blake, feeling as naked and vulnerable as a high school student called to the principal's office.

"Blake, I'm sorry. I really wanted to tell you."

"Then why didn't you? Why did you let me tell you all about the accident? You cried. I thought you felt sympathy for me, when all the while you were sitting on a secret."

"It wasn't like that." She *had* felt sympathy for him.

And for Alexis.

She'd also remembered her father, and knew if she told Blake her part in the tragedy, she'd lose him. He was so hostile toward the people in the other car. Everything about the accident was their fault. They were on the wrong side of the road. They caused a head-on collision.

"All right, Ellie." He stood across from her, his gaze and his body as hard as marble. "How was it?"

Ellie swallowed. Blake hadn't asked her to sit down or offered her a drink. On the table was a bottle of water and a glass. Ellie took the seat opposite it.

"I didn't grow up in San Francisco," she began. "I was born here, but we moved to New York State when I was young." Blake had never asked where she was from. Few people did. They assumed a California girl was a California girl, and people from the state never wanted to live anywhere else. "My family lived in the town next to the one where you grew up."

Blake folded his arms and remained standing. She

wished he'd be more relaxed, more ready to listen. His stance indicated distance, closed-mindedness and an unwillingness to believe anything she said.

"I took ice-skating lessons and I was on a team. We practiced every morning and every night when a competition was coming up." She paused, hoping she'd get some indication from Blake that her words were getting through to him.

She got nothing.

"My father was driving." Ellie's voice cracked. She knew what she was about to say, and the words had begun to choke her. "We were also arguing."

"About what?" Blake spoke, making her heart beat even faster than it was already.

"Me driving. I had a learner's permit, and I was allowed to drive. I wanted to, but he said no. The argument is trivial now. At the time, it was important to me. I wish I'd been driving. If I had, we wouldn't be here."

How many times had Ellie replayed that night and the possible outcomes a single change would have made? They wouldn't have been fighting, and the sequence of events wouldn't have resulted in the death of a teenage girl. And, Ellie told herself, she wouldn't be in love with the man standing in front of her.

"My father had a heart attack. We had one of those old vintage trucks. He loved it and spent hours every weekend maintaining it." Tears threatened as Ellie remembered working with her dad, rebuilding the carburetor and learning what a timing belt did. Conversations they had had on the way to her ice-skating lessons came back to her. Seeing him sitting on the bleachers, watching her as she went through her routines or fell on her butt when she miscalculated a move, made her proud and happy that he was her father.

"He fell sideways. One arm went through the big steering wheel, and his foot wedged the accelerator down. I grabbed the steering wheel when the car started to veer across the road, but I was restricted by the seat belt, by his heavy arm and by his weight. I didn't know it then, but he was already gone. I pulled at the wheel, but all that happened was the truck veered to the right."

Ellie could not go on. She held the tears at bay, but they were in her throat and she refused to shed them.

Finally Blake moved. He went to the kitchen, returning with a bottle of water. After twisting the cap off, he handed it to her.

She took a sip.

Blake moved the water glass and bottle from the coffee table and took a seat in front of her.

Ellie saw the darkness under Blake's eyes. He looked as if he hadn't slept in days. Try as she might, she couldn't help feeling sorry for him. They looked at each other for a long time. Ellie's heart fluttered. She raised her hand to smooth the frown from his brow. Blake caught her wrist before she could touch him. She pulled her hand free and leaned back.

"I didn't mean..." Ellie stopped. She didn't know what to say. She understood that he didn't want her to touch him. She should be grateful he allowed her in the same room with him.

"Blake, I'm sorry." The words sounded hollow, inadequate for the depth of grief she'd caused. The fact that Blake wasn't responding was disconcerting to her. "I know I should have told you who I was when we first met, and I wanted to, but it didn't seem like the right place. Later, I wanted to be with you, and I knew if I told you it would be the end of us."

Again she waited for him to say something. But he withstood her scrutiny. Ellie's shoulders dropped in defeat.

"The least you could do is say something, but I see you're so angry with me that speech is beyond you. I truly am sorry, Blake."

Ellie stood, moving around the table so there was at least ten feet between them. She took one final look at the man she loved. She knew she'd never see him again. Turning around, she went to the door and opened it. Refusing to look back and be humiliated any further, she went out and closed it behind her.

Ellie walked slowly to the elevator and punched the down button. Obviously Katherine Thorn had expected a different outcome would ensue. The car was gone when Ellie reached the street. She walked to the condo's entrance and got into a taxi. She didn't go home, but called Judi and agreed to meet her.

After her third margarita, Ellie felt a lot better. Everything Judi said was funny. When the music began, Ellie was the first one on the floor, dancing. She had no partner, but that didn't matter. She felt like moving. She wasn't going to let Blake Thorn ruin her night or her life. The fact that he didn't return her love was something she could get over.

"I think we should leave," Judi said when Ellie gained a partner.

"Not yet. I'm having fun." Ellie danced. She knew Judi disapproved, but as her friend, she would protect her. The music got louder, and while her drinks were replaced with nonalcoholic punches and soft drinks, Ellie still took to the floor with every song.

Until…

Suddenly she wanted to cry. Leaving the dance floor, she returned to the table where Judi was standing. The jukebox was playing the song that had been on the radio that night. It kept playing after the truck hit the car. Metal crumpled, radiators hissed and rain beat down, but "Endless Love," playing on an oldies station her father enjoyed, continued despite the chaos that began in her life at that moment. Her father told her he loved that song because it was the one he and her mother danced to at their wedding. And when Ellie was born, he knew there was such a thing as endless love. Ellie bought into the romance of it. She even had the song on her phone.

But of all the songs in the world, why was that one playing when he died?

Returning to the table, Judi looked at her and stood.

"I'd like to go home now," Ellie said.

Blake paced the floor after Ellie left. Her story was sorrowful, but he would not be moved. She should have told him who she was ages ago.

He stopped pacing and walked to the windows. The curtains were open and the sun had set. Lights from boats winked back at him. The distant hills looked like spangled stars instead of houses across the bay.

*Talk to her*, his mother had said. Blake hadn't done that. She'd talked to him, but he found it impossible to utter more than a few words. He hadn't even said he was sorry when she told him her father died.

Blake's uncle had died, and his cousins came to live with them. The six boys were reared as brothers, but Blake still remembered the nightmares and crying episodes of his grieving brothers. He couldn't imagine life without his father. How much would he have missed without his dad to talk to, to learn things from?

Ellie must have missed out, too. She was an ice-skater. If she practiced twice a day, she had to be good. The accident had changed her lifeline just as it had altered his.

She wasn't totally at fault. Really, she wasn't at fault at all. A teenager arguing that she wanted to drive was normal. How many arguments had he had with his dad? Blake couldn't count them, but he knew some of them had occurred in the car, while his dad was at the wheel.

The outcome of his and his dad's differences could not compare to Ellie's loss. Blake felt he should have said something, been more compassionate.

He went back to pacing the floor. What else could he do? When he reached his bedroom, papers lay wasted about the small writing table and floor. On the edge of the chair facing the bed lay the ring box, with the diamond he'd planned to present while on his knee.

He sneered at it, then picked it up and opened the blue velvet lid. A large blue diamond, ringed with multifaceted white diamonds, caught the chandelier light, reflecting prisms of colors up at him. Blake could almost imagine it on her finger. It reminded him of the shoes she'd worn their last night together, the ones encrusted with pearls and stand-up butterflies.

He snapped the box closed and dropped it on the table. Closing the box, however, didn't close that chapter of his life. It had taken him ten years to get Alexis out of his system. It would take longer for him to purge all the feelings he had for Ellie, if that were even possible.

# *Chapter 11*

The security office was on the third floor. Blake hadn't checked in with the teenagers in a couple of days. He'd barely spoken to anyone for longer than a casual greeting. His conversation with Ellie came back to him time and again. He was aware of everything she'd said, every gesture of her hand or movement of her head.

Blake felt as if he had a photographic memory when it came to her. He was in love with Ellie. He even had a ring in his pocket, ready to ask her to spend her life with him. Then that piece of paper had fluttered to the floor.

All the memories of the past ten years had come back to him, and he had lashed out at her. Ellie wasn't the cause of the accident. He was the wrong one. She'd left his condo and refused to take his calls. Blake couldn't blame her. He'd been a jerk and needed to apologize to her. Like his mother said, they needed to talk. Actually, Blake needed to talk. Ellie had tried, but he hadn't been ready to listen. He was ready now, and even if Ellie wasn't ready, he needed to see her.

He'd tried the conventional method, the phone. Since that hadn't worked, his only course was to try her office. She couldn't refuse to talk to him there. Blake wouldn't force her to talk, but he would look her in the eye and tell her he was wrong.

By the time he reached the security office, he had a plan. He knew he had to talk to Ellie, and he had to tell her the full truth. He had to tell her that he believed the accident wasn't her fault. It was no one's fault. He pulled out his phone and called the offices of the Give It to the Girl Foundation. Darlene, whom he'd met at the gala, answered the phone and told him Ellie wasn't there. She was taking a few days off.

His optimism fell, but he opened the door and went into the behind-the-scenes office. Will Jerome sat at one of the computer screens, his concentration intense.

"Will." Blake said his name, and the young man jumped as if surprised.

"Oh, hi," he said, his expression instantly transforming into a smile. "I was just checking the shoe department. I think I saw someone I knew."

Blake looked over his shoulder.

"Isn't that Ms. Judi? I've seen her with Ms. Ellie."

Blake bolted out the door without a word. He didn't

go to the elevator, but bounded up the stairs two and three at a time.

He opened the employee door that led to the shoe department and came out from a back room. Looking one way and then the next, he saw Judi browsing a pair of dress shoes. Ellie's shoes came to him. Images of her, dressed in red with the pearl shoes, shot into his mind. His body started to react the same way it had on seeing the real, flesh-and-blood woman, smiling and walking toward him.

"Judi," he called.

She turned, saw him and then started to walk away. Blake blocked her escape.

"Where is she?" he asked.

"She doesn't want to see you."

He blinked when she said that, yet it was not a surprise.

"I want to see her. I want to explain, apologize."

"You could have done that when she needed it. But all you did was stand in front of her and let her struggle for a way to explain why she didn't tell you about the accident sooner."

"I know. I understand now."

"You don't," Judi contradicted him. "Ellie is in love with you and you're too stupid to see that."

"I'm in love with her, too." Blake stopped her with his declaration. "I want to tell her."

Judi seemed stunned.

"Where is she?"

"You don't know?" Judi asked.

Blake shook his head.

"Think about what she loves. Where would she go to find comfort and love? That's where you'll find her."

Blake stared at nothing for a long moment. Then he grabbed Judi, startling her, kissed her on the cheek and was off and running.

He made it to the garage in record time, and breaking all speed limits, he was up in the hills, heading for the Purple Cloud Farm.

Ellie loved this place. She came here often, she'd told him. He rounded thc curve, passing the clearing where they had shared their first kiss at a speed that would get him a high-priced ticket for dangerous driving. He saw her car before he had time to stop. Braking, Blake left a layer of rubber and a cloud of toxic smoke on the roadway as he brought the Jeep to a stop. He reversed, backing down the road until he got to the clearing.

He parked next to Ellie's car and jumped out of the Jeep. His heart was pounding as hard as his footsteps. He ran to the clearing, stopping on a skid as he saw Ellie looking at the city.

"What do you want?" she asked, not turning around.

"I want to apologize."

Ellie's back stiffened, but she didn't turn around. Blake held his breath.

"Ellie, I'm sorry. I should have listened to you." He waited, willing her to give him a chance. "I know you were asking me to believe in you, give you a chance when you were in my apartment. I didn't. I've thought of nothing else since."

Blake took a few steps toward her. She didn't turn

to him, but she didn't step away, either. He took that as a good sign.

"I know I should have been more forgiving. When I thought about it, there was nothing to forgive. It was an accident. You tried everything, but what happened wasn't your fault." He paused. "The truth is, no one is at fault, least of all you. You tried to save your father and prevent the accident."

She finally turned. Blake thought his heart would burst.

"I was the one who was arguing with Alexis. I thought I was in love with her." His breathing was slowing, returning to normal. "But I wasn't. I didn't know what love was. Now I do. Because I'm in love with you."

Ellie's face softened just a bit. Her shoulders moved down, loosening.

"Alexis was in love with someone else, and I know how she felt. I can't think of anything better than having children with you. I want to wake up with you, argue with you, have fantastic sex with you. I want you with me every day and everywhere. I love you."

Blake took a step forward. He was close enough to her to use a normal voice. He lowered it even more. "I was hurt and angry. Alexis told me she was pregnant by another man. I demanded to know who. She never got a chance to tell me. The accident happened."

"I'm sorry," Ellie said. "I tried—"

She got no further. Blake rushed to her, pulling her into his arms and capturing her mouth in a desperate kiss. They could sort out the details later. Right now, it was enough for him to hold her and know that she was his. He was hers, too, and would always be.

When Ellie moved her mouth to breathe, Blake kept her close. He looked over her shoulder at the city. The sun was setting. Long streaks of oranges and reds colored the horizon. The breeze was light, and he wasn't letting Ellie go.

Holding her hand, he bent down on one knee.

She gasped. "Blake?"

He lifted the blue velvet box that had been in his pocket. "Will you marry me?"

Ellie stared at his open hand and the box lying on his palm. Expressions crossed her face too fast for him to capture any of them.

"Yes," Ellie whispered. Then louder she said, "Yes, yes."

Blake wasn't sure if there were tears in her eyes, but he could hear them in her voice. He understood them. His own throat was clogged with an emotional love that he'd never felt before.

He gave her the box, still refusing to break contact with her. Blake stood up, slipping his arm around her waist and pulling her into his side. She opened the box, and the breathy sound she made was nothing short of a climax.

* * * * *

**Leo held her close to his chest and inhaled the wonderful scent of her, clean, fresh and subtly spicy. If he kissed her, he knew she'd taste like cinnamon. Or some other sweet-smelling spice.**

His right hand was at the base of her neck. Her thick hair felt like silk. Her warm skin, beneath the fleece jacket, enticed him. He wanted to touch her bare skin but knew that would be an invasion somehow. He was happy to just hold her. That was a major improvement.

He fought the urge to bury his face in her fragrant neck. She resisted the urge to raise her mouth to his in silent surrender.

He felt her body tremble slightly. She felt the muscles in his arms and thighs grow tense, as if he was summoning up all the restraint he could muster.

They stood there for nearly two minutes before the dogs jumped up on them, breaking the spell. Laughing, they succumbed to their pets' playfulness and let them romp all over their humans on the living room floor.

"What are we going to do about these two?" Leo asked, laughing. "It's obvious they're wild about each other."

"We should set up a playdate," Meghan suggested. "Maybe next Saturday?"

Leo smiled at her. "It's a date."

**Janice Sims** is the author of over thirty titles ranging from romance and romantic suspense to speculative fiction. She won an Emma Award for Favorite Heroine for her novel *Desert Heat*. She has also been nominated for a Career Achievement Award by *RT Book Reviews*, and her novel *Temptation's Song* was nominated for Best Kimani Romance Series in 2010 by *RT Book Reviews*. She lives in central Florida with her family.

## Books by Janice Sims

### Harlequin Kimani Romance

*A Little Holiday Temptation*
*Escape with Me*
*This Winter Night*
*Safe in My Arms*
*Thief of My Heart*
*Unconditionally*

Visit the Author Profile page
at Harlequin.com for more titles.

# UNCONDITIONALLY

Janice Sims

This book is dedicated to the memory of
our daughter, Rachel Renata Sims,
who passed away on October 12, 2015.
She was my inspiration to become a writer.
Now she's become my inspiration to continue to write!

**Acknowledgments**

My sincere thanks to Senior Executive Editor Glenda Howard, who, first of all, displayed such patience and kindness when I had to take some time off to recover from a health crisis. Then she also offered wonderful editorial suggestions that gave Meghan and Leo's story more depth and meaning. Also, to my line editor, Rachel Burkot, whose comments were so wise and warm, they made revising this book a pleasure. Lastly, to my readers who knew what I was going through the past three years. Your encouraging messages kept me going. God bless you all!

Dear Reader,

It gives me great pleasure to bring you Meghan and Leo's story. It's a different kind of romance because Leo has a serious condition that causes him to suffer from self-doubt. While you're reading it, I ask you to be open-minded and be patient with him. After all, isn't love supposed to be unconditional? While writing it, I asked my husband if Leo's behavior in this tale was believable and he said yes. Even he would have had a hard time telling the woman he loved the secret Leo was hiding. I'm currently working on the fifth book in the Gaines Sisters series: Petra and Chance's story. Please post your thoughts wherever you buy books online and let me and other readers know what you thought of this book. Feel free to friend me on Facebook!

Continued blessings,

*Janice Sims*

# Chapter 1

Meghan Gaines kept checking her cell phone, a habit she reverted to when she was nervous. Every few minutes, her gaze would flicker to the café's entrance. It was a Saturday in mid-October and she was meeting someone for the first time at noon, and it was already a quarter past. She had chosen Annie's Café because she knew the owner and it was between Raleigh, where she lived and worked, and Durham, where Leonidas "Leo" Wolfe lived and worked. Plus it served fresh, delicious, locally grown food.

The restaurant was open concept and reminded her of a well-appointed Southern kitchen. Diners could see into the cooking area, with its stainless steel counters and pristine white cabinets, and watch the staff bustling about, preparing orders. Soft rock music played in the background and lush greenery was everywhere. Annie's Café had a very relaxing atmosphere.

What was up with his name? Leonidas? His parents must have been ancient Greek history buffs, since *Leonidas* was the name of a king of Sparta. The one who'd led three hundred people to their deaths at Thermopylae in 480 BC. Of course, all most people knew about Leonidas was what they'd learned watching the actor Gerard Butler portray him in the movie *300.*

She made a mental note to definitely not ask him about his name. She nervously bit her bottom lip. She hoped her sister Mina wasn't trying to fix her up with her soon-to-be brother-in-law. Mina and DEA Agent Jake Wolfe had recently gotten engaged, and after his twin brother, Leo, said he was moving from Atlanta, where he was an English professor at Spelman College, to Durham, where he'd been offered a position at Duke University, they'd asked Meghan to show him around the area.

Even though Meghan suspected a setup, she couldn't refuse because Leo was going to be a part of their family soon, and you didn't start off familial relationships by avoiding new family members. That was bad manners.

She heard the bell chime over the café door. A tall, handsome black guy the color of roasted chestnuts, with a bald head and a goatee like the one actor/musician Common sported, strode in, wearing jeans, a casual shirt, a tan leather jacket and a startlingly white pair of athletic shoes. His eyes scanned the place and locked onto her. Her breath caught in her throat. Dear God,

Mina had told her he looked like Jake (whom she'd already met), but the resemblance was uncanny!

She turned off her cell phone and shoved it into her shoulder bag. She wasn't going to miss a minute of this.

She knew she was staring at him as he walked over to her table, but she couldn't stop. He chuckled as he hesitated before pulling out a chair. "If you're not Mina's sister, you ought to be," he said, his light brown eyes twinkling with humor. She saw his brief perusal of her body and was sure he'd noted that she was dressed casually in jeans, like he was, and her brown suede jacket was hanging on the back of her chair. She was glad she hadn't glammed it up.

"I *am* Mina's sister," she said, sounding foolish to her own ears. His voice, on the other hand, sounded like a cross between Morgan Freeman and James Earl Jones. Deep, but sexy as hell. "And you have to be Jake's brother, Leo. Otherwise the universe is out of whack. You look just like him."

He sat down and offered her his hand. They shook. "Hi, Meghan, or is it Meg?"

"Meghan," she told him, smiling and finally relaxing enough to take a deep breath. She peered closely at his face. "I take that back. You don't look exactly like Jake. His nose is different. And, of course, he doesn't have a shaved head."

"True," Leo said with an amused smile. "His nose has been broken once. Mine hasn't. Also, if you look closer, you can tell that I have a scar on my right cheek from a cut I got when I fell out of a tree when I was eight."

"What were you doing up a tree?"

"Trying to prove I could go higher than Jake, of course. We were very competitive back then."

"I hope you didn't break anything," Meghan said.

"Nah, just a few scratches, some more severe than others," he said, his hand going to his cheek. He let out a relaxed sigh as he picked up the laminated menu. "So, Mina tells me you teach history at Shaw University. The oldest historically black university in the South. How do you like it?" His eyes met hers over the menu.

She smiled at him. "Easy question to answer. I love it. I love the sense of history, the dedication of the teaching staff and administration, and the potential I see in my students. I'm very happy at Shaw. You also worked at an HBCU in Atlanta, right?"

"Spelman, yes," he replied. "Great school. I would've been there the rest of my life if I hadn't started feeling like things were beginning to become stagnant. I'm forty. I'd been with Spelman since I got my doctorate fifteen years ago."

Meghan flashed him another grin. "I got my doctorate at twenty-five, too."

"And you're how old now, if you don't mind my asking?"

"I'll be thirty in July," Meghan answered, bracing herself for his reaction.

"You look twenty," he said incredulously.

She groaned inwardly. People were always telling her she looked younger than she was. She couldn't help how she appeared to others. It wasn't as if she dressed like a teenager. Or tried in any way to cut years off her age.

"You look good for your age, too. I could show you my driver's license," she joked. Then, after they'd finished laughing, she said, "Please go on. You were telling me you felt stagnant."

"Yes, as if I were standing still," Leo said. "I mean, in my work I always tried to be innovative, changing it up for my students to keep things fresh. It was my personal life that wasn't going anywhere. So I published a couple of novels to prove I wasn't just an English professor who couldn't master the language, only teach it. But I still felt like I needed a change, so when the recruiter from Duke phoned me with a very nice offer, I took it."

"Back up. You casually mentioned you'd published a couple of novels. I read a lot. Especially black authors, but I don't recall seeing your name on any novels."

Leo smiled sheepishly. "My name isn't on the novels. I use a pen name. Jeremiah Jacobs is the author of the dystopian novels *Monkey See, Monkey Do* and *The Silverback*."

Meghan was once again staring at him. "Set in the near future and an alternative history in which Africans were never enslaved in the United States, but discovered the country, instead."

"You read them?" He looked surprised by the possibility.

"More like devoured them," Meghan told him, smiling with pleasure. "You're very talented."

"Thank you," Leo said sincerely. "But the market

was glutted with dystopian novels, especially young adult ones. My books were well reviewed, but weren't exactly bestsellers. Although they did earn back their advances, and the publishing company wants another one."

"Are you working on it?" Meghan eagerly asked. "Because I'm dying to know what happens next."

"No, not really. My heart hasn't been in it. Writing's a lot of work. I know it may seem like it isn't. People think writers have it so easy because it's a compulsion with most of us, and the words should just come flowing out like a wellspring. But sometimes it's hard to come up with the inspiration to do it."

"Mmm," Meghan said, considering his words. Publish or perish. Many academics believed you couldn't get tenure without being a published author. She'd published articles herself, and had written three historical novels she hadn't shown anyone.

"I've always been in awe of those who can create a world just out of their imaginations. But I suppose it can be a frustrating process. I hope you get your mojo back."

"Thank you," Leo said. "You know, with both of us having worked at HBCUs, I thought you might be a little judgmental about my signing on with Duke. I've had other colleagues call me a sellout."

He was watching her intently, his full mouth turned up in a half smile and his translucent brown eyes taking in every contour of her face.

She blushed. It wasn't every day a handsome man observed her with such unconcealed interest. She wasn't imagining that warmth emanating from his body to hers, was she? It was cold outside, and the temperature inside wasn't too warm, either. So it had to be her body reacting to his. Which was surprising. It had been a long time since she'd felt attuned to someone right off the bat.

So, to be cautious, she naturally drew away from him.

He reacted by looking puzzled. "So I was right. You feel that way, too."

She gently smiled at him. From now on she'd pay closer attention to her body language. "No, no," she assured him. "That hadn't even crossed my mind. I believe a person ought to follow his heart. And if you think Duke will be a better fit for you, I wish you the best."

She laughed shortly, "In fact, my godmother is the head of the English department at Duke, and because I have a master's degree in English, she's always trying to get me to join the faculty. But history is my first love."

"Dr. Langdon is your godmother?" Leo asked. "Small world. She's the person who recruited me."

"I'm not surprised," Meghan told him. "Marjorie Langdon's goal is to make her department the best that Duke has ever seen. She might be only five-two and a hundred and ten pounds, but there's a lot of strength and resolve in that woman."

Leo chuckled softly. "I did get the feeling that she wasn't going to take no for an answer when I spoke with her. Then, when I met her, I had the distinct feeling I was being hypnotized. I couldn't have refused her if I'd wanted to."

"She does have that effect on you," Meghan said. "She and my mother, Virginia, have been best friends since they were five years old, and I swear, both of them are the kind of women who get their way, no matter who they have to cajole or charm, and I know one of them is going to get me for saying this. You must be good at what you do for her to go out of her way to get you."

"I'm both pleased by that comment and strangely frightened." Leo couldn't help smiling. He was enjoying himself, talking to this delightful woman. Delightful because he'd only known her for a few minutes and he already felt at ease in her presence. Delightful, too, because she was wonderful to look at: mounds of naturally curly black hair that fell down her back, smooth brown skin that fairly glowed with good health and features that would make any cover girl green with envy, like high cheekbones, a well-shaped nose (not too big, not too small), a luscious, full mouth. Did she have on any makeup? If she did, she'd applied it so expertly, he couldn't tell.

But what he liked most about her so far was how self-effacing she was. She didn't appear to care that she was beautiful. Many beautiful women he'd met in the past were haughty and seemed to put great importance on being admired for their beauty. This girl was so down-to-earth, it was as if she didn't give looks a second thought. Also, she had her doctorate degree. He knew how hard it was to earn a doctorate because he'd earned one himself. It took a lot of work and discipline. He admired that in anyone.

After they'd ordered, Meghan told him, "I thought we'd have lunch together first, then I'd give you the grand tour. I'll drive, and afterward I'll bring you back here to pick up your car. Is that all right with you?"

"I'm yours to command," Leo said lightly.

Meghan couldn't help thinking of a few naughty things she could command him to do to her. Then she reined in those inappropriate thoughts and smiled prettily. "It's a beautiful day to see the area. Have you already purchased or rented a home, or are you still staying in a hotel?"

"Oh, I moved fast on that. I started shopping around when I was still living in Atlanta. I found a sweet Southern-style cottage in an older neighborhood in Durham. The owners had completely renovated it. And it even had enough land for a garden."

Meghan looked at him with newfound admiration. A modern black man talking about gardening. He was as rare as the unicorn, in her opinion. "I love gardening, too," she said wistfully.

Leo had never met a woman quite like her. On the one hand, they had so much in common, which should make him excited because he hadn't recently been lucky in love. On the other hand, her youth, her vibrancy, even the fact that she, indeed, seemed like a good love match for him, told him he should not encourage such thoughts or get his hopes up. There was no future for them.

He would enjoy their day together, and that was all.

While he was thinking these thoughts, Meghan, in her youthful exuberance, was telling him how well her winter garden was doing, especially her collard greens.

"You've got to come over and pick some," she offered.

Leo was thinking he'd love to see her garden, among other things, when the server showed up with their meals. She was short and stout and had a cherubic face. She was smiling widely at the moment.

"Meghan!" she cried happily. "I heard you were out here. How are you, girlfriend?"

She placed the plates in front of them and straightened up.

Meghan stood up, and up (Leo hadn't realized she was so tall—around five-nine, he'd guess) and hugged the woman.

"Annie, it's good to see you, girl," she said warmly. "I brought you a new customer. This is Leo, Jake's brother."

"Jake, who's marrying our Mina?" Annie asked as she openly admired Leo. She looked around thirty, had flawless dark brown skin and wore her dark brown hair in a short Afro that beautifully framed her heart-shaped face.

She brushed her right hand across the apron she was wearing and offered it to Leo. "Pleased to meet you, Leo. Welcome to my humble establishment."

Leo smiled warmly. "The pleasure's all mine, Annie. From the mouthwatering aromas, I'm sure I'm in for a treat."

"Annie and I went to high school together," Meghan explained. "This girl could always throw down in the kitchen, even when we were teenagers. I knew she'd end up a famous chef."

"I don't know about famous," Annie said modestly. "But I'm doing okay." Then she started talking about what was on their plates. "This is the best time of year for crabs. Those just came in this morning, and I made crab cakes and also a nice bisque to warm your insides on this chilly day. I know you didn't order the bisque, but you've got to try it. It's on the house."

With that, she hastily kissed Meghan on the cheek and said, "Enjoy!" after which she returned to the kitchen.

Leo and Meghan dug into their meals, eating the delicious food with pleasure. Meghan knew she'd chosen the right place for their first meeting when Leo polished off the bisque, moaned softly and said, "You're right, Annie definitely knows her way around a kitchen."

Meghan was busy devouring a crab cake that was delicately spiced, the crabmeat still firm and the vegetables crisp while the outer coating was crunchy. She swallowed. "I'm glad you're enjoying yourself."

They looked into each other's eyes, neither of them seeming to want to look away first. Then Leo lowered his eyes to his plate momentarily, raised his gaze back to hers and said, "Forgive me if I'm being rude, but I believe we should address the elephant in the room before we go any further—namely, my brother and your sister are trying to fix us up. What do you think about that?"

Meghan laughed, "I had my suspicions from the get-go, but I was willing to ignore it. I'm glad you brought it up, though, because now we can proceed without any uncomfortable feelings between us. I'm not actively looking for anyone special right now."

"Neither am I," Leo said quietly. "And even if I were looking, I think ten years is too big an age gap."

"If you say so," Meghan said.

*If he doesn't like me, he doesn't like me*, she thought, *but to come up with some asinine excuse like he's too old for me?*

*That's just pitiful!*

"I don't think I'm going to fit," Leo said as they approached Meghan's cherry-condition, baby blue 1965 Mustang convertible in the parking lot. Since it was a cold day, the top was up.

Meghan unlocked his door, then went around and got behind the wheel of the muscle car. "Give it a try," she encouraged him. "This car used to belong to my dad until I won it off him in a card game. He's about your height."

Leo fitted just fine, with plenty of legroom. She turned and gave him a smile. "See?" Then she added, "Buckle up."

Leo did as he was told, admiring the white leather seats, soft as a baby's bottom, and light blue interior. Everything looked clean and well cared for, and the air smelled faintly of lemon oil. "You really love this car," he said.

"I do," Meghan said with pride. "She's my baby. I took auto shop in high school just so I could help Dad whenever he was working on her in the garage on Saturday afternoons. That was his stipulation, but I didn't care as long as I got to spend time with her."

Once again, Leo had to tamp down his growing admiration for this woman. He fiercely told himself to stop romanticizing everything she said that made his heart do somersaults. So what if she had a thing for muscle cars, just as he did? That didn't make her The One. The one woman who could accept him as he was, unconditionally, and not wish he were perfect.

"...all that stuff you probably already know anyway," Meghan was saying as she backed out of the parking space and began heading toward the adjacent highway.

Leo had missed what she said while he'd been daydreaming. "I'm sorry, what did you say?"

Meghan laughed softly, "I forgot you old people are sometimes hard of hearing. I was saying you already know Raleigh is the capital of North Carolina, is in Wake County and is part of the Research Triangle, comprised of Raleigh, Durham and the town of Chapel Hill, which produces many of the tech and medical jobs in the region."

"Look, I know I put my foot in it when I said I was too old for you, and I apologize, so could you stop mentioning it?" Leo ground out good-naturedly.

"I'll try," Meghan said. "But you know us young

folks—we're impetuous and hardheaded and rarely take advice from old folks." She pulled onto the highway, driving in the direction of downtown Raleigh. "All joking aside, Leo, I apologize, too. It's just that I hate it when people tell me I'm too young for anything. I realize this was a setup by our siblings, and the fact is, you don't need anyone to show you around. You're a big boy who no doubt has been managing to do things for yourself for quite some time. So, if you like, I'll turn around and take you back to your car. But if you're game, and would just like to have some fun on a beautiful Saturday afternoon, then stick with me."

She looked sideways at him, a mischievous smile crinkling the corners of her beautiful mouth.

Leo didn't hesitate. "I'll take the fun Saturday afternoon."

Meghan laughed softly, "Way to go, old dude."

"Meghan," Leo warned through clenched teeth.

"Last time," she promised with a saucy smile.

## *Chapter 2*

"I'm going to show you the soul of Raleigh and Durham," Meghan said as she pointed the Mustang toward downtown Raleigh and East South Street. "Or the history. Just by living here, you'll find out about the great restaurants in Raleigh and that it has the most live music anywhere in the state. You can find a live band playing somewhere here 24/7. And if you like museums, you can't go wrong with the North Carolina Museum of Natural Sciences or, my favorite, the North Carolina Museum of History."

"Stands to reason that would be your favorite," Leo said as he took in the views of a busy Saturday afternoon in Raleigh. The day was sunny and bright, and there were a lot of folks out and about enjoying themselves. Traffic was pretty heavy, but you could expect that in a city of almost half a million people.

Meghan drove competently. She seemed to be having a good time, if the fact that the smile hadn't left her face since they'd begun the tour was any indication. In the close confines of the Mustang, with the heater on low because it was in the forties outside, she smelled wonderful. Like the air in springtime, fresh and with a hint of jasmine.

"Yes, and I apologize if I get too historical on you, but that's my drug," she joked.

She turned to smile at him before returning her attention to the road. The sunlight was in her eyes, and he noticed her eye color was like melted caramel. *What is wrong with me?* he inwardly chided himself. *I don't usually wax poetic over a woman's eye color.*

"...look fit," Meghan was saying. "What do you do to stay in shape?"

While he'd been daydreaming, he'd missed what she'd said again. He thought he could save himself some embarrassment by answering her last question. "I run, hike and enjoy weightlifting."

"Oh, there are some good trails in William B. Umstead State Park. My sisters and I go there pretty often. Raleigh has some great spots for runners, too. North Wake Landfill Park has some steep hills, if that's what you like. Great views, too. I like Lake Lynn Park. You can run laps around the lake. It's in North Raleigh. Pretty spot where you can catch glimpses of wildlife sometimes, and in fall, it's gorgeous."

A few minutes later, they were on the campus of Shaw University. Meghan parked the car in a visitor's lot and they got out. The campus grounds were immaculately kept, some of the redbrick buildings quite old, like Estey Hall.

"Welcome to Shaw University," Meghan said brightly. "It sits on around sixty-five acres, and it's been here since 1865. The same year slavery was abolished in America."

She gestured for him to follow her toward a four-story Italian-style building. "Shaw had a rather funny beginning," Meghan said as they walked. "At least, it is to me. The founder was a white Baptist minister from Massachusetts, Henry Martin Tupper. After the Civil War, he decided he was going to stay in the South and teach newly freed slaves how to read and write. So he bought some land from a white landowner, not mentioning why he wanted it. When the landowner found out he was building a school for freedmen, he saw red and said if he'd known the land was for blacks, he'd never have sold it to that Yankee! Of course, you know he didn't use the word *black* when he said that." Meghan ended with a laugh.

Leo was laughing, too. "No, he probably used stronger language than that. Interesting story. It also proves that our ancestors *did* have some white benefactors."

"True," Meghan said. "There have been quite a few throughout African American history."

She pointed at the four-story building. "That's Estey Hall. It was built in 1873. It's on the National Register of Historic Places. When Shaw first opened, women weren't allowed to attend. But after a few years they were, and Estey Hall was built for them. It served the school until 1970, when it was closed and they started talking about tearing it down. But then the Estey Hall Foundation was born and the building was restored to its original glory. Today, the school's president has her office there, along with other administrative staff."

Leo had to admit, looking up at that handsome edifice, which was painted salmon red and trimmed in a creamy off-white that made it look slightly like a wedding cake, Meghan made history come alive. No wonder she was a history instructor. He was torn between admiring Estey Hall and admiring her with her glowing face.

Meghan must have caught him looking at her with his admiration showing because she looked down suddenly, blushing.

"Anyway," she said as she continued walking and he fell into step beside her on the sidewalk, "black colleges and universities helped create the black middle class. Whole neighborhoods sprang up around these kinds of institutions. For example, around Saint Augustine's College, another nearby HBCU, it was the neighborhoods of Idlewild and College Park. You may have heard of Idlewild. There was a movie a few years ago of the same name starring André 3000 and Big Boi."

"Oh, yeah, I remember that movie," Leo said. "Paula Patton was in it, too."

Meghan laughed shortly. "That's the one. The movie was filmed here in North Carolina. There are so many things I could tell you about Raleigh that I love," she said. "But if you make this area your home long enough, you'll come to love it, too."

It was a workout keeping up with her as she showed

him around the campus, weaving their way through students who were going from building to building or just relaxing in the sunshine. It was chilly out and the students were dressed in hoodies and sweatshirts with the school's mascot, the Shaw Bear, on them. The school colors must have been a deep red and white, the most frequently occurring colors he saw.

"Shaw's colors are red and white, huh?" he asked.

"Garnet and white," Meghan said.

They were suddenly interrupted by two students, a male and a female, hurrying up to them across the lawn, one of them calling, "Hey, Dr. Gaines. You just can't stay away from here, can you?"

Meghan stopped in her tracks, laughing. "Hailey, it's good to see you, too. I'm showing Dr. Wolfe here around the campus. How is that paper coming along?"

"Good to meet you, Dr. Wolfe," Hailey, a tall, athletically built young woman with long blond-tinted dreadlocks, said with a grin.

"Hello, Hailey," Leo said, smiling at the girl.

She beamed at him, then said to Meghan, "And, you know, the paper's coming slowly, but it's definitely coming!" She was one of Meghan's favorite students. Playful, but very serious when it came to academics.

The boy with her was on the basketball team. Six-six and shy. Except on the court. On the court, he ruled. Meghan thought they made a great couple. The intellectual and the jock.

"Hey, Jordan," she said.

"Hey, Dr. Gaines." He cautiously met her eyes, then looked down.

Hailey elbowed him in the side and said, "We were headed to the cafeteria for a late lunch. See you, Dr. Gaines."

"Bye," Meghan said with a smile.

She and Leo continued walking. "Nice kids," Leo remarked.

"Yes, they are. Our students are, for the most part, pretty serious about getting an education and not wasting their parents' money."

Leo glanced into her upturned face as they were walking. "Is it true what Hailey said about you? That you're always here?"

He didn't know why he was curious as to what she did on her off time. He had already decided he wasn't going to see her again, hadn't he? But it tugged at his heart to imagine her so wrapped up in her career that she didn't take time for herself, so he'd asked.

"I stay pretty busy," Meghan said with a contented smile. "I garden, I work on my house, which I bought for a great price about three years ago. It's in South Park, one of those black neighborhoods that sprang up around a college. Many of Shaw's faculty members have lived in South Park over the years. Nowadays, the city of Raleigh consists of mostly mixed neighborhoods, so it's not exactly a black neighborhood anymore. The street I live on is nice, with huge oak trees and well-maintained houses with manicured lawns. The owners take pride in their homes."

"Yeah, I live near Duke and was told my neighborhood also has been the home of a lot of Duke's faculty members," Leo told her.

"Duke," Meghan said, "was originally called Trinity College."

"Do you always know every historical fact about everything?" Leo asked with a note of wonder.

"I know, I'm weird," Meghan laughed. "But yes, I have a lot of historical trivia running around in my head. It was an endowment by the Duke family, who made their fortune from cigarettes, that financed the university. And it's ironic, really. Cigarettes have killed so many people, but today Duke University's hospital has some of the best doctors in the country. It's almost like the family made a conscious effort to make up for all the bad they did by selling tobacco."

Leo smiled at her. "I knew the history of Duke, but I never looked at it that way. Why some philanthropists choose to give money to an institution. Maybe you're right, and the family did want to make up for all the harm caused by selling cigarettes."

It was then that Leo knew Meghan Gaines was a woman to be reckoned with and was much more mature than she looked. She had a good head on her shoulders.

Back at Annie's Café, Meghan parked the Mustang next to his late-model SUV. They got out and stretched their legs, neither of them seeming in a big hurry to end the day. It was still beautiful out at half past five. A brisk breeze came from the south, and the sky was a crystalline blue with barely any clouds.

"I had a good time," Leo said, smiling at her. "And I learned a lot about the area. Knowing the little details about how our people had a hand in making Raleigh and Durham thrive does actually boost my appreciation of my new home. Thank you, Meghan."

Meghan had to force herself not to be too effusive in her appreciation of that compliment. She was normally a very enthusiastic person, but sensed in Leo a more reserved soul. So she merely smiled and said, "It was my pleasure, Leo."

She wanted to hug him but restrained herself.

Leo wanted to kiss her cheek and breathe in her essence one last time. But he shook her hand, instead.

"There's no point in saying goodbye because our siblings are getting married, and I know I'll be seeing you again soon," he joked. He handed her his card.

"True enough," Meghan agreed, palming the card. "See you soon," she said softly as she turned away and got back into the Mustang. Leo reluctantly drew his gaze away and got into his car. But he didn't start it until she'd driven away.

"Oh, my God, I've got it bad," he groaned. "She's adorable!"

In the Mustang, Meghan breathed a longing-filled sigh. "What a great guy. Too bad I talked his ears off and generally made an ass of myself!"

At home, Meghan parked her car in the garage and went into the three-bedroom, two-bath Southern-style bungalow through the garage door. Entering the laundry room, she yelled, "Mommy's home!"

She could hear the frantic *click* of Chauncey's nails on the tile floor as her two-year-old cocker spaniel came running. She knelt and hugged the dog, allowing her face to be licked to within an inch of its life. Rising, she rubbed Chauncey's golden-brown head. "I bet you're ready to go outside, aren't you, girl?"

Meghan got her keys out of her shoulder bag, dropped them into her jacket pocket, then deposited her bag onto the shelf above the washer and dryer in the laundry room. She grabbed the leash that was on a hook by the door and attached it to Chauncey's collar. "Let's go to the park. I feel like walking off a little steam myself. I met a gorgeous man today, and I need someone to talk to about him other than your aunties, who'll probably give me a lot of bad advice and then get mad at me for not taking it."

Chauncey looked up at her with big soulful brown eyes, as if in sympathy. "I know, I know," Meghan said. "It's not easy being the baby of the family. Everybody wants to tell me how to live my life. My sisters are all—except for the rebel, Petra, and Desiree—happily taken by some man and are deliriously happy. And now they're targeting me."

They strolled down the sidewalk, and as they passed her neighbor's house on the right, she saw Dr. Johnson in the yard putting up their Christmas lights. Dr. and Mrs. Johnson were always notoriously early decorating their house for the holidays. The elderly man was standing on a ladder and Meghan didn't want to startle him by yelling hello, so she and Chauncey walked quietly along without saying anything. But she was only a few steps past when he called out, "Good afternoon, Miss Meghan and Miss Chauncey. How are you two ladies?"

Meghan laughed. A retired professor of economics, Dr. Leland Johnson was seventy-nine years old, but he looked around sixty with his dark skin, bald head and the neatest moustache Meghan had ever seen. "We're doing just fine, Professor," she politely replied. "How are you and Mrs. Johnson doing today?"

"We're both in excellent health and spirits," Dr. Johnson said brightly. "Getting the house outfitted for the season. We're expecting our children this year. They're going to stay a whole week. It will be bedlam, but we're going to enjoy every minute of it."

"Sounds like my family," Meghan told him. "But good on you. I haven't even begun to think how I'm going to decorate the house this year."

"Your White Christmas theme was lovely last year."

"Thank you," Meghan said. "All the snow we got last year kind of canceled it out, though. I may go for a Kwanzaa theme this year."

"That would be interesting," Dr. Johnson responded.

Chauncey whined miserably. Dr. Johnson looked down at the dog and chuckled. "Am I holding up your walk, Miss Chauncey? Well, go on with your delicate sensibilities."

When he said that word, *sensibilities*, it made Meghan think of Leo. That was who he reminded her of. A Jane Austen character. Not a character from *Sense and Sensibility*, though, but *Pride and Prejudice*: Darcy. Darcy with his proud manner and self-sufficiency. Until he fell in love with Elizabeth Bennett, Darcy had needed no one except himself.

She said goodbye to her neighbor and let Chauncey lead her to the nearby park, a place the dog knew quite well.

When Leo got home, he opened the two-car garage with the remote and parked the SUV next to his candy-apple-red 1967 Pontiac GTO. He smiled when he saw it. That baby had a four-hundred-cubic-inch V-8 engine that delivered 360 horsepower. It reminded him of Meghan now. Meghan with her 1965 Mustang. Some purists didn't even consider pony cars like the Mustang to be muscle cars. But from riding around with Meghan that afternoon, he knew her particular Mustang deserved the title. There was power under that hood. And Meghan handled it beautifully.

What was wrong with him when he considered her driving skills to be damned sexy?

He got out of the SUV and, leaving the garage door open because he was thinking of going out to dinner later, walked to the front door and unlocked it.

Malcolm, his chocolate Labrador retriever puppy, ambled into the room from the kitchen. Malcolm had such a calm personality that even his master's return home rarely fazed him. He walked up to Leo and sat down, lifted his head and cocked it to the side, looking at Leo with a benign expression on his face. Leo knelt, scooped Malcolm up into his arms and hugged him. "I hope my pessimism isn't rubbing off on you, fella. You're a puppy. You're supposed to be bouncing off the walls."

He peered into the puppy's eyes. "Maybe you need to rip and run for a while. Do you want to go outside?"

Malcolm licked his cheek. "I'll take that as a yes," Leo joked.

He went and opened the back door that led to the yard. Putting Malcolm on the floor, he watched as the puppy sprinted for the wooden fence. On the other side was the neighbor's tomcat, sitting there glaring at Malcolm through the slats.

"Don't let him scare you, Malcolm. You own this yard!"

Leo turned away to go into the kitchen and get a bottle of water from the refrigerator. As he was reaching for the bottle, his cell phone rang. Looking down at the display, he saw that it was Jake.

No matter what, he always answered when family called.

"Hey, bro," he said.

"Well, what do you think about Meghan?"

"I think you knew what I'd think when you set me up with her," was Leo's reply.

Jake laughed, "I knew you'd find her beautiful. All of Mina's sisters are beautiful. And I hoped you'd have a lot in common. But other than that, I didn't know if you'd hit it off or not. So, what's the verdict? And Mina isn't here, so you can be brutally honest."

"Okay," Leo said. "She's the biggest history nerd I've ever met. She talks a mile a minute, and she has the tendency to blush a lot. She says she's thirty, but she looks twenty."

"Does that mean you don't like her?" Jake asked, sounding confused. "Because I definitely didn't think that was going to happen. Everybody likes Meghan. She's one of the sweetest girls on earth. Did you know she goes to see her old elementary school teacher who's in a nursing home, practically every Sunday?"

"She sounds like a saint. The last thing I need is a saint," Leo told his twin brother. "What I need is a woman who thinks out of the box. A woman who won't be cowed and afraid when I tell her that, in spite of how I look or how I perform in the bedroom, I'll never be able to give her a child. I need somebody strong enough to accept me as I am."

Jake let out a frustrated sigh. "What makes you think Meghan isn't strong enough to take you as you are, Leo? The question is, are you brave enough to let down your guard and find out?"

"Are you calling me a coward?" Leo asked indignantly.

"Yes, I am, baby brother," Jake said. "And I suggest you grow a pair!"

With that, he hung up.

Leo looked down at the phone in disbelief before turning it off and placing it on the kitchen counter. He couldn't believe his brother had said that. He might have been really pissed off if Jake hadn't been right. He *was* a coward. But he had reason to be. Natalie had broken off their engagement three years ago when he'd confided in her that he'd been born with a condition that caused him to be sterile. Plus, he had a congenital heart defect. Basically, he could drop dead any minute. And there was no cure for it. All he could do was live as healthily as he could and wish for the best. And should it look like his heart was going to fail him, they could rush him to an operating room and give him a new heart. But he didn't hold out much hope of finding a donor in time to save his life.

He'd always held the opinion that life had royally screwed him. Natalie had freaked out when he told her. She stopped taking his calls and totally cut him out of her life, finally saying after a month of silence that she wanted children who looked like her. Children who came from her body. Children with a biological connection to her and her husband. She didn't even mention the heart condition in her explanation. Leo figured the subject was too scary to touch. When she'd looked at him, he'd known why: there was pity in her big, beautiful brown eyes. That was worse than anything. It had made him feel less than a man.

Leo couldn't find fault with her reasoning. Most people did want children who looked like them. But it still hurt like hell. He'd loved Natalie with all of his being. She'd been the only woman he'd ever loved, and she'd ripped his heart out when she'd dropped him so easily. He'd thought love could fill the void. He'd thought love was everything and made all the difference in the world. But love had made not one iota of difference for Natalie. It had made no difference that he was an accomplished human being. It had made no difference that he was a wonderful, giving lover.

It had made no difference that he earned a very good living and they would live comfortably together. Nothing took the place of a biological child. Last thing he heard about her, she'd married someone a year after she'd broken up with him and had a child the following year. So her dreams had come true, while his had turned to dust.

Jake had had the nerve to call him a coward. He wasn't a coward. Not really. He was a realist. The adorable Miss Meghan Gaines would run for the hills if he told her he could never father a child, not to mention the heart condition. She was pushing thirty, too, which made some women think their clocks were ticking and there was no time to lose.

No, she was definitely not a possible soul mate for him.

# *Chapter 3*

Jake called back five minutes after hanging up on him. "I didn't mean to call you a coward. I know you're not a coward. But it frustrates me to see you give up like you're doing!"

Leo listened patiently. He knew his brother better than he knew anyone else on the planet. Jake wanted him to be as happy as he was right now with the lovely Mina. Even though Jake had been born only a few seconds before him, Jake had always considered himself the big brother. So when he saw his baby brother struggling in life, he naturally wanted to lend a helping hand.

"If you had let me finish talking," Leo said now, "I would have told you that I like Meghan a lot. She's, frankly, an angel. But I'm not going to pursue it."

"Why not?" Jake practically yelled.

"You. Know. Why," Leo said, enunciating every word. "She's a saint. And a saint deserves someone she can count on to give her the life she wants. I'm not that guy. So please don't continue talking me up to Mina or anyone else in her family. Just let me be the brother who occasionally shows up at family gatherings with one anonymous woman after another on his arm."

"Sometimes I think there should be violins playing in the background when you're talking, brother. Look, all right, when Mina asks me why you're not interested in her gorgeous baby sister, what am I supposed to tell her?"

"I've already told Meghan I think I'm too old for her," Leo offered. "After which she ribbed me big-time about it. I have to admit, she makes me laugh."

Jake chuckled. "Believe me, you want a woman like that in your life." Then, with a more serious tone to his voice, he asked, "Did she like you?"

"Attracting women has never been my problem. It's hanging on to them that eludes me." Leo wasn't bragging, just stating the facts.

"If I had the time, I'd come to Durham and knock some sense into you, but since I'm on a case, you get a free pass."

"Yeah, how is that going?" Leo asked, knowing full well his DEA agent brother couldn't disclose any details of his present assignment.

"You'll have to read about it in my memoirs when I retire," Jake told him. "Okay, if Mina asks why you're not in hot pursuit of Meghan, I'll say you're just crazy as hell."

"That's how I feel right now," Leo admitted. "She's so perfect, I can't imagine why she's not already taken."

"Are you interested enough to hear the reason?" Jake asked. "Because I'll tell you if you really want to know."

Leo couldn't resist finding out as much about Meghan as he possibly could. "Tell me."

"It's a common story, really," Jake began quietly. "When she was an undergraduate at Shaw, she fell in love with the football team's quarterback. By the time they were seniors, it was a pretty widespread belief that they were destined to get married. He was picked in the first-round draft to go to the Dallas Cowboys. She'd already been accepted in the English master's program at Duke."

"She didn't even mention that," Leo said.

"About her attending Duke? Bad memories, probably," Jake said. "Anyway, he went off to Dallas and broke up with her via email, the creep!"

"Poor kid," Leo murmured, his heart thudding in sympathy for Meghan's broken heart.

"So, you see, you're not the only one who was stomped on by love," Jake said. "Gotta go. But I just want to say one more thing first. Don't burn your bridges where Meghan's concerned right now. If you don't want to date her, at least be friendly when you see her—and you will see her. Mina wanted me to tell you that they're having Thanksgiving in the mountains this year. You're invited."

"I can't do that," Leo said regretfully. "That's about six weeks from now. Six weeks of my not trying to get in contact with her. If I showed up, I'd make her very uncomfortable."

"Then you like her," Jake pointed out.

"Were you not listening?" Leo asked a little irritably. "That's why I can't see her—because she's adorable and seeing her would just make me want to get to know her more. I couldn't even resist knowing about her broken heart!"

Jake laughed, "I'll never understand you. What if happiness is yours to take, and you never reach your hand out for it?"

"I'll just have to take that risk," Leo said stubbornly.

"You *are* coming to our wedding, aren't you? Meghan will be there."

"I'm your best man," Leo reminded him. "I can't very well shirk my duties."

"You'd better not!"

"I'll be there. By that time I should have my Meghan-avoidance maneuvers down pat."

"Uh-huh," Jake said doubtfully. "You've got me so confused, I don't know what I'm going to say to Mina about you and Meghan, and she *will* ask. Bye, brother. See a psychiatrist!"

"I did. Didn't help," Leo told him, chuckling. "Bye, bro."

As Meghan knew there would be whenever her family gathered together, there was high drama at Thanksgiving dinner in the Great Smoky Mountains. Mina and

Miss Mabel, their grandfather's lady love, had made a delicious feast. Mina had told her that when she'd phoned their mother, Virginia, the day before to confirm they were coming, she'd told Virgina she didn't need to bring anything except herself. However, Virginia, who had taken an unreasonable dislike to Miss Mabel since she'd started dating her father, showed up with a twenty-five-pound baked ham. Mina was livid because she knew how controlling her mother was and feared this was only the first shot in Virginia's campaign to break up her father and Miss Mabel, who Virginia thought was a gold digger trying to replace her mother—and her—in her father's heart.

Meghan was watching Mina's face after their mother told her she'd brought a ham. Mina's eyes had gotten cold, and she'd bared her teeth in a moment of sheer rage and frustration, but then she'd taken control of her emotions and smiled at her mother. Virginia Gaines said nonchalantly, "It's just a ham."

Meghan had held her breath, thinking Mina was about to say something scathing to their mother. Mina surprised her by saying, "Thanks, Momma. That was very thoughtful of you."

After that, Meghan and Desiree had each taken one of their mother's arms and pulled her up the steps of the huge log cabin and out of Mina's presence.

*One of these days*, Meghan thought, *I'm going to find out why our mom tries to control everyone around her.*

They all sat around the table: Meghan plus her sisters—Mina, Desiree and Lauren (unfortunately

Petra had not been able to come home from the Democratic Republic of the Congo this year)—and Lauren's hubby, Colton. Alphonse and Virginia, their parents. Their grandfather Benjamin Beck and Miss Mabel Brown, who up to that point was thought to be merely the cook at Ben's mountain lodge. She was obviously more than that to their granddad.

The table was laden with every conceivable Thanksgiving Day edible—a beautifully roasted turkey, dressing, giblet gravy, green bean casserole, glazed carrots, collard greens and sweet potato pies. Oh, yeah, and the ham her mother had insisted on bringing. Seeing all that food made Meghan wonder what Leo was doing for Thanksgiving. Maybe he'd gone to see his parents in Florida. Mina had told her that while he and Jake had been raised in the Bronx, where their parents were teachers, when their parents retired they'd moved back to Florida, where they were born, to take over the family farm in Crystal River. When Meghan learned Leo's grandparents had been citrus growers in Florida for over fifty years, she realized why he was a gardener: farming was in his blood.

Now she gazed around the table at the people she loved most in the world. Her mother was a small copper-skinned woman with long, wavy black hair with silver streaks in it. Her skin color and hair texture had been inherited from a Native American mother and an African American father. Right now she had her hair in a bun at the nape of her neck, looking like the scholarly woman she was. She was the principal of a large high school in Raleigh and had earned her PhD in education while almost single-handedly raising five daughters. Their father, Alphonse, had been an army man and was away quite often when they were growing up. He'd earned the rank of general before retiring about a decade ago. He was sitting beside Virginia, still looking soldierly with his tall frame, bald head and thick moustache.

She and her sisters favored each other, but still had distinct characteristics. Mina, for example, had practically the same skin color as her four sisters, a reddish brown that was a mix between their mother's coppery skin tone and their father's medium brown. However, for some reason, Mina's hair was thicker and kinkier than that of the other sisters, who wore their naturally curly hair down their backs. Mina had a glorious full Afro that she sometimes wore in braids, but that she preferred to let run wild, à la Diana Ross in the rain at that concert in Central Park. Or that was what Meghan thought, enviously, whenever Mina wore her hair in an Afro.

All the sisters had warm brown eyes, noses proportionate to their faces and full lips. And ranged in height from five-three, Petra, to five-ten, Lauren. Lauren was practically glowing now because she was expecting Colton's child.

Meghan sighed happily. Her first niece or nephew. She loved children. She wanted to match her mother in the number of children she had, five. Three girls and two boys. She'd grown up with all sisters and thought there should be some gender diversity in there.

Mina, who was sitting next to her at the table, interrupted her thoughts by asking, "What did you think of Leo?"

Meghan's happy thoughts of her future children immediately vanished. Her face flushed with embarrassment. "I blew it," she told Mina. Then she went on to tell her she thought she'd talked too much. Had probably given him too many impromptu history lessons. While she'd thought there was some mutual admiration going on throughout the day that Saturday, she wasn't so sure anymore because he hadn't phoned her once since then.

Mina looked mortified. Then she looked angry, and Meghan could guess what was going through her warrior sister's mind. *How dare he reject my sister?*

So Meghan told her she didn't want to talk about Leo anymore. It hadn't worked out. For whatever reason, he simply wasn't interested in a woman who was too young for him, as he'd put it.

"Okay, I won't mention it again," Mina promised, searching Meghan's face a moment, her expression both sympathetic and curious.

*"C'est la vie,"* Meghan said, as carefree as she could manage. The truth was, she was still hoping Leo would come around. But she hadn't heard from him in six weeks.

On a brighter note, their mother then got into an argument with their eightysomething grandfather about Miss Mabel (more than twenty years younger), during which he stood up and proudly announced Miss Mabel was his new wife.

Another wonderful, drama-filled Thanksgiving.

* * *

Leo drove to Crystal River, Florida, with Malcolm as his lone companion. Malcolm even managed to look excited about it from his perch in his puppy car seat. The elevated seat allowed him to see outside, and he seemed to be enjoying the view.

The trip was about a nine-hour journey, farther than when Leo had lived in Atlanta. But he wanted to see his parents and grandparents, so he left Durham on Wednesday night. He spent the night in a hotel in a small Georgia town to rest, was back on the road early Thursday morning and was soon in Crystal River. In western Florida, it was called Crystal River for the crystal clear natural springs within its boundaries.

The farmland his folks had owned for more than half a century boasted a spring where he and Jake used to swim when they were kids. The property was nearly a thousand acres, many of which were orange groves, plus a long tree-lined road that led up to the main house.

It was a beautiful day, and warmer in Florida than North Carolina. As he got out of the SUV, he raised his face to the sunlit sky and took a deep cleansing breath. Somehow the air smelled better at home. He stretched his jeans-clad legs and rolled the kinks from sitting so long out of his shoulders, then went around to the passenger side and got Malcolm out of his puppy seat.

Malcolm wiggled mightily. Leo put him down, and Malcolm calmly walked over to the nearest plant and peed on it.

"Who is that peeing on my roses?" Leo's mother's

voice came from the direction of the porch of the well-maintained farmhouse.

"It's not me this time," Leo joked, jogging over to give his mother a big hug.

Katherine Williams-Wolfe had a good grip, and by the time she let go of her son, his chest ached a little. Leo looked down into his mother's lovely face. At sixty-two, she was around five-six and trim. He and Jake had gotten their love for physical activity from her. She was a runner from way back, and had had them doing it by the time they were old enough to show some interest in the sport. He and Jake were still runners.

His mother was the parent from whom he and Jake had inherited their clear brown eyes. Hers were twinkling up at him now.

Behind them, Leo's father opened the screen door. He was sixty-five, and although he didn't exercise as much as his wife, he was in pretty good shape. His short Afro—not receding yet, Leo noted—was solid silver these days, and he wore a short beard that was fuller than Leo's and more luxuriant, too, Leo thought a bit enviously. He was one suave-looking senior citizen.

"Leonidas!" his father shouted. "Welcome home, my boy."

It was his mother who'd named him Leonidas, after the Spartan king, and named Jake Jason, after a mythological Greek hero who was the leader of the Argonauts. His dad was the only one in the family who called him Leonidas, though.

Leander Wolfe was six-three. The same height as his sons.

He looked into his son's eyes now and asked, "What's wrong?"

Leo laughed shortly. His father had the uncanny ability to know when something was weighing heavily on his mind.

"There's this woman," Leo started to explain.

Malcolm chose that moment to run up the steps onto the porch, and his mother, who loved puppies, bent down, scooped him up into her arms and exclaimed, "I finally get to meet my grandson, Malcolm X."

"It's just Malcolm, Mom," Leo said, smiling. "He's too mild mannered to be Malcolm X."

Katherine held Malcolm at arm's length, peering into his beautiful brown-green eyes. "Oh, I don't know. He looks like he's going to grow up to be a good guard dog to me. As soon as he was finished watering my rosebush, he came straight to his master." She looked up at Leo. "How old is he?"

"Nine months," Leo answered.

"Oh, you're just a baby," his mother cooed at Malcolm, who licked her face appreciatively.

Katherine turned and walked into the house. "Come on in. Your grandmother and I are cooking dinner. Did you stop for breakfast? I can whip you up something real fast."

"No, we're fine," Leo told her. "We stopped at Cracker Barrel."

He walked into the familiar house, which had high ceilings and was open concept. The living room, kitchen and dining room were one big space. He could see his grandfather sitting on the couch watching the morning news, and his grandmother in the kitchen stirring something in a big white ceramic bowl.

He felt that old sick feeling he got in the pit of his stomach whenever he saw his parents and grandparents. It was a mixture of love and regret. He loved them so much, and he regretted he wasn't around them more, sharing in their lives. They wouldn't be here forever, and he would miss them terribly when they were gone.

He went and shook his grandfather's hand. At ninety-four, Ellis was his oldest living relative. He used to be over six feet, too, but the years had shrunk him a couple of inches. Not a very demonstrative man, Ellis was satisfied with a handshake. But he could tell by the happy expression in his eyes that he loved his grandson.

His grandmother, Etta Mae, was ninety, but she still got around rather well. She quit stirring whatever was in the bowl and came toddling over to him. Her small body was clothed in her ever-present outfit of knit pants and long-sleeved blouse with comfortable shoes. No matter the season, that was her uniform. Leo didn't think she ever got warm enough to wear short sleeves. She was around five-two and slender, so maybe she did need the extra layers to keep warm.

"Leo!" she shouted, her voice strong in spite of her size and years. "What a lovely surprise!"

Leo gently hugged her frail body. Then he kissed her soft cheek. She smelled like baby powder. "I told you I was coming," he reminded her.

She looked at him through her thick glasses with a puzzled expression on her softly wrinkled face. "You did?"

"Yes, I did."

"Well, I must have forgotten because I don't remember," she said with a sweet smile. "Where's Jake?"

"Oh, he had to work," Leo told her.

Then he was swept up in the daily routine of his parents and grandparents, being monopolized by one or another of them all day long. He caught up with their lives, listening to them relate their aches and pains and problems with the business. Because that was what family meant to him: sharing their ups and downs. Meanwhile, Malcolm had the run of the house, his nose to the floor, experiencing new smells and sensations and having the time of his life.

And in the middle of all that, somehow his dad got him alone and they talked about the feelings he was having for Meghan and what he could possibly do about them.

Leo couldn't imagine a more perfect day and was glad he'd taken that nine-hour trip to once again be in the arms of his family.

# *Chapter 4*

"Dad told you what?" Jake asked, incredulously. Leo could tell his brother was about to bust with pent-up laughter. He was standing in the middle of the kitchen, cordless phone to his ear, barefoot and wearing his robe, after showering following a five-mile run on Monday afternoon. He had returned from Florida last night, his spirit refreshed and his refrigerator now stuffed with his mother's and grandmother's home cooking. The five-mile run was to ward off weight gain after eating too much of that home cooking.

"I don't know if I want to tell you if you're going to start laughing. This is serious business."

"Okay, I won't laugh," Jake promised. He cleared his throat, and his voice sounded totally devoid of hilarity when he added, "Go ahead, I'm ready."

"He said I would be a fool to avoid a woman like Meghan. He said life gives you only so many chances at happiness, and I shouldn't blow this opportunity. He also said that the next time he talked to me, he hoped I'd have some good news on the Meghan front. That's what he called it, as a reference to war because he said I should fight for that woman."

Jake guffawed. He laughed so loud and hard that he started coughing toward the end. "Good old Dad," he got out once he was in control of himself again. "He always did have a way with words." Then he started laughing again.

Leo couldn't help it; he joined in, and then they were off and running, talking about their parents and grandparents, how the farm was doing. Their cousin, the son of one of their father's brothers, had just graduated from the University of Florida with an agricultural degree and was eager to begin working with their father and grandfather to learn the business and eventually take over, thereby keeping it in the Wolfe family.

"He seems solid," Leo told Jake. "We can stop feeling guilty now because we chose different careers."

"The family understood," Jake said. "I didn't feel guilty, you did. But maybe now you'll begin to realize that it's okay to be happy. To live your own life. You deserve happiness. And let's not get off the subject of Meghan. What are you going to do about her?"

"One thing I'm *not* going to do is shut her out," Leo said. "But after weeks of ignoring her, I can't think of a way to get back in. She's probably done with me. Who wouldn't be?"

"So you're going to wait and hope she contacts you?" Jake complained. "Haven't you ever heard that faint heart never won fair maiden? Or something like that. Be aggressive, brother. Think of something soon because our wedding is coming up real fast, and I want to see you and Meghan dancing up a storm. Dust off your dancing shoes."

"I think you're enjoying yourself a little too much at my expense," Leo accused him.

"You're right, I am," Jake admitted. "Mina and I are rooting for you. But you're right about one thing. Meghan is pretty down on you. She's calling you Mr. Darcy. I don't know what that's in reference to. Mina says it's a character in a romance novel."

Leo frowned. Meghan thought he was proud and picky and possibly a snob? Nah, she couldn't believe that. "I know to whom she's referring," he said quietly. Then it dawned on him. Because he'd told Meghan he thought she was too young for him, she'd concluded that he was coming up with all sorts of excuses not to date her because he thought she wasn't good enough for him. Just like Darcy first rejected Elizabeth because he thought she was beneath him due to her exasperating family. But that didn't apply to him. He didn't think he was too good for Meghan. He thought she deserved someone better than him. She didn't know that, though. She thought he'd rejected her because he thought he was better than she was.

He shared his theory with Jake.

Jake said, "Mmm, dude, if that's true, you're in real

trouble. I don't have any idea how you're going to get out of this one. I have no advice."

"I finally stumped you, huh?"

"You did. Do you want me to pass it by Mina? She may have a suggestion."

"No, I'll figure it out," Leo told him. "It's my fight."

"The wedding's soon," Jake said. "Get busy."

"That's all I need, more pressure," Leo groused. "Goodbye. Give my best to the lovely Mina."

"Will do," Jake said and hung up.

Leo put the phone down on the island's countertop and sat perched on one of the high wooden stools, suddenly feeling hopeless. Mr. Darcy? Him?

He racked his brain, thinking back to that Saturday afternoon, trying to recall when he'd behaved haughtily or had done anything that could be construed as arrogant or unfeeling. No, he couldn't remember any of that kind of behavior on his part. He'd even downplayed his success as a writer. Fact was, he was doing pretty well. Not raking in millions, but his savings account had grown fat from his book earnings. It had to have been that *I'm too old for you* remark he'd made. Meghan had apparently interpreted that to mean he just didn't like her. Which was far from the truth. He couldn't get her off his mind.

He got up and went to his bedroom to get dressed. He had to do something about their miscommunication. The question was, what? He cleared his throat. Why was his throat feeling sore and scratchy? He never got sick. He prided himself on taking good care of himself. Running, weight lifting, long hikes. The heart doctors had always told him he needed to keep his heart muscle in shape. That included eating right and exercising.

He shrugged out of his robe and hung it behind the door in the bathroom of the master bedroom. Was it hotter in the house than normal? He placed his hand on his forehead. He felt a little warmer than usual. But how could he accurately tell when he didn't have a thermometer in the house? Parents kept thermometers to monitor their kids' temperatures during illnesses. He'd never had a need for one.

Then he thought back to his trip to Florida. He'd taken a long run in the Florida sunshine without his shirt on. The temperature had been in the mideighties, not unusual for November in Florida. But when he'd gotten back to North Carolina, the temperature was in the low fifties. He had just run five miles in fifty-two-degree weather. Could the temperature change have weakened his immune system enough to allow a nasty virus to catch hold?

He chuckled, remembering his mother's warning when she'd seen him leaving the house bare chested. "Put on a shirt, baby. You don't want to catch a cold."

But he'd had that encouraging talk with his dad, and he'd felt so strong and invincible that he'd thrown his mother a confident kiss and continued right on out the door.

After he'd put on jeans and a T-shirt, he glanced in the bathroom mirror and smiled at his reflection. He certainly didn't look sick. His black beard was still damp from the shower, and the water droplets made it shine even more. His brown eyes were clear. No reddening at all. He was fine.

He told himself that for four days straight.

By Friday morning, though, he had to admit he was certifiably sick. He had body aches and was feverish. Worst of all was his lack of energy. He was used to being very active. But this morning he'd had to drag himself out of bed in order to feed poor Malcolm and let him outside to relieve himself.

Malcolm, so grateful to have been let out, tried to lick his master's face in gratitude when he came back inside, and Leo prevented him, saying, "Better stay away from me, boy. I doubt if you can catch this, but who knows?"

Malcolm had whined, looked at him sorrowfully and, finally resigned to no playtime, trotted back over to his favorite spot by the fireplace in the living room and lay down.

Leo trudged back to the sofa and lay down. The coffee table nearby held tissues, water bottles and cold medicine that he'd been faithfully taking every four hours.

He felt miserable. He hadn't caught a cold in years. Maybe he was getting old, after all. Maybe the fates had conspired against him. *Maybe you ought to quit being melodramatic*, he told himself, *and stop acting like a baby.*

As soon as he got settled in a comfortable spot, his cell phone rang. He dug it out from between the sofa cushions. How it had gotten there, he didn't know. The display read *Mina.*

"Mina, what's up?"

The first thing out of her mouth was "You sound terrible. You caught a cold in Florida, huh?"

*What is it with women and their sixth sense about colds?* Leo wondered. He laughed shortly, "I'm afraid so."

"Flu's been bad this year. You'd better take care of yourself. Speaking of which—do you have everything you need to fight it? Chicken soup? Plenty of liquids? Cold medicine?"

"I'm good, really, Mina," Leo tried to claim. Although the sympathetic tone in his soon-to-be sister-in-law's voice made him feel a little less alone.

"I'm sending someone over," Mina said decisively. "Don't even try to argue with me." She cut him off when he tried to say something.

Leo fleetingly wondered who Mina, who lived in the mountains, could command to come check on him. He was beginning to wonder just how powerful these Gaines girls were. Jake had told him some stories that were hard to believe. Like Petra lived in an African jungle. Lauren had saved her ex-husband's life when a crazed woman tried to kill him. To say nothing of Mina rescuing Jake from a plane crash. What was to be his Gaines girl's miraculous feat? He wanted to be there to find out.

Even though Mina had warned him not to argue with her, he had to give it his best shot when she told him what she was planning. "You're not serious about sending Meghan over here, are you?"

Mina laughed, "Leo, don't look a gift horse in the mouth. Just take the gift."

"What if she doesn't want to see me?"

"It isn't you she's coming to see," Mina said, sounding mysterious. "Now, make yourself presentable and expect company soon."

"Mina?" Leo tried. But she had hung up on him.

Meghan was walking across campus to her car when her phone started ringing. She had taught her last class of the day and was looking forward to getting home, unwinding and starting a pot of homemade chicken soup, which she'd been craving for weeks. For some reason, when the weather was cold she wanted comfort food like thick homemade soups in her system.

At school, she dressed professionally. No jeans for her. Today she had on a dark gray skirt suit with black pumps and accessories. Her wavy black hair was pulled back in a ponytail. Her briefcase was in one hand, her shoulder bag tossed over her right shoulder and her laptop in its case in the other hand. She set the laptop on the Mustang's roof when she got to the car, and dug into her shoulder bag to answer the persistently ringing cell phone.

"Mina, are you okay?"

"Why is it you always think something's wrong if I call you on a workday?" Mina asked.

"It's just my anxious nature," Meghan said. She was the youngest of the Gaines girls, but the biggest worrywart. She mothered her sisters much more than they mothered her.

"It's about Leo." Mina dropped the bomb and waited for Meghan to respond.

"What about Mr. Darcy?" she asked warily.

Meghan was trying to sound uninterested, but she knew she couldn't fool her sister and mask how intensely interested she was in what Mina had to say next.

"He's sick," Mina said.

It took about five seconds for Meghan to cry, "With what? Mina, don't play with me, girl."

Mina laughed, "Then you do care! Calm down. It's just a cold."

Meghan sighed, "Of course I care. He's the one who doesn't care. I thought we were clear on that."

"Nothing's been clear between you and Leo since you met," Mina told her. "But that's neither here nor there. I'm calling because while he's sick, he's having a problem taking care of his puppy. He's a nine-month-old chocolate Lab called Malcolm."

"They're adorable," Meghan said breathlessly.

"So I wondered if you'd go over to Leo's and pick him up and keep him for a few days while Leo recovers. You two aren't that far away from each other, according to Google Maps. Only about twenty minutes."

"You do have an eye for detail," Meghan said.

"It's my army training," Mina said. "Oh, and while you're over there, maybe you can take him something to eat. What are you cooking today?"

"Who said I was cooking today?"

"Girl, I know you're going to have something good cooking on your stove shortly after you get home from work. And it's cold outside, too. What is it? Chili? Vegetable soup? You and Lauren make some damn good beef vegetable soup."

"Chicken soup," Meghan said, laughing softly. "You know me too well."

"I hear it's good for a cold," Mina said.

"Okay, I'll do it," Meghan said at last. "But I can't promise I'm going to have one good word for Mr. Darcy."

"Actions speak louder than words," Mina said.

By the time Meghan rang the doorbell at Leo's circa 1960s renovated cottage in a quaint neighborhood near Duke University in Durham, Leo had showered to get the smell of Vicks VapoRub ointment, which his mother highly recommended, off his body, put on fresh pajamas, brushed his teeth and straightened up the house. Although there wasn't much to clean up because he was compulsively neat. Another of his psychological quirks. Life was messy and disorganized, but at least he could keep his personal space neat and clean.

He answered the door almost immediately, and restrained himself from looking too glad to see her. Because he was definitely happy to see her. She, too, he could see, was going to play it cool. Dressed in jeans, boots and a black leather jacket under which she had on a gold-colored blouse that complemented her creamy, flawless brown skin, she had an insulated food container in one hand, her shoulder bag slung over her right shoulder and a pet carrier in her other hand.

She looked him straight in the eyes. "Hello, Leo.

Mina told me you needed help with Malcolm until you feel better." She stepped into the room and he moved aside, inhaling the fresh, sensual smell of her skin and hair.

He closed and locked the door. Then he realized he hadn't said a word, and felt foolish and inadequate in her presence. One part of him hadn't really believed she'd show up. Now that she had, he didn't know what to do about it.

"She did?" he asked, confused.

Meghan set the pet carrier down, and he noticed the cute cocker spaniel inside. "You brought me another pet?"

"I brought Chauncey over so she and Malcolm can get to know each other on his home turf before he comes home with me," Meghan said. "Mina told me to come over here and pick up Malcolm so that I can take care of him until you recover."

Her eyes raked over him and a soft sigh escaped from between her lips. Lips that were entirely too delicious looking to his feverish eyes. He could tell he was making her impatient. But what had Mina been thinking, telling Meghan he needed her to come pick up Malcolm and telling him quite another thing? Actually Mina hadn't told him much of anything. Obviously, she was just throwing them together and letting them figure out what to do. It was sink or swim.

So he started swimming.

"Yeah, that's right. I'm sorry. My brain is just not functioning at full capacity right now." He met her gaze. “Thank you for agreeing to take him. He’s only a puppy and he needs a lot of care.”

Meghan tossed her shoulder bag onto the sofa, put the insulated food container on the coffee table and then bent to take Chauncey out of her pet carrier. Meanwhile, Malcolm had come closer to investigate, tail wagging with enthusiasm.

As soon as Meghan let Chauncey out she went straight to Malcolm and started cautiously sniffing around his furry brown face. Malcolm stood still and let her, trembling with excitement.

Leo sat down on the sofa, smiling and shaking his head in wonder. “I haven’t seen him this happy in a long time,” he told Meghan.

Meghan took her jacket off and looked around. She liked the midcentury aspects of Leo’s house. Upon entering the house she was delighted with how spacious it was. There were large windows that she imagined brought in a lot of natural light in the daytime and the way he’d decorated the place, the various living areas maintained their distinctive functions. The floors were hardwood, the finishes high quality and the kitchen ultramodern but still homey. She’d expected Mr. Darcy’s space to be cold and impersonal. It was neat, but warm and welcoming.

She walked over and hung her jacket on a coat tree by the front door. Turning back around, she saw Chauncey and Malcolm nudging each other with their noses in a friendly manner. No growls or baring of teeth.

She looked at Leo, who was looking at the dogs

and smiling. She decided then that if Malcolm and Chauncey could get along, so could she and Leo.

She was a mature woman, after all. Not a schoolgirl with a crush. Therefore, she smiled when she walked over to the sofa and sat down on the other end from Leo. "How are you feeling?"

His eyes raked appreciatively over her face. He gently smiled. "Terrible."

He had dark circles under his eyes, which were watery, no doubt from the effects of the cold. But otherwise, he was as handsome as ever. Her heartbeat hadn't calmed down yet from her first glimpse of him after several weeks. She willed it to slow. "Are you hungry?"

"Famished."

She smiled. "Good. I made chicken soup."

"You made it from scratch?" He sounded surprised.

"It's homemade, yes," she said, rising. "I'll get you a bowl. I forgot saltines. Do you have any?"

"Top shelf, pantry," he said, his eyes following her as she picked up the chicken soup in its container and went to his kitchen. He watched her, in his kitchen, in his house, as she wasted no time locating a bowl and the crackers in the pantry. She looked so competent and relaxed. It was almost as if she were over here every day, doing mundane things like this.

Malcolm and Chauncey were chasing each other around with abandon. "Chauncey, behave yourself," Meghan called from the kitchen. Leo was surprised when Chauncey continued playing with Malcolm but in a slower and gentler manner, as if she fully understood Meghan's words.

"How long have you had her?" he asked Meghan.

"She was six months old when I adopted her a year and a half ago," Meghan replied. She walked back over to the sofa with a bowl of soup, saltine crackers and a bottle of water on the tray he kept on a shelf in the pantry.

She set the tray before him. She'd wrapped a napkin around a soup spoon. "You don't have any food allergies, do you?"

"No, I'm good." Leo tasted the soup. "Mmm, it's delicious."

"Thank you," Meghan said, pleased.

"Go on, tell me more about Chauncey."

"I got Miss Chauncey from the pound. I took one look at her and she took one look at me, and it was love at first sight. I can't imagine life without her. She's very smart and affectionate. Very protective, too. We were in the park one day and this guy approached me, and she got between us and wouldn't let him near me. He was trying to talk to me, and she kept growling at him. Wouldn't be quiet even when I ordered her to. He finally walked off, and not two minutes later he snatched an elderly lady's purse and ran off. She was all right. I waited with her until the police came and gave them a description of the guy."

Leo ate his soup, listening intently while she talked. The soup was wonderful, made with big chunks of boneless chicken in a savory broth with carrots, celery, tomatoes, potatoes, sweet onions, jalapeño peppers, red pepper flakes and okra. He loved the added okra, which was a surprise to him, but it made the broth thick and hearty.

"Did they catch him?"

"Oh, they sure did," Meghan said, glancing at Chauncey with pride.

Chauncey and Malcolm had settled down in Malcolm's favorite spot, Malcolm displaying his belly to her. Leo laughed. "What is up with him?" he asked, puzzled by Malcolm's behavior.

"I think he's welcoming her to his house," Meghan said. "Some dogs display their bellies to other dogs they consider to be higher ranking or more experienced. He's showing respect."

Chauncey responded by nudging Malcolm back onto his feet, and they started chasing each other around the room again.

"Then what's she telling him?" Leo asked, looking Meghan in the eyes.

Meghan smiled at him. "To stop being foolish? Miss Chauncey doesn't go in for rules and such. She just likes to have fun."

"Some of us humans should follow her example," Leo said. "Like a certain Mr. Darcy?"

At that moment, with that tender expression on his bearded face and the warmth emanating between them, all she wanted to do was hug him. But she didn't dare.

"So you've heard about that. I'm sorry if the nickname is hurtful. I didn't mean it to be. Darcy happens to be one of my all-time favorite romantic heroes."

"I'm an English professor," Leo said. "I've read all

of Jane Austen's novels. I enjoyed them in spite of the fact that she tends to make dunces out of the men."

"Is she really making dunces out of the men, or are men just naturally dunces?" Meghan asked with a smile.

Leo laughed, "I can see you're a die-hard Austen fan."

Meghan was laughing, too. "I'm also a die-hard Jeremiah Jacobs fan. Has he written anything lately?"

Leo was happy to tell her that he, in fact, had been writing again. He didn't tell her that she was his muse, though. He'd save that bit of information for later. Perhaps as a romantic gesture, he would let her read it before anyone else once he'd finished.

"I'm so happy for you," Meghan said with a sigh that was probably simply an exhalation of air for her, but for him was the height of sensuality. Or maybe being sick was somehow heightening his senses, because everything about her—her voice, her scent, the way she moved—was arousing him in ways he hadn't felt in a very long time.

He finished the soup and set the bowl back on the tray. "Thank you, Meghan. You're a godsend."

"You're welcome, Mr. Darcy."

Leo smiled at her. "I don't mind it so much when you say it like that."

"Like what?"

"Like you're calling me darling," he said.

"Your cold is making you delirious," Meghan said with a sexy smile. She got up, took the tray into the kitchen and made short work of washing the bowl and spoon and putting them in the dish rack to drain.

Going back to the living room, she sat down again. "I didn't come here to tempt you, Mr. Darcy. I came here on a mission of mercy. To help you with Malcolm." She looked over at the two dogs, who were now lying next to each other in easy camaraderie, perhaps even settling down for a nap. "Mission accomplished. They look like old friends. So I'll put them in their carriers and head back to Raleigh now."

"But they look so comfortable over there," Leo said, trying not to whine like a child. "Why don't you and Chauncey spend the night here? I don't like the idea of you on the road tonight."

"It's barely nine o'clock," Meghan said. "I'm a big girl. I've driven much later, and farther, at night. It's only a twenty-minute drive."

"Malcolm was given to me when he was barely weaned," Leo said. "We've rarely been apart since then."

Meghan stood up, determined. "Where's his carrier?"

"It's in the garage, just inside the door," Leo told her. "But won't you consider staying?"

"You can rest easy tonight," Meghan said, walking toward the garage door off the kitchen. "Malcolm will be fine with us, and tomorrow I'll phone to see how you're doing. Now, may I have his food? And are there any instructions I should have about his care and feeding?"

Leo gave her everything she asked for, albeit reluctantly.

He felt almost jealous when Malcolm went into his

carrier without a fight. Normally he had to chase the puppy to put him in there.

Chauncey also went quietly, tail wagging when her mistress called her and told her it was time to go home, and that they'd be having a guest for a while.

Meghan went to put Malcolm's food and bedding in the car and came back inside.

Ready to leave now, with her shoulder bag slung over her right shoulder and a doggy carrier in each hand, she smiled at Leo and said, "Good night, Mr. Darcy." Her tone was intentionally light, and her eyes danced with humor.

"What if Malcolm falls for Chauncey? It'll break his heart when he can't see her every day," Leo said in a last bid to get her to stay.

"Oh, don't worry about that happening," Meghan said as she stepped onto the porch, Leo holding the door open for her. "Chauncey's two years old. She's *way* too old for him."

# *Chapter 5*

Meghan phoned Leo an hour after leaving his house to let him know they'd arrived home safely. Leo had moved from the living room to the bedroom and stretched out on the bed. He'd been camping in the living room because he'd had to let Malcolm outside so often.

"Malcolm isn't giving you any trouble, is he?" he asked as he sat propped up on pillows.

"No, Chauncey is showing him around the place. I just saw her demonstrate how to use the doggy door in the kitchen a minute ago. She's taking good care of him."

"And how are you?" he asked, his voice husky.

In Raleigh, Meghan was sitting on the sofa in the living room with her legs stretched out. She'd changed into pajama pants and a thin sleep T-shirt, both in white.

This was the first time she'd spoken to him over the phone. His voice sounded sexy in spite of his cold. Or maybe she hadn't built up an immunity to his charms as she'd pretended to have done. "I'm fine. Don't worry about me. Just concentrate on getting better."

"I would hate for you to catch my cold," he persisted.

Meghan laughed softly, "Leo, I didn't touch you once when I was there. I wash my hands a lot. So don't worry."

He was well aware that she hadn't touched him. Of course, logically, he hadn't wanted her to risk catching his cold and had understood her reluctance to touch him. On the other hand, he'd craved her touch so badly, it had been painful being so close to her, knowing it wasn't going to happen. Now, he remembered their day together that Saturday with nostalgic fervor. When he'd shaken her hand as they were parting, he'd wanted to hold on longer but hadn't wanted her to think he was strange.

"What are you doing?" he casually asked.

"I'm sitting on the sofa in my jammies," Meghan said lightly. "Watching a movie."

"What's it called?" Leo asked. "No, let me guess. *Sense and Sensibility? Pride and Prejudice?* Or *Persuasion*?"

"None of the above, Mr. Darcy. I'm watching the magnificent story of the Delany sisters," Meghan said smugly.

"*The Magnificent Story of the Delany Sisters?* I didn't know Jane Austen wrote a book with that title."

"That's because she didn't," Meghan informed him, smiling.

Leo could hear the smile in her tone, and he smiled, too, imagining her face as she spoke. "Okay, I'll tell you what I'm watching, but you have to promise not to roll your eyes."

"Done," Leo quickly agreed.

"It's a 1999 drama about Sadie and Bessie Delany, sisters from Raleigh who lived to be over a hundred years old."

Leo didn't roll his eyes, but he wasn't surprised in the least that she was watching a movie about history. "They really existed?"

"Do you remember me telling you about Saint Augustine's College, another HBCU in Raleigh?"

"Yes." He coughed. "Excuse me a sec," he said, and he put the phone down and blew his nose. Picking it up again, he said, "I'm back. Go ahead and tell me about the Delany sisters."

"Their father, Henry Beard Delany, was the first African American Episcopal bishop. He worked at Saint Augustine's, and that's where he and his wife raised their ten children, Bessie and Sadie among them."

"Wow, people had big families back then," Leo commented.

"Yeah," Meghan agreed. "Women were made of better stuff back then. I'd be happy with half that many."

Hearing that, Leo's hopes for something meaningful to happen between the two of them were dashed to pieces. Five children. Meghan wanted five children. He could imagine her with five children, too. That was the part that hurt the most. Five children, a young, robust man to father them and a beautiful house in the suburbs where she would garden and haul all those children around in a big SUV.

Even after that devastating revelation, he soldiered on. "Are you actually going to give birth to those five children, or adopt one or two?" he jokingly asked.

Meghan laughed, "I'm strong and healthy. I think I can have them the old-fashioned way. But I'm not averse to adopting. There are a lot of kids out there who need homes, and I'm not stuck on my children having to come from my body." She stopped suddenly. "I feel like I've said too much."

"No, no," Leo reassured her. "You've said just enough." He didn't have to fake a yawn. He really was exhausted, and the impact of Meghan's revelation had done a number on his psyche.

Fight, his father had told him. He wished he were more confident about the outcome of this fight. Did he actually have a chance of winning?

Hearing his yawn, Meghan quietly said, "Get some rest, Leo. I'll phone you tomorrow and let you know how your baby boy is doing."

She glanced at Chauncey and Malcolm, who had curled up in front of the fireplace and were sharing Chauncey's comfy bed.

"I think they've decided to go to sleep for the night," Meghan told Leo. "I'm going to snooze right here on the sofa so I can keep an eye on them for a while. Good night, Leo."

"Good night, Meghan. Thanks again for your help. You're a sweetheart."

Meghan sighed after she'd hit the off button on her cell phone. "Leo, Leo, what is it about you that I like so much? I need my head examined!"

Fluffing up her pillows on the sofa, she snuggled into them and turned the DVD player back on. On the screen, Ruby Dee and Diahann Carroll were having a lively conversation about men. Both actresses had undoubtedly needed to spend a long time in the makeup chair in order to portray the Delany sisters, Bessie and Sadie, who were in their hundreds in the scene that was being played out. They were talking about how neither of them had had long relationships with men. Their longest relationship was with each other. Were they trying to say women who didn't have a man in their lives lived longer?

Meghan laughed quietly so as not to disturb Chauncey and her houseguest. There could be something to that theory. Here she was thinking about a man who clearly didn't give her a second thought.

Yawning, she closed her eyes and soon was asleep, the remote still in her hand.

Chauncey licked her face to awaken her the next morning. Meghan sprang up, wiping her face and laughing. "Ugh, morning breath!"

She stood up and Chauncey and Malcolm danced around her long legs, obviously ready for their breakfast. "Okay, okay," Meghan cried, heading to the kitchen and the pantry. "Good thing it's Saturday and I have all day to be at your beck and call."

After filling their bowls with food and freshening up their drinking water, Meghan left them to their repast and trudged to the bathroom.

Once she'd seen to her more urgent needs, she lingered at the sink and examined her face in the mirror. She wiped the sleep out of the corners of her eyes and grimaced. She liked her face, even though she didn't consider herself to be beautiful.

She liked her nose, even though it was a little too long. She liked her unruly hair, especially in the morning when it was all over the place, and she rarely cut it so it was nearly to her waist. Her sister Petra's was at her butt. Petra didn't get to a salon often since she lived mostly in the equatorial jungle in Central Africa.

Meghan was grateful for what God had given her. It was simply that she didn't care so much about the physical face other people saw when they looked at her. She cared more about the person inside and the legacy she would leave behind.

If that made her strange, then so be it.

"Wonder how Mr. Darcy's doing this morning," she murmured and then checked herself. They said talking to yourself was the first sign of madness. *In which case all of us are a little crazy.* She smiled at that and went to the kitchen to make herself some breakfast.

She turned the TV to the Weather Channel and listened as she scrambled a couple of eggs and made wheat toast. As soon as she sat down to enjoy her meal and a glass of orange-pineapple juice, her cell phone, next to her plate at the island in the kitchen, rang. Recognizing the ringtone as belonging to her mother, she started to let it go but thought better of it. Virginia Gaines was not a woman to be ignored.

"Good morning, Momma," she answered pleasantly.

"Good morning, Meggie," Virginia said, her tone sweet.

*Uh-oh*, Meghan thought. *She wants something.* Normally her mother's voice was no-nonsense. When she phoned, it wasn't to chitchat. Virginia Gaines wasn't one of those mothers who tried to be best friends with her children. She was the mother, and that was perfectly clear.

"I was wondering if you're free for lunch today. Marjorie and I would like to speak with you about your career path. We can go to that place your little friend from high school works at."

"Mother, Annie owns that café, and she's doing very well. She's a formidable businesswoman."

"Sorry I ruffled your feathers this early in the morning." Virginia came back with the guilt, which she was an expert at.

Meghan sighed softly. "I'm sorry, too, but I'm busy today. We'll have to make it another time. I'm babysitting a puppy for a friend of mine who's sick."

"A friend?" Virginia asked, curious. "Which friend?"

"You don't know her," Meghan said. There was no way in Hades she was going to discuss Leo with her mother. Virginia Gaines would want to do a full background check on the poor man.

"Oh, I have the perfect solution," Virginia cried.

"Marjorie and I will come to you! I'll pick up takeout for us on the way. We'll be there around noonish."

Meghan glanced down at the time on her cell phone. That meant she had around three and a half hours to make her place spick-and-span clean. Her mother was a stickler for cleanliness. Meghan was surprised she didn't carry a supply of white gloves in her designer bag specifically for random inspections.

"That's fine," Meghan agreed. "Bye, Momma. Love you."

"I love you more," Virginia stated before hanging up.

"There goes my peaceful Saturday!" Meghan groused and continued eating her breakfast. It had gotten cold while she was talking to her mother.

It wasn't that she didn't love her mother. She adored her. All of her sisters adored Virginia. That didn't erase the fact that their mother had a problem. She liked to micromanage their lives, or try to. She and her sisters had learned how to reject their mother's interference and stay on speaking terms with her. That didn't mean spending time with her wasn't sometimes frustrating. Such was life, and it was one of the things they'd learned to live with because even though Virginia seemed to be improving a little, she was never really going to change her psychological makeup.

Meghan was hoping her mother would mellow with age. But so far, that hadn't happened.

She concentrated on the Weather Channel while she finished eating. The weatherman said that it looked like they were in for a warm-up this weekend, but not to get too excited because the forecast showed the beginning of December and possibly all of December promised to be very cold indeed. Meghan shuddered, remembering last winter when half of America had been plagued by snowstorms. Even the South hadn't been spared tons of snow.

Chauncey trotted up to her, resting her forepaws on Meghan's thigh, her brown eyes pleading for a taste of Meghan's scrambled eggs. Meghan gave her a little. "Now, go play while you can. You don't know how long Malcolm's going to be here. His dad might be feeling a lot better today. Speaking of which..."

She stood up and drank a little of her juice to clear her throat before dialing Leo's number.

He answered on the second ring. She smiled. She hoped that meant he'd been anticipating her call.

"Good morning, Miss Elizabeth," he said, with a note of laughter in his voice.

Meghan laughed shortly, "So it's like that now, huh? I'm actually flattered. Elizabeth Bennet had a lot of qualities I admire in a heroine. She was smart, funny and was able to admit when she was wrong. You sound a lot better today. Did you get a good night's rest?"

"I did," Leo said. "I feel more energetic this morning. I didn't realize how beneficial a good night's rest is."

Meghan smiled again at his word choices. He sounded just like an English professor.

"Yeah," Meghan said. "Uninterrupted rest is the best thing for a cold. Any illness, really, since it's when you're asleep that your body gets the chance to heal."

"I can't thank you enough."

"Stop, you've already thanked me enough," Meghan told him. "I just called to let you know Malcolm is doing fine. He's having fun. When do you want me to bring him home? Chauncey is enjoying him so much I was hoping you'd let him stay at least another night."

In Durham, Leo was pacing the kitchen floor in his robe and a pair of Adidas slides. He had made himself a fruit smoothie this morning. The blender was still on the counter, and a tall glass of frothy smoothie was in his left hand as he held the cell phone to his ear with his right. He wanted to see Meghan as soon as possible and was about to say he'd like Malcolm back home today, but he didn't want to be selfish. If Chauncey was enjoying Malcolm's company, the least he could do was let Meghan's dog have her day. "Tomorrow will be soon enough," he said. "What are your plans today with them?"

"I'll probably take them to the neighborhood park and let them romp later on today. But first, I'm going to have company. Remember I told you about my mom and my godmother, who are both educators?"

"Uh-huh," Leo said, with a note of interest in his voice.

"They're coming over today to give me their annual pep talk, or rather, their 'so what are you doing with your life, Meghan?' talk. I call them the Higher Education Mafia because they usually make you an offer you can't refuse. Or, according to them, you *shouldn't* refuse if you have any sense."

"They don't approve of your working at Shaw?" Leo asked.

"They have nothing against Shaw," Meghan said. "They simply have something against remaining in one place too long. Or not living up to your full potential. They believe black folks need to be strivers, always trying to improve their positions. On a personal note, they also believe I'm at Shaw out of some exaggerated sense of loyalty since I was an undergraduate there. Although I got my master's from Duke and my doctorate from Howard."

On his end, Leo was setting his glass on the countertop and climbing onto a stool at the island. Recalling what Jake had told him about Meghan's broken relationship with the quarterback she'd met at Shaw, he wondered if that was the reason her mother and godmother thought she had an unusual attachment to the school. Memories of a lost love? He dared not broach that subject, though, because then Meghan would know he'd been digging up information on her behind her back. That wouldn't be good.

Or would it? Meghan struck him as someone who appreciated honesty. There were some things he couldn't come right out and tell her, like he had a heart condition and was sterile. Essentially, a dead man walking. But he could at least be honest about other things.

"Meghan, I hope you won't think I've been prying into your business," he said cautiously, "but Jake told me about the guy you were involved with at Shaw."

He heard her sharp intake of breath and thought she was about to hang up on him or say something cutting. But she only exhaled and said, "Yeah, but that was a long time ago and I'm totally over Chauncey Evans."

"Chauncey," Leo said. "I *thought* that was a male name."

"I named her Chauncey after him just to prove to myself that I could use his name on a daily basis and not react negatively to it. I don't feel anything for the first bearer of that name, but I dearly love the second bearer of it."

Leo sat on his stool, feeling stunned by her admission. Stunned and totally in awe of her strength and resilience. "I wish I were there to hug you, Meghan Gaines. Even if I do have a cold and you might catch it."

"I wish you were here, too, Mr. Darcy," Meghan said, her voice breaking. She cleared her throat. "I'd better go. The Higher Education Mafia will be here all too soon. Bye for now, and spoil yourself today. Watch *The Godfather*."

"How do you know I love that movie?"

"You're a red-blooded American male, aren't you?" Meghan said with a note of laughter.

The Mafia arrived promptly at noon. Meghan's mom, Virginia, looking positively glowing in her winter togs of expensive dark brown lined wool slacks, a caramel-colored V-neck cashmere sweater and a faux-fur-lined jacket. On her small feet were leather boots with three-inch heels nearly the same shade as her sweater, and she was surrounded by an appropriately understated cloud of her signature perfume, Chanel No. 5.

Her best friend, Marjorie, who dressed much more casually, was wearing designer jeans, a long-sleeve T-shirt in jade, a cute little black leather jacket and a pair of black Nikes. She was the first one through the door and hugged Meghan tightly. She wore her black hair in a pixie cut and used minimal makeup. Her golden-brown skin was smooth and showed very little aging, except for crinkles around her hazel eyes.

Meghan kissed her cheek. "Hello, Auntie Marjie," she murmured close to her godmother's ear. Meghan had been calling her godmother Auntie Marjie since childhood.

"Hello, sweetheart," Marjorie cooed affectionately.

Meghan had to bend a little to hug her godmother. Marjorie was five-two and around 110 pounds. Her mother was shorter and a tad heavier than Marjorie, but not by much.

While Meghan was hugging her godmother, Virginia set the takeout she'd brought on the island's countertop in the kitchen. Chauncey and Malcolm ran to her, hoping she'd pet them, maybe share a little of that delicious-smelling food she was carrying, but she merely glared at them until they lost their nerve and hightailed it for the relative safety of the living room.

Meghan released Marjorie and went and hugged her mother, who squeezed her tightly, with an exaggerated moan at the end. Looking around, as she removed her jacket, Virginia said, "The place looks good." She inhaled the pleasant Febreze-scented air. "No pet smells."

Her mother didn't allow pets in her house. She believed there was no way to prevent a house from smelling like its occupants, human or animal. "Just because you have pets doesn't mean your house has to smell bad," Meghan said. "Not if you keep your house and your pets clean. Which I do."

Her godmother gave her a sly encouraging nod. Marjorie was a pet lover, too. She went over and gave Chauncey and Malcolm warm pats on their heads. "Hello, pretty girl. Who is this handsome guy, mmm?"

Chauncey and Malcolm wagged their tails in appreciation for her kindness. Marjorie looked at Meghan. "Who is this? You got Chauncey a companion?"

"That's Malcolm. He belongs to a friend," Meghan explained. "I'm just taking care of him for a day or two."

"Well, he's gorgeous," Marjorie said. She joined Meghan and Virginia in the kitchen.

Meghan went to get plates and silverware while her mother started removing the takeout from paper bags. The food turned out to be hickory-smoked barbecue from an African American–owned soul food restaurant the family had frequented for a number of years.

Meghan looked at her mother with appreciation. The woman knew her food. "My favorite," she said with a smile.

Virginia smiled. "I know." Then she added, "Better get the big white dish towels so we can protect our clothes from barbecue sauce."

Meghan looked in the drawer next to the stove. She

had the dishcloths and towels in there. She selected three towels, returned to the island and handed them out.

They all tucked them into the necks of their shirts like bibs and then filled their plates with barbecued ribs and chicken, coleslaw and baked beans. There was cheesy corn bread, too, with jalapeño peppers and whole corn kernels in the batter.

As they consumed the food, Meghan looked at her mother and godmother and said, "To what do I owe the pleasure of your company today?" They liked it when she behaved like a proper Southern belle. She obliged them as long as it didn't entail losing herself in the role. She loved listening to them regale her with tales of what it used to be like to be a black woman in the South. All the things they'd had to go through to maintain their dignity. To keep their families together. To support the men in their lives and help them maintain their sense of purpose. They were incredible women, and a lot of their advice was solid gold. However, she took everything they told her and weighed it against her own goals in life. She was, after all, her own woman.

Virginia wiped her hands on her towel and put it down on the countertop. She looked her daughter in the eye. "Marjorie and I think it's time you seriously considered a position at Duke. I'll let her explain."

"I'm taking the English department in a new, exciting direction," Marjorie said with a smile. "Much more African American lit. The whole African diaspora, really. I've hired a professor who is doing wonderful things with African American literature. He's a dynamic speaker, has written numerous, well-received articles and a couple of acclaimed novels. He is heading the new program, but I want you to work closely with him. He'll supervise you for a while but, depending on your performance, that won't last long. I want you on my team."

Meghan realized her godmother was talking about Leo. She looked from her mother's expectant face to her godmother's. Were these two education mavens doing some not-so-subtle matchmaking? Did Marjorie realize Jake and Leo Wolfe were twins? It was true that Marjorie hadn't met Jake yet, so maybe she hadn't connected the two men who had the same last name. To say nothing of very similar faces.

Yet Meghan wrinkled her nose. Something didn't smell right here.

She had a few pertinent questions she needed answers to. "What is the name of this super professor?" she asked Marjorie.

"Leo Wolfe," Marjorie answered innocently enough.

"And when did you start considering hiring him?"

"Oh, more than a year ago," Marjorie said nonchalantly. "I like to be sure about my choices. I'd been looking at him for quite a while before I contacted him about nine months ago. After I made an offer, he took his time weighing his options."

Meghan inwardly breathed a sigh of relief. If what her godmother said was true, then hiring Leo had had nothing at all to do with her. She didn't believe Marjorie would lie to her. She was the type of woman who would gladly own up to matchmaking if that was what she was engaged in.

Therefore her godmother could not have possibly hired Leo with the intention of setting him up with her.

But was her mother also in the dark about who Leo really was?

She hadn't spoken to anyone in the family about Leo except Mina. Mina and Jake apparently hadn't made an announcement to the family about Leo's moving to the area. If they had, Desiree and Lauren, who both lived in Raleigh, would have been calling her and making plans on how best to welcome their new soon-to-be in-law to the area.

Mina and Jake must have had a reason to remain silent about Leo. Had Leo asked them to let him have his privacy for as long as possible? That made sense to Meghan.

Therefore, she didn't tell her mother and godmother she knew Leo. She simply smiled at them and said, "I'll consider the offer and get back to you, Auntie Marjie. Thank you for your continued faith in me."

From the relieved expressions on their faces, Meghan knew she'd made them happy with that reply. The other times her godmother had asked her to join the faculty at Duke, Meghan had politely turned her down. The Mafia probably thought her actually considering the offer was a step in the right direction.

# Chapter 6

Meghan returned Malcolm to his human the next day around eleven in the morning. She was met at the door by a much-improved-looking Leo, wearing jeans that could have been sculpted to his hard body and a gray short-sleeve T-shirt that made her jealous. She wished she could be that close to his muscular chest.

He smiled at her, and her legs went weak. She handed him the pet carrier with Malcolm in it and Malcolm went nuts inside the carrier, he was so happy to see Leo. She turned around and started walking back out to her car.

"Where're you going?" Leo anxiously asked. "You're not staying awhile?"

"To get Chauncey," Meghan called over her shoulder. "She put up such a ruckus when I put Malcolm in his carrier that I brought her, too."

Leo laughed as he carried Malcolm inside, set the carrier on the foyer floor and let Malcolm out. Malcolm jumped up on Leo's legs with delight. Leo knelt and let Malcolm lick his face. "I missed you, too, buddy."

He heard Meghan coming into the house. He glanced up to see her carrying Chauncey in her arms, a smile on her face. She set Chauncey down, and Chauncey wasted no time joining Leo and Malcolm. Leo scratched her behind the ears and she snuggled closer.

The scene melted Meghan's heart. A man who loved animals was high on her list of priorities when it came to choosing someone to be with. Leo looked up at her and their eyes met across the room.

He rose, leaving Malcolm and Chauncey to entertain themselves, which they were more than happy to do. He walked over to Meghan, his eyes never leaving her face.

"Good day, Miss Elizabeth. You look lovely."

Meghan pushed a tendril of hair behind her ear. "Oh, this old thing?" she joked, referring to the black jogging suit she was wearing. Her hair fell down her back in loose curls, and she was wearing her favorite white Nikes. She'd planned on taking Chauncey for a walk after they'd brought Malcolm back home.

She felt like an awkward teen trying to talk to the hottest boy in school. Timid and shivery. "You look good yourself, Mr. Darcy."

Leo gave her an appreciative once-over, then met her eyes. Meghan fell deeper under that magnetic gaze and started moving closer to him as if she had no will of her own. “Do you think it would be okay if I hugged you?” Leo softly asked. “I won’t breathe on you, I swear.”

“I think that would be okay,” Meghan said and went into his open arms. Her body immediately relaxed in his embrace. She let go. That was the only way she could describe it. She let go of the hurt feelings, the invisible barrier she’d erected around her heart to keep it from being damaged by yet another insensitive male. Most of all, she let go of the lies she’d been telling herself about Leo. Foremost, the one that stated she didn’t care about him. Because, the fact was, she did care about this mysterious man.

Leo held her close to his chest and inhaled the wonderful scent of her, clean, fresh and subtly spicy. If he kissed her, he knew she’d taste like cinnamon. Or some other sweet-smelling spice.

His right hand was at the base of her neck. Her thick hair felt like silk. Her warm skin, beneath the fleece jacket, enticed him. He wanted to touch her bare skin, but knew that would be an invasion somehow. He was happy to just hold her. That was a major improvement. The fact that she was not drawing away from him and her body felt relaxed in his arms gave him hope that one day she would feel totally safe in his embrace.

They stood there for nearly two minutes before the dogs jumped up on them, breaking the spell. Laughing, they succumbed to their pets’ playfulness and let them romp all over their humans on the living room floor.

“What are we going to do about these two?” Leo

asked, laughing. "It's obvious they're wild about each other."

"We should set up a playdate," Meghan suggested. "Maybe next Saturday?"

Leo smiled at her. "It's a date."

Meghan's cell phone rang as she and Leo were getting up off the floor. She reached into her jacket pocket and glanced at the display. Lauren. Her heart immediately started beating fast. Lauren was nine months pregnant and could deliver at any time.

"Lauren!" she cried. "I'm here. Are you all right?"

"No," Lauren moaned. "I'm in the delivery room right now and my husband just passed out. I need you, M!"

"Girl, you should have called me when you went into labor. You promised me you would do that."

"Don't chastise me now, Mommy," Lauren joked. "Colton swore he could handle it. He wanted it to be an experience the two of us could share for years to come. Now he's out cold and I'm by myself."

"I'm on the way," Meghan told her. "Bye."

After she'd hung up, she turned to Leo. "I guess you got the gist of that. My sister's in labor." She looked around, a desperate look in her eyes. Then her gaze met his. "Will you watch Chauncey for me?"

"Of course," Leo immediately answered. "She'll be fine here."

Meghan threw herself into his arms and planted an impulsive kiss on his cheek. Leo gave a dazed smile. "Go, go, and call me later, please."

Meghan was running for the door. "I will, and thanks so much, Leo!"

Leo was just happy to be able to return the favor—just happy that she didn't consider him to be untouchable anymore.

He went to the door and watched her run to the Mustang, start it and drive away.

He felt excited for her and her family. A new life coming into the world was a momentous occasion. It was something that made you contemplate the divine.

By the time Meghan got to the hospital, her parents and her sister Desiree were sitting in the birth-and-delivery waiting room, all looking nervous. Her mother rushed to her when she walked in.

"Lauren won't let anyone back there except you. What is wrong with that girl? A mother should be with her daughter when she gives birth."

Meghan hugged her mother tightly. She had no time for histrionics. Her sister needed her. "Momma, just pray. I'm going back there." She turned her mother in the direction of her father, who had risen when she walked in, too. Alphonse pulled his petite wife into his arms. "Come on, Ginny, sit down and let the girl do what she came to do—help calm Lauren so she can bring our grandchild into the world."

Desiree, who always had her sisters' backs, winked at Meghan. "Go on, sis, tell her she's got this!"

Meghan had to check in at the nurses' desk, after which a male nurse outfitted her with a gown, gloves and a cap and instructed her on how to properly wash her hands before she could go into the delivery room where Lauren was.

Meghan was pleased to see Colton there, over his fainting spell now, standing next to Lauren's bed, holding her hand. Or, rather, Lauren was squeezing his hand while she was going through a painful contraction. Lauren gave a high-pitched squeak when she saw her sister and Meghan hurried to her bedside.

Meghan didn't judge Colton harshly when he stepped aside, a slight look of relief on his face, and let Meghan hold Lauren's hand. "How long have you guys been here?" Meghan whispered as she leaned toward him.

"Four hours," he said, his gray eyes haunted. "I can't stand to see her in so much pain." All of this was said in low tones to keep Lauren from overhearing.

But she overheard anyway. "I'm fine, Colton, don't worry about me and the baby. Now that Meghan's here, I want you to go take a breather. I'll be all right until you get back."

"But..." Colton protested. He looked exhausted, not so much from physical exertion but from fear and worry.

"You have my permission to leave the room," Lauren insisted as another contraction ripped through her body. Her beautiful brown eyes stretched wide as the wave of pain reached a crescendo, then lessened.

Colton went and kissed her cheek, then beat a hasty retreat, suddenly deciding to do as she asked. Meghan guessed he didn't want to add more stress to this situation. She knew he didn't want to leave Lauren. He probably felt, like most fathers, that he wasn't a man unless he had the courage to stick by his wife's side while she did all the work and gave birth to his child. Yet it was also his job to do whatever she said when she was in this physical state. So he granted her wish.

When he was gone, Lauren grabbed Meghan around the neck and pulled her close to her perspiring face. "I love that man, but when he took a look down there he blacked out so fast I was afraid he was going to crack his skull on the floor. Good thing we're in a hospital." Then she laughed uproariously, and Meghan laughed with her. Meghan knew that her sister was going to be fine.

She hugged her tightly and looked her in the eyes. "Desiree said to tell you you've got this!"

"Of course I've got this," Lauren said as she released Meghan and lay back on the pillows in the hospital bed. "I just don't want to be alone when I give birth, that's all. The pain's worse than I imagined. Don't let anyone tell you giving birth is a breeze. But I'll do whatever it takes to deliver a healthy child. He's who I care about. I love this boy so much. I can't begin to describe how much of my heart he's already claimed, and I don't even have him in my arms yet."

Meghan smiled down at her. "Oh, I think I can imagine how much."

Lauren grabbed her hand, moaned loudly and started squeezing so hard the pain almost brought Meghan to her knees. "Another contraction?" Meghan croaked.

"Uh-huh," Lauren said and groaned as the pain sharpened. "Only two minutes apart now. This boy is coming soon."

The fetal monitor began beeping like crazy. A nurse swiftly came into the room, smiling. "Let's get this show on the road!" she said cheerfully.

She was followed by three more hospital personnel, one of them Lauren's obstetrician, an African American woman in her midforties.

Meghan glanced at the stitched name on the doctor's white coat: Dr. Gladys Tulloch. Dr. Tulloch started giving orders and the nurses around her sprang into action, positioning Lauren in the bed so she could begin pushing, configuring the bed to support her body more efficiently. Then she looked at Meghan. "Your sister, I presume," she said to Lauren. "Is she staying for the big event?"

Lauren looked at Meghan with pleading eyes. "Yes, I'm staying," Meghan told Dr. Tulloch.

"And would somebody please go tell my husband it's time?" Lauren asked.

One of the hospital's personnel exited the room to do so.

"All right, Lauren," Dr. Tulloch said. "It's okay to push now, but concentrate for me. Push, but try not to strain. Slowly and gently."

Lauren closed her eyes and grasped Meghan's hand tightly.

A couple of minutes later, Colton returned and Meghan handed Lauren off to him and stepped aside. She stood in the back of the room, making sure Lauren could see her there, knowing her presence was a comfort to Lauren. Then she watched the miracle of birth. Up close and personal. And when her nephew came into the world, screaming his lungs out, she cried with relief and happiness.

Lauren came through like a trouper, and the baby was a bruiser at nearly nine pounds. Colton was crying, too, as the doctor handed the baby to him after she'd cut the umbilical cord and wrapped him in his swaddling clothes. Lauren, understandably exhausted, fell back on the pillow, laughing softly with tears streaming down her face. "Bring him to me, babe. Let me look at him."

Colton lifted the baby close and Lauren peered into his face. The baby's eyes were still closed and he seemed to be trying to suck on his balled-up fist. "He's got your healthy appetite," Lauren joked. "He's already looking for something to eat."

Meghan moved closer. Her nephew had a headful of black curls and was possibly the most beautiful baby she'd ever seen. She smiled. Wasn't that how everyone felt about babies? They were all beautiful.

She took her cell phone out and asked the new parents' permission to take a few photos. Permission granted, she took several of the proud parents with Colton, Jr. between them.

She sent the photos to all of her sisters, her parents, grandparents, godmother and a few other relatives on her contact list. Before she'd even walked back down the hall to the waiting room, she'd gotten a message from Petra in Central Africa: Our first nephew!!! He's so handsome. Give my love to the new parents. I wish I could be there.

* * *

The next few weeks, the family was obsessed with the arrival of Colton, Jr., or CJ, as everyone was calling him. Meghan visited as often as she could to lend a hand with whatever Lauren and Colton needed. They were both taking time off from work, though, so little was needed except for the occasional babysitting to give both of them a chance to get out of the house for an hour or two.

Shaw closed for the winter holidays in early December, and classes weren't set to resume until the beginning of January, so Meghan had time on her hands. She and Leo met once a week for playdates for Chauncey and Malcolm, and while the dogs raced about the park, content to be together, they chatted about anything and everything.

They hadn't had any physical contact since Meghan had kissed his cheek, and even though she knew from the lingering looks he gave her that hc wanted more, she was not going to go there. He had to be the one to initiate the next move. She didn't know what was preventing him from making that move, but she knew it was something deeply personal. She'd probably read too much Jane Austen, about social rules and people who dared not cross them, but she also felt that there was something to those stories. Like the notion of waiting for true love and not rushing into a relationship.

Sure, Leo hadn't pulled her into his arms and ravished her, and something told her that was as it should be. Whatever happened between them had to take its natural course. So she was content with being his friend and occasionally catching him watching her with longing evident in his gaze. That look made her skin tingle. It gave her hope, too. One of these days, she was sure, he was going to act on those sensual thoughts and she would reap the rewards for being so patient.

The weekend of Mina and Jake's wedding arrived. Leo went to Florida and picked up his parents and his grandparents because, although they dearly wanted to be at the ceremony, his grandparents had never been on a plane in their lives and they weren't going to start flying in their nineties.

They stayed with Leo for a couple of days, and then they all piled into Leo's SUV the day before the wedding and he drove them to the Great Smoky Mountains and the town of Cherokee, where the wedding would be held at the lodge Mina's grandfather had owned for years but which Mina now managed. Her grandfather had retired after remarrying in his eighties.

The lodge was a magnificent three-story pinewood building with guest rooms on every level, and the property was dotted by cabins on the perimeter. Benjamin Beck, the girls' grandfather, had combined two cultures when he'd designed it: his, African American, and his first wife's, Native American. The two-story entrance had a huge door with a totem pole on either side. The intricately carved double wooden door had images of deer, bears, foxes and elk, all taken from Native American lore. Inside, the spacious lobby was decorated with both African and Native American art. The highly polished dark hardwood floors shone, and the sofas and chairs were done in light earth tones with Native American print throw rugs and African sculptures in wood and stone on pedestals at strategic places in the big room.

Leo got a kick out of seeing his grandma Etta Mae craning her neck to take in all the sights, her eyes stretched wide behind her thick glasses. "This is like something out of a fairy tale," she said softly, sounding awestruck.

The five of them walked up to the registration desk in the lobby and were warmly greeted by the young woman behind it. "Good afternoon, welcome to Beck's Wilderness Lodge. How can I help you?"

Leo didn't get the chance to reply because Mina came rushing toward them, a huge grin on her pretty face. Her glorious natural hair was in braids that were parted in the middle, beautifully framing her features. "Leo," she cried. "You're here!"

Leo wasn't surprised that Jake wasn't with her. Jake had told him he had some business in Atlanta, but would return later that afternoon.

Leo moved forward and hugged her, after which he moved aside. Mina hugged each of his parents and grandparents in turn. But she held on to his mother a little longer, saying apologetically, "Thank you for traveling so far to be here. The day wouldn't have been complete without you."

Leo stood back and watched her interact with his family. He could see by the expressions on his folks' faces that they were utterly charmed by Mina. And he was proud and happy for his brother to be marrying such a sincerely kind woman. Of course, that brought thoughts of Meghan to the forefront. He was looking forward to seeing her today.

In the last few weeks, they'd been able to forge a friendship. He was enjoying her company. He believed she was enjoying his, too. Now, if he could put aside his fear of rejection, maybe they could take their friendship to the next level. His folks had asked a lot of questions about her on the drive up here. Obviously his father had been talking about his predicament with the rest of the family since Leo's visit on Thanksgiving. He just hoped his father would be able to contain his joy when he finally introduced him to Meghan and wouldn't say something that would make her wonder just how much he'd told his father about her.

In retrospect, it had been presumptuous of him to dream of a real relationship with Meghan Gaines so soon after meeting her.

What if his assumption that she was attracted to him was wrong? He would look like a lovesick fool.

"Let me show you to your rooms," Mina said excitedly. Leo stopped daydreaming about Meghan and followed her sister to a couple of suites on the ground floor. He suspected she'd thoughtfully given them downstairs rooms because of his grandparents' advanced age.

After he'd gotten his folks settled in their rooms, he went for a walk to stretch his legs after the long trip and to phone the kennel that was boarding Malcolm for the weekend.

The temperature was in the low thirties, but the day was bright and clear, and the lodge was surrounded by beautiful pine trees, which gave the air a sharp, aromatic smell. He breathed deeply as he walked.

The kennel staff member told him Malcolm was well, if a little quiet, which was not unexpected as far as Leo was concerned. He thanked her and hung up.

Glancing in the direction of the lodge, which was about fifty yards away by now, he spied Meghan walking toward him with Chauncey on a leash. It occurred to him that he could have brought Malcolm if only he'd had the presence of mind to ask if pets were allowed on the premises.

She spotted him and waved, then they began walking swiftly toward each other. When they met up, Leo bent and gave Meghan a hug. "Hi, how are you two? Did you have a nice trip up?"

Meghan squeezed him tight before letting go. "We're doing just great. And the trip was interesting. My parents, Desiree, Lauren, Colton and the baby rode together in the general's Hummer. With Chauncey in the back in her carrier. And with Momma worrying that maybe the baby shouldn't be in a car breathing dog-infested air. Oh, I swear, that woman is going to make me crazy before it's over."

Leo laughed, "Sounds like she's got some serious issues with pets. What happened? Was she bitten by a dog when she was a little girl or something?"

"I don't know," Meghan said, laughing, too. "But I'm going to get to the root of the problem." She took a deep breath and exhaled. "How was your trip? Mina told me you went to Florida to pick up your folks. How are they enjoying North Carolina so far?"

"They love it," Leo told her. "You should have seen my grandma's face when she walked into the lobby. She said it looked like something out of a fairy tale."

"Aw, she's sweet," Meghan cried, beaming. "So, when do I get to meet them? Tonight at the dinner they're having for us at the lodge, or tomorrow at the reception?"

"Why not right now?" Leo asked, his light brown eyes taking in the way her full lips curved when she grinned like that.

Meghan smiled even wider when she caught him looking at her mouth. "I'd love to."

His parents and grandparents were relaxing in one of the suites when he and Meghan got back to the lodge. The room was large, with two king-size beds and a sitting area with two sofas facing each other, a coffee table between them. There was a football game on the big-screen TV, and his father and grandfather were sipping beers while his mother and grandmother were enjoying glasses of white wine.

Meghan's first impression of them was that they certainly knew how to enjoy themselves. And her second thought was that Leo looked just like his parents. He had his mother's eyes and his father's build and facial construction. Now she knew how he would look when he was older. He'd still be a handsome man.

Meghan was hugged by everyone, including Leo's grandfather, who normally didn't hug anyone. Leander muted the TV so they could sit down and chat awhile.

Meghan sat on one of the sofas beside Etta Mae,

and Chauncey sat at her feet and laid her head on her paws. Katherine smiled at the pooch. "She's beautiful. What do you call her?"

"Chauncey," Meghan said with a warm smile.

"She's so well-mannered," Katherine said. "Did you train her yourself?"

"We're both works in progress," Meghan said jokingly.

Katherine chuckled. "Isn't that the truth? Sometimes pets teach their owners more than their owners teach them!"

Meghan was inundated with questions about herself, and although she was glad Leo's family was showing an interest and were such nice people, it did make her wonder exactly what Leo had told them about her.

By the time she got up to leave, she'd decided that maybe Leo had talked her up just a little to his loved ones. That meant maybe, just maybe, Leo Wolfe was softening.

# *Chapter 7*

"Oh, my God, did Jake shave his head, grow a beard and start dressing like he just stepped off the pages of *GQ*?" Desiree exclaimed rather loudly.

Meghan, who was sitting at a table with her family in the dining room of the lodge that night for dinner, didn't even need to glance up to figure out her sister was referring to Leo, who happened to be entering the dining room with his parents and grandparents.

She was grateful that the other fifty or so diners, some of whom she knew, and all of whom were dressed in varying degrees of semicasual attire, were carrying on lively conversations around them, so Leo probably hadn't heard Desiree's comment.

He did look in their direction, though, saw her and smiled at her. She smiled back, then he and his party followed the hostess to their table on the other side of the room.

Her group consisted of her parents, her grandfather and step-grandmother, and Desiree, Marjorie and Marjorie's husband, Professor Rudolf Langdon. Lauren and Colton had opted to dine in their cabin, where they were watching over Colton, Jr.

Marjorie had been looking down at her cell phone when Leo and his party entered the dining room, but she raised her gaze to see what the commotion was about and exclaimed, "What is Leo Wolfe doing here?"

Then Virginia cried, "That's Dr. Wolfe?"

Alphonse asked, "Who the hell is Dr. Wolfe?" and after he'd put on his glasses and looked in Leo's direction, he followed with, "Somebody tell me what's going on here. That man looks exactly like Jake!"

"Well, not exactly," Meghan said with a grin. "Jake's nose was broken once and he doesn't shave his head. Plus, there's the matter of a scar on Leo's face that he got when he fell out of a tree as a boy."

Desiree looked at Meghan askance, admiration visible in her sable-colored eyes. "Baby's got secrets. Come on, girl, spill!"

So Meghan told her family that Leo was Jake's twin brother and he was living in Durham and, of course—she glanced at Auntie Marjie—working at Duke. However, she neglected to tell them she was falling in love with him.

Shortly afterward, Mina and Jake came into the dining room holding hands and looking like two people very much in love, to Meghan's satisfaction. Jake gave an impromptu speech as they stood in front of their guests. "Welcome! This is an intimate group of our closest and dearest family and friends. Mina and I are simple people who didn't want our wedding day to be a big production, but a meaningful, memorable day filled with love, and that's why you all are here. You are the people we love."

"That's right," Mina said. "And tonight is not for giving toasts or anything like that. We'll do that tomorrow at the reception. Tonight is for you to chill out from your trip, and some of you have come a long way to get here! Dinner's buffet-style. Help yourselves to the food and drinks, and also introduce yourselves to the other people in the room while you're at it. By tomorrow, I want all of you to be, if not friends, acquaintances. Most of you already know each other, anyway. But if you don't know someone, then walk up and introduce yourself! And when you go back to your rooms or cabins, make sure you get your rest, because tomorrow, we party!"

Cheers went up and guests rose from their seats and started forming lines at the buffet tables, the sound of their happy chatter filling the room.

Mina and Jake walked over to Meghan's table, and Jake was bombarded with questions about his brother. "Why didn't you tell us your brother was moving to North Carolina?" Virginia asked, standing for full effect, though she was barely five feet tall.

Jake went over to her and playfully pulled her to his side. "Leo wanted to get used to his new job first and then start socializing. Plus, Mina and I wanted it to be a pleasant surprise. Now, aren't you pleasantly surprised?"

He kissed her cheek. Virginia, much shorter than he was, smiled up at him. "I'll let it slide this time. But only because you're so charming."

Everyone around the table laughed good-naturedly.

"Why don't we go over and say hi before everyone starts chowing down?" Mina suggested.

They got up and made their way across the room to Leo's table.

Meghan was surprised by how quickly like souls paired up in conversation. Her father and grandfather and Leo's father hit it off immediately. Her mother and step-grandmother and Leo's mother were soon laughing at something or other. Marjorie and Rudolf wanted to know all about growing citrus from Grandpa Ellis, who hadn't gotten out of his seat, so they pulled up a couple of chairs to sit with him. Meghan couldn't hear what exactly any of them were saying because she and Miss Etta Mae were at the buffet table discussing the merits of boneless chicken versus chicken with the bone in. Miss Etta Mae preferred the bone in because she liked to suck all the juices off them after the meat had been devoured. Meghan fell in love with her sassy attitude.

The two groups wound up shoving tables together to accommodate everyone and had a very pleasant evening.

During dinner, Meghan would sometimes look in Leo's direction at the other end of the table, find his gaze on her and feel that now-familiar tingling on her skin. His piercing eyes seemed to see into the depths of her soul. That look inflamed her passions. She drank the ice water in front of her, but that didn't help.

She fanned her face with a napkin.

Desiree, sitting beside her, asked, "Is it too warm in here for you?"

"No," Meghan said and lowered her gaze from Leo's.

Keen-eyed Desiree had followed her line of sight, though. "I think there's something you're not telling me. But that's okay. I think we should compare notes."

Meghan immediately understood what Desiree was alluding to. Or rather, whom.

"Decker Riley?" she asked.

"He's getting to me," Desiree admitted. "He keeps sending flowers and I keep sending them back to him. He's relentless."

"And sexy as hell," Meghan said.

"That, too."

"Well, at least he lets you know how he feels about you," Meghan said. "I know you think he's a player and not worth your time and possible heartache, but you'll never know until you get to know him better."

"I realize that," Desiree said, a little sadly. "I don't think I'm ready to risk my heart again. Love hurts."

"No kidding," Meghan said, her gaze drifting back to Leo.

He was laughing at something and his profile was to her, but, oh, what a profile. Formerly, she hadn't been a big fan of beards, but his made him look ultra-masculine. She wouldn't mind him rubbing that beard all over her body.

"Maybe you ought to step outside to cool off," Desiree suggested.

Meghan looked down at the napkin in her right hand. She'd been fanning herself with it so furiously that it was falling apart. She dropped it onto the table. "No, what I need is a tall drink of water."

Desiree chuckled softly because her sister was looking at Leo Wolfe when she said that.

The wedding took place right there in the lodge. Keeping it simple, Mina descended the staircase on the arm of Alphonse, who handed her off to Jake with the words "Be happy, you two."

Her sisters stood behind her for support, and Leo stood next to Jake as best man. A young female violinist played "La Vie en Rose" as the processional song. The notes floated on the air so beautifully, the wedding criers had already been in full force before Mina took one step on the staircase with her dad. There were around one hundred guests in attendance, all in formal wedding finery: the out-of-towners whom Mina and Jake had welcomed last night, plus guests who'd driven a shorter distance to get there.

Later, at the reception, Meghan was chatting with her mother when Leo walked up to her table.

"Excuse me," he said in his gentlemanly fashion. "Would you like to dance?"

Her mother started to open her mouth, but clamped it shut, her eyes on Meghan. Meghan breathed a sigh of relief and got to her feet. She was surprised by his gesture, but tried not to show it as she took his offered hand.

"I'd love to," she said and reminded herself to breathe.

Eyes locked, they moved onto the dance floor. "I've been admiring you in that dress," Leo told her.

"Thank you. I've been admiring you in that tux," she said, reveling in the moment.

The dress was made of a thick cotton fabric in off-white. A raised jacquard design was woven into the material, and the dress itself was sleeveless and A-line with a scoop neck that revealed just enough cleavage, which Meghan had been abundantly blessed with. The hem fell three inches above her knees.

Leo was wearing a traditional black tuxedo that fitted his muscular, fit body wonderfully well. He'd taken off the jacket, and Meghan could see his biceps and chest muscles straining against the long-sleeve shirt. He must have left his black silk bow tie with his jacket because she knew she'd seen him wearing it during the ceremony.

The song playing was "Thinking Out Loud" by Ed Sheeran. Leo gently pulled her into his arms and they began to move to the music. Meghan could tell by the way his hand caressed the small of her back that he knew what he was doing. Some of her partners in the past had been unsure of exactly where their hands should go for any given dance.

Meghan relaxed after the first couple of minutes, realizing that something monumental was happening to her. Ever since she was a little girl, taking dance lessons that Virginia insisted she needed in order to become a well-rounded young lady, she had envisioned her dream dance partner. Someone who would simply take her in his arms and with whom she would instantaneously begin dancing as though they'd been dancing together all their lives.

And it had finally happened to her.

Leo swept her around the dance floor like Prince Charming twirled Cinderella the night of the ball. Meghan felt light as a feather.

"Where did you learn to dance like this?" Meghan asked, astonished.

"Where did *you* learn to dance like this?" Leo countered.

"I took dance for nine years," Meghan divulged. "Momma forced me, at first, but then I got hooked on it. I took ballet, jazz and ballroom. But I gave it up when I realized I was never going to find a partner who actually loved it as much as I do."

"I do," Leo said, smiling at her. "I got ridiculed because I took ballroom dance lessons. I admit, I took them because I wanted to impress a girl I knew who loved to dance. But I kept going even after she broke up with me."

"Was it for your high school prom?" Meghan asked.

"Yes," Leo laughed. "She broke up with me before the prom, so I never got to show her my skills."

"Well, she missed out big-time," Meghan said. "Dip me, Mr. Darcy."

So he did, elegantly and with sensual intensity. Meghan thought she might have an orgasm right there on the dance floor. His strength as he held her was formidable.

The DJ changed up the music then and put on an upbeat Bruno Mars song, and she and Leo smoothly transitioned to a salsa. The syncopated beat encouraged complicated footwork and swift movement topped off with a hot sexuality that Meghan found exhilarating. Leo moved with the assured confidence that the movements required, his body's lines on point. She'd known he was in good shape, but, Lord, in formal clothing, his muscles flexing sensually, he owned the dance floor.

Leo was grinning. Did she know how hot she was? She killed in that dress. She was flinging her hair with abandon, her hips in sync with the music and her legs so long and shapely.

Where he led, she followed. It was as if theirs was a dance partnership made in heaven.

Several dances later, they were so wrapped up in each other they didn't notice when the other guests surrounded them and started clapping, cheering them on. All they knew was that it felt like a miracle that they matched each other's passion for dance.

After about the sixth song ended Meghan and Leo stopped dancing and finally noticed the other people in the room. They were greeted with thunderous applause.

They gave exaggerated bows and walked off the dance floor hand in hand, heading in the direction of their table. "Would you like to go somewhere a bit more private than this?" Leo asked softly.

"We can go to my cabin," Meghan suggested, matching his tone. "Everyone I'm sharing it with is in this room, so we should be alone, for a while, at least."

They collected their coats and walked outside into the blisteringly cold night. Meghan gazed up at the starlit sky.

It was in the low thirties, but there was no accompanying breeze, so the cold was manageable.

When they got to the cabin, which had a living room, a kitchen, two bedrooms and two baths, they were leaped on by Chauncey, who was lonely. Meghan knelt on the pinewood floor of the living room and playfully ruffled the fur on the dog's head. "Wanna go outside?" In response, Chauncey wagged her tail. Meghan let her out the back door into the fenced area behind the cabin.

Coming back inside, she faced Leo, who was standing in the middle of the living room, watching her every move.

Meghan took off her coat and hung it on the coat rack next to the door. She went to Leo and helped him out of his jacket, then hung it next to hers.

"Leo, is there something you want to say to me?" she prompted him, hoping that, at last, he was going to declare that he wanted her. Declare something! Anything other than continuing to leave her in the dark the way he'd been doing.

When she was with him, she felt as if he were almost bursting with the need to talk to her about something important. She hadn't been able to fathom what he needed to tell her, but she knew in her gut that he was holding something back. Whatever that something was, she was sure it was the reason he devoured her with his eyes but kept his hands to himself.

Meghan stood in front of him and gazed deeply into his eyes. She went and placed both hands on his hard chest. Leo blinked, his face a mask of contradictory emotions. His translucent brown eyes were at once soft, then cold, then determined. “I wish I had the courage to ignore all the things about us that tell me pursuing you would be a big mistake, especially for you, my darling Meghan. You deserve someone who can make all of your dreams come true. You don’t know how much I wish I were that man. I’d give anything to be.”

Meghan stood on tiptoe and tilted her head back, inviting him to kiss her. When he didn’t take her up on her offer, just stood there like some flesh-covered robot, she sighed and said, “What’s her name? I told you about Chauncey, the human who was a dog. My Chauncey is more loving than he ever was. So now I want you to tell me about the person who broke your heart, Leo. At least give me that much, because I’m about to give up on you.”

Leo clasped her hands in his and held on tightly. Meghan waited patiently for him to answer. But after a few minutes, when it was evident he wasn’t going to say anything, she closed her eyes and tried to pull her hands free of his grasp.

“Her name is Natalie,” Leo told her. “I asked her to marry me and she turned me down.”

“Why?”

“I can’t tell you why.”

“What do you mean you can’t tell me why?” Meghan

asked, her tone fierce. Her first impulse was to fight for what she wanted, and she wanted Leo.

"Go ahead and give up on me, Meghan, because this isn't going to work."

He let go of her hands and started walking toward the front door. He turned around and faced her again. "I'm sorry I got your hopes up. I'm sorry I got *my* hopes up. But if I told you, you wouldn't want to see me anymore, either."

"Is it AIDS?" Meghan asked sorrowfully. "Are you sick?" She sounded like she was about to cry. Her eyes were wet with unshed tears.

"No, baby girl, it's not AIDS," Leo told her. "It's something worse." He looked away. The last thing he wanted was her pity. "I should go."

With that, he grabbed his coat from the rack by the door, opened it and was about to walk out when Meghan caught his arm and held on tightly.

"You can go," Meghan said, walking around and standing in front of him. "But this doesn't change anything between us, Leo Wolfe. I'm falling in love with you. There, I said it. Although, God knows, you've tried to dissuade me to the best of your abilities! Whew, talk about hard to get."

She was confident he'd changed his mind about bolting because she felt the muscles in his arm relax. She let go, her eyes on his. "I know you're not gay."

Leo laughed, "Not even a little."

"And you're not impotent," Meghan continued. "We were really close on the dance floor."

* * *

Leo's body was at that moment responding to the delectable scent of her, the sensory pleasure that her touch ignited deep inside of him. It wasn't just that he got hard. It was almost spiritual in nature. Her soul called his. He wasn't impotent.

"There's nothing wrong with my sex drive, which has been in high gear since I met you," he told her. "Given my situation, it would be unfair to you to have a love affair with you, that's all."

Meghan cocked her head and looked at him sideways, her hand on her hip. "That's all?" She narrowed her eyes. "Sometimes it *does* feel as if we're stuck in a Regency novel. You can't tell me something that's too harsh for my delicate female ears to hear? We look at each other like all we want to do is rip off each other's clothes and make love all night long, but you won't act on those feelings because it's not proper?"

Leo was standing there, drinking her in with his eyes, his mind half in a panic because he figured this was it. She was never going to be alone with him again. She'd run out of patience. This had been unforgivable. Asking her to go somewhere private. With the intention to do what? His enthusiasm had canceled out his normal protective instincts. A few turns around the dance floor and he'd gone nuts. He was so tired of having to keep his guard up.

Was it so wrong of him to simply want to kiss a beautiful woman whom he cared deeply for?

When they'd gotten to the cabin, he'd remembered who she was now. His in-law. Related by marriage.

In each other's lives from now on unless, God forbid, Mina and Jake broke up or one of them died. It was complicated. And life was already complicated enough without adding a sexual relationship with Meghan.

That was why he hadn't kissed her. It had hurt like hell to have to deny her a kiss. Every particle of his being had been anticipating that kiss. But until he was ready to come clean and tell her why a romantic relationship between them was a bad idea, he wasn't going to kiss her. If he did, he'd be all hers, and he knew it. She would own his heart and soul.

Ever since the day they had met, she'd been reeling him in.

It wasn't her beauty that drew him like a magnet. It was her kindness, her sense of humor, how she loved everyone in her life, how she adored Chauncey.

They'd been gazing into each other's eyes for a while when Meghan laughed softly and said, "It's obvious we aren't going to get anywhere tonight." She sighed. "I'm sorry you don't feel confident enough in our relationship to tell me what's going on with you. But I do understand. You don't know me well enough yet. I'm not going anywhere." She rose up and kissed him on the cheek. "I'm patient and we're family now. Like it or not, we're going to see each other. Plus, there's Malcolm and Chauncey's playdates to consider. You and I may not be on the best of terms, but those two love each other. I don't want to deny them time together, do you?"

"No," Leo said with a gentle smile.

Meghan walked him to the door. "Good night.

Thank you for the dances. I had a wonderful time. You're my best dance partner ever!"

"Ditto," Leo said. He gave her a regretful smile, then turned and stepped out into the chilly night. And that was how he felt, too, cold. Cut off from the warmth of the love that Meghan had offered him tonight.

# *Chapter 8*

"Lauren, slow down!" Meghan called to her fleet-footed sister. Not that she couldn't keep up with her, but Lauren had to learn to relax. Being a new mother, Meghan noticed, had turned her sister into a multi-tasking dynamo who stayed busy practically 24/7.

No sane person could maintain a schedule like that without eventually experiencing burnout, and Meghan wasn't going to let her sister go out like that.

"I don't have the patience to jog," Lauren said, running in place so that Meghan could catch up with her. "Lately, I feel like I have to hurry through everything. I know endurance running is your thing, but I just can't do it."

They were running in Lauren's neighborhood while Colton took care of CJ. It was the middle of February, so they were dressed for the below-thirty-degree weather.

"Endurance is good when you want to go the distance," Meghan said. "Lauren, your body has been through a lot lately. You should exercise, yes, but in moderation until you're fully healed. You can get back to running like Florence Griffith-Joyner in the near future."

"I don't have time for anything anymore," Lauren complained. "I'm sleep-deprived. I miss work. I never knew how much I loved designing buildings and homes for people to live and work in. I loved dreaming up a design concept and seeing it come to life from beginning to end. It made me feel powerful, indestructible!"

"Oh, my God, you sound like Donald Trump. You *are* sleep-deprived!" Meghan joked. "But now you've got to shove all of that aside and concentrate on the big change in your life, my dear sister. Namely, a husky fellow by the name of Colton, Jr. I hear you don't get any do-overs where watching your children grow up is concerned. Time goes by so quickly, you have to relish every minute. Relax and enjoy him. Don't worry about work. Work will be there when you get back to it."

Lauren slowed her pace further. She sighed. "We women are so caught up trying to do everything, trying to be everything to everybody. It's a vicious cycle. I know what I should be doing now. I'm just not sure I can stop being Superwoman. I've worn the cape for too long."

"It's an ugly cape, girl," Meghan said. "Get rid of

it. It doesn't do you justice. Wrap yourself up in the warmth of your family's love instead."

Lauren stopped running and, hands on hips, faced her sister, who'd also stopped. "We've been running for about two miles already. Let's go back to the house and get some cocoa."

"Got any mini marshmallows?"

"Virginia Gaines came over and stocked my pantry. You know she didn't forget those!"

Meghan laughed, "Not our mother. Do you remember when she'd make us hot chocolate? She would put exactly…"

"Five mini marshmallows in each cup," Lauren finished for her. They turned around and began retracing their steps, this time walking.

"So, how are things going with Leo?" Lauren asked.

Meghan didn't look surprised. If you told one sister a secret, nine times out of ten, the others found out about it pretty quickly.

"I haven't seen him since the wedding. But we have a standing playdate for the kids this weekend. I'll see what happens then."

"You sound like a divorced couple," Lauren said. And they both laughed.

"Nah, we're two sad humans trying to make sure our fur babies are happy," Meghan said.

"He sounds like a very sweet guy," Lauren said wistfully.

"He *is* a very sweet guy," Meghan agreed. *Unfortunately, he's also a very secretive guy*, she thought glumly.

* * *

Leo wasn't scheduled to begin teaching until the spring term started, but Marjorie Langdon asked him to show up for the next faculty meeting of the English department. That was where he was now, standing in the midst of his new colleagues, who were warm and welcoming and eager to get to know more about him.

Marjorie introduced him to so many men and women that he was sure he wouldn't remember them all, but there was one standout: Shari Dunbar, an English literature professor.

When Shari found out he was from Atlanta, she told him she'd been born there and practically all her relatives were still there.

"John and I are eventually going to end up there, no doubt," she said. She was an attractive African American woman in her late forties, he guessed, around five-five, fit, with shoulder-length dark brown hair she wore straightened and combed back from her widow's peak.

Marjorie had excused herself to go take care of something, and now it was just him and Shari. "I take it John's your significant other," Leo said. Or else she was another pet owner who named her pets after ex-boyfriends, like Meghan.

"My one and only," Shari said proudly. "He's a lieutenant colonel in the Marine Corps. He's overseas right now, but he's going to retire in a few months."

"How many years has he been in the military?" Leo asked, interested in this accomplished woman who taught English and lived a world apart from a husband who was serving his country.

"Twenty years," Shari told him. "Twenty-one in March."

"A career soldier," Leo said. "You must be proud."

Shari smiled, a happy light in her dark brown eyes. "Yes, I am. I'm singularly proud that he's doing what he wants to do and excelling at it. But the kids and I miss him a lot."

"How old are they?"

"They're both over eighteen," Shari answered. She seemed to Leo like the type of person who could feel at ease in any situation and was able to express herself with equal ease. "John and I were so young when we got married. I was eighteen and he was twenty. We've supported each other through everything. He was the one who encouraged me to pursue my doctorate."

Leo smiled, shaking his head in admiration. "I envy you, Dr. Dunbar."

Shari glanced down at his ring finger. "A bachelor?" she asked with mild surprise.

Leo chuckled softly. "Yes, but hopefully that condition won't last for much longer."

Shari's brows rose in curiosity. "Tell me about her."

Leo didn't know why he felt so comfortable with Shari Dunbar. Maybe because she adored her husband. Maybe because she was safe. Safe in that she was a perfect stranger.

While other faculty members chatted around them in the big conference room, he finally told someone besides his family how he felt about Meghan. He left out the macabre information about his heart condition and sterility.

Shari, who was clearly a romantic at heart, listened raptly.

When he finished talking, feeling almost like he'd just made a confession to a priest, she looked up at him and smiled. "I like to think that's exactly how John feels about me. Thank you, Leo, for reminding me what it feels like to be newly in love. If there's anything that I can ever do for you and the lovely history instructor, who's nearly thirty but looks much younger, let me know."

"Same here," Leo said. "If there's anything I can do for you."

She smiled at him. "I'm a plainspoken woman, Leo. What do you think of Pink?"

"The color's not my favorite," Leo admitted.

"Not *pink* the color. Pink the singer!"

"Oh, I think she's talented."

"Then will you go with me to a concert at the end of the month? She's going to be at the PNC Arena."

Leo smiled, remembering Meghan had told him that you could find live entertainment in Raleigh practically any day of the week. "Sure," he said. "Why not?"

"Exactly," Shari said. "My man is halfway around the world and you feel like your lady is. We can support each other."

Meghan, who sometimes ran on the Shaw University track late in the afternoon when the track team was finished practicing and other faculty and students took over the track for personal use, was running there one day at the end of February when the assistant football coach, Andre Hanks, called to her. She held up two fingers to denote she had two laps left to run and would speak with him afterward, and he grinned at her.

Meghan wondered what he wanted. They used to date, but hadn't been intimate. Andre had been too much of a ladies' man for her. He was still quite the player according to what she heard from the college gossip mill. Her mind hadn't changed about him romantically, but sometimes she did like to run with him. He was a great athlete and made her work hard. He was also, she hated to admit, good for her ego. She wasn't proud that his continued interest made her feel feminine and appreciated by the male sex. After Leo's rejection, the way Andre looked at her boosted her poor self-esteem. Which also made her feel bad, because why should her self-esteem need a boost? That irked her.

After the two laps, she walked off the track and up to Andre. He was half African American and half Swedish. His father was a professional basketball player and his mother a former swimsuit model. The man was gorgeous. Six-five and 250 pounds of pure muscle. It was no wonder he was a chick magnet. Meghan didn't know if it was possible for him to be loyal to any one woman.

"Hey, girl," he said, grinning. His coppery brown skin was flawless, and his square-chinned face clean-shaven. His hair was curly and dark brown with blond highlights Meghan knew were natural. He'd always had them, and she'd known him since they were in their teens.

"Hey yourself," she said, smiling back. "How has life been treating you, Andre?"

"I've been great," he said. He gestured toward the gate that led to the parking lot.

"I was wondering if you have plans for Saturday night," he said shyly. Meghan smiled. In spite of his luck with women, Andre still got tongue-tied around them.

"Is this something you need a plus-one for?" she asked. They'd made a deal that occasionally they would serve as each other's platonic dates for certain events. A last resort thing. Meghan knew that Andre wasn't the right man for her, but she liked him as a friend. She didn't see any reason why they couldn't be civil and see each other based on those terms. He'd agreed, and they'd been there for each other for the past three years now.

"My sister's getting married," he said, frowning. "You know if I asked anyone I'm currently dating to go with me, she'd read too much into it."

"When is it?"

"This Saturday," Andre said, his tone regretful. "Sorry I couldn't give you more notice. I was thinking of going with Sharon, but she's been hinting that we should take our relationship further than I'm ready to take it, and I chickened out and didn't ask her."

Meghan thought his explanation had the ring of truth to it. She didn't feel good coming to his rescue at the disadvantage of another woman, though. However, she also didn't believe she should lecture him on his inability to commit to one woman. Andre was twenty-nine. Meghan didn't believe all men that young were commitment challenged, but she hadn't met one yet who wasn't.

"What time Saturday?" Meghan asked. She and Chauncey were supposed to meet Leo and Malcolm at William B. Umstead State Park at noon, weather permitting. They'd gotten flurries lately, but no heavy snow.

"Oh, it's an evening ceremony," Andre said cheerfully. "I'll pick you up at five in the afternoon."

"All right, then," Meghan said.

They arrived at her Mustang. She looked up at Andre. "I think you ought to know I'm serious about someone now."

Andre smiled. "A woman like you couldn't remain a free agent forever."

Meghan laughed, "You and your sports references."

William B. Umstead State Park was about the same distance from Meghan's house in Raleigh and Leo's in Durham. The weather was fine—a clear blue sky, very little wind and the temperature in the midthirties. The park was huge, but she'd told Leo which parking area she would be in, and shortly before noon he rolled up in the SUV. She waited by the Mustang until he and Malcolm got out of it and joined her and Chauncey. The dogs immediately said hello by nuzzling the sides of each other's heads.

Leo looked at her with tender emotions mirrored in his light brown eyes, and Meghan swallowed a lump in her throat. She wished she could control the physical reaction she had to him, but every time his gaze swept over her, she shivered with longing. She wondered how long it was going to take for her body to stop craving his touch.

"Hi, Meghan," he said, his baritone husky.

"Hi, Leo," she returned, her voice cracking. She cleared her throat, lowered her gaze and pointed to a wooden bridge nearby that led to one of the park's many trails for hikers. "Would you like to try that trail?"

Silently Leo got Malcolm's attention, and they all started walking toward the bridge, Malcolm and Chauncey leading the way.

"I see you're letting your hair grow out," Meghan commented.

Leo ran his hand over his head. "Yeah, I got tired of shaving my head every day."

As always, the park was busy. People were walking and running; parents were running while pushing babies in sports strollers. Meghan even saw people on horseback in the distance.

"You're not going to go into tour guide mode?" Leo asked lightly.

Meghan smiled at him. "Maybe I'd like to talk about more personal things instead of telling you that this park covers over five thousand acres and was once farmland."

Leo laughed, "Talk about anything you want to talk about. I'm just glad you're willing to talk to me at all."

"I'm afraid I'll pick a subject that will further alienate you from me," Meghan said candidly.

"Honestly, there's nothing you can say that will make me willingly pull away from you, Meghan."

"Conversely, there is nothing I can say that will make you take me in your arms," she couldn't help saying.

"You're wrong there," Leo said. "All you have to say is you'll accept me as I am, and I'm yours for the rest of my life."

Meghan noticed that he'd said *for the rest of my life*, not for the rest of *our* lives. She suddenly felt lost and hopeless. She wasn't one of those morose readers of novels with heroes or heroines who met tragic ends. She didn't like reading tearjerkers. She was a cockeyed optimist. A person who found something positive in the most depressing of situations. That was her gift, being certain that no matter what happened in life, there was always a silver lining.

She didn't like movies where the widow was shown grieving her young, handsome husband while figuring out how to live the rest of her life without him. No, that wasn't her. But she had a sneaking suspicion that if she allowed herself to fall in love with Leo Wolfe, she was going to be starring in one of those movies in real life. Yet she couldn't resist wanting to know more about him. What was more, she wanted to be the one who put a real smile on his handsome face. Was she a glutton for punishment?

She laughed and said, "In my imagination, Nina Simone is at the top of your life's playlist, Leo. When I'm with you, her voice is in my head singing 'Suzanne' or 'Black Is the Color of My True Love's Hair.'

I'm drawn to you, but I don't know why, because you withhold yourself from me. You're a perfect specimen of male beauty, and when you talk, I listen raptly, as though I can't bear to miss anything you have to say."

"I love Nina Simone," Leo said quietly.

"I knew you would," Meghan said mockingly. "Because you're my perfect match. That's the joke in this situation. There should be nothing keeping us apart because, to anyone looking on, you and I are a match made in proverbial heaven!"

"Don't you think I'm frustrated, too?" Leo asked, his voice anguish filled.

"Apparently you're not frustrated enough," Meghan told him. "Because if you were, you'd tell me what's wrong."

"It's not an easy thing to say," Leo said quietly. "When I told Natalie, she dropped me so fast it made my head spin."

"I'm a lot stronger than I look!" Meghan cried.

"I know you're strong, Meghan. You wouldn't be here now if you weren't."

"Damn straight," Meghan said huffily.

They stared at each other, her expression belligerent, his patient and loving, as though she were a recalcitrant child whose parent meted out kindness when the child acted out.

She could not stay mad at him. She heaved a huge sigh and said, "My sisters and I are planning an anniversary party for our parents. It's a surprise, so keep it on the down low. It's going to be a big affair. Petra is coming home from Africa to be here for it. You're invited. You can bring a date." She hadn't wanted to say that, but the affair was for couples and she didn't want him feeling like a third wheel. "You'll be getting a formal invitation in the mail. It's their thirty-fifth anniversary so we're going all out."

"I'll be there," Leo said without hesitation. Meghan could have screamed in frustration. There were those puppy-dog eyes again, causing her heart to beat double time and her female center to get ready for the sex that would not be forthcoming.

It was cold as hell where they were standing, tall pine trees and myriad other trees and plants all around them, but her body temperature was going up due to the Leo effect.

She met his eyes. "I'm not going to wait forever."

Leo nodded. "I know."

# Chapter 9

Several weeks later, Raleigh-Durham International Airport was as busy as usual on Sunday night when Meghan and Desiree went to pick up Petra. The sisters were waiting in the terminal when Petra walked in wearing jeans and hiking boots, a man's thick denim shirt and a lined safari jacket that had seen better days. She was a world traveler who packed lightly—she was only carrying a huge shoulder bag, also made of khaki, and one carry-on bag.

Desiree, the fashionista in the family, groaned while hugging her petite sister. "Oh, girl, it's so good to see you!"

"It's great to see you, too, sis." Petra grinned, her straight teeth in her sun-kissed medium brown face looking extra white in contrast to her skin.

She had her waist-length curly, dark brown hair piled on top of her head, with a wide black headband holding it in place. Her face was devoid of makeup and she smelled like eucalyptus oil.

"Do you have a cold?" Meghan asked after she'd hugged Petra.

"No, it's this jacket," Petra explained. "I'm usually covered in eucalyptus oil, a natural insect repellant, and I haven't had the chance to have the jacket dry-cleaned." She looked around the busy terminal. "This place is almost unrecognizable. It's gotten so big." She regarded her sisters. "Come on, let's get out of here. I'm hungry."

"Seriously?" Desiree asked, astonished. "You didn't bring any more clothes?"

"I've got a couple changes of clothes in here," Petra told her, indicating her carry-on bag. "How much clothes do you need?"

"For you, not me," Desiree said. "It's relatively warm here because we're down South, but I know that jacket didn't cut it in New York City. You must have frozen half to death. You were there for a couple days before coming here, weren't you?"

"Yes, but I was rarely outside in the weather," Petra said reasonably. "I was picked up by a limousine and taken to a luxury hotel. I ran from the hotel to the car. Was driven to the airport and got on the plane, and here I am."

Desiree gave Meghan an "I don't know what we're going to do about our sister" look and reached over to take Petra's carry-on bag, which was surprisingly heavy. "What the heck do you have in here?"

"My camera equipment, satellite phone, laptop, various essential oils and necessary clothing."

"I'm taking you shopping tomorrow," Desiree told her.

They began walking toward the exit. "What happened to your apartment in the city?" Meghan asked.

"I gave that up before I left for the Congo," Petra said. "I gave away all unnecessary items, so now I'm free of material things and much happier without them."

Desiree looked horrified. "Even those Louboutins you owned that I wanted to steal?"

"No, they're in the bottom of the carry-on," Petra informed her.

Desiree breathed a sigh of relief. "Your values are still intact, then."

Petra laughed, "Just kidding. I gave those away, too."

"I may faint," Desiree said, looking bug-eyed at Petra.

"Then you'd better let me drive home," Meghan joked, holding her hand out for the keys to Desiree's car.

"I'm driving," Desiree said, then turned her attention back to Petra. "I can't believe you gave away those beautiful shoes!"

"They were no use to me in the jungle," Petra said with a chuckle. "They were nothing but something to haul around, and my backpack was heavy enough with my research equipment."

Desiree opened her mouth to say something else

but Meghan cut her off with, "The shoes are gone, sis. And they're not going to miraculously reappear because you're upset about it."

Her cell phone rang and she dug it out of her shoulder bag. It was their mother. Meghan answered with, "Hi, Mom, what's up?"

"Marjorie and I were wondering if you've made up your mind about Duke yet. It's been weeks now."

"No, I'm afraid not," Meghan said. "I promise, as soon as I make up my mind, I'll phone Auntie Marjie."

"Don't wait too long," her mother warned her. "Opportunities like this don't come along every day."

"I won't," Meghan promised. "Bye, now. Have a good evening."

"You, too, sweetheart," Virginia said.

When Meghan hung up, she looked at her sisters with a panicked expression on her face. "Do you think she suspects?"

For years they had been trying to surprise their mother on her special days—birthdays, Mother's Day and anniversaries—but she always found out about the surprise party before it occurred and enjoyed having one-upped them. She would crow about it for weeks.

"No way," Desiree said confidently. "We've sworn everybody we invited to secrecy. She isn't going to win this time."

"It isn't a matter of winning," Meghan said.

"Oh, hell, yes, it is," Petra said stubbornly. "We've put up with her bragging for too many years. She's going down this time!"

Meghan took Petra by the arm. "Let's go get you something to eat. You get mean when you're hungry."

Leo had guests. Newlyweds Jake and Mina had come over for a meal while they were in town for Mina's parents' anniversary party.

He hadn't seen them since the wedding, although he spoke with both on a fairly regular basis. Jake was in the kitchen with him while Mina was on the living room floor playing with Malcolm, whom she'd fallen in love with the moment she saw him.

Jake couldn't help stealing glances at his beautiful wife, smiling happily while Malcolm jumped all over her.

"I can see that three months of marriage hasn't cooled your ardor one bit," Leo said.

"Huh?" Jake said, eyebrows raised in confusion. "Would you translate that into normal, everyday language for those of us who don't have a doctorate in English?"

"You know what I said," Leo returned. He now had a full head of dark brown hair, which was sheared close to his head, the waves in it following their natural pattern. His goatee was as neat and luxuriant as ever.

Jake's hair was the same color, but a bit longer, and his moustache and full beard were sculpted to frame his strong jawline. He continued to admire Mina. "Yeah, I know exactly what you mean. And, if anything, I've fallen even more in love with my wife in the last three months. I can't keep my eyes, or my hands, off her. Of course, as the next few months go by, I'll probably be in protective mode, knowing I have two people to protect now."

Leo set down the knife he'd been using to chop onions and turned around to face Jake. "Mina's pregnant?" he asked excitedly.

Grinning, Jake nodded. "I wanted you to be the first to know, bro."

Leo burst out laughing and hugged his brother tightly. "You two didn't waste any time! Congratulations. I couldn't be happier."

"Good," Jake said as they parted. He looked Leo in the eye. "We're going to announce it at the party tomorrow night, but Mina and I thought you should hear it privately."

Leo smiled, realizing his brother's meaning. Knowing Leo's particular situation, he and Mina had wanted to break the news gently. It wasn't that Jake thought Leo would be jealous or anything as trite as that. They just wanted him to have time to process the news and not have it be a shock to the system.

"I'm going to be an uncle," Leo said, his voice awe filled.

"The best damn uncle ever!" Jake said and hugged his brother again.

The next night, the party was in full swing when Leo arrived at the downtown luxury hotel in Raleigh and entered the ballroom with Shari on his arm. Shari looked lovely in a sophisticated white sheath dress with a scoop neck and a hem that fell just above her ankles. She reminded Leo of one of those black actresses from the fifties, like Dorothy Dandridge, who were always so well put together when they were photographed at Hollywood events.

He was wearing a tailored black tuxedo, his black dress shoes shined to a high gloss.

"I'm a little nervous," Shari whispered.

"You have nothing to be nervous about," Leo assured her. "These people are down-to-earth. They're going to make you feel welcome."

Sure enough, Meghan spotted them and came over to say hello. Leo's heart started its normal rat-a-tat in his chest at the sight of her. She looked gorgeous. She was wearing a black sleeveless dress, the neckline of which both accentuated her full breasts and displayed the lovely curve of her neck. The hem fell about two inches above her well-shaped knees. Her legs went on for days.

He was so mesmerized by her that he failed to notice the giant crossing the room at her side until they were almost upon them. But Shari didn't. "Who is that? Dwayne Johnson's younger, finer brother?"

*Who is that, indeed?* Leo thought, trying his best to beat down the green-eyed monster. "We're going to find out soon," he told Shari. "That's Meghan."

"Hi, Leo," Meghan said enthusiastically. "I'm so glad you could come. This is my date, Andre Hanks. Andre, this is Leo Wolfe. His brother, Jake, is married to my sister Mina."

"Oh, yeah," the giant said, grinning. "The other twin." Then he proceeded to shake Leo's hand off.

Leo had to rub the feeling back into his hand when Andre released it. "Hello, Andre. Nice grip."

Then he politely introduced Meghan to Shari. "Meghan Gaines, this is Shari Dunbar. Shari teaches English literature at Duke. Shari, this is my friend Meghan."

"Oh, yes," Shari said with a friendly smile. She placed her hand on Leo's arm. "The history instructor who looks more like a student than an instructor. It's a pleasure to meet you, Meghan."

There might have been something evil in Meghan's eyes for a split second. Leo wasn't sure, because she quickly schooled her expression and smiled at Shari. "Welcome, Shari. I hope you enjoy yourself this evening." Then, suddenly, she said, "Excuse me, won't you? I think my sister's trying to get my attention."

Leo noticed Desiree was beckoning her from across the ballroom.

The couples smiled at each other and then Meghan and Andre departed. Leo looked at Shari and said, "Something's rotten in the state of Denmark."

Shari laughed, "You can always rely on Shakespeare to have a pithy remark for any occasion." She glanced in the direction Meghan and Andre had gone. "That girl's in love with you, by the way."

Leo stared at her. "Why do you say that? She did nothing that would convince me she's in love with me."

Shari laughed, "Sometimes men can be so dense. For a second there, I feared for my eyes. I thought she might scratch them out. But, that aside, she's a lovely woman. I'm not holding that fierce territorial streak she has against her. I'm like that when a woman gets too close to John, too."

Before Leo could comment, he heard Jake call, "Hey, Leo, over here."

Leo escorted Shari across the ballroom. Jake was alone at his table. After Leo introduced Shari and they sat down, Jake said, "Mina's with her sisters. Apparently, Momma Virginia found out about the surprise party beforehand. No one knows who talked, but the girls are furious. But they have one more card up their sleeves and I think they're about to play it."

Her interest piqued, Shari asked Jake, "Did you say Virginia? Are you talking about Dr. Virginia Gaines?"

"That's right," Jake said. "Why, do you know her?"

"My kids went to her school," Shari exclaimed. She looked accusingly at Leo. "You never said Meghan was Virginia Gaines's daughter."

"I didn't think to mention it," Leo said, surprised by the intensity with which Shari was expressing her respect for Meghan's mother.

"That woman is awesome," Shari informed Leo and Jake. "When she became principal at my kids' school, it had the worst scores in the state. Inside a year, she'd turned that place around. I had even been considering sending the kids to a private school, but John was against it. He felt they should be in the public school system where, by God, they should be able to get as good an education as in an expensive private school. We argued about that for a while. But I let them stay and they graduated with honors from her school. And

John was right—they got an excellent education. Virginia Gaines fights for her students!"

"She's a fighter, all right," Jake had to admit.

Leo, who up to that point hadn't had much personal experience with Meghan's mother, now recognized some of her mother's spirit in Meghan. Apparently, neither of them gave up when they were faced with adversity. Maybe Meghan wouldn't give up on him yet.

"There they are," Jake announced while Leo was ruminating about Meghan.

Leo looked up to see Meghan and three of her sisters climbing the steps to the stage that had been set up for the night's festivities.

For the next few minutes, the Gaines girls entertained the audience with tales of what it was like to grow up with Alphonse and Virginia as parents. Their father had been the pushover and their mother the disciplinarian. But they allowed that it was because their father had often been stationed overseas and felt guilty for not being with them year-round that he tended to spoil them. Their mother, on the other hand, saw them day in and day out and knew they needed order and discipline in their lives. They said that, for this, their mother was often accused of being too strict with them. However, they loved her for encouraging them to work hard and push themselves beyond their comfort zones.

Then they asked their parents to join them onstage, and that was when they started talking about their fifth sister, Petra, who was reportedly in Central Africa doing research on the great apes. Mina stepped up to the mic. “In Petra’s honor, Momma and Daddy, we thought we’d play a song to remind you of her.”

The DJ, hearing his cue, played “The Lion Sleeps Tonight.” As soon as the music began, the double doors leading into the ballroom were shoved open and a beautiful petite woman in full African dress strode into the room to a collective sigh from those in attendance. Leo assumed she was the absent Petra, about whom the sisters had spoken so glowingly.

“My baby girl!” Virginia screamed and ran down the steps of the stage to throw herself into Petra’s arms.

“I thought I was your baby,” Meghan, who was the youngest, cried, at which everyone started laughing, Leo included.

For the next few minutes, it was pandemonium, with the Gaines family hugging each other and their guests applauding, getting out of their seats and joining the Gaineses to congratulate them.

Eventually everyone returned to their tables and dinner was served by the waitstaff amid constant excited chatter from the guests. The rest of the family joined Leo, Jake and Shari at the big round table in the center of the room, and lively conversation ensued.

Virginia had to point out that although her daughters did, indeed, surprise her with Petra’s appearance, she had bested them yet again by uncovering the details about the surprise party.

“Okay, you got me,” she said. “But next year you won’t be so lucky, I assure you.”

“Mom,” Mina said cheerfully. “This time next year you’re going to be a grandmother twice over.”

The whole family cheered and Virginia got up, ran around the table and hugged Mina.

Congratulations were given, and Mina and Jake were soundly hugged and kissed by everyone.

When it quieted down, Leo whispered to Shari, who seemed to be having a wonderful time, "Please excuse me for a few minutes."

Shari smiled at him. "Of course."

Leo got up and walked outside the ballroom into the wide corridor. People milled about, coming from and going to the nearby restrooms or sitting on the comfortable-looking upholstered benches that lined the walls.

He just needed a quiet moment. Things certainly hadn't gone as he'd imagined. He'd been hoping to get the chance to speak with Meghan alone. All evening he'd wondered what Andre Hanks meant to her. Leo hoped he meant nothing because she certainly didn't mean anything to Hanks. He'd been eyeing attractive women all night long.

Leo went to the men's room, and when he came back out, he walked from one end of the long corridor to the other. Just walking and thinking. Was Meghan actually dating this joker, or was he only a friend who'd agreed to be her escort, as Shari had agreed to be his plus-one?

He wasn't jealous. He had no right whatsoever to be jealous. Meghan was not his woman. Meghan could be his, if only he would be honest with her. That was a possibility. A real possibility. Or so he tried to convince himself. There were only two possibilities. She would accept him as he was, or she would react like Natalie had.

"I'm going to do it," he muttered. "To hell with the consequences."

A tall man in a dark suit gave him a funny look as he walked past him in the corridor. Leo figured the guy must have overheard him talking to himself.

He turned around and started walking back down the corridor toward the ballroom. Then he heard a soft voice say, "How's your evening going?" It was Meghan.

Leo spun toward her voice. They were, luckily, alone at this end of the corridor. He went up to her and grasped her by the upper arms. "Meghan, what are you doing with a guy like that? He's been checking out other women all night long. You deserve better!"

"Andre and I aren't exclusive," Meghan said dismissively. "I know he plays the field."

"And you're okay with that?" Leo asked, shocked by her attitude.

"I'm young, remember? I'm not mature enough for a serious relationship," Meghan taunted him.

Meghan didn't know why she was saying what she was saying. Why didn't she tell him Andre was only a friend? Because she was angry at him and wanted to lash out? For over five months she'd been trying to figure out what made Leo Wolfe tick, and she'd failed miserably.

"You know that's not what I meant when I said we shouldn't date each other," Leo accused her, keeping his voice low so it wouldn't carry.

"It doesn't matter what you meant," Meghan said ferociously. "The bottom line is, I want you, but you don't want me."

Her anger confused him. He started talking about her age compared to his. How she'd still be beautiful when he was a doddering old man. He couldn't believe the nonsense issuing from his mouth when all he really wanted to say was that he wanted to be with her.

"I don't care about tomorrow," Meghan cried. "What about now? Tell me once and for all you're not attracted to me and that's why you won't date me. Say the words so I can hear and understand, Leo. The way you look at me, it's so hot it makes my skin burn. It drives me crazy! Does that woman mean anything to you?" She took a deep breath and waited for his answer.

He looked at her in shock, as if he'd never expected those words to come out of her mouth. "Shari is just a friend, an acquaintance, a colleague. What the hell? She's a married woman who loves her husband. I'm not having an illicit affair. Who is he to you?"

It was her turn to look flustered. "Andre is a friend who I dated a long time ago, and figured out we should be friends only. And I mean *only.* We've never been intimate."

"I've got a congenital heart defect that could kill me without warning," Leo blurted out. He squeezed his eyes shut for a moment, and when he opened them again, he saw that the news had floored her.

Meghan went weak in the knees, and if he hadn't grabbed her just in time, she would have fallen. He held her until he thought she felt steadier on her feet. In the safety of his arms, Meghan peered up at him. Her eyes were so sad it tugged at his emotions. He'd done exactly what he'd been avoiding doing for five months. He'd hurt her, and he'd probably ruined his chances with her forever.

"Now you see why people keep secrets," he said softly. "Some things are better left unsaid."

He yearned to kiss her, just once. This could be his only opportunity. The way she was looking at him, he might as well already be dead.

Meghan stood on her own. She felt her strength returning to her. She wasn't Virginia Gaines's daughter for nothing. She looked Leo in the eye, her gaze determined.

"It's too late for dire warnings, Leo Wolfe, because I'm totally into you."

Leo smiled and breathed a sigh of relief. She hadn't said she loved him but what she'd declared had given him hope, so he kissed her.

This kiss had been a long time coming, so it had to be a good one. He pressed his mouth to hers softly, their clean, sweet breaths mingling, and they got closer until they were fully covering each other's mouths. His arms drew her into his embrace. Her arms encircled his neck, and nature took its course.

They were both trembling with pleasure, the pent-up longing finally released. The anticipation was not better than reality. When they came up for air, Leo breathed, "I want you. But I want so much more for you than I can give. That's why I tried to avoid you."

Meghan was silently crying. "The way I see it, we've wasted enough time. Let's start living. The day of the wedding, you said you were perfectly capable of having sex, right?"

"Mmm-hmm," Leo said against her fragrant neck.

"Then let's have some at your earliest convenience, Professor."

"Tonight?" he asked hopefully.

"You take Shari home, and by that time I'll be at your place," Meghan said, hurriedly formulating plans. "Thank her for me, will you? For coming with you tonight. Because tonight was our lucky night."

"Babe." Leo reminded her of what he'd just told her. "I may die at any time."

"And *I* may die at any time," Meghan said. "But I'm not spending another night without you. So go speak with your date and I'll go speak with mine, and I'll meet you at your place soon."

She stood on tiptoe and kissed him for good measure. It was as wonderful as the first one had been. "Now, get moving!" she ordered saucily.

"Yes, ma'am," Leo said, grinning. He was so relieved he hadn't scared her off, it was as if this good fortune were happening to another man. It felt like he was having an out-of-body experience, albeit a happy one.

Then something pertinent occurred to him and he spun around. "Hey, beautiful!"

Meghan turned, her smile never wavering.

Leo took his house key off his key ring and handed it to her. "You'll probably get to my place before I do, and I wouldn't want you to have to sit in your car waiting for me."

Meghan looked at him with admiration. "Good thinking. No alarm code?"

"No," he said and gave it to her.

"All right, then, see you later, Mr. Darcy."

He smiled and slowly followed her back to the ballroom entrance, thinking that maybe his luck was changing. And then he remembered that he hadn't told her about his sterility, which, if he were being honest, was probably the worst of his maladies. He closed his eyes and blew air between his full lips in frustration. More shocking news before they made love would not be well received. He was certain of that.

What was he going to do?

# *Chapter 10*

Meghan went around the table at the party whispering good-nights to her sisters and parents before telling Andre she was ready to leave. Her grandparents were on the dance floor.

Lauren looked aghast when Meghan whispered in her ear and got up to give her a quick hug. "You're leaving so soon?"

Meghan didn't want to get into it with Lauren, so she distracted her by saying, "Have you noticed that every Gaines girl here is with a mate or a potential mate? You've got Colton by your side. Desiree has Decker. Mina and Jake are expecting. And even Petra has that gorgeous Chance Youngblood looking at her like she's something good to eat."

"You didn't mention yourself," Lauren pointed out.

"I'm leaving to spend some quality time with Leo," Meghan said.

That was all she needed to say. Lauren kissed her on the cheek. "Well, thank goodness you two were able to finally get past whatever the hell you had to get past! Go, go, and be gentle with him. You haven't had any in about a million years."

Meghan laughed. That was the Lauren she knew and loved.

Andre didn't prove to be a problem. He was texting someone when she returned to her seat beside him. She took a quick glance at his phone's screen and saw it was Sharon.

He looked up guiltily and smiled at Meghan. "Sorry, she's been hitting me up all night. Says she misses me. We usually kick it on a Saturday night."

"It's still not too late," Meghan told him, "because I'm ready to leave."

Andre grinned. "Really?"

"Yes, let's go," Meghan said.

Leo, on the other hand, was reluctant to disturb Shari because she was having a blast talking to Virginia and Marjorie.

When he could get a word in edgewise, he whispered in her ear, "Meghan and I talked."

Quick on the uptake, Shari smiled at Virginia and Marjorie and said, "Ladies, it's been my pleasure." She rose and gave Leo a curt nod, denoting he should follow her.

Leo said his good-nights with alacrity, and followed Shari to the exit.

She beamed at him when they got outside the noisy ballroom where they could hear each other without difficulty.

"So you've worked things out?"

"Yes," Leo said triumphantly.

"You've made plans for later," Shari assumed. Her dark brown eyes were lit with excitement. She didn't even wait for Leo to confirm. She began walking toward the closest exit. "Come on, Leo. Take me home so you can get to Meghan."

Leo didn't have to be told twice.

When she got home, Meghan made quick work of packing an overnight bag for herself and Chauncey, who she was not going to leave in the house alone for however many nights she and Leo would be spending together. She was optimistic it would be more than one. It was just Saturday, after all. They had tonight and Sunday night to revel in before they both had to go to work on Monday.

She parked at the curb in front of Leo's house about an hour after she'd gone home to pack. She didn't pull into the driveway because she didn't want to block the garage. She went into the house with just her shoulder bag and overnight bag and disabled the alarm. Malcolm gave a half-hearted bark when she entered the house, recognized her and started happily wagging his tail.

"It's just me, boy," Meghan hastily said. "I'm going to get Chauncey now, then I'll let you outside." But she thought better of that. He was already excited and might not be able to wait.

She opened the door to the fenced backyard. “Be back for you soon!”

Once Chauncey was in the house and out of her pet carrier, she went in search of Malcolm. “Be patient. He’s outside taking care of business.”

Meghan made sure the house was secure, then she went in to find something to drink.

At her house, she’d changed out of her party dress and into a pair of jeans, a soft, long-sleeve T-shirt and a pair of black leather flats. She wanted to be comfortable but sexy, and those simple items of clothing all fitted her curves to perfection. Plus, she had to think of things like how easy Leo could rip them off her. They wouldn’t be hard to remove.

She found a good bottle of wine in the fridge and got two wineglasses from Leo’s very neat cabinet above the sink. Out of curiosity, she looked in other cabinets, which were all in perfect order. Was she getting involved with a Monk? She enjoyed watching the TV show about an obsessive-compulsive detective.

She decided she would let the wine sit on the counter next to the wineglasses until Leo got here. By that time it would be the perfect temperature to drink, not too cold, but not warm, either.

She was nervous. Excited, but nervous. And Leo’s heart. Dear God, why did life have to be so complicated? Sure, he’d been living with the condition since birth. He’d said it was congenital. She knew people could live with a heart murmur until they were senior citizens. Most of them didn't even take medication for it, but were advised to live life in moderation: eat right, exercise, avoid stress. Leo certainly did appear to eat right and exercise, but the mere fact that he was living with a condition that could kill him was stressful.

She adopted a Scarlett O'Hara attitude and told herself she would think about that another day. Tonight, she was going to make love to the man.

She heard scratching and looked behind her to see Chauncey at the back door. Her smart girl had figured out Malcolm had gone through that door. "All right, I'll see if the deed is done," Meghan said and went to check on Malcolm.

He ran into the house as soon as she opened the door and went straight to Chauncey. The dogs dashed into the living room to Malcolm's corner, where his bed was. Malcolm grabbed a toy from his bed with his teeth and put it at Chauncey's feet. Chauncey accepted it and took it in her mouth, shaking it and growling as though she were a hound after a rabbit.

It was while Meghan was watching this spectacle of dog behavior that the doorbell rang. Obviously, Leo didn't keep a key hidden somewhere outside like a lot of homeowners did.

She went and peered through the peephole. Yes, it was her handsome professor, smiling happily. She unlocked the door and pulled him inside. "I thought you'd never get here!" she cried, grinning.

Leo had taken off his bow tie, and his silk shirt's collar was unbuttoned. Both his hands held packages, yet he still managed to pull Meghan into his arms and kiss her soundly.

Joyful barking greeted him as the dogs ran circles around their legs. "Hold on, hold on," he said. "What's going on up in here? A man can't come home without everyone jumping all over him?" He grinned at Meghan. "With the exception of you, of course. You can jump all over me anytime you want to."

He went and set the packages on the island's countertop. Then he pulled Meghan into his arms again. Gazing into her upturned face, he said, "Listen, on the drive over here it occurred to me that we haven't even gone on a date yet. Well, not an official date. And we're already talking sex, so I thought I'd at least go through some of the dating rituals with you before picking you up and taking you to the bedroom."

Meghan laughed, eyeing the packages on the counter. "What do you have in mind?"

Leo showed her. From the plastic bags he pulled a dozen red roses, so fresh there were still minuscule water droplets on their petals, a box of Godiva chocolates and the cutest stuffed bear Meghan had ever seen, so small it could sit in the palm of her hand. She recognized the brand as belonging to a company that made chew toys for pets.

"Aw, thank you. You even brought a gift for Chauncey."

Leo chuckled. "To get in good with the woman, you've got to win the pet over."

"Smart man," Meghan said, then threw her arms around his neck and kissed him again. When they parted, she said, "I'm making up for lost time. Since I wanted to kiss you the first day we met, I figure you owe me about a thousand kisses."

"Okay," Leo swiftly agreed and bent to kiss her. "One, two, three..." After three, the kisses quit being pecks on the lips and transformed into foreplay.

Meghan sighed and relaxed, her body feeling light, as if with very little effort it could mold itself to fit perfectly against Leo's hard form. He was solid to the touch and warm, and he smelled wonderful. She breathed deeply, taking his heady essence into her lungs. His scent was woodsy and clean. All male and undeniably sexy. It had been hell keeping her hands off him for months.

Leo tried to slow down and enjoy every second of finally having Meghan in his arms. The pheromones were kicking in, though. He'd known they were physically drawn to each other. He'd felt it each time they were together, but to actually feel her in his embrace, her skin touching his, the warmth, the smell of her—it all worked to render him her slave.

When they broke the kiss, Meghan said breathlessly, "I took the wine out of the refrigerator and got two glasses. Would you like a glass?"

Leo didn't need a stimulant—he was already quite stimulated—but he sensed she wanted to slow down, and anything she wanted was his pleasure to give her. "Sure, I'll pour."

While he poured the wine, Meghan leaned on the counter and propped her shapely bottom up on a stool, a saucy smile on her face. He handed her a glass of wine and they playfully tapped the rims of the glasses together in a silent toast.

"I wanted to know more about your condition," Meghan said, trying to sound as though this were an everyday conversation, not one of the most important of her life.

"You want to know if you can kill me during sex." Leo interpreted her meaning.

She lowered her lashes and sighed. "Yes."

"Sex, like any other exercise, is good for my heart," Leo said with a gentle smile.

"Rough sex?" Meghan asked.

"Yes."

"The kind of sex that makes your eyes roll back in your head?"

"Yes, please."

"Screaming is allowed?"

"The more the merrier."

Meghan set her wineglass down and shot a very suggestive look his way. "Any condoms in those bags?"

Leo produced a box from the bottom of one of the bags. "I'm always prepared."

"Bless you, Mr. Darcy."

Leo's bedroom was very large. And made to look even larger than it was because the only furniture in it was a king-size bed with an upholstered headboard, nightstands on either side of it. Meghan assumed he stored all his clothing in the nearby walk-in closet. A glance revealed it was a large room with multiple shelves. There was also a spa-like master bathroom.

Leo switched on the lamps on the nightstands. He then took off his suit jacket and began unbuttoning his shirt. “Welcome,” he said. “This is my sanctuary, and I hope you’ll be comfortable here, too.” Meghan sensed he was saying all of this because he was nervous. “I’m a big man, so the bed’s big and the headboard’s upholstered because I like to read in bed, and a soft headboard is appreciated then. No dressers or bureaus, as you can see. I get dressed in the closet. It’s roomy in there and has a couple of floor-to-ceiling mirrors that show me how I look.”

Meghan went into the organized closet, and sure enough, his clothes were hanging neatly: pants with pants, shirts with shirts, jackets with jackets. There were shelves of folded sweaters and athletic wear. A large bureau with four drawers probably held his underwear. A six-tiered shoe rack was filled with several pairs of shoes. A tie rack was next to it.

It was like a mini men’s shop. *I am involved with Monk*, Meghan thought.

Leo joined her in the closet, and when she caught their reflections in the mirror, she gasped. He’d removed his shirt, and the man was breathtaking shirtless. She’d known his body was rock hard, but she hadn’t imagined how ripped he was. His arms, chest and stomach had the muscular definition of a professional athlete. The kind who hit the gym on a daily basis, not one who just got in shape for the season.

“Anal retentive, huh?” Leo said of his closet, his baritone seeming to reverberate off the closet walls.

“You’re organized,” Meghan said after calming

down enough to speak, "and that's a good thing. You're probably never at a loss for what to wear to work, are you?"

"I pick out what I'm wearing the night before," Leo admitted.

"Of course you do," Meghan said, turning into his embrace. They kissed briefly, and Leo started trailing kisses down the side of her neck. She turned, and he kissed her throat. She removed her T-shirt and presented him with her back. He unhooked her bra and her full breasts spilled into his big hands. They slowly moved back out to the bedroom while her clothing remained on the closet floor.

She unbuttoned her jeans and unzipped them. Leo was happy to roll them down off her shapely hips and she stepped out of them, leaving them on the hardwood floor of the bedroom. She'd kicked her flats off in the closet, so she was now standing in front of him in a pair of soft pink hip huggers. The pink went beautifully with the caramel color of her brown skin, Leo thought as he divested her of them, too.

After a quick perusal of the area below her belly button, he noted she didn't color her hair. "You're exquisite," he said, his breathing labored.

Meghan showed no embarrassment in being naked. It was obvious she worked out because she was toned, slightly muscular while still being curvaceous. Which was to his satisfaction, because he liked something to hold on to when he made love to a woman.

She held his gaze confidently and with just a little

arrogance, which made him smile. He was glad she knew her strengths and wasn't shy. She glanced down at the bulge in his pants. He'd tried to play it cool and will his erection to stay in control of itself, but hey, he was just a man, a horny one at that, and nature would not be denied. He was ready for her.

Her hand went to his slacks, which he regretted not doffing earlier. But he gently loosened her grip, saying, "I'd better do it. One touch from you in a sensitive area, and it might be over for a good twenty minutes."

Meghan smiled. "We wouldn't want that to happen."

Leo was out of his pants, briefs and socks in record time. They were in bed moments afterward, kissing, hands roaming over each other, reveling in the wonderful sensations and the utter miracle that was the human body.

"Oh, my God, you feel so good," Meghan moaned.

She caressed the backs of his arms, his biceps, his chest, his stomach. She kissed his ear and his cheeks, avoiding the beard, which was softer than she'd imagined. She kissed his forehead and ran her hands through his hair, which was soft, too. She straddled him and stroked her hands across his muscular chest. All the while, his member was growing larger. She could feel him move against her as she sat directly on top of him, her vagina throbbing. She wanted him so badly.

Leo cupped her gorgeous breasts while holding her gaze with his. He gently rolled her over onto her back so that he could feast on her. Her nipples were hard, and he licked them until they got even harder. She tasted sweet on his tongue, and the look of pleasure in her eyes made him mad with the urgency to give her as much as she could stand.

He glanced over at the two condoms in their packets he'd put on top of the nightstand when they'd gotten to the bedroom, just being certain the action wouldn't be interrupted by another foolish move on his part. Then he pulled her closer to him and went for the gold.

Meghan's closed eyes shot open when she felt Leo's head between her thighs. What was he doing? Did she need to guess?

This was a first for her. Call her a prude. Call her inexperienced. But don't call her in the next few minutes because she was going to be in the process of having her mind blown!

She'd heard about it. She'd read about it. But the moment Leo's tongue touched her clitoris, she felt like shouting about it. She melted. He was slow and gentle, then a bit rough and gentle again, as though he sensed just how she liked it. Which was impossible because she hadn't even known she liked it until now. The pleasure and the pain continued until it reached a delicious crescendo. She trembled with the release, her feminine center throbbing crazily, then she fell, and she didn't know whether she'd die right there or get up singing praises to the universe.

While her thighs trembled, Leo kissed the insides of them.

"Are you okay, my love?" he asked softly, a wickedly satisfied expression in his weirdly light brown eyes.

Meghan tried to focus as she came down from her

high, but all she could do was sigh and croak, "Give me a minute."

*And I thought I might kill him*, she thought with a smile.

Leo smiled knowingly and reached over to get a condom off the nightstand. He tore the packet open, then tossed it onto the nightstand and rolled the condom onto his engorged penis.

Meghan looked at his penis and grinned. It fitted the man. It was big, just like he was. She opened her legs wider.

Here, Leo needed to concentrate. He tried not to think of how long he'd been wanting to make love to Meghan. That just made him want to come faster. No, he had to think of things about the last few months with her that had infuriated him. Anger focused his energies. So he remembered how she'd started calling him Mr. Darcy just because he hadn't jumped on the Meghan bandwagon as soon as they'd met and started behaving like a lovesick schoolboy. That had been presumptuous of her.

To think that no man could resist her charms. Which, to be honest, he hadn't. He'd wanted her from the beginning. Okay, that scenario wasn't working. Besides, she felt so good. Her sex was tight and her walls caressed him and, oh, no, the woman had skills. She was squeezing the muscles of her vaginal walls around his member. Hard, too. Every time he thrust, she would parry. It was driving him crazy.

He yelled when he came. And he groaned in disappointment because he'd wanted to last longer.

Meghan, however, was not disappointed.

She pushed him onto his back and rode him until she had her second orgasm of the night, then she collapsed on top of him and let out a long sigh. Her ear on his chest, she listened to the rhythm of his heart. It thumped hard at first, and then it gradually slowed down. Leo inhaled and exhaled, his big chest raising her up with him. She rolled off him and they lay in bed face-to-face. She smiled. He smiled back.

"You are the best thing that ever happened to me," she said softly with a contented sigh.

"Next time," Leo promised, "I'll put on some Gladys Knight."

"Gladys who?" Meghan asked.

Leo laughed, "I knew you were too young for me."

Meghan giggled. "Psych! Of course I know who Miss Gladys Knight is. She and her brother Merald 'Bubba' Knight, along with two of their cousins, formed the group Gladys Knight and the Pips. She's a Southern girl, you know. She was born in Atlanta."

"Merald? You know Bubba's real name?" Leo exclaimed.

Meghan smiled, snuggled closer to him and sultrily said, "You just made love to a history nerd of the first order, Mr. Darcy."

Leo laughed and kissed her. "I adore you, you nut!"

# Chapter 11

On Sunday morning, Meghan was awakened by the smell of breakfast cooking. She slowly opened her eyes, relishing the feel of her body's faint soreness from making love more than once last night. Felt for Leo on his side of the bed and discovered he wasn't there. Then grinned at the memories she and Leo had made.

She sat up. Leo had left the blackout curtains closed so it was dark in the bedroom. She reached over and switched on the nightstand's lamp. Suddenly, the sound of scratching came from the door. She got up, realized she was naked and got her T-shirt off the closet floor. The shirt covered her sufficiently.

She opened the door, and Chauncey and Malcolm came running into the room and pounced on her. Leo was right behind them, laughing. "Sorry, they got away from me. I let them out and fed them afterward. Now they're bursting with energy." He stepped over to her and hugged her tightly. Looking down at the dogs, he exclaimed, "Out, you two!"

Instead, Chauncey sat down as if he'd told her to sit. To his surprise, Malcolm followed Chauncey's lead and sat, too.

Meghan laughed, "I guess she missed me last night, and doesn't plan to let me out of her sight for a while." She sighed. "I didn't think I needed my dog's permission to spend the night with you."

She met his eyes. "But then, this has never happened before, so how was I to know she'd think I was abandoning her?"

"You sleep with your door open," Leo guessed.

"Yeah, and she's awake half the night patrolling, and comes into my room to check on me several times during the night."

"In that case," Leo said, "last night must have been stressful for her."

Meghan affectionately rubbed Chauncey's chin. "Okay, girl, from now on, I'll remember to leave the door open at night. But right now, you and Malcolm need to leave so I can shower and dress. Today, we go visit Miss Lillie and her friends at the nursing home."

Chauncey's ears perked up when she heard the name *Lillie*. Meghan smiled at her pooch. Chauncey loved visiting the nursing home where Meghan's former teacher, Lillie Franklyn, lived.

Meghan stood up and in an authoritative voice said, "Go play with Malcolm, Chauncey."

Chauncey gave her one last sorrowful glance, then did as she was told. Leo watched the dogs leave the room, and after they were gone, he said, "I'm impressed. I haven't even begun to train Malcolm. He's still basically without any discipline."

Meghan went into his arms, put hers around his neck and gazed up at him. "Good morning. How long have you been up? Did my snoring wake you?"

"Good morning, beautiful. I've been up a couple of hours. My internal clock wakes me at six every morning, whether I have to go to work or not. And you don't snore."

"Even your internal clock is efficient," Meghan said with wonder. "Is there anything you're bad at?"

"Wait till you taste my cooking," Leo joked, then patted her on the behind, gave her another quick buss on the cheek and returned to the kitchen.

A few minutes later, they were sitting at the island in his kitchen chatting over a very delicious meal. "It seems you've exaggerated your ineptness at cooking," Meghan jokingly accused him, her eyes alight with humor. "Your eggs are fluffier than my mother's and Virginia prides herself on her scrambled eggs."

Leo eyed her over his coffee mug. "I've noticed you often refer to your mother by her first name. Why is that?"

"It's not out of disrespect, if that's what you're wondering," Meghan told him. "My sisters and I began doing it when we were little. We felt we needed to be a united front against her. She was our only parent in some ways, you see, because Dad wasn't home a lot. Desiree, who went into psychology in an effort to understand herself better, believes we did it to separate her 'mother' persona from her 'Virginia' persona, which was the disciplinarian. Mom was the lovable one, Virginia the impersonal rule maker who you didn't disobey. So I suppose I refer to my mom as Virginia when I'm thinking of instances when she was laying down the rules."

"Cooking scrambled eggs?" Leo asked skeptically.

"Cooking class was on Saturdays," Meghan told him. "And it was definitely like school. We got graded on our scrambled eggs. I remember I got an F when she tried to teach us how to cook grits, a Southern staple. My grits always stuck to the pot," she laughed. "Do you eat grits?"

"Only when I go visit my parents," Leo said. "Grandma Etta Mae knows how to cook grits, and they never stick to the pot."

Meghan laughed, "I knew I liked her for a reason."

Her cell phone rang, and she picked it up from the island's counter and glanced at the display. "It's Auntie Marjie," she said. "I know she's calling to see if I've made up my mind about the position she offered me." She looked into his eyes. "Do you remember my telling you she and my mom were visiting me that day I was looking after Malcolm while you were sick?"

"Yes, I remember," Leo said, smiling. "The Higher Education Mafia."

Meghan smiled, apparently pleased he'd remembered. "Well, she offered me a position in her department that day. I've been putting her off because she told me you would be my supervisor. I thought it would be uncomfortable for me, and you, if we were working together."

"What's their position on fraternization?" Leo asked. "I haven't looked into it since being hired."

"There are couples who work at Duke. Of course, your behavior should be respectful and aboveboard. As long as you're professional and are doing your job, you're okay."

"Personally, I want to spend as much time with you as I can," Leo said seriously. "You know my situation now. And like you said last night, we need to start living. Especially since I have no idea how long I have."

Meghan looked at him with sympathy. But then her expression became optimistic. "Duke has some of the best doctors in the country. When was the last time you got another opinion? Fresh eyes on the case. There could have been medical advances since the last time you were checked out."

"I go to the doctor every few months," Leo said.

"I know, but would you see a specialist here? Just to cover all the bases?"

Leo frowned. He hated going to doctors. He'd gotten so much bad news from doctors, he had developed an aversion to them. They were a necessary evil as far as he was concerned.

Meghan smiled. "I know you've already been through a battery of tests. Having this condition all your life, you must be tired of doctors. But would you try for me?"

Leo grasped her hand and squeezed it reassuringly.

"Okay, babe. If you'll accept the position at Duke, I'll go run on a treadmill for one of their brilliant heart specialists."

"I'll phone Auntie Marjie right now," Meghan told him happily.

Marjorie answered right away. "Where did you disappear to last night?" was the first thing out of her mouth. "Rumor has it you left at around the same time as my new English professor."

"Is no one's business private in this town?" Meghan cried, laughing.

Meghan hadn't yet read her messages this morning. But she'd noted that there were around forty new ones. Undoubtedly, her sisters and her mother had been blowing up her phone.

Meghan smiled at Leo while she talked to Marjorie. "Is it true that couples can work together at Duke?"

Meghan had to hold the phone away from her ear, Marjorie started screaming so loudly. "Yes," she said after she'd calmed down. "As long as you're the professionals I know you are and you perform your jobs well, we're always willing to work something out. Does this mean you're going to take the position?"

"Yes," Meghan said. "My contract will soon be fulfilled at Shaw. I was offered another, but haven't given them my answer yet. Auntie, you know I love that school."

"Yes, but no one there would dream of holding you back. They understand how hard it is to make a living as an academic. They'll wish you well, sweetheart. Besides, it's not as if you'll be abandoning them. You're an alumnus. You'll be at all the homecoming games and reunions."

"Go, Bears!" Meghan and her godmother cried in unison. Shaw was Marjorie's alma mater, too.

Leo laughed. He was getting used to the lively women around him. He sincerely doubted Meghan would ever stop surprising him with her enthusiasm for life.

Meghan said goodbye to her godmother and regarded him with a broad smile. "It's done," she said breathlessly. "Our lives will never be the same."

Leo smiled as if in agreement, but inside his emotions were a seething cauldron of misgivings. He should have told her about his sterility, and the fact nagged him. This morning, he'd gone out on the back porch to have a private conversation with Jake, who didn't sound pleased to be awakened at six o'clock.

"Why didn't you tell her at the same time you told her about your heart?" Jake practically yelled at him. Then he lowered his voice. "Mina's asleep beside me. Hold on, I'm going downstairs. I hope the general's not up yet. That man acts like he's still on army time." Leo imagined Jake going downstairs at his in-laws' house, trying not to make noise for fear he'd disturb Virginia and Alphonse's sleep.

He felt like an ass standing on his back porch, the air still filled with mist. The morning was crisp, but he knew the sun would come out and dispel the chill in the air, and the day would be bright and cloud-free. Such was April in Durham. It was a beautiful month.

Finally, Jake started talking again. He sounded a little breathless. "So, you're calling to ask me not to tell Mina you're sterile because it just slipped your mind when you told Meghan about the murmur," Jake deduced.

"Yeah," Leo confirmed. "And I hate to ask you to do that knowing you hate keeping secrets from your pregnant wife."

"Damn straight I do," Jake grumbled. "You're lucky I haven't said anything to her yet."

"You haven't?" Leo said, relieved. "But you told me you were going to tell her after you were married."

"It may come as a surprise to you, Leo, but I've got a life, too, and I've been busy living it. It slipped my mind, okay? I've been so wrapped up in Mina. I'm happy. I know the concept is new to you. But happiness is a state sought after by most red-blooded males. And while I'm glad you've finally found a woman who can stand you, I ask you—can that happiness be complete when you're not being honest with her? Now, handle your business. Tell Meghan as soon as possible. Tell her while she's in the throes of new love. That's my advice."

"I know what you're saying is true," Leo told his brother. "But telling the woman you love that you can never give her a child isn't as easy as you might imagine. She's a healthy, vibrant woman who loves children. Physically, she's perfection, and after last night I can say that with some authority."

"I don't want to hear anything too intimate about my baby sister-in-law," Jake warned him.

"I wasn't going to say anything," Leo assured him. "That's between me and Meghan. All I'm saying is now that we've been together, I feel even worse about deceiving her. It pains me, and yet I can't seem to form the words to tell her I'm not the man I appear to be."

"Tell me this," Jake said. "Did you tell her you love her?"

"I told her I adore her," Leo admitted. "And I meant it."

"Then you're up shit creek without a paddle," Jake told him. "Man, everything you say before you tell her you love her can be forgiven, and she'll reason that you did it before you told her you loved her. So it doesn't count. But anything after you've already said you love her? You come back with some new revelation? She's going to suspect you were never truthful with her in the first place. Which means when you told her you loved her, you lied. Because to women, when you say *I love you*, it's sacrosanct. Sacred, my brother."

"I do love her," Leo insisted. "With all my heart, body, mind, spirit and everything else I have."

"You just don't love her enough to risk losing her," Jake said. He sighed. "I understand what you're going through. I do. However, women can forgive a lot of things. Being dishonest isn't one of them. Ask any woman on the street which quality she wants most in a man and she'll tell you—honesty. So I feel for you. Plus, you've got that Dracula syndrome thing going for you, too."

"Dracula syndrome?" Leo asked, puzzled.

"Dracula was a creature who lived forever, but he only survived by sucking the blood from people's veins. Imagine how hard it was for him to sell a woman on that life. No woman wants to deal with that. I don't care if she never ages and has a figure like a supermodel for the rest of her life. She wants to go out in the sun sometimes! You're like Dracula, because deep inside you think no woman will ever want you because of your condition. So you set yourself up for failure each time you get brave enough to enter into a relationship. Like you did last night when you conveniently forgot to tell Meghan about your sterility when you told her about the heart murmur."

"I'm setting myself up for failure?" Leo cried incredulously.

"Hell, yeah," Jake said. "What other explanation is there for your actions?"

"Believe me, I don't want to lose Meghan," Leo said earnestly.

"Gotta go," Jake whispered. "The general's on the stairs. He still glares at me like he's not sure I'm the man for Mina."

Leo would have laughed if he weren't so depressed by their conversation. He said goodbye and went back inside, where Malcolm and Chauncey were chowing down on their breakfast.

Two hours later, he was sitting across from the woman he loved, wondering when would be the best time to wipe that look of happiness from her eyes.

Their lives would never be the same, she'd exclaimed happily after making a phone call that would put her on a new career path. Leo got up and pulled her into his arms. "Congratulations. I know you're going to love it at Duke. It's a great university, and the faculty is very welcoming."

Meghan smiled up at him. "I'm not worried. I can

get along with anyone. I just feel sad about leaving Shaw after five years. I'm going to miss the staff and, most of all, my students. They inspired me as much as they said I inspired them."

On Monday, Meghan gave a lecture on the rivalry between W.E.B. DuBois and Booker T. Washington, and afterward, Hailey Robinson, one of her favorite students, stood up and said, "Dr. Gaines, I read that W.E.B. DuBois was a communist and an atheist. We're a Christian school. How can you recommend him to us as a historical figure we can look up to?"

The class was packed, it being one of her most popular courses, History or Propaganda. In it, students were encouraged to make up their own minds about what they read in history books.

She stood before her class now, dressed in a black pantsuit and black pumps, her hair in a bun. She looked into their eager faces, happy that they were intellectually engaged and not bored.

"First, I congratulate you for doing your own research on DuBois. He was a perfect example of a man who didn't follow the crowd," she began. She gestured to Hailey that she should sit down and get comfortable. This might take a while.

The girl sat back down, a look of humor in her brown eyes. Meghan knew Hailey liked nothing better than a lively debate.

"W.E.B. DuBois was the first African American to earn a doctorate at Harvard. You know him as one of the founders of the NAACP, and from his most popular book, *The Souls of Black Folk.* Compared to a lot of African Americans in his day, his worldview was more expanded because he'd lived in foreign countries and got to experience their governments. He did say that Russia had a better social system than America at the time. That was because they treated all their citizens equally and America didn't. That doesn't make him a communist, though. That makes him open-minded.

"He said in *The Souls of Black Folk* that the problem of the twentieth century is the problem of the color line. He believed capitalism caused racism. As long as Americans could make a buck off black people, they were happy. But when the black man started wanting to participate in the system and get his fair share, there was a problem. And as you know, he wanted blacks to have a full share in the American economy. Not only be the servants, as Booker T. Washington promoted, but professionals with the right to fully participate in American society.

"You may call him a communist for thinking that way. A lot of people did. Or you can think of him as a visionary, someone who saw the future clearly. That's why he said that either America will destroy ignorance or ignorance will destroy America. As for his being an atheist, he believed that the church was not the black man's friend. It was his opinion that American churches were some of the most discriminatory institutions and said African American churches didn't support racial equality or the activists who were out there marching for freedom. We know that Dr. King came along and proved him wrong on that count.

"But the point is, Hailey, he was a product of his time. You have the power to decide whether or not you'll take his beliefs to heart, or discard them in favor of other beliefs. Think for yourself. He's not here to defend himself, but from everything I've read about him over the years, I don't believe he was a communist, although I do believe he was an atheist. He always refused to lead prayers when asked, and wrote that he did that because he didn't believe in organized religion. Does that answer your question?"

Hailey laughed and said, "Yes. I choose to believe some of what he said and I choose to respect him for his work in elevating our people and educating them."

"I'm sure he would take that as high praise," Meghan said with a grin. She looked down at the time on her cell phone sitting on the podium in front of her. "Class dismissed."

As the class filed out of the room, Meghan began gathering her belongings. Someone cleared his throat from the doorway. She looked up into thc smiling face of Andre. He was dressed in his usual athletic clothing.

"Hey," he said. "You got a minute?"

"You can walk me to my car," she said, having put everything into a huge leather tote.

They began walking companionably toward the exit. "I just wanted to thank you," Andre said sincerely.

"For what?" Meghan asked.

"For just being you, I guess. When I asked you to go to my sister's wedding with me, you went. No questions asked. Even though I knew you were dying to give me a lecture on my inability to commit to one woman. And then there was how you behaved at your parents' anniversary party. In the beginning, I thought you wanted me there to make Leo jealous, but that wasn't your goal. You simply didn't want to go dateless in case he showed up with a date, which he did."

Meghan laughed. Andre was more perceptive than she'd given him credit for. Here she was thinking he was just a man-child looking for easy gratification, when he was actually a sensitive guy.

"I sense you have something else to tell me," she said, smiling up at him as they continued across campus to the faculty parking lot.

Andre chuckled. "Sharon and I are engaged."

Meghan laughed delightedly, "Congratulations. I'm so happy for you!"

"Yeah," Andre continued. "After I took you home, I rolled up to her place and we had a serious conversation about where our relationship was going. She told me that after two years..."

"You've been dating Sharon for two years?" Meghan was dumbfounded. "That's a record for you, isn't it?"

"Hell, yeah," Andre confirmed. "So she says after two years of putting up with me, she was done. There was no future in it, and she couldn't devote any more of her precious time coddling my monumental ego."

"Your ego isn't the problem," Meghan said. "You just don't want to grow up."

Andre looked at her in amazement. "Exactly. You've put up with me for years so I guess that's why you know me so well. Anyway, I told her what you just said and she laughed in my face and said it was time I grew up!

She threw my ring at me and told me she didn't want to see me anymore."

"You gave her an engagement ring?" Meghan asked. "I mean, prior to Saturday night? I'm confused, Andre."

"No, it was a friendship ring," Andre told her.

Meghan laughed, "You're too old to be giving a woman a friendship ring. I'm surprised she took it. She must really love you."

Andre nodded. "Those were my thoughts exactly. So I got down on one knee and asked her to marry me."

"And she said yes!"

"Yes, and she's keeping the friendship ring until we can pick out an engagement ring," Andre said quietly. His smiling eyes got serious all of a sudden. "What happened with you and Leo Saturday night?"

"Well, he didn't propose, but we did come to an understanding," Meghan said.

"Good, good," Andre said. His cell phone buzzed in the pocket of his Shaw Bears jacket. He took it out and glanced at the screen. "Gotta take this," he said apologetically.

"Of course," Meghan said as she continued walking. "Congrats again, Andre!"

"Thanks," he called and returned his attention to his cell phone. Meghan smiled all the way to her car. To think that the biggest player she'd ever known was settling down. Love was definitely in the air!

# *Chapter 12*

We're having a girls' night out this Friday before Mina and Petra have to leave town, can you make it? Desiree asked via text message on Thursday of the following week.

Meghan had just come out of the shower. With a towel wrapped around her, she touched the screen and dialed Desiree's number.

It was the week after her parents' anniversary party, and she felt guilty that she hadn't spent more time with her sisters, but she had phoned them and explained why: she was in love. But she had not revealed anything about Leo's condition. She wouldn't do that until he said it was okay. They'd all been understanding and happy for her, but she could tell by the sound of their voices that they missed her. Her sisters were her best friends. They told each other everything, and to not be able to tell them exactly what she was going through with Leo didn't sit well with her. However, she fully understood that it was his prerogative to share, or not share, the information with whomever he chose.

Desiree answered with, "There you are, baby girl. What's the verdict? Are you going out with us Friday night?"

Meghan set her phone down on the nightstand after turning on its speaker function, and began slathering lotion on her body while she talked with Desiree. "Why go out?" she said. "Wouldn't it be fun to have a meal at one of our houses and include the guys? When was the last time we socialized as couples?"

"If you mean all of us at once, never," Desiree answered with a laugh. "It's not going to happen this time, either, because Petra sent Mr. Chance Youngblood packing right after the party."

"What? Nobody told me," Meghan complained lightly. "Why'd she do that?"

"He scares her, that's why."

"Are you psychoanalyzing your own sister?"

"Somebody's got to do it," Desiree returned, still laughing. "Our Petra believes if she gives a man her heart, she gives him her power. Chance, it seems, has a certain magnetic charm she finds hard to resist. She says he's not only brilliant and confident, but is the best lover she's ever had."

"We're not talking about that many lovers," Meghan pointed out. "She's always put her career first and foremost, which doesn't leave a whole lot of time for lovers. Plus, you don't meet many men in the jungle."

"Agreed," Desiree said. "However, it's telling the way she looks when she's talking about him—wistful and starry-eyed. I've never seen her like this before."

"Then she's definitely got to get rid of him if she's going to continue being an opponent of marriage and everything else she thinks stands in the way of a woman's independence."

"See?" Desiree said. "You've come to the same conclusion I did. She sent him away because she likes him too much."

"Just out of curiosity, did she say how she got him to go away? He doesn't seem like someone who gives up easily."

"She told him if he didn't, she wouldn't even consider seeing him again," Desiree replied. She sighed, and Meghan heard her whispering to someone. "So, Friday night at seven? We'll come pick you up."

"Okay," Meghan said. "But we can't stay out too late."

"I know," Desiree said. "I've got a man who wants me all to himself, too. Bye, sis."

"Bye," Meghan said. "Give my best to Decker."

Desiree laughed, "How did you know he's here?"

"Because your voice changed when he came in the room. You went from conversational to sexy in a heartbeat."

After they hung up, Meghan finished moisturizing her body and grabbed her robe from behind the bathroom door. Slipping into it, she went to the closet to choose a dress to put on. Something sexy, but not too revealing. Something comfortable and casual, just right for an evening at home entertaining her man. She gave a soft sigh at the thought of Leo being her man.

As she rifled through the section of her closet that held nothing but dresses, she wondered how long the Fates, God or the universe was going to give them. She hated thinking about macabre subjects like death, but no matter how much she would like to avoid thinking about it, death was a part of everyone's reality.

The doorbell rang as she was slipping her feet into a pair of low-heeled brown leather sandals. She was wearing a short sand-colored dress in soft cotton that clung to her curves and displayed her legs to perfection, but the bodice revealed very little cleavage. She looked in the mirror and fluffed her loose curls before going to answer the door.

Meghan opened the door, and Leo stepped across the threshold, set Malcolm down and swept her into his arms. The dogs danced around each other and ran off together.

While in his arms, Meghan pushed the door closed.

She laughed with joy. She'd never been picked up in a man's arms and twirled around like this. Of course, she'd never been in love like this before, either, so the territory was bound to be new to her.

Leo set her down and they gazed at each other. Then they were kissing hungrily, their bodies clinging in an effort to get ever closer. After a minute or two, they parted and just stared at each other. She had a peculiar feeling that she was seeing him for the first time.

*Everything old is new again.* That must be it. She was seeing the world through the eyes of love.

She loved everything about Leo. From his short, soft, curly dark brown hair and manly, smooth, close-trimmed goatee, to his square-jawed face with high cheekbones, a rather long well-shaped nose, full-lipped mouth and those thick-lashed eyes that were more golden than brown—a light brown whiskey color that was just as intoxicating as the spirit.

Tonight he had on jeans and a polo shirt in light blue with a pair of white athletic shoes. His biceps bulged every time he moved his arms, she noted. And those jeans didn't hide the play of muscles in his legs and thighs.

"Damn, I missed you," he breathed.

"I missed you, too," she said, grabbing his hand and leading him back to the kitchen, where she'd prepared dinner prior to jumping into the shower.

Her living room, kitchen and dining room was one large space. Dark hardwood covered the entire space and her furnishings were light colored, the sofas and chairs in leather and the accent tables in modern glass. She liked clean lines and didn't care for clutter, so she had few knickknacks around. There were family portraits on the walls, some original oil paintings and live plants and trees in huge pots in strategic places around the great room.

Leo looked around. "I like your home."

Meghan smiled. It hadn't occurred to her that this was the first time Leo had been here; she'd always gone over to his place. His home was larger than hers. But the manner in which she used space added to the appearance of room to stretch out in.

"It's a 1950s' bungalow that has been well maintained since it was built. The previous owners loved it, and in fact, the only reason I'm the new owner is because I'd known the couple who owned it for years before I started looking to buy. They knew I'd love it as much as they did, so they gave me a very good deal. They're retired now and living in Arizona."

"It's beautiful," Leo said, looking around appreciatively. "You have a minimalist style that's very peaceful."

"That's me," Meghan joked. "Peaceful."

Leo laughed as he gazed at her. His eyes held a mischievous glint. "Maybe you are in your quiet moments. But most of the time, the vibe I get from you is electric. You have lots of positive energy working for you. Whereas, I'm more…" He seemed to struggle for the right word to describe himself.

"Introspective?" Meghan said.

"You're intuitive, too," Leo complimented her.

Meghan was at the stove peering into the oven at the lasagna she'd made for dinner. She'd turned the oven off so there was no fear of it burning. She closed the oven door and regarded Leo. "I hope you like Italian."

"I do, and that lasagna smells delicious."

"It's vegetarian. I'm looking out for your heart." A bottle of red wine was alongside two wineglasses on the island's countertop. Meghan gestured to them. "Would you like a glass of wine?"

"I like vegetarian," Leo said. "But no, thanks, to

the wine right now." His gaze followed the lines of her body from head to toe. "I wouldn't mind a tour of the house, though."

"Of course," Meghan said, a bit nervously. Even though they were already lovers, he still made her blush when he looked at her with his intentions reflected in his expressive eyes.

She gestured toward the hallway adjacent to the kitchen. "This way. The house has three bedrooms and two and a half baths." She stopped at a bedroom on the left. "This is the smallest room."

They stepped inside, and Leo saw that she'd turned this bedroom into a home office. The room was around twelve feet by twelve feet and had a huge bay window under which was a padded seat. A very nice place to read. And he could tell she loved to read. One wall had floor-to-ceiling bookcases filled with hardcover and paperback books. In front of those bookcases sat a comfortable-looking chaise longue and an adjustable arc floor lamp. Her reading nook.

He smiled at her. "You told me you enjoyed reading, and now I see that you have a designated place for it."

He also noticed she had a desk in the room with a laptop on it, a good reading lamp and a clear glass jar filled with jelly beans. He walked over and picked up the jar. "Sweet tooth, huh?"

"Not particularly," she said, smiling. "They're a nostalgic reminder of when I first started writing as a teen."

His brows arched with surprise. "Why didn't you

mention you're also a writer when I told you about my novels?"

"Because I didn't know you then," she said reasonably. She went and sat down on the chaise longue, and Leo pulled the wheeled office chair from the desk and sat next to her. He had a feeling this might be a long story.

"I haven't shown anyone my work," she said shyly.

"Not even your sisters?" Leo asked softly.

"Especially not my sisters," Meghan told him. "They'd recognize themselves in my stories. Although all three novels are historical, they're also semi-biographical. The main characters in each book have the spirits of my sisters. The first novel is about Lauren, the second about Mina and the third about Desiree. Of course, the stories are set during different historical periods, but they're definitely about them."

"I see," Leo said. "And you believe that's something to hide from your sisters because you think they'll be angry that you wrote about them without their permission?"

"No, that's not it. I just don't want them to think I don't respect them. That I would exploit them for monetary gain."

"Therefore, you haven't tried to publish the novels."

"Right," Meghan said. She met his eyes, hers bright with excitement. "Writing is cathartic for me. I have to do it or I don't feel fulfilled. When I finish a novel, my first thought is not of accomplishment, but what I'm going to do next. I'm always working on something. I'm writing about a black woman now, who agreed to be a mail-order bride in the late 1850s to a wealthy rancher in Montana who passed for white. He fell in love with her and had to make a choice—marry her and give up the protective wall he'd built around himself because of the advantages he gained by passing for white in a white-ruled society, or give up the only woman he'd ever loved. The whole marriage scenario tells me I'm writing about Petra, who has an aversion to marriage."

Leo smiled, fascinated. "Are you going to let me read your stories?"

Meghan stared at him, shocked he'd even ask. "I don't think I'm ready for anyone to read them."

"You've read mine," Leo stated.

"Yes, but you published them. Anyone could read them. My stories are in files on my computer."

"Did you back them up? You don't want to lose them."

"Yes, I backed them up," she said, smiling because it was sweet of him to ask. Also, she was enjoying talking to a fellow writer. She'd been living in seclusion where her writing was concerned. It felt good to exchange views with another author.

"I'll think about it," she said. "But to me, my books are like my babies. I think they're cute. However, someone else might think they're ugly. It would devastate me if someone thought my babies weren't pretty."

"No, it wouldn't," Leo countered. "You would eventually grow a thick skin like the rest of us dreamers who are compelled to put their hearts and souls out there for the public to judge."

Meghan laughed, "We're dreamers, huh?"

"What else would you call someone who keeps writing even though they're not earning much? I read that only about three percent of writers are making a great living doing it, and the rest of them aren't even making a salary equivalent to a part-time job at a fast-food joint. They're dreamers—wishing and hoping that someone will finally notice their brilliance, and then they're on their way!"

"Dreamers or not," Meghan said, "I love them for sharing their souls with us. Books have always been my escape. I love to read them, and I love to write them."

Leo rose and pulled her into his arms. "Thanks for sharing your secret with me. I love you even more now, realizing that you're as big of a book nerd as I am."

Meghan spontaneously kissed him for that. She was so happy to finally have someone in her life she could discuss books and writing with.

Leo felt himself hardening and broke off the kiss. "Babe, you're turning me on. Unless you don't mind postponing dinner awhile, we should cool it."

Dreamy eyed in a way that told him she was turned on, too, Meghan shook her head. "Dinner can wait. I can't."

"Then maybe you ought to show me your bedroom," Leo coolly suggested.

Meghan beckoned to him as she sashayed out of her office. Leo followed and began pulling off his shirt.

Her bedroom was spacious, with a queen-size sleigh bed made of cherrywood and the accompanying dresser and nightstands. The floor was a light-colored hardwood, and he noticed she had a huge walk-in closet and adjoining master bath. In line with her tastes, the room was sparse in the sense that the furnishings didn't make the room feel crowded.

The covers on the bed had been pulled back. He smiled at that. She must have thought she was going to get lucky. Well, he didn't want to disappoint her. He helpfully unzipped her dress. Underneath it she was wearing black lingerie. The lace pattern left little to the imagination. He tried not to salivate.

"Condoms?" she asked, making even that word sound sexy to his ears.

"You don't have any?"

"No, I haven't bought them in a very long time," she told him. "No sex, no need for them."

He didn't ask her how long it had been since she'd been with another man. That wasn't important to him. He was a modern guy who didn't expect women to be celibate. That didn't mean he wasn't pleased she didn't sleep around. He didn't, either.

"Then I'll have to go out to the car," he said regretfully. "I put a few in the glove compartment, just in case."

Meghan smiled. "I'll put on something more comfortable while you're gone."

He looked down at her body in her lacy bra and panties. "You look pretty comfortable to me."

"You'll thank me later," she said mysteriously.

Leo's heart thudded excitedly. He put his shirt back on and turned to leave the room. "Be back in a hurry."

"You do that," Meghan said and headed to her closet to pull down a white box sitting on a shelf in there.

The dogs were glad to see Leo as he rushed through the house to the front door. He had to calm them down a bit before they would allow him to open the door. Finally, he was able to close the door behind him and jog down the front steps to his car.

An elderly gentleman was walking his Jack Russell terrier. He seemed very interested in Leo's movements. In fact, he stopped on the sidewalk in front of Meghan's house and called, "Hello there! You must be a friend of Meghan's. I'm Dr. Leland Johnson. My wife and I live next door."

He walked up to Leo and offered his hand. Leo, a little taken aback by the elderly guy's temerity, shook his hand. Deciding to give tit for tat, he introduced himself with his credentials out front, too. "Hello, Dr. Johnson. I'm Dr. Wolfe. Yes, I'm a friend of Dr. Gaines's."

Leland Johnson nodded and said in pleasant tones, "Wonderful, wonderful. Mrs. Johnson and I look out for Meghan. A young woman living alone and all that. You understand."

Yes, Leo understood and was suddenly thankful that Meghan had neighbors who kept their eyes open and cared about her well-being. "Absolutely," he said. "You can't be too careful. Well, I was just going to my car. It's a pleasure meeting you, Dr. Johnson."

"Same here, Dr. Wolfe," Leland Johnson returned,

and continued down the sidewalk with his energetic dog, who was pulling on the leash.

There was another attempt by the dogs to get him to play with them when he got back inside with the condoms tucked in his jeans pocket, but he deftly slipped past them.

In the bedroom, Meghan had dimmed the lights. When he walked in, though, she was nowhere in sight. "Meghan?"

The light in the closet came on and there, framed in the doorway, was Meghan, wearing a white, see-through robe and nothing else. She'd tied the sash as though she were interested in modesty. Leo smiled lasciviously. There was no way in hell she could look modest in that particular item of clothing. Her luscious body was plainly outlined beneath it. He felt emotional at that moment. As though he were the luckiest man alive.

Slowly, he loosened the sash at her waist and pulled the garment off her silken shoulders. "You're a goddess," he whispered.

Meghan smiled appreciatively. "I'm just a woman in love with a man, hoping that I please him."

She moved into the circle of his arms and offered him her mouth. This kiss made a promise that what followed would be memorable.

Afterward, Leo shed his clothing right there in the closet and they fell to the thickly carpeted floor.

On their sides, they kissed hungrily and then Meghan straddled him and rolled the condom, which he'd had the presence of mind to get out of his pocket while he was doffing his jeans, onto his hard penis.

She was wet and ready for him. She positioned herself over him and gently impaled herself. Leo couldn't take his eyes off her. Her eyes were closed as she exulted in the pleasure he was giving her. This knowledge made him even harder than he already was. The urgency to come grew. But he held on because he wanted to witness her face when she achieved the height of her pleasure. Mesmerized by her beautiful face, he thrust upward, his powerful leg muscles burning with the effort after a while. This, however, joined with the passion of the moment and enhanced his enjoyment.

Meghan moaned softly. Her eyes shot open and she met his gaze. "Why didn't you get here sooner?" And she came, quivering with the release. Leo held her a moment, his eyes moist because she'd undone him with those words. Why hadn't he gotten here sooner? *Dear God, please inspire me to come up with a solution to my problem so I can have a future with this wonderful woman.*

He carefully turned her over onto her back and made love to her until she cried out with another orgasm. Then he took his pleasure and they lay on the floor in the closet, their gazes locked, with satisfied smiles on their faces.

# Chapter 13

"Okay, this is the last time we're going to be together for a long time," Lauren said, raising her glass of cranberry juice and Sprite in a toast to her sisters. "So let's make this night count!"

They were in a bar that catered to young professionals in downtown Raleigh. It was loud and rowdy, but in a fun way. The music playing on the sound system was a mixture of hip-hop and contemporary rock.

"Let's get the serious stuff out of the way before some of you get too drunk," Meghan said. She was limiting herself to two glasses of white wine.

"What serious stuff?" Petra asked, tossing back a whiskey with ease. Desiree, who had earlier promised to take her shopping, had fulfilled that promise and now she was as trendy and fashionable as Desiree in a short dress, sexy, strappy sandals and a short denim jacket. She had her hair in two braids down her back.

"You know," Meghan said. "Our 'where are we now' and 'where do we want to go' dreams thing we do whenever we're all in one place. Are we working on our goals, ladies, and do we maybe have some new ones to add to the list?" She ended by giving Petra a meaningful glance.

Petra laughed, "Not you, too, baby sister."

"Well, I don't understand why you couldn't give Chance a chance!" Meghan said, laughing, too.

"Oh, you've got jokes," Petra said, eyes sparkling with humor. "I'll tell you why I don't want to get serious about Chance Youngblood. His family is astoundingly wealthy. His grandfather started out as a newspaperman and built the family publishing business into a multimedia empire. Chance was born rich. I don't need a man with that kind of mind-set. I want someone who knows what it is to struggle and to have to fight for what he wants. A man like that might be able to keep up with me. Chance would expect to have everything his way. I would be a disappointment to him because I'm stubborn, independent and I don't give a rat's ass about living in luxury. I live in the jungle where there are no amenities. It wouldn't work."

"Point taken," Meghan said. "Opposites attract, though. And you did say he was the best lover you ever had."

"I can count on one hand the number of lovers I've had," Petra said. "He hasn't had much competition."

"You like him," Desiree stated with conviction.

"With a passion," Mina put in. She was nursing a ginger ale. No alcohol for her since she was expecting.

"We saw the way you two were looking at each other," Lauren said with a sigh. "When Colton looks at me like that, my clothes are off the moment we're alone!"

Petra laughed. "I hate it when you gang up on me like this. But I'll give you this much," she said in an appeasing tone. "I'm leaning toward doing the show with Chance's company. My research is coming along well, and I'm looking for more funding. The deal he's offering is the answer to my prayers."

"Then you're going to be working closely with him," Meghan pointed out.

"Yes, but that doesn't mean anything," Petra said firmly. "I made the mistake of jumping into bed with him before I was aware of who he was. Now I'm..."

"Back up," Desiree cried impatiently. "You mean he deceived you?"

"No, I'm not saying that," Petra said. "I was in a bar in Manhattan having a drink because I was a little nervous about a meeting I had to go to the next morning. A meeting at which I was expected to impress a potential investor who might be funding my work if I hit a home run, and he sat down beside me. It was lust at first sight. We struck up a very suggestive conversation. Long story short, I liked him, I was lonely and the next thing I knew I was naked in his arms."

"Whoa," Meghan said, amazed. "That's never happened to you before."

"No," Petra said. "And it's never going to happen again."

"When did he tell you who he was?" Lauren asked.

"He didn't tell me," Petra said. "I'm not proud of it, but I sneaked out the next morning and went back to my hotel to get ready for that important meeting I mentioned. Five minutes after I got to the meeting, guess who walked in?"

"How did he know where you were?" Desiree asked, eyes stretched in horror.

"You don't get it," Petra said. "He was the investor. I'd slept with the investor and then I had to convince him that the research organization that funds my work is worth backing! Getting up in front of everyone and talking about my work with images of him and me the night before running in my mind was the hardest thing I've ever done. But, by the grace of God, I did it."

"I've never been more embarrassed in my life," Petra continued. "I left the meeting while he was preoccupied with one of the suits and hightailed it for the airport."

"I just have one question for you. Did he agree to support the organization?" Meghan asked.

"Yes, he did," Petra replied with an exaggerated sigh. "For which I'm grateful, believe me. But I'm not going near that particular rich boy ever again."

Then she held up her empty glass and called to the nearby waiter, "Sweetie, another whiskey, please!"

The waiter—a tall, good-looking African American in his early twenties, with a hard body and a ready grin—called back, "Coming right up!"

* * *

Meghan missed her sisters the next few weeks, but she was so busy, she hardly had time to wonder what they were up to. She made the transfer from Shaw to Duke. It was a longer commute to work, but she didn't mind.

Also, Leo had been right when he said her new colleagues would be friendly and welcoming. Shari Dunbar, especially, proved to be a fast friend.

Marjorie had assigned her to introductory courses for freshmen, which Meghan wholeheartedly agreed with, since she liked teaching students who had not been indoctrinated in a certain way of studying literature. She wanted them to be inquisitive and eager to learn.

How her students expressed themselves was also important to her. She stressed the usefulness of being a competent speaker as well as a competent writer, along with inculcating in them the love of reading. To her, this method produced a well-rounded student. A student who would grow into a mature scholar who loved literature for the sake of literature, not simply showing enough interest in it to earn a passing grade in her class.

Her teaching style was unorthodox in some ways. This was brought home to her when Leo, as her supervisor, sat in on her classes a few days to observe. When it was time for him to give her his opinion of her performance, he asked her to come to his office.

Meghan was careful not to treat Leo with anything but professional courtesy when they were working.

She knocked before entering his office, and when he called, "Come in!" she strode in wearing a dark gray skirt suit with black pumps and accessories, including her briefcase. Her hair was in a neat French braid, and she wore minimal makeup.

Leo had on a dark blue suit with a white long-sleeve shirt, a striped tie and black dress shoes.

He gestured to the chair in front of his desk as he sat on the corner of the desk, a sheet of paper in his hand. "Please, sit down."

Meghan sat and looked expectantly up at him.

"Meghan, I monitored your class a few times last week," he began gravely.

"Yes, I saw you," Meghan told him. When her class was being monitored, she was advised that she should not acknowledge it but simply go on teaching in her normal fashion. Which was what she had done. On the whole, she believed she had all the qualities a good instructor possessed. In fact, she had never gotten a bad evaluation from any of her past supervisors.

So she wasn't prepared when Leo said, "I don't think you take this position seriously. You give your students reading assignments and ask them to either write essays relating to those assignments, or they can give an oral report that includes spoken word or rap. Which, I admit, is very entertaining, but does it improve their understanding of the literature they've just read?"

"How kids today absorb information is different from the way kids used to," Meghan said. "If allowing them to speak their own language helps them to remember facts, then I don't see why they shouldn't be free to express themselves in that way. It might have seemed like a foreign language to you, but they get it."

"I like rap as much as the next person. But what if they're not learning as much as you think they are?" Leo queried. "Midterms are coming up, and if this department shows a decline in our students' grades, that's not going to look good, Meghan. Please, just stick to the tried-and-true method of having them write down their thoughts." He glanced down at the sheet of paper in his hand, after which he raised his gaze back to hers. "I hope you'll take my suggestion in the manner it was intended—to make sure our students get a sound education."

Meghan rose. "Of course. That's my goal, as well. Is there anything else?"

"No, that's it," Leo said.

"All right. Thank you for your advice." She turned and left, silently closing the door behind her.

As she walked down the hallway, she felt a little stunned, but not angry. On the contrary, she was worried about Leo because he'd looked so serious, as if it pained him to have to give her a bad evaluation. In her opinion, although she and Leo had some things in common, like they were pet lovers, enjoyed running and long walks, were both quite organized and were close to their families, deep down their philosophies on life were extremely dissimilar. She knew they weren't going to agree on everything. She was positive that when the results came in after the midterm tests, her methods would be proven worthwhile.

* * *

Leo sat in the chair behind his desk, wondering if he had been right to suggest Meghan teach her classes in a less modern manner. The proof, after all, was in the test results after the midterms. On one hand, he had faith in Meghan's abilities; on the other, as her supervisor, it was his duty to offer suggestions on how she could improve those abilities if he saw something lacking in her performance. The question was, had he come to his conclusions because he was too set in his ways? Was his opinion based on his personal beliefs? And was he trying to mold Meghan in his image?

He needed to speak with Marjorie and ask her those questions. Maybe his working with Meghan wasn't such a good idea, after all. He had to be unbiased as her supervisor. Yet he cared very much about her well-being, and the thought of her making a fool of herself when it got back to the other members of the faculty that she was allowing her students to rap for a grade rankled.

Also, on a personal front, he was tense because he'd gone to a heart specialist who'd put him on the treadmill for a stress test and had him get an echocardiogram, blood work and myriad other tests to determine what shape his heart was in, and he hadn't gotten the results yet. He had an appointment with the doctor to get them this afternoon. Frankly, he was on pins and needles worrying about those results.

As for Meghan, she was a trouper. She was supportive and loving and everything he wanted in a mate.

He loved her more with each passing day. However, he also grew more and more certain he was going to lose her because he still hadn't told her about his sterility. The guilt was eating him alive. He was putting so much stock in those test results. If they came back in his favor, at least he would have one thing working for him. Then, perhaps, he could break the bad news to her. *I'm sterile, sweetheart, but at least I'm not going to suddenly drop dead on you!*

Later that day, Leo was able to catch up with Marjorie in the faculty lounge near the English department's offices. The place was pretty busy, with the buzz of voices of other faculty members conducting lively conversations. Marjorie was at a table with her laptop open before her. She was sipping coffee when she looked up and saw Leo approaching.

She smiled and set her coffee down. She looked sharp today in black slacks and dark gold silk blouse with bold black onyx earrings in her lobes and black three-inch-heeled pumps. Her hair had grown, and now she wore it in a sophisticated, sleek pageboy.

"Ah, Leo, how did your meeting go with Meghan? I got your email. Though I haven't had time to respond to it."

Leo's hand was on the other chair at her table. "May I?"

"Please do," Marjorie said casually. She picked up her cup and took another sip, her keen eyes on his face.

Leo told her about his fears that he might be imposing his own feelings on Meghan's teaching style, and he wanted to run it by Marjorie to make sure he wasn't doing that.

"Of course you're doing it," Marjorie said. "We all impose our views on others. We've always done that. People feel comfortable around the familiar. However, Meghan's style can only be judged on its value by how the students respond to it. Therefore, we should wait and see." She smiled warmly. "I hope that answers your question."

Leo sighed with relief. "I thought I was being hard on her."

Marjorie laughed, "Meghan's tougher than that. She probably feels bad for *you*." She suddenly raised her brows as if a thought had just hit her. "Oh, I'm glad you sought me out. I wanted to tell you that I'm sending you and Meghan to a professors' conference in San Francisco so you can mingle with teachers from all over the country and pick their brains and let them pick yours. Then you two can come back here refreshed and ready to rock our world with your ideas. In other words, you two can duke it out at the conference. Maybe you're right and Meghan should tone down her style of teaching. On the other hand, maybe you're a stick-in-the-mud who should try something new," she laughed. "At any rate, I think we'll all benefit. Are you game?"

Leo looked skeptical. "When is it?"

"In a couple of months," Marjorie informed him. "The midterms will be over with by then, and school will be out for summer vacation."

"Have you spoken with Meghan about this?"

"Nope," Marjorie said happily. "You're the supervisor. You talk to her. I'll have my assistant email the information to you."

"All right," Leo said, rising. "Thanks, Marjorie."

"My pleasure," Marjorie said. "You're doing a good job as supervisor, Leo. We work as a team to make this department as effective as we possibly can. That means we have to exchange ideas. Meghan is a professional. She understands that."

Leo was confident that what Marjorie said was true. He still didn't know what kind of reception he was going to get from Meghan when he saw her next. After he'd had his say earlier, she'd walked out of his office without a backward glance, so he had not seen the expression in her eyes. That would have given him some clue as to how she felt about his evaluation.

"I'm sure you're right," he said and made himself scarce.

# *Chapter 14*

"Can I have that in writing?" Leo asked, his heart, his healthy heart, beating excitedly.

His new cardiologist, Dr. Aaron Lindsey, had just told him he couldn't find anything wrong with his heart. He told him even though he'd been diagnosed with a heart murmur when he was a child, children often grow out of them, and apparently, that was exactly what Leo had done. "The cardiac catheterization and echocardiogram, which I see from your medical records you've been getting done at least once a year, plus an excellent stress test, show me a normal, healthy heart, Dr. Wolfe."

"Oh, please call me Leo."

"Leo, I'm surprised no one has seen fit to put you through more extensive tests over the years. I've seen this happen many times before—a person lives with the fear of sudden death when, all along, they're as healthy as the next person. I'm sorry you've had this experience."

While Leo was supremely relieved nothing was wrong with his heart, he was naturally upset no other health professional had seen fit to look into the possibility that his condition might have changed. "Why do you think no one spotted this before you did?" he asked the doctor.

"Because medical professionals are not good at communicating," the cardiologist told him. "I hope it's getting better. I bet every time you had an echocardiogram, you were told your heart sounded normal and you interpreted that to mean your heart's valves weren't worsening. Therefore you were doing all right and you should continue eating right, exercising and not smoking. Am I right?"

Leo nodded. "Yes, I thought I was doing what was necessary to live longer."

Dr. Lindsey laughed shortly, "And you were. You're in great health. I wish all my patients were as healthy as you are. Oh, wait, then I'd be out of a job."

They laughed. Leo shook the doctor's hand. "Thank you. Now if I can find a good fertility specialist, I'll be set."

"Life gave you a double whammy, huh?" the cardiologist asked sympathetically. "I have a recommendation for you." He opened his desk drawer and retrieved a notepad. He quickly scribbled a name on it and handed the slip of paper to Leo. "Dr. Angela Omoro is a very thorough physician with an investigative mind. A good doctor has to be a good detective, you know."

Leo breathed a sigh of relief. He wished he'd run into one of those investigative physicians when he was younger. Maybe he wouldn't have developed such a pessimistic view of life. There were years of negativity he had to purge from his system. Living with the possibility of sudden death had surely helped shape the man he was today.

He thanked Dr. Lindsey again and left, feeling much lighter and more optimistic about life than he'd felt in years. He couldn't wait to share the news with Meghan.

However, by the time he'd gotten to his car, he'd decided that it would be a better idea to wait until he'd gone to the fertility specialist and gotten the results of what would probably be quite a few tests to determine if, indeed, he'd been born without the vas deferens, the main pipelines from the testicles, which made it possible to impregnate his partner.

He'd been lucky once. Maybe his luck would hold out and he'd be given more good news. Whatever the results were, he had made up his mind he was going to tell Meghan the truth as soon as he had the results of the fertility tests.

As he walked to the parking garage where he'd left his car, he pulled out his cell phone and asked Google to find the phone number for Dr. Angela Omoro. He wasn't surprised to learn she was affiliated with Duke University Hospital, just as Dr. Lindsey was.

Meghan was barely home from work when her mother phoned her with a request. "I want you and

Leo to come to brunch tomorrow. Your father and I think it's about time we met him."

"You've already met him," Meghan said. "You met him at Mina's wedding and your anniversary party."

"You know what I mean," Virginia said testily. "You two were not dating then. We want to meet the man who has the temerity to date our baby girl. I can't make it plainer than that."

Meghan winced. No, she certainly could not.

"First of all," Meghan began, her brain trying to come up with an excuse not to go. "You've got to tone it down a bit. I won't have you putting Leo through the third degree. Second, if we come, we'll have to bring the dogs because it's too late to find a puppy sitter. And you don't like dogs."

Virginia harrumphed. Then she laughed softly. "This time, I'm going to make an exception. Bring your pets. The backyard is fenced. They'll be fine out there for a couple of hours. Remember to bring your little blue bags."

Meghan tried not to laugh, but ended up doing so anyway. Her mother had her. "Fine. What time should we be there?"

"Eleven," Virginia answered, a satisfied note to her voice. "Dress casually. We're eating on the deck."

"All right. Thank you for inviting us," Meghan said.

"Thank you for agreeing to come," Virginia said politely.

Meghan hung up. *Temerity* her mother had said. Excessive boldness or audacity. What made her mother say such things?

As if Leo had to be brave to date her. As if her mother thought no one was good enough for her.

She just had to laugh at her mother's behavior sometimes.

Right this minute, though, she needed to jump into the shower because it was Friday night, and Leo would be there in two hours. She wondered how he was going to behave after giving her a bad evaluation today. Would he be shy and hesitant to bring up the subject? She hoped not, because she had no hard feelings about the situation. It was her wish to keep business separate from their personal lives. Their workday was over, and now it was time to be a loving couple.

When she opened the door for him, he stood there with a beautiful bouquet of flowers that he thrust at her, a huge grin on his face and his beautiful brown eyes shining with joy.

Malcolm squeezed between his master's leg and the doorway, barking hello to Meghan and running over to Chauncey, who affectionately nudged the side of his head with her nose.

Meghan accepted the flowers, stepped back to allow Leo entrance and, if truth be told, sniffed him as he came in for a kiss because she thought her Mr. Darcy might have been imbibing a little wine, he looked so happy. But no, he didn't smell or taste like alcohol. They did an awkward dance there in the foyer with her arms full of flowers, his enthusiasm and the dogs attempting to trip them.

"Hello, beautiful," he said, his normal greeting lately.

"Hello yourself." She smiled as she walked past him

and went to the kitchen to find a vase. Leo followed. "You look especially joyful tonight," she said. "Did something unusual happen to you today?"

"I'm just happy to see you," Leo said. "And happy that you don't seem upset by my evaluation today."

He sat on one of the island's stools while she was reaching into the cabinet above the sink where she kept a couple of crystal vases. After grabbing one, she filled it with water and put the flowers in it.

"We need to keep work and our personal lives separate," she said. She came and set the vase in the middle of the island. "I don't care what you say to me as my supervisor, Leo. I'm not bringing that home."

She walked around the large island and into the circle of his arms. Looking into his eyes, she said, "Thank you for the flowers. I love you unconditionally. That means I'm going to love you when we have disagreements and when everything is wonderful between us."

Leo buried his nose in the side of her neck, inhaling the enticing scent of her skin. Honeysuckle tonight, with a hint of cinnamon. At that moment, he wanted to tell her everything so badly that he was trembling inside with the desire to do so. But he didn't. He had a plan. When he finally told her, it was going to be in San Francisco at a luxury hotel, where the backdrop would be undeniably romantic. He would give her the good news first: no heart murmur. Then, if he was lucky, he would tell her that for years he had thought he was incapable of fathering children and the knowledge had made him severely depressed, but everything had changed since he met her. Then he planned to ask her to marry him.

Of course, if the news was bad concerning his infertility, he would still confess everything. It was the asking her to marry him part that might not get said. Because once she found out he couldn't perform the one imperative every male on earth, animal or human, was obsessed with, that of propagating and spreading his seed, she would undoubtedly leave him standing on that balcony he envisioned in the dream scenario in his head.

"I love you, too, babe," he said, kissing her forehead. "I love you so much, I'd do anything to keep you in my arms. Anything."

Meghan beamed with pleasure. "That sounds good to me."

They kissed again, and when they came up for air, Leo said, "Oh, I do have some news for you. Marjorie wants to send us to San Francisco this summer to attend a professors' conference. What do you think of that?"

Meghan's smile got broader. "I've always wanted to go to one of those, but I never got the chance. Budget cuts and all that."

"Well, I read the information Marjorie's assistant emailed me, and it looks like the school will pay for everything—travel, registration fees and accommodations."

"That sounds wonderful," Meghan said. "I can't wait!"

Leo squeezed her. "I'm glad you're excited about it.

And I want you to know that I'm going to take every opportunity to spoil you."

"You already spoil me every day just by loving me," Meghan said. She kissed him high on his cheek. "You don't know how much your love means to me. I thought I would never find a man who could love me just as I am. I'm a peculiar woman, Leo. I know my strengths and my weaknesses. I'm stubborn and opinionated."

"I wouldn't say that," Leo interrupted her. "Being stubborn can be a good quality when it makes you stick to your beliefs. You've got a lot of faith in mankind, Meghan. It's one of your sweetest characteristics, your utter faith that we're all deserving of kindness and happiness. You're patient with those of us who're more cynical about life. I have to admit, I'm more optimistic since I met you. You're good for me."

Meghan had tears in her eyes as she gazed up at him. "And you're good for me," she said softly. Putting her arms around his neck, she offered him her mouth. "Now, be good to me, Mr. Darcy, and make love to me."

Leo bent his head and met her mouth in a passionate kiss filled with all the love inside of him, past, present and what was to come. Meghan was his everything. He didn't know what he would do if he ever lost her.

Later, they lay wrapped in each other's arms, smiling contentedly. "My mother wants us to come to brunch tomorrow. I've already accepted for us, but if you'd rather not, I'd understand. She can be intimidating, and if you're not ready for the 'meet the parents' stage yet, we can put it off."

Leo chuckled. "I wouldn't think of it. I'm not afraid of Virginia Gaines."

Meghan laughed, "Oh, my God, I was just reminded of that movie starring Elizabeth Taylor, *Who's Afraid of Virginia Woolf?*"

"Yeah, my last name and your mother's first," Leo said. "Your mind does go to odd places sometimes, my love."

"You don't know the half of it," Meghan said. "Last night I was working on my latest book, and as I was writing a description of the hero, I realized I was describing you. You're creeping into my subconscious. I had to go back and rewrite the description to match how I've described the hero in the rest of the book."

"I'm flattered," Leo said. "You might as well know that you're the reason I'm writing again. Your interest in my work encouraged me to get back to the computer and be productive. You're my muse now, so if the book's a total failure, you can blame yourself."

Meghan laughed, "I'll take that risk. Just keep writing because I've got to know what happens to Jess Harper."

"You like Jess, huh?"

"Jess is my kind of man, yes," Meghan cooed, snuggling closer.

"I might just kill Jess," Leo joked.

"Beware of killing Jess," Meghan warned, smiling enticingly. "You probably have lots of female readers who like Jess as much as I do."

"And since studies show that women read more than

men do, especially fiction, I'd be wise to let the stud live," Leo concluded.

"You're a smart man," Meghan said and rewarded him with a kiss.

At ten o'clock the next morning, Leo pulled up to Meghan's house behind the wheel of his candy-apple-red, mint-condition, 1967 Pontiac GTO. Meghan, who was waiting at the curb with Chauncey in her pet carrier, melted at first sight of the beautiful muscle car. She had previously seen it in his garage, but never on the road in all its glory.

"Whitewall tires!" she exclaimed. She put Chauncey on the back seat in her carrier next to Malcolm in his. Leo had gotten out to help her, but saw she didn't need his help and was slipping back behind the wheel when Meghan said, "Let me drive her!"

Leo grinned and walked around the car. The two of them met in front of the GTO, and he handed her the keys and went around to the passenger side. "Okay, enjoy yourself but I get equal time with the Mustang."

For a moment, Meghan hesitated. No one drove her Mustang except her. Then she laughed and said, "Deal."

She got behind the wheel, started the engine and put her hand on the gearshift. Looking at Leo, she said, "You won't have to work hard to get on Dad's good side when he sees this baby."

"I was counting on that," Leo said with a conspiratorial smile.

Meghan pulled away from the curb and thrilled at the feel of the powerful car underneath her direction.

Even the sound of its motor turned her on. "Truly, this car is foreplay in its purest sense. Too bad we're going to spend the afternoon with my parents. But watch out when I get you alone again."

Leo laughed, "I'm not above reminding you of that promise later."

"You won't have to," Meghan assured him. Then she drove in silence, joining the Saturday morning traffic and pointing the GTO to the outskirts of Raleigh and her parents' sprawling, two-story updated farmhouse.

Alphonse and Virginia had bought the house over twenty years ago, and it was where the girls had spent their formative years. It had undergone various renovations over time. Still, Meghan felt nostalgic each time she entered the house with its five bedrooms and three and a half baths. The people her parents had bought the land from had been farmers, so Alphonse and Virginia continued to refer to the house as a farmhouse. The only farming they did was to turn a patch of land in their vast backyard into a garden. They'd fenced in the rear of the house because their property backed up to an undeveloped wooded area.

When Meghan and Leo got to the house, Alphonse, who undoubtedly had heard the rumble of the GTO's engine, came outside and greeted them with a huge smile on his handsome face.

Meghan parked the GTO in the driveway behind her father's metallic blue Super Duty Ford F-250—he'd finally traded in his Hummer—and got out to run into her father's open arms.

"Hey, Dad, we're here."

Alphonse was dressed in a blue polo shirt, plaid cotton knee-length shorts and a pair of white athletic shoes. He hugged Meghan tightly and kissed her cheek, but Meghan could tell he only had eyes for the GTO. "Hey, baby girl," Alphonse said, his gaze on the car.

Leo was busy getting the pet carriers out of the back seat. He walked around the car with a carrier in each hand. "Hello, Mr. Gaines," he greeted Alphonse.

"Leo," Alfonse said cheerfully. "Is this yours?"

Leo smiled. "Yes, it is. Would you like to take her for a spin?"

"Is the sky blue?" Alphonse asked eagerly.

Leo gestured to Meghan to hand her dad the keys. "I'll go with your father," he said.

Meghan took the pet carriers from him. "Okay, sweetie. Have fun."

By the time she'd walked onto the front porch, a carrier in each hand, her mother had stepped out of the house. "Where are they going?" she asked, puzzled. She watched the back end of the GTO as it sped down the country lane, dust and gravel kicking up in its wake.

"Dad wanted to drive the GTO," Meghan told her mother.

"That man and his obsession with cars," Virginia grumbled, frowning, then she glanced down at Chauncey and Malcolm in their pet carriers. "So you actually brought them."

"I told you I was going to," Meghan reminded her as she squeezed past. "Don't worry, I'm going to put them in the backyard and set up their dishes on the deck. They won't even walk on your floors."

"Good," Virginia said. "They won't be underfoot."

Meghan walked straight through the foyer, great room, dining room and kitchen until she reached the French doors that led out to the deck. She placed the carriers on the deck and opened first Malcolm's and then Chauncey's. The dogs were happy to be out of their cages and ran right back into the kitchen, where Virginia was rinsing vegetables at the deep, ceramic sink. Meghan ran after the dogs but was too late to prevent their jumping up on Virginia's legs and trying to play with her.

"My clean apron!" Virginia cried. She dropped the cucumber she'd been rinsing into the sink and pressed herself against it, a look of consternation on her face. "Meghan, get these beasts out of here!"

Meghan grabbed Malcolm and Chauncey by their collars but did not immediately herd the dogs outside. "Quiet now," she said calmly to the animals. "Show your host that you can behave yourselves."

Chauncey was the first to respond to her voice, then Malcolm stopped quivering with excitement. After a few seconds, both dogs sat down at Meghan's feet and looked up at her as if awaiting further instructions. Meghan was proud of them, especially Malcolm, who, in the last few months, had learned how to curtail his enthusiasm. Also, Leo had put in a pet door at his house, and Malcolm was now going outside to do his business on his own. He'd become quite the responsible pooch.

Meghan stood there, smiling at her mother. "You see, Mom, they're not savage beasts. They won't hurt you."

Virginia hastily removed her now-soiled apron and

regarded Meghan with a sour expression. "I just don't want to be near them, that's all."

"Why?" Meghan asked plaintively. "Why do you hate dogs?"

Virginia held her daughter's gaze awhile before opening her mouth to impatiently say, "Okay, if you must know, it's because when I was a little girl, I had a dog, a chocolate Labrador that looked just like that one." She pointed at Malcolm. "And he got killed, stupid dog. He ran into the street and somebody ran over him and kept going."

Tears were forming in her eyes. She grabbed a paper towel from the holder on the counter closest to her and dabbed at her tears. "I know it was years ago, but I still remember it as clearly as if it happened yesterday. Coco was his name. I was seven years old and I loved that dog. Daddy buried him in the backyard, and I would visit his grave and cry every day. I swore I would never own another pet because it hurt too much when they died."

At this point, Meghan was crying, too, and hugging her mother with Chauncey and Malcolm gently licking any surface of the humans' skin they could reach, trying their best to comfort them.

"It's all right," Meghan said soothingly. "I understand how you feel. Chauncey's my first pet, but I know I'd be devastated if something happened to her."

Virginia looked up at her daughter through tear-filled eyes. "It hasn't escaped my notice that you named her after that brute who left you in college."

Meghan laughed, "Yes, Momma. Nothing escapes your notice."

Virginia blew her nose while cradled in her much taller daughter's arms. "And I haven't missed the fact that you and Leo are in love. Anyone who sees you together can see that." She narrowed her eyes. "I'm just worried that history is repeating itself. You fell in love with that football boy at Shaw, and you're in love with Leo at Duke. If I had known you two were already seeing each other prior to Marjorie offering you a position at Duke, I would have intervened. But, unfortunately, you don't talk to me, so it was too late to do anything by the time I heard about you two."

"Momma, you just ruined a tender moment between us. You don't need to worry about me and Leo. We're doing fine, and I don't believe he'd ever do anything to hurt me."

"You didn't believe that other one would do anything to hurt you, either. Until he did something to hurt you."

"What do you want me to do, be alone for the rest of my life? Or wait until you personally pick the perfect guy for me?"

"No, I want you to be happy. I want all of my daughters to be happy. I just worry about you the most because you're the last one I'll have the chance to give advice to and actually see my advice put to good use."

"Oh, I see where you're going with this," Meghan said as she shooed Chauncey and Malcolm back outside onto the deck. Virginia followed. "You know that you'll never influence Petra to get married and give you grandchildren, so I'm your last chance."

"Exactly," Virginia readily admitted. "Petra is a die-hard man hater. I wouldn't be surprised if she's gay and is just not telling me. Five daughters and no one's gay. What are the odds?"

"Petra isn't a man hater or gay," Meghan informed her mother.

She watched as Chauncey and Malcolm safely climbed down the steps that led to the backyard. She breathed in the fresh air, admired the blue sky and felt the spring breeze on her face.

"Now, let's go finish preparing brunch. I'm hungry."

Virginia started to say something else, but Meghan stopped her. "And another thing—if you want to micromanage someone's life, you ought to get a pet. You can train him any way you want to, and he'll obey you much more eagerly than any of your daughters will."

"I was just going to say I know I'm overbearing sometimes, and it's something I'm working on, but when I see one of you going in the wrong direction, I wouldn't be a good mother if I didn't try to point you in the right direction."

"Answer me this, Momma," Meghan suggested. She waited for her mother to meet her eyes and show some sign that she was actually listening.

Virginia looked straight at her and sighed softly. "Okay, I'm in the moment with you."

"Good," Meghan said. "Are you proud of us?"

Virginia frowned and forcefully said, "Of course I'm proud of you!"

"Well, then, you've done your job as a mother. You can relax and enjoy your first grandchild, CJ, and the grandchildren to come. It's not that your daughters don't need you. We do. It's that we've got to make our own decisions and mistakes if that's what we're going to do. And don't tell me you took every piece of advice Grandma and Grandpa gave you because I know you didn't. Grandpa didn't want you to marry Dad, but you defied him!"

"It was bad advice," Virginia said. "The advice I give you girls is good advice."

Meghan laughed and went inside. "I'm wasting my time trying to reason with you."

"My advice to you about Leo is marry him and have a houseful of children!"

Meghan spun around, pointing a finger in her mother's face. "I can't believe you're trying to use reverse psychology on me!"

Virginia laughed, "I can't win with you! I tell you I like Leo and you turn on me."

"What's going on here?" Alphonse's booming voice asked from the front of the house as he and Leo came through the door. "Ginny, why're you yelling at Meghan?"

"I wasn't yelling at Meghan," Virginia claimed. Moving quickly, she went to a deep drawer next to the dishwasher, retrieved a clean apron and put it on. "I was telling her I thought she and Leo make a lovely couple, that's all."

Leo went to put an arm around Meghan's shoulders. "You okay?" he asked softly.

Meghan smiled. "Sure, sure I am," she replied and took a cleansing breath.

"Please go hug your mother," he whispered. "I think she's about to cry."

Meghan glanced at her mom. Sure enough, she looked teary-eyed, her bottom lip trembling. Her father was rubbing her arm, trying to be supportive.

Meghan went and hugged her mother. "You know I love you," she said in her ear. "And I know you love me. As of this moment, I won't react to what I consider to be negative comments from you about my life. I know you mean well." She held her mother at arm's length and met her gaze. "Now, let me help you finish preparing brunch and let's have a good time today."

"Okay," Virginia said, her voice soft and hesitant. She sighed. "I got you some fresh cherries for dessert."

"I love cherries!"

Later, as the four of them were sitting at an umbrella-topped table on the deck, drinking mimosas and eating bing cherries after consuming the delicious meal Virginia had planned to perfection, Malcolm came up to Virginia and licked her offered hand. She scratched him behind his ear, and he sat down at her feet.

This small gesture of kindness from her mother to Malcolm made a lump of emotion form in Meghan's throat. Maybe her mother was mellowing out.

# *Chapter 15*

Leo wasn't able to get in to see Dr. Angela Omoro until late May, which was cutting it close as far as his plans were concerned. The conference was in early July, and he knew it would take weeks to schedule tests and wait for the results.

However, luck was on his side and he was able to see Dr. Omoro, have the suggested tests done and get the results back before he and Meghan flew to San Francisco for the conference.

Therefore, when he and Meghan boarded the plane for San Francisco the day before the conference was to start, he had in his wallet two folded sheets of paper with test results for his heart and the results determining whether he was absolutely sterile or not. Prior to the tests, he was hoping that even if they proved he was sterile, there might be a small chance of impregnating Meghan. He just needed something to pin his hopes on.

Meghan had the window seat, and he was in the middle. He hoped that the passenger in the aisle seat would be someone easy to get along with. The nonstop flight was going to last over six hours.

Meghan closed her eyes. He remembered she'd said she'd spent more hours writing last night than she planned to. Now the lack of sleep was catching up with her. "Relax and lay your head on my shoulder," he told her. Meghan opened her large brown eyes and smiled at him. "This is our first big trip together, and I don't want to miss anything."

Leo laughed shortly, "I consider our trip to the Great Smoky Mountains a big trip. It's not every day you run into a bear in the woods."

"A very nice bear," Meghan said.

"How do you define a nice bear?"

"He didn't try to eat us. He just looked us over, decided we didn't look tasty and ambled on to his destination, wherever that was."

"He almost gave me a heart attack," Leo said.

"You didn't seem scared at the time. You pushed me behind you and held me tightly by my hand because you sensed I was getting ready to sprint. You were my hero." She kissed his cheek, then she scowled at him. "But don't even mention your heart. I'm still mad at you for not going to the doctor when I asked you to. It's been months, and you've avoided it. How do you think that makes me feel?"

"As if I don't care about your opinion?" Leo asked.

"Believe me, sweetheart, I care deeply about your opinion, and I'm doing something about my health. I'll have results for you soon."

"I don't like to nag," Meghan persisted.

"You're not nagging," Leo countered. "You're gently reminding me to take care of myself. And I hear you. Now, can we talk about the midterms? You proved me wrong. Your students did very well, and it looks like word of mouth is working in your favor. Pre-enrollment shows students are signing up for your classes in droves. So I'm formally apologizing for calling your style too modern."

Meghan grinned. "Apology accepted, Mr. Darcy. And I want you to know no one is more relieved than I am. I'll come back next term and really give my students everything I've got!"

Leo kissed the tip of her nose playfully. "You already do that."

Meghan sighed and laid her head on his shoulder. She closed her eyes. "I think I *will* take a short nap."

A couple of minutes later, she was sound asleep and Leo was left alone with his guilty thoughts. Was he selfish for not telling her everything? Yes, he was selfish because he didn't want a good thing to end. But the time to end his silence was fast approaching. He would tell her on this trip. No matter what, they would return to North Carolina with everything out in the open.

The question was, would they still be a couple?

He was gazing into Meghan's face when their seatmate arrived. The guy cheerfully said, "Hey, man, I'm Gary." He offered his hand and Leo shook it. "Leo."

Gary, an African American in his midthirties, smiled

in Meghan's direction. "Sleeping beauty. You two together?"

"Yeah," Leo said and smiled at Meghan.

Gary stowed his bag in the overhead compartment and sat down. "Lucky man. Me? I'm still looking."

Then they had a long conversation about women and the fact that neither of them truly understood them, but the sisters were definitely worth all the effort.

In San Francisco, they took a cab from the airport to Loews Regency on Sansome Street. Meghan especially enjoyed the scenery. She was rubbernecking while Leo was checking his phone, into which he'd put the trip's itinerary. "We don't check in until four," he was telling Meghan. "The three-hour difference puts us at only two o'clock here. But we can leave our bags at the hotel and go sightseeing until it's time to check in."

"And get something to eat," Meghan said. "It feels like mealtime to me."

Leo chuckled. "Of course, my love. I'm sure we can find somewhere nearby to have a bite to eat, but I made reservations tonight at a West African restaurant in the Mission District. They have good Senegalese food and great cocktails. Plus world music to dance to."

"Is it a place you discovered on your book tour?" Meghan asked. Leo had told her he'd been to San Francisco on a book tour three years ago.

"Yeah, and after we get something to eat, we can go to City Lights. It's a bookstore on Columbus Avenue. Great place."

Meghan squeezed his arm in excitement. "I've heard great things about that bookstore!"

The Loews Regency San Francisco occupied the top floors of a forty-eight-story tower in San Francisco's Financial District. Leo held out his hand to Meghan when they arrived and helped her out of the cab. Both of them gazed up at the tall building. "It's a good thing I'm not afraid of heights," Meghan commented dryly.

"You won't know you're on one of the top floors once you're up there," Leo said. "The views are spectacular. You can see a lot of the city and the Bay."

A doorman greeted them and directed them to the front desk. At the desk, Leo told the clerk they had a reservation and needed to leave their luggage with them until it was time to check in.

"No problem," the young man, a redhead with light lashes and a ginger beard, said happily. He attached tags to their luggage and handed Leo a couple of brochures about the hotel, which Leo passed on to Meghan, who leafed through them while their luggage was being taken care of. Only a few minutes later, the two of them were walking across the luxurious lobby in the direction of the exit.

"This says there's a restaurant here called Brasserie S&P," Meghan said, reading from the brochure. "Says it serves innovative San Francisco cuisine daily for breakfast, lunch and dinner. But it probably costs an arm and a leg."

Leo smiled. "Don't worry about the price. I can afford a sandwich, I'm sure."

She was right. The prices were high, but the food was delicious and the service exceptional.

As they were leaving, Meghan joked, "No wonder

rich people are so slim. It's painful paying that much for so little food."

Next they took a cab to City Lights Bookstore on Columbus Avenue. Meghan noted how the old merged with the new in San Francisco. Old buildings were juxtaposed with skyscrapers like the hotel they'd just left. The streets were uphill and downhill, and the sidewalks were busy with pedestrians.

The bookstore had hardwood floors and aisles of bookcases. Every inch of space was used, which made it feel a little claustrophobic, but it was the type of atmosphere she loved, and she immediately felt at home.

Leo saw the expression on her face and smiled to himself. She was indeed a woman after his heart—she loved books as much as he did. "Your books could be on these shelves," he said. "All you have to do is let someone read them besides me."

He'd read all three of her finished novels and told her they were brilliant. He didn't think she believed him, though.

"Maybe one day," Meghan said distractedly. She was busy reading a passage from a book.

She bought two books, Leo bought one and they got a cab back to the hotel to check into their suite. The suite had a king-size bed, trey ceilings, luxurious furniture in caramel and lighter earth tones, and a spa bath with a huge soaking tub plus a glass-enclosed shower. The views were breathtaking. The day was clear and Meghan could see all the way to the Golden Gate Bridge as she stood at one of the two big windows. Leo hugged her from behind. "Happy?"

She turned in his arms to look up at him. "You are a beautiful man!" And she kissed him, which led to their christening the bed in that elegantly appointed room.

That night they dressed up and went to Bissap Baobab Village, a West African restaurant that served Senegalese food, and dined on *maafe* (with lamb), a peanut stew and seafood *coco*, which was prawns in a spicy coconut curry. For dessert they had the bananas flambé and a chocolate soufflé. A live band played world music while they danced. Afterward, when they returned to the hotel, they sat on the terrace, Leo's arm around her and her head on his shoulder, admiring the city's night lights.

"This has been one of the best days I've ever had," Meghan said softly.

"I'm glad," Leo said. "You deserve lots of days like these."

Meghan peered into his eyes. "Is there something you want to tell me?"

Leo's heart thudded in alarm. "Why do you ask?"

"You seem more pensive than normal, and you're already quiet and absorbed in your own thoughts."

"Am I?"

"You know you are," Meghan said softly.

"Okay, babe, yes, you're right, I do have something on my mind, and all will be explained soon. I promise."

Meghan snuggled closer. His arms tightened around her. "I'll try to be patient. But you know that's not my strong suit," she warned lightly.

Leo laughed, "Yes, I know that about you."

The next couple of days were spent attending the

conference, which had sessions running concurrently. They attended different sessions, picking and choosing what interested them most. Each of them sat on panels and met like-minded individuals with whom they traded ideas. Meghan found it very illuminating, and she wound up exchanging contact information with a couple of the conference attendees.

They dined at a different restaurant each night and went dancing afterward. By the last day of the conference, they felt as though they'd absorbed a lot of knowledge they could take back with them to Duke.

There was a ball the last night of the conference, during which the attendees were encouraged to wear formal attire and mingle with each other over drinks.

Meghan wore a sleeveless high-neck lace-and-glitter gown in pale salmon with her long, wavy black hair down her back. Strappy sandals in gold leather were on her feet, and she kept her jewelry to a minimum, with just a slim gold bracelet on her left wrist and simple gold drop earrings.

Leo wore a tux with a white silk shirt, a black bow tie and highly polished dress shoes. His beard was neatly trimmed and had a healthy shine. Meghan took one look at him and cried, "Damn, you're fine. There's nothing finer than a gorgeous black man with a beard in a tuxedo."

Leo grinned appreciatively and secretly hoped that she would still believe that after the ball. "I'm happy you're pleased, my queen."

They had to descend a winding staircase to enter the ballroom, and Leo noticed that there was a photographer snapping pictures of couples as they entered. Undoubtedly the photographer would be selling copies of them, and he made a mental note to make sure he got one later.

There was a band playing songs Leo considered American standards by composers like Gershwin and Sondheim. As the evening progressed, he also heard some Duke Ellington. He and Meghan danced every dance, enjoying the feel of their bodies moving smoothly together. It wasn't their favorite music to dance to—that was salsa—but they were definitely enjoying themselves.

Toward the midnight hour, he said in Meghan's ear, "Let's get some fresh air."

There was a terrace through French doors across the ballroom. Leo took Meghan by the hand and they walked out there. Meghan was once again captivated by the view, so she didn't notice Leo removing a couple of folded sheets of paper from his inside jacket pocket.

"Meghan, um…" he began. He took a deep breath and started again. "Meghan, I have to tell you something that's been weighing heavily on my mind for months now."

Hearing this, Meghan's attention was riveted to him. Eyes wide, she cried, "Oh, my God, you got the results from the doctor and it's not good news!"

Leo placed an arm around her. "Now, don't get ahead of yourself. It's not all bad news. I'm just going to tell you—Meghan, my heart is fine. Dr. Lindsey says medical incompetence kept me from learning that years ago. Or miscommunication. At any rate, no one was thorough enough to examine me more closely. Otherwise they would have found out my heart is healthy."

Meghan burst out crying and hugged him tightly. "Thank God for that." She kissed his cheeks repeatedly. "I'm so happy."

"I hope you'll keep that feeling," Leo said ominously. "Because the bad news is, I'm sterile. I went to see a fertility specialist because I'd been told that I was born without the vas deferens, the main sperm pipelines from the testicles. It's a birth defect."

Meghan went still in his arms. He hoped she wasn't going to pass out like she'd almost done when he'd told her about his heart condition. He held on to her.

After a moment she rallied and sighed tiredly. "Keep talking," she said softly. "You're not finished telling me everything."

"It's not totally a lost cause," Leo told her. "Twenty-five to thirty-five percent of couples will eventually have children. There's no guarantee, though. So, if you decide to leave me, I'll understand. I've held this inside for months because I was afraid of losing you. That was a cowardly thing to do, and I deserve anything you dish out."

He pressed the folded sheets of paper into her hand. "These are copies of the results."

Meghan gave them right back to him. "I don't need to see them. Give me a minute to think."

Leo stuck the papers back into his pocket and waited. Emotions threatened to choke him if he didn't plead his case, but he remained silent.

Meghan stared at him with an expression of disbelief

on her face. She just shook her head. The disbelief transformed into sadness. Leo looked up at the sky. She hadn't pushed out of his arms yet, and he took that as a good sign. She wasn't finished crying, though. He heard her sniffling. He couldn't bear to look into her sweet face.

After a few minutes of silence, Meghan cleared her throat and asked, "Is there anything else?" She looked him in the eye and with the force of her will alone demanded he maintain eye contact with her.

"No, that's all," he said softly, hopefully.

"Because if you come back months from now with something else world-shattering to tell me, I'd have to slug you, Leo Wolfe. And don't think I can't lay all six feet three inches of you out, because I can. I only threaten violence so you'll understand how serious I am at this moment. I'm normally not a violent person. But you've pushed me to the limit. This is the limit. I can't take any more secrets! Now, I'd like to hear a better reason for not telling me about this when you told me about your heart condition."

"I guess I thought I'd lead with what would probably kill me first," he joked. "At any rate, I tried to warn you off me, didn't I? I made every excuse I could, but I just couldn't resist you. Then, when I got the good news that there was nothing wrong with my heart, I started hoping I'd be lucky twice, so I went to a fertility specialist, but unfortunately my luck had run out. If you're brave enough to marry me, babe, I'll be the best husband and, hopefully, father to our adopted children I possibly can be!"

"Wait," Meghan cried. "Did you just propose?"

"Not formally, but I did have plans to, if you didn't freak out and tell me it's over between us after I told you I'm sterile."

Meghan huffed. "Do I look like I'm freaking out?"

"No," Leo admitted. "You look in control."

He reached into his pocket and produced a beautiful five-carat white diamond in a platinum setting. He took her hand and slipped the ring onto her finger. "I adore you. Would you do me the honor of becoming my wife and the mother of my future children, whether they're adopted or by some miracle come here the old-fashioned way?"

Meghan smiled at him, her expression tender. "Yes, you crazy man, I will. And we *will* have children because we've got a lot of love to give. Chauncey and Malcolm can't be the only creatures we lavish love on. Besides our families, of course."

Laughing, Leo bent down to kiss her. "I love you so much!"

After the kiss, Leo gazed lovingly into her eyes and said, "In the beginning of our relationship I jokingly wondered what miraculous thing you would do that would compare to your sisters' acts of heroism."

Meghan smiled. "You mean like Mina rescuing Jake from that plane crash? I could never top that."

"But you did," Leo said softly. "You made a cynic like me believe in love again."

Meghan's response was to kiss him soundly.

* * * * *

SPECIAL EXCERPT FROM

HARLEQUIN®

*Savion Monroe's serious business exterior hides his creative spirit—and only Jazmin Boyd has access. Beautiful, sophisticated and guarding a secret of her own, the television producer evokes a fiery passion that dares the guarded CEO to pursue his dream. But when she accidentally exposes Savion's hidden talent on air for all the world to see, will he turn his back on stardom and the woman he loves?*

*Read on for a sneak peek at*
Forever with You,
*the next exciting installment in*
*the Sapphire Shores series by Kianna Alexander!*

Savion held on to Jazmin's hands, feeling the trembling subside. He hadn't expected her to react that way to his question about her past. Now that he knew his query had made her uncomfortable, he kicked himself inwardly. *I shouldn't have asked her that. What was I thinking?* While his own past had been filled with frivolous encounters with the opposite sex, that didn't mean she'd had similar experiences.

"I'm okay, Savion. You can stop looking so concerned." A soft smile tilted her lips.

He chuckled. "Good to know. Now, what can you tell me about the exciting world of television production?"

One expertly arched eyebrow rose. "Seriously? You want to talk about work?"

KPEXP0319

He shrugged. "It might be boring to you, but remember, I don't know the first thing about what goes on behind the scenes at a TV show."

She opened her mouth, but before she could say anything, the waiter appeared again, this time with their dessert. He released her hands, and they moved to free up the tabletop.

"Here's the cheesecake with key lime ice cream you ordered, sir." The waiter placed down the two plates, as well as two gleaming silver spoons.

"Thank you." Savion picked up his spoon. "I hope you don't mind that I ordered dessert ahead. They didn't have key lime cheesecake, but I thought this would be the next best thing."

Her smile brightened. "I don't mind at all. It looks delicious." She picked up her spoon and scooped up a small piece of cheesecake and a dollop of the ice cream.

When she brought it to her lips and slid the spoon into her mouth, she made a sound indicative of pleasure. "It's just as good as it looks."

His groin tightened. *I wonder if the same is true about you, Jazmin Boyd.* "I'm glad you like it."

A few bites in, she seemed to remember their conversation. "Sorry, what was I gonna say?"

He laughed. "You were going to tell me about all the exciting parts of your job."

"I don't know if any of what I do is necessarily 'exciting,' but I'll tell you about it. Basically, my team and I are the last people to interact with and make changes to the show footage before it goes to the network to be aired. We're responsible for taking all that raw footage and turning it into something cohesive, appealing and screen ready."

"I see. You said something about the opening and closing sequences when we were on the beach." He polished off the last of his dessert. "How's that going?"

She looked surprised. "You remember me saying that?"

"Of course. I always remember the important things."

Her cheeks darkened, and she looked away for a moment, then continued. "We've got the opening sequence done, and it's approved by the higher-ups. But we're still going back and forth over that closing sequence. It just needs a few more tweaks."

"How long do you have to get it done?"

She twirled a lock of glossy hair around her index finger. "Three weeks at most. The sooner, the better." She finished the last bite of her cheesecake and set down her spoon. "What about you? How's the project going with the park?"

He leaned back in his chair. "We're in that limbo stage between planning and execution. Everything is tied up right now until we get the last few permits from the state and the town commissioner. I can't submit the local request until the state approval comes in, so…" He shrugged. "For now, it's the waiting game."

"When do you hope to break ground?"

"By the first of June. That way we can have everything in place and properly protected before the peak of hurricane season." He hated to even think of Gram's memory park being damaged or flooded during a storm, but with the island being where it was, the team had been forced to make contingency plans. "We're doing as much as we can to keep the whole place intact should a bad storm hit—that's all by design. Dad insisted on it and wouldn't even entertain landscaping plans that didn't offer that kind of protection."

She nodded. "I think that's a smart approach. It's pretty similar to the way buildings are constructed in California, to protect them from collapse during an earthquake. Gotta work with what you're given."

He blew out a breath. "I don't know about you, but I need this vacation."

*Don't miss* Forever with You
*by Kianna Alexander, available May 2019*
*wherever Harlequin® Kimani Romance™*
*books and ebooks are sold.*



KPEXP0319